25

NEW YORK TIMES BESTSELLING AUTHOR

LISA KLEYPAS

is

"A REAL JOY."
Kathleen E. Woodiwiss

"A MASTER OF HER CRAFT."
Publishers Weekly (★Starred Review★)

"WONDERFULLY REFRESHING."
Johanna Lindsey

"DELIGHTFUL!"
Jill Barnett

"A DELICIOUS TREAT FOR ROMANCE READERS."
Mary Jo Putney

"WONDERFUL . . . GRATIFYING AND DELIGHTFUL."
Denver Rocky Mountain News

"MS. KLEYPAS DOESN'T LET TRUE ROMANTICS DOWN."
Cincinatti Enquirer

LISA KLEYPAS

PRINCE OF DREAMS

AVON BOOKS

An Imprint of HarperCollinsPublishers

AVON BOOKS
An Imprint of HarperCollins*Publishers*
10 East 53rd Street
New York, New York 10022-5299

First Avon Books paperback printing: August 1995

Avon Trademark Reg. U.S. Pat. Off. and in Other Countries, Marca Registrada, Hecho en U.S.A.
HarperCollins® is a trademark of HarperCollins Publishers Inc.

Printed in the U.S.A.

20 19 18

To my husband, Greg

Thanks for making my life wonderful!
I love you forever.

LK

PRINCE
OF DREAMS

PART I

Strange, the way we met. In a drawing-room circle
     With its empty conversation,
   Almost furtively, not knowing one another,
        We guessed at our kinship.
   And we realized our souls' likeness
Not by passionate words tumbling at random from our
   lips,
   But by mind answering mind,
   And the gleam of hidden thoughts.

—KAROLINA PAVLOVA

❧ One

"*W*AITING FOR SOMEONE?" A man's voice cut through the rustling quiet of the garden. The Russian accent was soft and guttural, falling pleasantly on Emma's ears. Turning with a wry smile, Emma watched as Prince Nikolas Angelovsky stepped out of the shadows.

With his golden skin, his sun-streaked hair, and his unpredictable cruelty, Nikolas was more like a tiger than a human being. Emma had never seen such a perfect blend of beauty and menace in any other man. She knew from personal experience that there was good reason to fear him. But she was an expert at handling dangerous creatures. The only sure way to be hurt was to show her fear.

Emma relaxed her spine and settled more comfortably on the stone bench, located in the most secluded section of the formal estate garden. "I'm certainly not waiting for you," she replied briskly. "Why are you out here?"

He smiled at that, his white teeth gleaming in the darkness. "I felt like taking a walk."

"I'll thank you to walk somewhere else. I'm trying to meet someone in private."

"Who is it?" He slid his hands into his pockets, walking around her.

"Go away, Nikolas."

"Tell me."

"Go away!"

"You can't order me about on my own estate, child." Nikolas stopped a few feet away from her. He was a tall man, one of the few in London whom Emma didn't tower over. He had big hands and feet, and a spare, powerful build. A shadow fell across his face, obscuring all but the piercing yellow gleam of his eyes.

"I'm not a child. I'm a full-grown woman."

"So you are," Nikolas said softly. His gaze swept over her, taking note of her slender figure wrapped in a simple white gown. Emma's face, as always, was unpowdered and unpainted. Her hair had been pinned into a tight chignon, but exuberant curls sprang around her face and neck. Her hair was a sublime shade of red, burning with bronze and cinnamon lights.

"You look beautiful tonight," he said.

Emma laughed. "Don't flatter me. 'Attractive' is the best I can do, and I know it. It's hardly worth having my head stuck with hairpins and my ribs crushed with tight lacing until I can't breathe. I'd much rather go 'round wearing boots and breeches and be comfortable, as men are. If one can't be beautiful, one shouldn't have to try at all."

Nikolas didn't argue, though he had his own opinion on the matter. Emma's unique attractiveness had always fascinated him. She was a strong, resilient woman, with the grace of a tall-masted ship. Her face was a composition of delicate angled cheekbones, a lush mouth, a scattering of golden freckles across the bridge of her nose. Long-limbed and slender, she reached a height of nearly six feet, even in her flat slippers. Nikolas topped her by a scant two inches. He had often imagined her body matched exactly to his, her legs and arms wrapped around him.

They were right for each other. Strange that no one else could see it, but it had been clear to Nikolas for years, ever since he had first met her. She had been a devil-child, an explosive bundle of gangly limbs and wild red hair. Now she was a young woman of twenty, with a ruthless honesty that was a perfect foil for his own secretive nature. She reminded him of the women he had known in Russia, women with fire in their souls . . . so unlike the tepid European creatures he had known for the past seven years.

Aware of his inspection, Emma made a face at him. "I don't mind being plain," she said. "As far as I can tell, beauty is a terrible inconvenience. Now you really must go, Nikolas. With you hovering around, no man will dare come near me."

"Whomever you're waiting for, he won't last any longer than the others."

Emma scowled in sudden defiance. "This one will."

"They never stay," he continued idly. "You send them all away, in the exact order they come to you. Why is that?"

Emma's vivid flush clashed with her hair. She clamped her lips together. His arrow had found its mark. This was her third Season after having been presented. If she didn't marry soon, she would be considered a failure in the marriage market and on a rapid road to spinsterhood.

"I don't see why I need a husband," she said. "I don't like the idea of being owned by someone. You probably think that makes me unwomanly."

"I consider you very much a woman."

Her auburn brows inched upward. "Is that a compliment or mockery? With you, it's hard to tell."

"I never mock you, Emma. Other people, yes. You, no."

She gave a disbelieving snort.

Nikolas came forward then, stepping into the light that spilled gently from a garden lantern. "You will accompany me back inside now. As your host—and a distant cousin—I can't allow you to stay out here unchaperoned."

"Don't try to claim any kinship between us. You're my stepmother's relative, and you have no ties to me whatsoever."

"We're cousins by marriage," he insisted.

Emma smiled at that, knowing that as cousins, they could have a far more informal relationship, calling each other by first names and talking privately without the need of a chaperone. "Whatever you say, Your Highness."

"Perhaps you would like a tour of my art collection," Nikolas suggested. "I have an icon wall that might interest you. Many of them are works from thirteenth-century Novgorod."

"I don't care for art, and I certainly don't want to look at any gloomy old icons." Emma gave him a skeptical glance. "Why do you keep them? You're

the last person I'd expect to collect religious paintings."

"Icons are the windows to a Russian's soul."

Emma's wide mouth curled derisively. "I've
never seen any evidence that you have a soul."

"Perhaps you haven't looked closely enough."
He took a step forward and then another, until his
feet nearly touched the flowing hem of her white
dress.

"What are you doing?" she asked.

"Stand up."

For a moment Emma didn't move. Nikolas had
never spoken to her like this. He seemed relaxed,
his ungloved hands loose at his sides, but she
had seen such calculated stillness before, in a cat
about to strike. Emma obeyed uneasily, straightening as tall as possible until they stood almost
nose to nose.

"What do you want, Nikolas?"

"I want to hear more about this friend of yours.
Does he hold you in his arms? Does he whisper
love words to you? Does he kiss you?" His fingers
closed over her arms, the warmth of his palms
sinking through the fragile silk sleeves.

Emma jumped and made a small sound in her
throat. Her heart began to beat painfully hard. It
was unimaginable, undreamed of, to feel Nikolas
Angelovsky's hands on her, to stand so close that
her breasts touched his chest. She tried to pull
away, but his grip tightened.

"If you're finished amusing yourself, Nikolas,
then kindly remove your royal paws. I don't appreciate your sense of humor."

"I'm not making a joke, *ruyshka*." His arms slid
around her, locking her against his body. At her

gasp of bewilderment, he explained, "That means 'little redheaded one.' "

"I'm not little," she said, straining to break free. He contained her struggles without effort. Although they were almost the same height, he was double her weight, his body muscled and big-boned, his shoulders broad as church doors.

He continued to speak softly, ignoring her gasping protests. "You could easily pass for a Slav, you know, with your red hair and fair skin. Your eyes are the color of the Baltic Sea—the darkest blue I've ever seen."

Emma thought of calling for help. Why was he doing this? What did he want from her? She recalled all the rumors she had heard about Nikolas. His past was filled with betrayal, murder, treason. He had been permanently exiled from Russia for crimes against the Imperial government. Many women found his aura of danger exciting, but she wasn't one of them.

"Let me go," she said breathlessly. "I don't like your games."

"You might."

He held her so easily, as if she were a doll or a kitten. She sensed that he relished his power over her, that he wanted her to know how much greater his strength was. Her head fell back, her eyes closing. Any moment she would feel his mouth on hers. She held her breath, waiting, waiting . . .

One of his arms loosened, and his hand came up to her throat, fondling lightly. His thumb stroked the driving pulse beneath her jaw. The unexpected lightness of his touch made her shiver. Emma lifted her trembling lashes and looked at him. His face was very close to hers. "Someday I will kiss you," he said. "But not tonight."

Emma jerked away in an offended flurry. Retreating a few yards, she folded her long arms across her chest. "Why don't you return to your guests and play host?" she snapped. "I'm sure there's any number of women inside who are dying to be near you."

Nikolas remained in the lampglow, his hair glittering, his mouth twitching with a smile. In spite of her annoyance, Emma couldn't help noticing how indecently beautiful he was.

"Very well, cousin. Enjoy yourself in the arms of your . . . friend."

"I will." Emma didn't move until she was sure he was gone. She made her way back to the bench and sat, sprawling out her long legs. Nikolas had left her shaken . . . and strangely disappointed.

Someday I'll kiss you . . . He had only been mocking her, of course. She was hardly the kind that men lost their heads over. Emma remembered all the childrens' parties when spotty-faced boys had made fun of her for being taller than anyone else in the room; and her coming-out, when all the bachelors had ignored her in favor of the pretty, petite girls nearby. She had been a wallflower at seventeen, even though she had the attraction of a large family fortune behind her.

But now she finally had a suitor of her own. She was in love with Adam, Lord Milbank. He had been courting her secretly for months now, since the beginning of the Season. Her heart thumped impatiently at the thought of him. Adam should have been here by now. What was taking him so long?

* * *

The Angelovsky garden was laid out in a series of "rooms," each bordered by hedges, flower beds, or trees. Nikolas circled the clearing where Emma sat, keeping himself concealed behind a row of towering Irish yews. Finding a good vantage point, he stopped and waited for Emma's mysterious suitor to appear.

Thinking herself alone, Emma fidgeted on the bench, tried to flatten her red curls, and arranged her legs several times to make them appear shorter. Evidently deciding her efforts were useless, she slumped in resignation. Nikolas smiled at her antics. Emma rose to her feet, brushed off her skirts, and stretched her back, standing in profile to him. Nikolas admired the elegant length of her body, the roundness of her breasts. She paced around the bench and broke off a sprig of honeysuckle from a hedgerow.

A man's voice cut through the serene rustling of the garden. "Darling!"

Emma turned, dropping the honeysuckle. A dazzling smile appeared on her face. "You're late," she accused, and rushed to the visitor. Flinging herself into his arms, she lavished a storm of kisses on his face.

"I had to sneak away without causing suspicion." The young man laughed as he tried to defend himself. "You know nothing would stop me from coming to you."

"Every time I see you across the room, I want to run into your arms."

"Soon we'll be together."

"How soon?" she asked impatiently.

"Very. Now, hold still so I can kiss you." He

grasped Emma's curly head in his hands and pressed his mouth to hers.

Nikolas watched the lovers, his eyes narrowed and intent. The man's back was turned to him. Patiently Nikolas circled them. He pushed aside a low-hanging branch to get a good view.

The man drew back slightly, the light falling on his face. It was Lord Milbank.

Suddenly Nikolas relaxed. "Perfect," he said under his breath, and meant it.

Now he understood Emma's need for secrecy. Milbank was an impoverished viscount. A fortune hunter. Emma's father would never allow his only daughter to marry a penniless manipulator like Milbank. No doubt Stokehurst had forbidden them to see each other. Nikolas turned and walked back to the ballroom, almost purring with satisfaction. It would be easy to get rid of Milbank. Nothing would stand in the way of his having Emma.

Emma linked her arms around Adam's neck. She breathed in his smell, clenched her hands in his jacket, luxuriated in his nearness. He was a tall, good-looking man of twenty-four with an appealing boyishness. "I'm more in love with you every day," she said, staring into his velvety brown eyes. "I think about you all the time."

Tenderly Adam stroked the side of her face. "You've bewitched me, Emma." He kissed her for a long moment, his mouth warm, his arms locked around her narrow back. When he lifted his head, they were both slightly out of breath. "We'll have to return to the party soon," he said. "Separately, of course. It won't do to have anyone suspect us. And don't scowl like that. You know it's necessary."

"It seems as if we've been doing this forever, Adam. Ten minutes here and there . . . it's not enough. Now that we're both certain of how we feel, we should confront Father together. And if he won't give his blessing to our marriage, we'll elope."

"Hush, darling," Adam soothed, his face shadowed with sudden wariness. "I don't want to hear the word 'elope' from your lips ever again. I know how important your family is to you. I won't be the cause of a separation between you and your father."

"But Papa may never approve."

"He'll come around in time." Tenderly Adam kissed her furrowed forehead. "I can be very patient, Em."

"I can't." Emma gave a frustrated laugh. "Patience may be one of your virtues, but not mine."

"Try talking to your stepmother," Adam suggested. "If you can win her to our side, she might soften your father's heart toward me."

"Maybe," Emma said thoughtfully. Her stepmother, Tasia, had always been like a kind older sister, unfailingly sympathetic to Emma's problems. "I suppose if anyone could change Papa's mind, it would be Tasia. But if that doesn't work—"

"It *has* to work. Em, you must understand how important it is to have your father's approval. We can never be married without it."

She drew back in surprise. "*Never?* Why not?"

"We won't have any money to live on."

"But money isn't as important as being to-gether."

"That's a very nice sentiment, sweetheart, but you've grown up with the finer things in life. You have no idea what it's like to do without. And re-member, without a dowry you would have to give up your menagerie, and sell your animals to zoos and private buyers."

"No," Emma said, horrified at the thought. "My animals would be terribly mistreated. I couldn't allow that to happen." For years she had kept a menagerie on her family's estate, taking in strays and wounded creatures of all kinds. She harbored horses, bears, wolves and dogs, mon-keys, and even an Asian tiger. "They depend on me . . . very few of them would survive without special care."

"Then you understand that it's necessary for us to have your family's consent?"

"Yes," Emma said reluctantly. She longed to goad Adam into confronting her father. If only Adam would stand up to him, and demand his permission to marry her. It would never happen, though. Poor Adam hated arguments, and he, like everyone else, was in awe of her father.

It was understandable. Her father, Lord Stoke-hurst, intimidated people easily. In his eyes, no one was good enough for her. Several months ago he had flatly forbidden Adam to court Emma. Adam had been too terrified to argue. Instead he had slunk away in defeat, and now the whole situation was impossible.

Emma squared her jaw. "I'll talk to my step-mother," she said. "Somehow I'll make her understand that you and I belong together. Then she'll convince Papa to allow the match."

"That's my good girl." Adam smiled and kissed her. "You return to the ball first, Em. I'll wait out here for a few minutes."

She hesitated, staring at him wistfully. "Do you love me, Adam?"

He pulled her close against his lean body, nearly crushing the breath from her. "I adore you. You're the most precious thing in the world to me. Don't be afraid—nothing is going to keep us apart."

Emma found her stepmother in the circular ballroom, a sumptuous cavern of gold leaf and carvings and mirrors. Sipping from a glass of wine and smiling at the easy chatter of her friends, Tasia looked like a girl in her teens rather than a matron of twenty-five. She had the same air of mystery that made her cousin Nikolas Angelovsky so fascinating. They were both full-blooded Russians, compelled by circumstance to make their home in England.

Emma went over to her stepmother and pulled her aside. *"Belle-mère,"* she said urgently, "I have to talk to you about something important."

Tasia regarded her without surprise. There was little that escaped Tasia—at times it seemed she had the power to read minds. "It has to do with Lord Milbank, doesn't it?"

"Who told you?"

"No one. It's been obvious for months, Emma. Every time you disappear at a ball or *soirée,* so does Lord Milbank. You've been meeting each other in secret." Tasia gave her a chiding glance. "You know I don't approve of doing things behind your father's back."

"I've been forced into it," Emma said guiltily. "All because Papa won't be fair about letting Adam court me."

"Your father doesn't want anyone to take advantage of you, least of all a fortune hunter."

"Adam is *not* a fortune hunter!"

"He's certainly given everyone that impression. There was that dreadful business with Lady Clarissa Enderly last year—"

"He explained that to me," Emma said, wincing at the reminder that before he had begun courting her, Adam had been caught trying to elope with a naive young heiress. The outraged Enderly family had threatened Adam within an inch of his life, and quickly married their daughter off to a wealthy old baron. "It was a mistake. A misunderstanding."

"Emma, your father and I want to see you with a husband who values you, who is worthy of you—"

"Who's rich enough," Emma interrupted. "That's what this is all about. You and Papa don't like it that Adam doesn't have a great family fortune behind him."

"And if you were penniless?" Tasia asked softly. "Would Adam still want to marry you? Of course money isn't the only reason he wants you—but you can't deny that it's a factor."

Emma scowled. "Why is it so impossible for everyone to believe that a man could actually love me? He doesn't care about my fortune, not in the way you think. All he wants is for me to be happy!"

Tasia's eyes were soft with sympathy. "I know

that you love him, Emma, and you believe he feels the same way. But your father would think so much more of Adam if he had the courage to come to him and say, 'Lord Stokehurst, I want you to reconsider your decision about forbidding me to court Emma, because I want a chance to prove how much I respect and love her' . . . but no, Adam has talked you into this very suspicious hole-and-corner arrangement—''

"Can you blame Adam for being afraid of Papa?" Emma asked in a fierce undertone. "*I* certainly don't! There are quite a number of people who think Papa is an ogre!"

Tasia laughed, her pale blue-gray eyes finding the broad-shouldered outline of her husband in the crowd. "So did I, once. But now I know better."

As if he sensed Tasia's gaze, Stokehurst turned and glanced at her. He was striking rather than handsome, with strong masculine features and vivid blue eyes. Some people were disconcerted by the sight of the silver hook in place of his left hand. Long ago he had lost the hand in an accident, trying to save Emma and her mother from a deadly house fire. Emma had lived through the disaster, but her mother hadn't. Sometimes Emma wondered how she might have turned out if she'd grown up with a mother. Instead there had only been her father, loving, domineering, and far too overprotective.

At the sight of his wife and daughter, Stokehurst excused himself from a casual conversation and began to make his way over to them.

"You deserve a man like your father," Tasia murmured as she watched her husband approach.

"He would do anything for the people he loves, even sacrifice his life for them."

"There are no other men like that," Emma said ruefully. "Good Lord, if I have to hold every suitor up to those standards, I'll *never* find anyone to marry."

"You'll find someone who's worthy of you. It will just take a little time."

"It will take forever. If you haven't noticed, there aren't exactly crowds of frantic bachelors running after me."

"If you would show them the side of yourself that your family sees, you *would* have crowds of bachelors chasing you. You have so much natural warmth and charm, but when you're around men, you turn as stiff as a statue."

"I can't help the way I am." Emma let out a long sigh. "But I'm different around Adam, *Belle-mère*. He makes me feel special . . . even beautiful. Please try to understand. You have to talk to Papa for me, and make him invite Adam to the house."

Perturbed, Tasia patted Emma's arm and nodded. "I'll see what I can do. But don't expect too much. Luke isn't going to like the idea at all."

Emma's father reached them, and though his smile encompassed both of them, his gaze lingered on Tasia. For a moment they seemed lost in a private world. It was rare to see a husband and wife so passionately in love with each other. After his first wife had died, Luke had never expected to marry again, but from the moment Tasia had entered his life, he had been bewitched by her. Since their marriage, she had given him two dark-haired sons, William and Zachary. There were times when

Emma felt separate from their close-knit circle, in spite of their efforts to include her.

"Are you enjoying yourself?" Luke asked Tasia, staring into her smoky cat-eyes.

"Yes," she replied softly, smoothing the wide lapel of his black evening jacket. "But you haven't yet asked your daughter to dance."

Emma interrupted quickly. "I'd rather be a wallflower than have my father as my only waltz partner for the evening," she said. "And no, I don't want you to procure a partner for me, Papa. No one likes duty dances."

"I'm going to bring over young Lord Lyndon for an introduction," Luke said. "He's an intelligent man with a quick wit—"

"I've already met him," Emma said dryly. "He strongly dislikes dogs."

"That's hardly reason to condemn a man."

"Since I always seem to be covered in some sort of animal hair and smelling of dogs or horses, I don't think we'd get on well. Don't start matchmaking, Papa—you're beginning to terrify me."

Luke smiled and tugged lightly at one of her brilliant red curls. "All right." He turned to Tasia. "Will you do me the honor, madam?" The pair went to the dance floor, and Luke took his slender wife into his arms. Relaxing into the rhythm of the waltz, they were able to exchange a few words in private.

"Why isn't Emma socializing with anyone?" Luke asked. "She seems to be withdrawn tonight."

"She's interested in only one man."

A scowl crossed Luke's face. "Still Lord Mil-

bank?'' he asked grimly. ''I thought I had taken
care of that problem.''

Tasia smiled. ''Darling, just because you forbade
them to see each other doesn't mean their feelings
cease to exist.''

''I'd rather marry her off to anyone but that
spineless fortune hunter. *Anyone* would be better.''

''Don't say such things aloud,'' Tasia cautioned,
her fine brows drawing together. ''You always like
to tempt fate.''

Luke grinned suddenly. ''You and your superstitious Russian nature. I meant what I said. Who
could possibly be a worse son-in-law than Milbank?''

Left to her own devices, Emma wandered over
to the wall and leaned her back against it. She
sighed fretfully, wishing she could leave the ball,
or at least meander by herself through the Angelovsky manor. It was filled with ancient Russian
treasures, magnificent works of art, intricately
carved furniture, priceless panels thickly covered
in jewels. Nikolas had brought it all with him—
along with an army of family retainers—when he
had come to England.

Nikolas's home was like a museum, breathtak-
ingly opulent, intimidating, richly gloomy. The
central hall was lined with fifteen towering gold
pillars—an extra having been added in deference
to the Russian superstition that even numbers were
bad luck. A grand staircase with blue-and-gold
spindles arched delicately up to the second and
third floors. Dove-colored walls were highlighted
with rich stained glass, rising from black-and-gray
marble floors.

The manor was set in the middle of fifty thousand acres of cultivated land just to the west of London, covering territory on both sides of the Thames. Nikolas had bought the estate three years before, and had decorated it to his taste. It was a splendid setting worthy of a prince, but it must be small compared with the palaces Nikolas had owned in Russia. He had been permitted to take a tenth of his fortune with him in exile, and that fraction alone was estimated to be thirty million pounds. Nikolas was one of the richest men in Europe, and by far the most eligible. A man with all that wealth should be very happy, yet Nikolas seemed like one of the least happy people Emma had ever met. Was there some elusive thing he wanted but couldn't have, or some private desire that had never been fulfilled?

A delicately brittle voice interrupted her thoughts. "Why, look, Regina, it's our friend Emma, standing at the wall as usual. I'm surprised they haven't put a plaque there to mark your special place . . . 'Here Lady Emma has waited thousands of hours in hopes of an invitation to dance.' "

The speaker was Lady Phoebe Cotterly, accompanied by her friend Lady Regina Bradford. Phoebe was the success of the Season, possessing the magical combination of gleaming blond beauty, a revered family name, and the assurance of a generous dowry. Her only problem was deciding which of her legions of suitors she would marry.

Emma smiled uncomfortably, feeling like a towering giant as she loomed awkwardly over the two of them. She slumped her shoulders and retreated until her back was plastered against the wall. "Hello, Phoebe."

"I know why she looks so out of place," Phoebe said to Regina. "Our Emma feels much more at home in a barnyard than a ballroom. Isn't that right, Emma?"

Emma felt her throat tighten. She glanced across the room at Adam, who was involved in a conversation with friends. Taking courage from his distant presence, Emma told herself that Adam loved her, and therefore this girl's snide comments shouldn't matter one bit. But they still hurt.

"What a wholesome, unaffected girl you are," Phoebe purred, digging her claws in deeper. "So *unique*. You should have men flocking around you. I simply don't *understand* why they don't appreciate your rustic charms."

Before Emma could reply, she was startled to discover that Prince Nikolas had suddenly appeared at her side. Blinking in surprise, she looked up into his inscrutable face.

"I believe it's time for the dance you promised me, cousin," he said softly.

Emma was temporarily speechless, as were the other girls. Here in the glittering splendor of the ballroom, dressed in severe black-and-white evening clothes, Nikolas was too extraordinary to be real. The light gleamed on his austere features, highlighting each golden curve and angle, turning his eyes into iridescent pools of yellow. His gold-tipped eyelashes were so long, they had tangled at the outside corners.

Phoebe Cotterly's lips drooped open with dismay as she realized that Nikolas had overheard her petty taunts. "Prince Nikolas," she said breathlessly, "what a marvelous evening this is—and what an exceptional host you are! I'm enjoying myself very much tonight. Everything is perfect, the music, the flowers—"

"We are pleased that you approve," Nikolas interrupted coldly.

Emma struggled to suppress a laugh. She had never heard Nikolas use the royal "we" before, but it was quite effective.

"Did you call Emma 'cousin'?" Phoebe asked. "I wasn't aware you were related."

"Distant cousins, by marriage," Emma explained, ignoring the faint smile that had appeared on Nikolas's mouth.

"Our dance?" he prompted, holding out his arm.

"But, Your Highness," Phoebe protested, "you've danced with me only once before, at the Brimforth Ball. It was an experience worth repeating, don't you think?"

Nikolas's speculative gaze traveled down to Phoebe's dainty feet and back up again. "I believe once was enough, Lady Cotterly." He reached for Emma and led her to the dance floor. Phoebe was left speechless, while Regina appeared bemused.

Emma curtsied in response to Nikolas's bow and put her hand in his. She stared at him with a smile of guilty delight. "Thank you. I've never seen anyone put Phoebe in her place before. I owe you for that."

"Then we'll consider you in my debt." He slid his arm around her waist and drew her into a sweeping waltz. Emma followed his steps with ease, their long legs moving in perfect unison. She was momentarily stunned into silence. She had

never danced so well with anyone. It was like flying, the skirts of her white gown whirling and
flowing around them, her feet taking on a life of
their own. She realized that people were looking at
them. Some couples even retreated to the side to
watch. Emma hated being the focus of attention. A
hot flush spread over her face.

"Relax," Nikolas murmured, and she became
aware that she was clutching his hand.

"Sorry." Instantly Emma loosened her fingers.
"Nikolas . . . why have you never asked me to
dance before tonight?"

"Would you have accepted my invitation?"

"Probably not."

"That's why I didn't ask."

Emma stared curiously at the man who held her.
It was impossible to tell if he was enjoying himself
or not. There was no expression on his face. He
moved very lightly for a tall man. His body seemed
to be made of muscle and springs, like a cat's.
There was a pleasant smell about him, the mixture
of warm male skin and birch soap, and the trace of
sugared tea on his breath.

At the place where his golden skin met the crisp
white edge of his collar, Emma saw the tip of a
scar. She lowered her gaze to his shoulder, suddenly remembering when he had come to England
seven years before, nearly at the point of death. She
had followed her stepmother to his sickbed, and
had stared at him intently. She would never forget
how Nikolas had looked, so gaunt and pale, barely
able to lift his head. And the scars . . . an ugly map
of them spreading over his chest and wrists. She
had never seen scars like that before. Somehow Nikolas had managed to capture a lock of her hair in

his thin fingers. *"There,"* he had said softly. *"I know a Russian folk tale about a girl who saves a dying prince . . . by bringing him a magic feather . . . from the tail of the firebird. The bird's feathers were a color between red and gold . . . like your hair . . ."*

Emma had pulled away scornfully, but her curiosity was sparked by his strange words. Later she had asked Tasia what had happened to him, and why he had been wounded in such a way. *"Nikolas was tortured,"* Tasia had said quietly, *"and exiled for treason."*

"Will he die from his wounds?"

"Not from his physical wounds, no. But the inner ones are much worse, I'm afraid."

For a while Emma had tried to feel sorry for him, but it was impossible. Nikolas was too arrogant to inspire pity, no matter how he had suffered for his sins.

Her thoughts were jerked back to the present as they waltzed by Adam Lord Milbank, who was standing at the side of the room. Adam was watching her with astonishment. What must he be thinking? Emma's spine stiffened, and her movements became stilted as Nikolas guided her across the floor. If only she could rush over to Adam and explain the situation!

"Your friend must be watching us," Nikolas said.

Emma was surprised by his perceptiveness. "Unfortunately, yes."

"A taste of jealousy never hurts a love affair."

"I suppose you would know. You've found your way into quite a few beds, haven't you?"

Nikolas looked amused. "Do you ever guard your tongue, *ruyshenka*?"

"Does it offend you?"

"No."

"Sometimes I try to be polite and restrained. It lasts for a half hour or so, and then I'm back to my old ways." Emma twisted impatiently to glance at the musicians in their flower-covered alcove. Her movement caused Nikolas to miss a step. "Isn't this waltz nearly over? It seems to have lasted forever."

"You're not enjoying yourself?" Nikolas asked, compensating for the lost step and reestablishing their rhythm.

"Not with all these people watching us. You may be used to it, but it makes me nervous."

"I'll end your torment, then." Drawing her to the side of the room, Nikolas released her waist. He brought her hand to his mouth in a perfunctory gesture. "Thank you for the dance, cousin. You are a most charming partner. I wish you luck with your friend."

"Oh, I don't need luck," she replied confidently.

"One never knows." Nikolas bowed and strode away, thinking to himself that all the luck in the world wasn't going to help Emma's cause. She would never belong to any other man. He had always known she was meant for him, only him . . . and soon he would have her.

The Milbanks were the brand of European aristocrat that Nikolas despised most, living off an ever-shrinking pool of resources that they were either too lazy or too proud to supplement—except by marrying their children off to wealthy families. They would never work except at some nominal position at a bank, law firm, or insurance company. And they clung too tightly to their dwindling hoard of money to ever make a profitable investment.

Standing at the front door of the Milbanks' London home, Nikolas returned the butler's mildly startled expression with a level gaze.

"I'm here to see Lord Milbank," he said, extending a calling card.

The butler took the card and recovered himself at once. "Certainly, Your Highness. I believe Lord Milbank is at home, but I could be mistaken. If you will wait in the entrance hall . . . ?"

Nikolas answered with a single nod and came into the house. His expressionless gaze swept over the hall, lingering at the frayed edges of carpet on the stairs, and on the polished but scuffed woodwork. The smell of mustiness and decay hung in the air. As he had expected, the place was badly in need of repair and refurbishing.

In approximately two minutes, the butler returned. He didn't meet Nikolas's eyes as he spoke. "Regrettably I was in error, Your Highness. It seems Lord Milbank is not at home."

"I see." Nikolas allowed a long silence to pass, his hard stare boring into the butler's blank face. The butler tensed, his brow turning clammy with sweat. "You and I both know he's here," Nikolas said quietly. "Go back to Lord Milbank and tell him I need to discuss a business matter with him. It won't take long."

"Yes, Your Highness." The butler vanished in such haste that one of his polished shoes left a scuff mark on the marble floor.

Soon Milbank appeared in the entrance hall. "Prince Nikolas," he said with a wary smile. "I can't fathom what brings you here. Business matter, is it?"

"Personal business."

They exchanged assessing stares. Milbank took an involuntary step backward, perhaps sensing the dislike behind Nikolas's remote expression. He looked younger than Nikolas remembered, with smooth features and brown, puppy-dog eyes.

"Shall we take some refreshment in the parlor?" Milbank offered hesitantly. "Some tea and toast?"

Tea and toast. A typical English offering—generous, even. Refreshment wasn't routinely offered to guests in this country. In Russia, the tradition was to welcome any acquaintance, whether friend or foe, with special food and drink. Thinking longingly of the traditional table of Russian "small bites"—dishes of pickles, caviar, salads, and buttered bread, all washed down with glasses of cold vodka—Nikolas repressed a sigh. He had made a home for himself here in England, but he would never feel entirely comfortable in a culture so different from his own.

"No refreshment, thank you," he murmured. "This won't take long. I've come to talk to you about the Stokehursts. One Stokehurst in particular." He paused deliberately, watching Milbank's face grow taut. "I want your involvement with Emma to end."

The soft brown eyes widened in surprise. "I-I don't understand. Did the duke ask you to warn me away from his daughter?"

"Don't be a fool," Nikolas said. "Stokehurst is capable of doing that with no help from me."

Milbank shook his head in confusion. "Then

you're asking for yourself? Wh-what is your motive?"

"You don't need to know."

Milbank drew a sharp breath. "I saw you dancing with Emma last night. My God, what's going on? You couldn't possibly have a personal interest in her."

"Why not?"

"There's nothing you could want from a girl like Emma. You certainly don't need her dowry."

Nikolas arched a tawny brow. "You think money is all Emma has to offer?"

"I didn't say that," Adam replied quickly.

Nikolas kept his face blank, but contempt spilled into his voice. "The Season will be over soon. As usual, there will be some leftover heiresses who were not sufficiently appealing to catch a husband. They would gladly bestow their plump little hands in marriage to you. Since it's money you want, take one of them. Stay away from Emma Stokehurst."

"The hell I will!" Adam's chin trembled in what seemed to be rage or fear, or some volatile mixture of the two. "I intend to take my chances with Emma. I happen to love her. Now get off my property, and don't ever return."

Nikolas's mouth curved with a chilling smile. No matter how convincingly Milbank played the part, Nikolas saw through the pretense, the lies, the manipulation. "I don't think you understand," he murmured.

"If you're trying to frighten me—"

"I'm not giving you a choice regarding Emma. There will be no visits, no correspondence, no secret meetings. If you try to see her, you'll only bring needless suffering on yourself."

"Are you threatening me?"

The touch of amusement disappeared, and Nikolas replied in deadly seriousness. "I'm promising to make your life such a misery that you'll curse your mother for ever bearing you." He waited calmly, while the air turned thick with frustration. He enjoyed the sight of Milbank's distress, the internal struggle between greed and fear. Milbank was a cowardly jackal, wanting Emma and her money, but not enough to risk his own safety.

Milbank turned scarlet. "I've heard of all the lives you've destroyed. I've heard about your brutality . . . your cruelty. If you dare to hurt Emma, I'll kill you!"

"No one will be hurt . . . as long as you defer to my wishes."

"Why are you doing this?" Milbank asked hoarsely. "What plans do you have for Emma? I have a right to know!"

"Where Emma is concerned, you have no more rights." Nikolas bowed with exquisite grace before taking his leave, while Adam Milbank trembled in bewildered fury.

Emma whistled cheerfully as she strode into the Stokehursts' London villa on the Thames. The mornings in June were still cool enough to allow for a vigorous ride in Hyde Park. Her horse, a beautiful but nervous two-year-old, had been difficult to manage today. Red-cheeked and sweating from exertion, Emma unbuttoned the short jacket of her riding habit as soon as she came into the entrance hall.

"Miss Emma." The butler proffered a small silver tray with a sealed letter on it. "This arrived for you not long ago."

"Thank you, Seymour. I wonder who . . ." Emma's voice faded as she recognized the small, perfectly formed handwriting. The letter was from Adam. Emma's heart gave an extra beat of excitement, and she glanced quickly at the butler. "Does Papa or Tasia know about this?"

"Neither of them has seen it," he admitted.

She gave him her most appealing smile. "I don't think there's any need to tell them, do you?"

"Miss Emma, if you're asking me to deceive them—"

"For heaven's sake, Seymour, I'm not asking you to lie to anyone . . . just don't say anything unless you're asked. All right?"

He released a brief, almost unnoticeable sigh. "Yes, miss."

"You adorable, wonderful man!" Emma threw her arms around the shocked butler, hugged him violently, then fled upstairs to read the letter in private.

After locking the door to her room, she flung herself on the bed, ignoring the dirt crumbs that fell from her skirts and boots onto the embroidered linen. She broke the brown wax seal and unfolded the letter. Tenderly her fingertip moved over the first few words.

My dearest Emma,

I wish I could find the words to tell you how much I love you . . .

Emma stopped for a second and pressed the letter to her mouth. "Adam," she whispered, tears of happiness gathering in her eyes. But as she lowered the paper and continued to read, the smile faded from her lips, and the blood drained from her face.

My life has been changed for the better, knowing you these past months and having the occasional joy to hold you in my arms. It is with deepest sorrow . . . no, anguish . . . that I have come to realize any sort of relationship between us is impossible. Your father will never approve of us. Rather than subject you to a life of hardship and sacrifice, I must give up my dream of happiness. It is difficult not to be selfish, my sweet love, but I am compelled by honor to let you go. I am leaving the country for a while, with no idea of when I will return. Do not wait for me. It is my fondest wish that someday you might find happiness with someone who will be able to provide for you in the way your father expects. In closing, I will not say au revoir, *but* adieu.

Ever your
Adam

Emma's mind was blank for a while, but she was conscious of a terrible pain lurking behind the nothingness, waiting to swamp her. "No, I can't bear it. Oh, God . . ." She rolled onto her side and clutched the letter to her midriff, struggling to breathe. Her face was dry. It would hurt too much to cry. "Adam . . . you didn't have to leave me . . . you said you would wait. You said . . ." Her throat contracted. She wasn't aware of holding her breath until a burst of air came into her lungs, and then another. "Adam," she gasped, then was silent, wondering desperately if she would ever be able to feel anything again.

Luke lounged on the hearthrug, staring into the fireplace while Tasia leaned back against his chest. They shared a brandy, sipping from the same glass, occasionally kissing to share the flavor. The sitting room, attached to their private suite, was filled with golden fireglow.

"Where are the children?" Luke asked.

Tasia swirled the brandy in the snifter and offered him another sip, gently tilting the crystal rim against his mouth. "The boys are playing in the nursery. It's almost time for their baths . . . I suppose I should go up to them now."

"Not just yet." His large hand closed over her arm. "This is my favorite part of evening, when I have you all to myself."

Tasia laughed and nuzzled the soft spot beneath his bristled jaw. "I really must go help Nurse, or the boys will splash water everywhere. And I want to check on Emma. She's been closed up in her room all day. I had Cook send up supper for her, but I don't know if she touched it."

Luke scowled slightly. "Probably pining over Milbank."

"Probably."

"I was certain Emma would have gotten over him by now. Can't we do something to hurry it along?"

"Obviously you have never suffered the pangs of unrequited love," Tasia said dryly.

"I did with you."

"Hardly! You decided you loved me, and two days later you came to my bed."

"It was the longest two days of my life."

Tasia laughed at his heartfelt tone. She set aside the brandy and slid her arms around his waist. Her hands settled lightly on his muscled back. "And we've been together almost every night since."

"Except for Prince Nikolas's interference," Luke said darkly.

"Shhh." Tasia pressed her lips to his. "We agreed to forgive and forget about all that. It's been seven years."

"I haven't forgotten."

"And you don't seem to have forgiven either." Tasia stared into his narrow sapphire eyes and shook her head slowly. "You, my darling, are the second most stubborn person I've ever known."

"Only the second?"

"I think Emma may actually surpass you by a narrow margin."

Luke leaned over her and grinned. "The Stokehurst blood," he informed her. "Neither one of us can help being stubborn."

Tasia giggled, turning her face to avoid his kisses. "The Stokehurst blood is your excuse for everything!"

He used his weight to hold her down, and nibbled amorously on her throat as she squirmed beneath him. "Stubborn and very passionate . . . Let me show you."

"I've already had ample demonstration," she said, gasping with laughter.

All at once their play was interrupted by a sharp knock on the door. Tasia looked in that direction and had an upside-down view of Emma's tall figure. She drew apart from her husband, struggling to a sitting position. "Emma, dear . . ." She paused and blinked as she saw the girl's face, white and brittle, as if she'd received some dreadful shock. Luke must have seen it at the same instant, for he sat up and said his daughter's name in a questioning tone.

"Pardon me for interrupting," Emma said coldly.

"What's the matter?" Tasia asked in concern. "Has something happened? You look upset—"

"I'm all right." Opening her fist, Emma tossed a sheet of crumpled paper at Luke's feet. The firelight played across it in flickers of red and gold. "I hope this pleases you, Papa."

Silently Luke picked up the letter, while his eyes remained on his daughter's drawn face.

"Read it," Emma said tersely. "It's from Adam. He's given up any hope of marrying me. He's leaving the country for a while. Thanks to you, I'll never have anyone." The tiny muscles of her cheeks twitched violently. "I'll never forgive you for taking away my only chance to be loved."

There was a troubled look on Luke's face. "Milbank didn't love you," he said quietly.

Emma's mouth curved in a bitter twist. "Who are you to decide that? What if he did? What if it was real love? Can you be so certain you haven't made a mistake? My father, so noble, so wise . . . so bloody damn perfect that you can see inside a man's heart and judge him in a glance! It must be nice to be absolutely infallible!"

Luke didn't answer.

"You don't want me to be married," Emma continued in rising vehemence, "unless it's to some spineless puppet whom you can control as you do everyone else—"

"That's enough," Tasia interrupted.

Emma's anguished gaze turned on her. "You don't think I've *hurt* my father, do you? You have to love someone in order to be hurt by their words—and I'm not privileged to be on the very short list of people Papa cares about."

"That's not true," Luke said, his voice rusty. "I love you, Emma."

"Really? I thought loving someone meant wanting them to be happy. Well, you can keep your so-called love, Papa. I've had enough of it for a lifetime."

"Emma—"

"I *hate* you." A visible shudder of emotion ran through her body. In the blanket of silence that descended, she turned and walked away.

❧ Two

TASIA WAS THE first to move. Carefully she pried the letter from Luke's hand and read in silence. Luke remained sitting with his head bent, all thoughts concealed.

After finishing the letter, Tasia set it aside with a sound of disgust. "What melodramatic prattle," she said flatly. "He's painted them as a pair of star-crossed lovers, with you cast as the villain, of course. Adam is leaving her 'for the sake of honor'—and he blames you for keeping them apart."

Luke raised his face. He was pale, and his mouth was taut. "Who else is to blame but me?"

"You did what you felt was best."

His wife's quick defense brought a warm gleam to his eyes, but then Luke shook his head wearily. "Emma was right. I should have allowed for the possibility that Milbank did love her, but—" He broke off and scowled. "You and I both know he's nothing but a parasite."

"I'm afraid it's clear to everyone except Emma."

"Should I have allowed him to court her when I knew he would hurt her? Christ, I don't know anything about headstrong daughters! All I know is that she's far too good for Milbank. I couldn't stand by and let him take advantage of her."

"No, of course not," Tasia said gently. "You love her too much for that. And Mary would never have wanted a man like him for her child."

The mention of his first wife seemed to be Luke's undoing. He turned away with a groan, staring into the fire. "There were so many lonely years for Emma after Mary died . . . I should have married someone right away for my daughter's sake. She needed a woman's influence. I should have thought about what it was like for her to grow up without a mother, instead of thinking only of myself—"

"You're not to blame," Tasia insisted. "And Emma doesn't hate you."

Luke laughed without humor. "She gave a hell of an imitation."

"She's angry and hurt because Adam deserted her, and you're the most available target. I'll talk to her when her temper cools. She'll be all right." Tasia took his jaw in her small hands and urged him to look at her. Her blue-gray eyes were filled with love. "And you may be right about Emma needing a mother when she was young," she whispered. "But I'm glad you didn't marry someone else. I'm so selfishly glad you waited for me."

Luke lowered his face to her rounded shoulder, drawing comfort from her nearness. "So am I," he said, his voice muffled. Tasia smiled and stroked his black hair, lingering on the threads of silver at his temples. To the rest of the world, Luke was a powerful, confident man who rarely allowed his emotions to show. Only with her did he reveal his doubts and feelings, trusting her with all the secrets of his heart.

"I love you," she said against his ear, touching the lobe with the tip of her tongue.

Luke sought her mouth and kissed her hungrily, his arms drawing tightly around her. "Thank God for you," he said, and pulled her down to the carpet.

Now that the London Season was officially over, the Stokehurst household—family, servants, and animals—was transferred to its sprawling country estate. Set on a broad hill overlooking the tidy village below, Southgate Hall was a romantic home built on the remains of the original castle, a Norman fortress. With its lofty turrets and intricate front of brick and glass, it would have been the perfect setting for a fairy tale. The family would relax for the next few months, far from the humid, fetid atmosphere of London. There would be an occasional house party, a few visits paid by friends and relatives, and the activity of the summer harvest.

Emma spent most of her time riding alone through the green countryside or working in the menagerie, located a quarter mile from Southgate Hall. The endless tasks of caring for her animals helped to take her mind off Adam. During the daylight she worked until her muscles ached, and at night she slept from exhaustion. But it was always there, the knowledge of what she had lost. She found it hard to accept that she would never be with Adam again.

The worst part of the day was suppertime. Emma gulped down her food and left the table as soon as possible, unable to endure her family's presence. She had never been so angry with her father. Every moment of loneliness was his fault. Every night of solitary sleep was because of him. Her father had made a few apologetic overtures to her, but she had remained coldly unforgiving. As far as Emma was concerned, there was no chance they would ever resume the close relationship they had once had. Something had been broken that could never be repaired.

It didn't matter that there was some truth to her father's claim that Adam had wanted her dowry. Of course the money had appealed to him—Adam had made no secret of that. But he had also cared for her. They would have had a good life together. Now that was gone, and Emma knew she would never be anyone's wife. She didn't intend to settle for some fat old widower or some half-witted bore just for the sake of being married.

By now she had lost all her value in the marriage market. There were too many younger, prettier girls who came out each Season, and they were the ones who caught the only decent bachelors available. Her father and Tasia were blind to the flaws that everyone else saw in her. They didn't seem to realize that Adam had been her only hope.

"Emma, do animals ever marry?" her six-year-old brother, William, asked one day as he watched her cleaning the chimpanzee pen. Its aging occupant, Cleo, combed her leathery fingers through William's black hair in a fruitless search for insects. The door to the building was left open, inviting any breeze that might find its way inside.

Emma stopped her work and leaned on the rake handle, smiling at him. "No, William, not the way people do. But some kinds of animals mate for life. Wolves, for example. Or swans."

"What is a mate?"

"It's like your mother and father—two creatures that stay faithful to each other their whole lives."

"Do monkeys mate for life?" William pushed Cleo's inquisitive hands away and glanced into her soulful brown eyes. The chimp pursed her lips and made a few inquiring grunts, reaching for his hair once more.

"No," Emma replied dryly, "they're not so discriminating."

"Do tigers?"

"Not tigers either."

"But people mate for life."

"Most people," she agreed. "When it's possible."

"And when they don't, they're spinsters. Like you and Cleo."

Emma laughed as she pulled clinging strands of straw from her clothes. "Something like that."

All at once a new voice entered the conversation. "Your sister is too young and lovely to be a spinster."

Emma and William both turned to see Prince Nikolas standing at the threshold, in a patch of blinding sunlight. With a critical glance at the chimp, he added, "I'm afraid I can't say the same for Cleo."

Cleo squeaked and hooted as William rushed eagerly to the newcomer. It seemed, Emma thought wryly, that no one was immune to Nikolas's potent mixture of charm and mystery. "Prince Nikolas!" the boy said breathlessly. *"Zdráhstvuyti!"*

"Zdráhstvuyti, William," Nikolas said, crouching down to the boy's height. He smiled as William

repeated the word perfectly. "What a fine accent. Your mother has taught you well. Only a boy with Russian blood like yours could say it so clearly."

"I have Stokehurst blood too," William said proudly.

Nikolas looked over the boy's dark head at Emma. "A powerful combination, *nyet?*"

Emma regarded him stonily. Although it was Nikolas's habit to pay infrequent visits to Southgate Hall, drinking pots of Chinese caravan tea and conversing with Tasia in rapid-fire Russian, he had never made a side trip to the animal menagerie. This was her private world, and no one was allowed here unless specifically invited. "What do you want, Nikolas?"

He gave her an oblique smile. "I've never seen your collection of animals before. I would like to have a look."

"I'm working," Emma said curtly. "I'm sure you can find better entertainment than watching me feed animals and rake manure."

"Not necessarily."

Her mouth twisted. "Stay if you like, then." She finished raking a pile of dirty straw from the chimp's pen and replaced it with a fresh scattering. Then she gestured for Cleo to go inside. "Back in there, old girl. Go in." The chimpanzee shook her head vigorously, baring her teeth. "Yes, I know," Emma said, pointing to the pen. "We'll play later, Cleo. Later."

The chimp muttered resentfully as she picked up a rag doll from a small pile of toys. In a flash, Cleo's small, wiry body ascended a ladder bolted to the side of the wire pen. When she reached the top, she seated herself on a wooden perch and frowned down at them. Emma closed the door of the cage and turned to her little brother. "William, it's time for you to go back to the house."

"Can't I stay with Cleo?" the boy pleaded, staring wistfully at the chimp.

"You know the rule—no visits to the animals unless I'm with you. We'll come to see her later this afternoon."

"Yes, Emma."

As the child left, Emma turned her attention to Nikolas. He was dressed in dark riding breeches and a white shirt that emphasized his tawny coloring. His hair looked more brown than blond today. A light sheen of perspiration had given his skin a smooth shimmer, as if he were a sculpture cast in precious metal. The thick lashes that framed his yellow eyes gleamed like filaments of light.

For the first time since Adam's desertion, Emma felt a stirring of something other than anger inside, a mixture of nerves and confusion and awareness. Realizing she was staring, she turned and picked up a metal bucket. She went to the large iron slop sink in the corner and worked the pump until a steady stream of water emerged.

Nikolas came forward, reaching for the pump handle. "Let me help you."

"No," she said quickly, elbowing him aside. "I can do it."

Nikolas shrugged and stood back as she labored over the sink. He watched her intently. The taut muscles of Emma's shoulders strained beneath a sweat-blotched shirt. Snug gray trousers outlined the slender shape of her bottom and thighs. Briefly he remembered her appearance at the ball in London, the cool white dress, the tightly pinned hair.

He preferred her this way, strong, capable, flushed from exertion. She was extraordinary. He had never known an aristocratic woman who worked like a peasant. Why did she tend the animals when she could order her servants to do it?

"It's not often I have the chance to see a woman in trousers," he said. "In fact, this may be the first time."

Emma straightened in a snap. She gave him a wary look. "Are you shocked?"

"It takes more than that to shock me." He let his admiring gaze sweep over her. "You remind me of a phrase by Tyutchev . . . 'the face of beauty flushed with the air of spring.' "

Apparently deciding he was mocking her, Emma glared at him and turned back to the sink. "I don't like poetry."

"What do you read, then?"

"Veterinary manuals and newspapers." She lifted the heavy bucket from the sink, breathing hard with the effort.

Automatically he tried to take it. "Allow me—"

"I'm used to it," she said gruffly. "Let go."

Nikolas raised his hands in a mocking gesture of surrender. "By all means."

Emma's thick auburn brows lowered in a scowl. She pointed to another bucket nearby. "If you want to help, carry that."

Nikolas complied, rolling up his sleeves in a few deft twists. The bucket was filled with approximately twelve pounds of fresh meat scraps. The scent of blood filled his nose, and he hesitated before picking it up.

"Squeamish?" Emma taunted. "This sort of work is rather beneath you, isn't it?"

Nikolas didn't reply, although she was right. There had never been any need or question of his performing this sort of labor. Like the other men of his social circles, he took his exercise in the form of riding, hunting, fencing, and boxing.

As he grasped the bucket handle and lifted it, the blood smell became stronger. Rich, salty-sweet... His fingers locked, and he went still as a memory sprang to mind... dark and sickening images... He struggled to push them away, but they rushed over him in a red tide.

Blood oozed and trickled over his chest. His back was scored with lash marks, while the coarse rope around his wrists had torn a deep channel through skin and muscle. Peotr Petrovich Ruvim, the Imperial interrogator, touched his face with gentle fingertips, blocking a salty trickle of sweat from falling into his eyes. Although he was fiendishly proficient in the art of torture, Ruvim did not appear to enjoy it. "Isn't it enough?" he asked quietly. "Won't you confess now, Your Highness?"

"I've done nothing," Nikolas croaked.

It was a lie, and they all knew it. He was a murderer. He had killed Samvel Shurikovsky, the tsar's favorite adviser, but since nothing could be proved, they had accused him of treason. In these turbulent days of reactionaries and reformists, there was danger for the tsar everywhere. Evidence wasn't required to imprison a man indefinitely; suspicion was all that was necessary.

For a week Nikolas had been subjected to daily sessions with Ruvim and other government officials in which they inflicted pain just short of the limit that would kill him. He was no longer human. He was only a suffering beast, waiting for the time to come when the misery ended and he could take his secrets to the grave.

Ruvim sighed and spoke to the others. "Bring the knout again."

"No," Nikolas said, while a shudder racked his naked body. He couldn't stand the whip anymore, the searing crack of it ripping through his flesh until it reached bone . . . and all the time, questions buzzing in his ears—"Do you have sympathy for the Nihilists? Do you agree with the tsar's policies?" The irony was, he had never concerned himself with politics. All he cared about was his land and his family.

Ruvim pulled a hot poker from the pit of coals and held it close to Nikolas's face. "Would you prefer this to the knout, Your Highness?"

The flare of heat made Nikolas shiver violently. He nodded and let his head hang forward, sweat and tears dripping from his jaw—

"What is it?" Emma asked. She glanced at his bare arms, and her expression went blank. Her eyes returned to his face. "Oh," she said softly.

Nikolas stiffened. He always kept his shirtsleeves buttoned over his wrists. Strange, that he would forget to hide them around Emma. But they were no surprise to her. She had seen them before, when she was a child.

He let out a slow breath and forced himself to relax. "You seem irritable today," he said with deliberate casualness. "Have I offended you, cousin?"

Taking his cue, Emma began to walk away from the building. To his relief, she didn't mention the scars. "Lately your entire gender offends me," she replied pertly.

"Because Lord Milbank abandoned you?"

"He didn't abandon me, he was *driven* away, and—" She turned suddenly, water sloshing over the rim of her bucket. "How did you know? Oh,

God, is it being talked about in London? Have the gossips gotten wind of it?''

''There are rumors.''

''Damn.'' Emma flushed. ''Well, I don't care what anyone says. Let them do their worst.'' Her shoulders hunched defensively. ''It wasn't Adam's fault, you know. My father behaved like a modern-day Genghis Khan. Adam had no choice but to leave me and go on with his life.''

''Milbank was too weak for you.''

''You don't know anything about it.''

''If he wanted you, he should have fought for you.''

''Adam is more civilized than that,'' she said defensively.

''Civilized?'' Nikolas repeated, holding her gaze. ''Is that the kind of man you want?''

Suddenly there was a twinkle of reluctant amusement in Emma's eyes. She glanced down at her dirt-streaked shirt and trousers. ''Well, yes. I'm so terribly *un*civilized that I need someone to balance me. Don't you agree?''

''No,'' he said softly. ''You need someone who will allow you to be as uncivilized as you want.''

Emma's smile remained as she shook her head. ''A pretty sight that would be.'' She led him to the next building, where a rust-colored fox darted back and forth inside a large pen. The animal was sleek and healthy, but it moved in uneven hops. Nikolas quirked his brows as he saw that the fox's front left paw was missing.

''I named him Presto,'' Emma said, ''because he's so quick and agile.''

''Evidently not agile enough to keep all his feet.''

Nimbly the fox hopped to the water dish that

Emma had filled to the brim. A few laps, and then the fox turned his full attention to Emma, watching with bright, dark eyes as she drew out an egg from the depths of her pocket.

"I have a treat for you, Presto," Emma said in a tantalizing voice. She peeled the boiled egg and held it through the bars of his enclosure. Trembling with eagerness, the fox inched closer.

"He was caught in a trap." With practiced skill, Emma let go of the egg just as the fox snatched it. Presto gobbled the delicacy in two saliva-drenched bites. "He was half-dead from exposure and loss of blood. He'd been gnawing his leg off to escape. If I hadn't found Presto when I did, he'd probably be an adornment for some fine lady's mantle or muff—"

"Please," Nikolas said politely, "save your speeches for that club you belong to—friends-of-the-animals, or whatever it's called."

"The Royal Society for the Humane Treatment of Animals."

"Yes, that one."

Emma surprised him by looking over her shoulder with a grin. No other woman on earth had such a smile, a sly and irresistible sunburst. "If you want to visit my menagerie, Nikki, you have to listen to my speeches."

Nikolas started slightly at the Russian diminutive of his name. Only a few friends from his boyhood had ever called him that. It sounded odd coming from Emma's lips, pronounced in her crisp English accent. Suddenly he felt the need to escape her artless smile, the childlike clarity of her eyes. But he stayed, driven to finish what he had begun, carefully luring her into the snare he had set.

"I don't see any point in making speeches," he heard himself say, "until you find replacements for the products they supply—including the meat for your table."

"I'm a vegetarian." Seeing that the word was unfamiliar to him, Emma explained. "That's English for someone who doesn't eat meat." She laughed at his expression. "You look surprised. Aren't there vegetarians in Russia?"

"Russians have three requirements for their diet: meat to make the bones strong and the blood red, dark bread to fill the stomach, and vodka to impart joy in life. Give a Russian a plate of green weeds, and he'll feed it to the cow."

Emma didn't appear to be impressed. "I'll take weeds any day."

"I think you take your opinions to an extreme, *dushenka*." Nikolas stared at her with growing amusement. "When did you decide to stop eating meat?"

"I think I was thirteen, maybe a little older. One night I was in the middle of supper, listening while everyone talked around me, and as I stared down at the roasted game hen in front of me, I felt as if I were picking a little corpse apart . . . seeing all the tiny rib bones, the muscle, the fat and skin. . . ." She grimaced at the memory. "I excused myself, went up to my room, and was sick for hours."

He smiled. "You're an odd child."

"So people say." Emma gestured for him to come with her, and they went to a small door that led to a connecting building. As they walked, Emma gave him a sideways glance. "What was that Russian word you called me?"

"*Dushenka*."

"What does it mean?"

"Perhaps someday I'll tell you."

Her brows drew together at his response. "I'll ask my stepmother tonight."

"That wouldn't be wise."

"Why? Is it a bad word? An insult?"

Before Nikolas could reply, they had entered the next building. A pungent cat-smell crept to Nikolas's nostrils, in spite of the plentiful air and light that circulated through grates and barred windows. He forgot the smell as soon as he saw the huge striped animal padding toward Emma, prevented from reaching her by a row of iron bars. The magnificent tiger had a deep reddish-orange coat scored with thick black stripes. A distinctive burst of long hair adorned its neck and back. Nikolas had never seen such a large tiger—definitely over forty stone—and certainly not one at this close range.

"You brought him to me as a kitten, remember?"

"Of course," Nikolas said quietly. It was the only gift he had ever given Emma, when she was twelve years old. He had found the sick tiger cub in a ramshackle shop filled with exotic animals and had bought it for her. He hadn't seen the animal since then.

Emma crouched close to the bars, cooing and making baby noises. "Manchu, this is Prince Nikolas." The great cat settled nearby with a half-lidded, drowsy look of pleasure. An opening had been cut in the wall, allowing Manchu access to an outside enclosure where he could sun himself. His legs and belly were soaked from his lounging in a shallow tank of water. "Isn't he beautiful?" Emma asked with maternal pride. "Look at the size of those paws. Tigers have killed more humans than any other cat, you know. They're wonderfully unpredictable."

"Wonderful," Nikolas agreed dryly. His breath caught as Emma reached between the bars of the cage and scratched the tiger's neck.

"In Asia, where Manchu is from, the tiger is a symbol of reincarnation." Emma glanced from Manchu to Nikolas. "You look alike, actually. Maybe you were a tiger in another life, Your Highness."

"Don't reach in there." Nikolas's voice was soft, but it held a note that caused both Emma and the tiger to look at him questioningly.

Emma slid her arm farther into the cage and rubbed the cat's neck harder. "If you recall, he has no claws," she said. "They were pulled out by his first owner. Now Manchu will never be able to provide for himself. He'll never have freedom, the poor little kitten." She looked at Manchu with loving pity. An affectionate gurgling noise began in the tiger's chest, and he stared at her with the love of a cub for its mother. Nikolas tensed visibly until Emma withdrew her arm.

"There's no need to worry," she said. "Manchu thinks of me as a friend."

"Or an afternoon snack." Nikolas lifted the bucket of meat scraps. "I assume this is for him?" The tiger's head lifted, and he regarded the bucket with sudden alertness.

Emma rose to her feet and took the bucket from Nikolas. Expertly she shook the sopping mess into the cage. "*Bon appétit*, Manchu." The tiger gurgled with appreciation and applied himself happily to the meal. "Ghastly." Emma made a face and laughed. "I'm surrounded by carnivores." She wiped her hands on her trousers and grinned at Nikolas. "How does it feel to have dirty hands, Your Highness? A new experience for you, I imagine."

He approached her slowly. "I believe you're trying to bait me, Emma." Reaching for her slender wrist, he lifted her hand and looked at it palm-up, then turned it slowly.

Emma's smile vanished as she flinched in embarrassment. Her hand was reddened and callused. Her fingers were long and slender, but the nails had been filed to ruthlessly short crescents. Tiny white scars, most of them scratches or tooth marks, were scattered from her fingertips to her wrist. After the well-groomed women Nikolas was used to, she must be a horror. "Not the hand of a lady, is it?" she said.

He smoothed his thumb over the fine tracing of blue veins on her skin. "It's the hand of a woman."

Nervously Emma tried to pull away. "What do you want from me? Why are you here?"

His grip tightened. "I enjoy your company."

"You couldn't possibly."

"Why not? You're intelligent, entertaining . . . and very beautiful."

"You arrogant bastard," she said, her temper exploding. "Don't you dare mock me!"

"Do you really think so little of yourself? It's not mockery." He took her other wrist, ignoring her burst of outrage. "My red-haired one," he murmured. "In the old Russian, we used the same word for 'red' and 'beautiful.' "

Emma yanked at her imprisoned hands. "What are you doing?"

"I said I would kiss you someday. I always keep my promises."

Her muscles strained against his hard grip as she tried to wrench free. "If you don't take your hands off me, I'll blacken both your eyes. If you haven't noticed, I'm as tall as you are!"

Nikolas pushed her easily against a nearby wall. Her shoulders hit the wooden boards with a soft thump. "Not quite." He leaned over her, pinning her arms at her sides. "And you're only half my weight."

"I-I'll tell my father!" The few times in the past she had used those words, they had produced a magical effect. Everyone was afraid of her father.

"Will you?" His eyes gleamed with amusement. "That should be interesting."

Emma turned her face away, knowing she had made a mistake. She should have reacted with contempt, should have laughed and said he was being ridiculous. Instead she had lost her temper, the only sure way to keep his interest.

He released her hands and leaned closer, using his body to press her against the wall. Deliberately he wrapped her braid around his hand, and exerted enough force to pull her head back. His mouth hovered just above hers. She could feel the heat of his breath wafting against her lips in a soft, even rhythm, and she began to tremble. She spoke in a thick voice that didn't seem to be her own. "Whatever you're going to do, get it over with. I have work to attend to."

All at once she felt his mouth on hers, in a hard assault that was over as quickly as it had begun. He lifted his head, staring down at her with those golden-lashed eyes. Emma's mouth tingled from the bruising kiss. Tentatively she licked her lips, discovering a faint sugar-and-tea sweetness. "Now leave me alone," she said unsteadily.

The edges of his wide cheekbones seemed sharper than usual. His face looked exotic, almost Oriental in its austere calm. "I'm not finished."

Emma moved suddenly, trying to push him away. His arms closed around her, and she struggled until she was crushed by the power of his body. Nikolas bent his head again, kissing her with a force that wiped away the memories of all other men. Never again would she be able to recall the fumbling sweetness of her first kiss with a village boy, or even the tender embraces she had shared with Adam. Nikolas took it all away, branding her with a brutal passion which left no room for anything else. Emma was dizzy from the speed at which everything had changed. No longer was he the darkly glamorous figure who had hovered at the farthest edges of her life. Suddenly he was real, immediate, making her recognize him in a way she had never dared to before.

His large hands spread over her back, traced the length of her spine until he came to the swell of her hips. Beneath her shirt and trousers, she wore only a chemise and thin linen drawers . . . no corset, stays, laces; no protective layers that would disguise the shape of her body. She knew he could feel the softness of her breasts, the natural curve of her waist. Shame and sensation collided within her, making her sway dizzily against him. She shook with the effort not to clench her arms around him, pull him harder, closer, twine her fingers in his beautiful hair. Her flesh ached wherever it pressed his . . . breasts, legs, stomach . . . she wanted to bring his hands to her body . . . God, she wanted . . .

His lips broke from hers, and she gave a little moan of frustration. Her hands worked in the folds of his shirt, grasping aimlessly. He murmured something in Russian, his breath sinking through her hair to her scalp. Gradually her hands relaxed on his shoulders. Opening her eyes, Emma looked over his shoulder and saw that Manchu was watching them with unblinking yellow eyes, his tail flicking in an idle pattern. She snatched her hands away from Nikolas and tugged nervously at her shirt and belt.

Nikolas drew back and stared at her without emotion. "If you ever need anything," he said quietly, "you can come to me. I want to be your friend, Emma."

"I should th-think you have quite enough friends."

He used his thumb to smooth the crimson silk of her eyebrow. "Not like you."

"Friends don't kiss like that."

He flicked his forefinger lightly against her cheek. "Don't be a child, Emma."

The remark stung, and she replied in the haughtiest tone she could manage. "What could either of us have to gain from friendship?"

She stiffened as he slid his fingers beneath her chin. His lips almost brushed hers as he answered, "Perhaps we'll find out, *ruyshka*."

Then he released her. She stood with her eyes half-closed, leaning against the wall while he walked away.

* * *

As the rest of the week passed, Emma could think of nothing except Nikolas's visit and the possible reasons for his behavior. She didn't understand what he wanted. Surely Nikolas wasn't angling to have an affair with *her*, the eccentric daughter of an English duke, when so many beautiful women in London were eager to have him in their beds. And she wasn't stupid enough to believe he really wanted her friendship. He had the company of innumerable aristocrats, intellectuals, artists, politicians, all ready to come running whenever he snapped his fingers. He was never at a loss for companionship of any kind.

Just when she decided that the episode had been a temporary amusement for Nikolas, he came to visit again. Emma was in her room, reading a novel and basking in the morning light that streamed over her cushioned window seat. Her dog, Samson, a mongrel with a large dose of wolfhound, looked up expectantly at the sound of footsteps.

Tasia appeared in the doorway and tapped on the frame with her knuckle. "Emma," she said in a strange voice, "Nikolas is here."

The book wavered in Emma's hands. She looked at Tasia with open surprise.

Tasia continued softly. "He asked if you would care to go riding with him."

Emma was filled with a storm of confusion that made her want to leap up and pace around the room. Instead she turned toward the window and fixed her gaze on a point in the distance. "I don't know," she said, unnerved by the thought of being alone with Nikolas. What would he say? What did he want? Would he try to kiss her again?

"I don't think Luke would approve," Tasia said tentatively.

Emma scowled. "I'm sure he wouldn't! Papa wants me to stay alone and never see anyone. I don't care if there's hell to pay when he comes back from his meeting in London—I'm going to do as I please. Tell Nikolas I'll be down in five minutes."

"You're not being fair to your father."

"Has he been fair to me?" Emma stood and went to her armoire, opening the top drawer and searching for riding gloves.

"You need a chaperone."

"Why?" Emma asked scornfully. "Nikolas is a cousin, isn't he?"

"Not really. Perhaps a case could be made that he's an extremely distant relation by marriage."

"Well, I doubt there's any possibility of scandal if I go riding with him. No one in his right mind would believe Nikolas Angelovsky has taken a sudden interest in carrot-topped spinsters."

"You're not a spinster."

"I'm not the toast of London either." She kept her back to Tasia, continuing to rummage through the armoire.

There was the sound of Tasia's soft sigh. "Emma, when will you stop being so angry at your family?"

"Maybe when you stop interfering in every part of my life. I feel as caged as those poor animals in my menagerie." Resolutely Emma kept her back turned toward Tasia until she heard the sound of retreating footsteps. She glanced defiantly at Samson, whose furry face was wreathed in puzzled dismay, his tongue drooping limply from the side of his mouth. "Don't look at me like that," Emma muttered. "She's taken Papa's side, as always." The dog continued to stare at her, ears twitching with curiosity. Suddenly he flipped over onto his back and stretched out his paws in an invitation to a tummy scratch.

Emma's rebellious anger faded, and she went to him with a muffled laugh. "Silly old dog. Silly boy." Squatting next to him, she scrubbed her short nails through his rough coat while he whined and wriggled happily. Emma gave a deep sigh. "Oh, Samson . . . how many thousands of secrets have I told you? You're my best friend." She smoothed his long ears as she continued to talk wistfully. "I wonder why I can't be calm about everything the way Tasia is. She always manages her feelings so well. Mine are always exploding out of control. Phoebe Cotterly was right—I am more at home in a barnyard than a ballroom. Thank God I don't have to be clever or sophisticated or well behaved around my animals. All I have to do is love you, and you love me right back. Isn't that right, Samson?" She smiled bleakly as the dog nudged her hand with his moist nose. "Maybe Adam's love for me would have faded in time. I don't think I would be a good wife for anyone. Love isn't enough. A woman needs to be obedient and devoted, and beautiful, and helpful to her husband . . . instead I'm plain and wild and . . ."

She looked down at herself, wrinkling her nose at her usual combination of trousers, boots, and white shirt. She preferred to ride astride, in men's clothes. It was far more comfortable, not to mention easier for controlling the horse. But for some reason she didn't want to appear in front of Nikolas Angelovsky in her outlandish breeches today.

She returned to her armoire and opened a gleaming paneled door, pushing back layers of garments until she found her blue riding habit. The smartly tailored jacket and broadcloth skirt were dyed a shade of indigo that matched her eyes. Rummaging deeper in the armoire, Emma located a pale blue veil to wear with her high-crowned black silk hat.

She turned and grinned at her attentive dog. "Prince Nikolas is waiting. What do you think, Samson? Should I surprise him by dressing like a lady?"

If Nikolas was surprised or pleased by her appearance, he gave no sign. He waited in the great hall, half-sitting on the edge of an octagonal stone table with casual elegance. He held a riding whip in one hand, tapping it lightly against his fawn breeches and polished boots. Sunlight poured in from the solar windows at the top of the hall, turning his hair to a golden blaze. As he watched Emma descend the grand staircase, there was an insolent glint in his eyes, as if they shared a secret. And they did, Emma reminded herself with sudden discomfort. Somehow Nikolas had known that she wouldn't tell anyone he had kissed her.

She had considered it, of course. But there seemed to be no point. And the thought of her father's reaction, the reprimand he would try to give Nikolas—no, it would all be too humiliating.

He smiled as she approached him. "I'm glad you agreed to see me, cousin."

"I was bored," she said flatly. "I thought you might provide some diversion."

"How fortunate for me that you had no better offers." His tone was light, almost cheerful.

As she studied him, Emma realized that he was

pleased at the prospect of riding with her. Smug, actually. She narrowed her eyes in suspicion. "What do you want, Nikki?"

"To provide some diversion for you." He crooked his arm invitingly.

Emma ignored the courtly gesture. "I don't need to be escorted to my own stables," she said, motioning for him to follow her. "And if you dare lay a finger on me today, I'll cripple you."

Nikolas smiled and matched his legs to her brisk stride. "Thanks for the warning, cousin."

The mount that Emma chose, a supple and energetic chestnut, was a good match for the black stallion Nikolas had brought. They rode in perfect balance, after the stallion's fretful temperament had been worked out. Emma couldn't find fault with the way Nikolas rode. He was patient with the animal, using just the right amount of discipline to keep him under control. But she sensed the contest of wills between them, the way Nikolas dominated the stallion. Almost all men rode that way, as if one had to be superior and the other inferior. Emma treated her horses as equal partners. Because she worked with them and communicated with them, they were far more responsive to her commands.

Emma and Nikolas rode from the broad hill that Southgate Hall was founded on, down to the outskirts of the busy town below. The day was bright and warm, the air stirring with a pleasant breeze. After crossing a small creek, they cut through the oak forest that bordered Southgate, and raced across a wide green meadow. The stallion easily overtook Emma's chestnut, and she slowed the horse's pace, laughingly acknowledging defeat.

"I would give you some real competition if I weren't riding sidesaddle," she called.

Nikolas reined in the stallion and grinned back at her. "You ride like no other woman I've ever seen, Emelia. Like a swallow in flight."

"Is that the Russian version of my name?"

He nodded. "My distant grandmother was named Emelia. It suits you." He circled the stallion around her. "Shall we walk for a little while?"

"All right." Emma dismounted easily, before he could offer to assist.

Nikolas slid from the saddle, clicking his tongue against his teeth as if she were a willful child. "You're independent to a fault, *ruyshka*. Is it such a crime to take a man's arm every now and then? To let someone help you down from a horse or climb a flight of steps?"

"I don't need help. I don't want to depend on anyone."

"Why not?"

"Because I might get used to it."

"Is that so terrible?"

She shrugged impatiently. "I do much better on my own. I always have."

They left the horses grazing beneath the branches of an ancient oak tree, and walked across another wide green meadow. The grass was alive with the drone of bees harvesting pollen from a carpet of wildflowers. Emma glanced at Nikolas frequently, struck by the sight of him walking beside her with the grace of a prowling cat. In her whole life she had never known such an unpredictable man. The first time she had ever seen him, he had torn her family apart. They had all hated him. But somehow in the following years he had stolen his way into

their lives. If not exactly welcomed into the Stokehurst household with open arms, at least he had
become a tolerated visitor.

"I never thought we would be walking together
alone like this," she commented.

"Why not?"

"To begin with, my father doesn't like you, my
family doesn't trust you, and everyone I know says
you're a dangerous character."

"I'm not dangerous," he said, a smile playing on
his lips.

"According to the stories, you are. A scoundrel,
betrayer, seducer of married women . . . some even
say a cold-blooded murderer."

Nikolas was quiet for a long time. Somewhere in
the midst of their grass-muffled footfalls came a
soft reply. "All those things are true. Even the last.
I left Russia because I killed a man. But there was
nothing cold-blooded about it."

Emma stumbled a little, fixing her startled gaze
on him. His expression was closed, the tawny crescents of his lashes veiling his eyes. Why on earth
would he admit this to her? She felt her heart
pound in an agitated rhythm. Nikolas kept walking, and she followed uncertainly. They reached a
shaded cart path bordered by a wooden fence.

Nikolas stopped in the center of the path, his
muscles tensing. It had been a calculated risk, telling Emma about what he had done. But she would
find out anyway, and it was better to have heard
it from him. A mist of sweat broke on his forehead,
and he wiped at it with the cuff of his sleeve in a
controlled gesture. "Would you like to hear about
it?"

"I suppose," she said diffidently, but he sensed

the intense curiosity behind her stillness.

"The man I killed was named Samvel Shurikov-sky." Nikolas paused and swallowed hard. Five Imperial interrogators and two weeks of torture hadn't been able to wring those words out of him. It was a trick of the imagination, but suddenly his scars seemed to burn and itch. He continued with difficulty, rubbing absently at his wrists. "Shuri-kovsky was the governor of St. Petersburg, and the tsar's favorite adviser. He and my brother, Mikhail, were lovers. When Mikhail broke off the relation-ship, Shurikovsky went mad with rage . . . and stabbed him to death."

"Oh," Emma said, her mouth slackening in astonishment, trying to comprehend that not only had his brother taken a male lover, but he had been murdered by one of them. It was a shocking reve-lation, especially uttered in such a casual tone. Sub-jects such as sex and murder had never been discussed in her presence, except for Tasia's moth-erly lectures on morality.

"Mikhail was all I had," Nikolas said. "I was the only one who ever gave a damn about him. He was my responsibility. When he was killed, I . . ." He paused and shook his head. Sunlight moved over his golden-brown hair in a shower of sparks. "The only thought that kept me breathing and eating and living was to find his murderer."

Slowly Nikolas forgot he was speaking. The memories came over him in a blur. His eyes were open but unseeing. "First I thought that Tasia had done it. As you remember, I followed her from Russia to England in an effort to make her pay for the murder. But then I learned that Shurikovsky was the one responsible for my brother's death . . .

and I knew there would never be justice unless it came from my hands."

"Why couldn't you let the proper authorities handle it?"

"In Russia, politics take precedence over everything else. Shurikovsky was the companion-favorite of the tsar. I knew he would never be prosecuted for murdering Mikhail. He was too influential."

"So you took your revenge," Emma said tonelessly.

"I was careful to leave no evidence, but I came under suspicion nonetheless. And I was arrested." Suddenly the words stuck in Nikolas's throat. There was so much he couldn't tell her, things that could never be expressed, nightmares that seethed deep inside him. With an effort, he assumed his usual calm mask. "The government tried to force a confession from me, if not for murder, then for treason. When I refused to talk, I was exiled."

He fell silent then, concentrating on the hard-baked ground. A breeze filtered through the damp locks on his forehead. Exile from Russia had been worse than torture or even death; it meant being cut off from the very source of life. Even the most reviled criminals were pitied when they were sent away from their beloved country. *Neshchastnye,* they were called—"unfortunates." Russia was the great mother, and her children were sustained by her frosty air, her dark forests, and her great cradling arms of earth and snow. Part of Nikolas's spirit had withered after he had left St. Petersburg for the last time. Sometimes he dreamed he was still there, and he awoke with an unbearable ache of longing.

"Why tell me?" Emma asked, interrupting his bleak thoughts. "You never do anything without a reason. Why did you want me to know?"

Nikolas looked at her, smiling sardonically into her serious face. "Don't friends confide in each other?"

"How do you know I won't tell anyone?"

"I'll just have to trust you, *dushenka*."

Emma stared at him intently. "Are you sorry you killed Shurikovsky?"

Nikolas shook his head. "I don't believe in regret. It doesn't change the past."

"You're an amoral man," Emma said, her blue eyes fixed on his. "I should be afraid of you. But I'm not."

"How brave you are," he mocked, amused by her bravado.

"I even think . . . if I had been in your place, I might have done the same thing."

Before Nikolas could reply, he felt her touch his wrist. He froze, realizing that he had unconsciously been rubbing the scars on his chest as they talked. His hand stiffened beneath her slim fingers. There was no pity in Emma's face. She regarded him with a strange acceptance, as if he were a savage creature who couldn't be faulted for his own nature.

"Then you don't blame me for the murder?" he asked, his voice gruff.

"It's not my place to judge you. But I understand why you did it." Her bare hand rested lightly on his. "I'll keep your secrets, Nikki."

Nikolas didn't move. His muscles locked against a sudden shiver of feeling. He had no idea why her touch, her words, had such power over him. All he knew was that he wanted to hold her, hurt her, kiss her . . . he wanted to bear her down to the ground, here, and tug her red hair loose, and take her in the field as if she were a peasant girl. Instead he drew back and pulled his hand from hers. His voice was pleasant, friendly, as he replied, "I believe you will, Emelia."

She gave him a cautious smile and began to walk again, her skirts brushing through the clods and wheel ruts on the dusty path. Nikolas kept pace with her, his hands jammed in his pockets. She hadn't reacted as he'd expected. She had accepted his story too easily. Her family had sheltered her too much, allowing her to live her life as if it were something out of a novel. She was even more unworldly than he'd suspected. *You poor little fool,* he thought, glancing at her through the amber screen of his lashes. *Why must you make it so easy for me to take advantage of you?*

"May I see you again tomorrow?" he asked.

Emma hesitated, her teeth catching on her bottom lip. "No," she finally said. "I'll be in London for the rest of the week."

"A social engagement?"

"Actually, I'm attending a meeting of the R.S.H.T.A. I've been asked to say a few words about the most recent animal protection laws."

"Will your family be accompanying you?"

Emma's jaw hardened. "No. They have no interest in my crusades, and even if they did, I wouldn't want them there."

"Ah," he said softly. "So you haven't yet made peace with your father."

She shook her head. "My father drove away the love of my life. If someone did that to you, I doubt you'd be so quick to forgive them!"

"Perhaps not. But I need no one, whereas you . . . you've lost your love and your family all at once." Nikolas watched for a reaction from her, but she concealed her emotions well. He made one more soft-voiced comment, well timed and carefully aimed. "It's not easy to be lonely, is it? Emptiness, silence, unwelcome solitude . . . it can turn a palace into a prison."

Emma turned a wondering gaze toward him, her blue eyes wide. Heedless of where she was walking, she stumbled on the edge of a deep wheel rut. Nikolas reached for her immediately, lending her his balance. Before she could protest, he grasped her hand and drew it through the crook of his elbow. An easy smile curved his mouth as he stared into her flushed face. "Take help when it's offered, cousin. It's just a temporary arm to lean on."

The Royal Society for the Humane Treatment of Animals conducted its annual general meeting at a lecture hall in London, not far from Covent Garden. The small building had been converted from an old hotel located on a street of auctioneers, booksellers, and publishers. Looking around the room, scored with light that came from the half-shuttered windows, Emma felt a sense of kinship with the crowd of two hundred Society members. Middle-aged men, most of them, some of them slender and stiff in their mahogany chairs, some of them plumply overlapping the small, square seats. There was a sparse peppering of women, the youngest of them exactly twice her age.

Emma knew that they all didn't have the same motivation for being there. Although some shared her passionate concern for the well-being of animals, others were there merely because it was a popular political concern. But that didn't matter, as long as they were working together for an important cause.

Feeling someone's gaze on her, she looked down the row to her right. A young man with a narrow face and lively dark eyes was sitting several places away. While they exchanged a discreet smile, Emma tried to remember his name. Mr. Henry Dowling, or maybe it was Harry. They had spoken once or twice before. If she remembered correctly, he held a position at a publishing company, but his real interest was collie dogs. He was known as one of the foremost breeders of collies in England. His charmingly sharp-featured face reminded her of Presto, her fox. Emma's smile widened for a second before she looked away. She still felt that he was staring at her, however, and a warm blush burned at the tops of her cheeks.

The meeting progressed through several speakers. There was a great deal of rustling paper as the members took notes or prepared their own speeches. The wooden chairs squeaked as legs were crossed and uncrossed. Once in a while there were interruptions as members sought to clarify certain statements or information. After the fourth speaker, it was Emma's turn. Lord Crowles, the president of the Society, asked for a report on the manual for animal-protection laws, and Emma's mouth went dry.

All at once the room seemed very quiet. Carefully Emma made her way to the front of the room, holding a thick sheaf of paper in her arms as if it were a shield. Her stomach flip-flopped with excitement and nerves. Hunching her shoulders defensively, she gripped the papers tightly and stared at the rows of faces before her. She was surprised to hear her voice come out clear and steady.

"Gentlemen, I have brought the proposed revisions for the animal-protection manual. It has been rewritten according to many wise and helpful suggestions from the distinguished officers of the Society. If the manual is found to be acceptable, then a large-scale printing will be ordered and distributed to the public."

An elderly gentleman near the front of the room spoke up. "Would Lady Emma care to describe the nature of the revisions?"

Emma gave him a brisk nod, her shoulders relaxing a little. "Yes, sir. The manual gives a more detailed explanation of the procedures for making complaints about animal abuse. Certain evidence must be gathered at the time of an offense in order to conduct a successful prosecution. The public is well aware of the animals being abused in the streets . . . we've all seen horses beaten with whips, cudgels, or shovels; livestock mistreated on the way to market; stray dogs and cats being tormented. Many people are distressed by the cruelty they witness, but they don't know what they can do to stop it. The manual contains guidelines for recognizing an offense, and procedures for reporting criminals to the proper authorities."

To Emma's surprise, Mr. Dowling asked a question. "Lady Emma, what about the area of scientific experimentation? Does the manual mention the practice of vivisection?"

Emma shook her head regretfully. "The medical

and scientific communities claim that they need to perform vivisections—the procedure of dissecting live animals—in order to further their knowledge. But they have no proof that it accomplishes anything, except to cause thousands of animals a cruel and painful death. I would have made mention of this subject in the manual, but there are no guidelines at present. We have no way of knowing which scientific practices are necessary and which ones are merely experiments in torture. Perhaps the members of the R.S.H.T.A. might consider it worthwhile to appoint a committee to study the situation . . ."

Emma would have continued, but something drew her eyes to the back of the room, a familiar flash of gold, a man's form swathed in dark clothes. It was Prince Nikolas. Even at this distance, the amber shade of his eyes and hair was vivid. Confusion seized her. She was barely conscious of Lord Crowles's agreeable response to her previous suggestion, the motion being made and seconded. Somehow she managed to rip her gaze away from Nikolas. She handed the manuscript to the secretary of the club, who was waiting nearby. The men in her row stood politely as she made her way back to her seat.

The meeting lasted another hour. Emma kept her gaze pinned on the back of the chair in front of her, unable to concentrate. Somehow she resisted the temptation to glance back at Nikolas. He was here because he wanted something from her. That was the only explanation for this deliberate pursuit. Unease and anger tangled inside her. But . . . was it possible she also felt a flicker of pleasure? Nikolas was a handsome and powerful man. Many women would do anything to capture his attention just for a few minutes ... and here he was, waiting for her.

As Lord Crowles's concluding remarks signaled the end of the meeting, the assemblage rose to leave. Emma made her way to the end of the row and found herself in the company of Mr. Dowling. A smile lurked in the depths of his dark eyes.

"Lady Emma, I'm going to suggest to Lord Crowles that your name be included in the manual as recognition of the splendid work you've done."

"Oh, no," Emma said earnestly. "Thank you, but I haven't done all that much. And I don't want any sort of recognition. I just want the animals to be helped."

"If I may say so, you're as modest as you are attractive, Lady Emma."

Confused and pleased, Emma lowered her gaze.

Mr. Dowling spoke again, this time on a more tentative note. "Lady Emma, I was wondering if you would consider—"

"Cousin." A soft Russian accent cut through the conversation. "How nice to find you here. But you seem to have lost your chaperone. You must allow me to see you back home safely."

Emma's head snapped up, and she scowled at Nikolas, who knew perfectly well that she often discarded the basic etiquette of chaperones. It was one of the benefits of being eccentric. Realizing introductions were in order, she crossed her arms over her chest and gruffly did the honors. "Prince Nikolas, may I present Mr. Dowling."

The men shook hands briefly. Nikolas turned a shoulder to Dowling, rudely indicating that the meeting was over. "You look very fine today, Emelia."

Mr. Dowling hovered nearby, his eyes meeting with Emma's. She smiled apologetically. "Good day, Lady Emma," he said hesitantly. "My best wishes to you and your . . . family." He eyed Nikolas uncertainly, clearly wondering if the blond Russian fit in that category. As he left, he seemed to fade away like a puff of smoke.

Emma glared at Nikolas. "What are you doing here?"

"I'm concerned about animal protection," he said mildly.

"Like hell you are. This was a closed meeting. How did you get in?"

"I purchased a membership."

"You can't buy a membership, you have to fill out papers and go through interviews, and then there's a committee vote—" She stopped abruptly. "You bribed your way in."

"I made a donation," he corrected.

Emma gave an exasperated laugh. "Is there anything your money can't get for you? What do you want now?"

"I intend to escort you home, cousin."

"Thank you, but I have a carriage waiting outside."

"I took the liberty of dismissing it."

"Presumptuous man," she said without heat, sliding her hand into the crook of his proffered arm. "Do you always get your way?"

"Almost always." Nikolas escorted her from the building, ignoring the curious stares that followed them. "I like to watch you make speeches, Emelia.

I admire a woman who doesn't try to hide her intelligence."

"Is that why you followed me to London? Because you admire me so much?"

He smiled at her impudence. "I'll admit to having taken an interest in you. Would you condemn a man for that?"

"Condemn, no. But I have plenty of suspicions. Especially where you're concerned. I think you're nothing but a great big mass of ulterior motives, Nikki."

A low laugh of delight came from his throat. He led her to the curb, where a splendid lacquered carriage awaited them. It was drawn by a team of four gleaming black Orlovs, the finest carriage horses in the world. A pair of tall, black-liveried footmen attended the vehicle.

Emma preceded Nikolas into the carriage and settled herself on upholstery of burgundy velvet in a shade so dark, it looked black. The interior was filled with gleaming panels of precious inlaid wood. The windows were framed in gold and crystal, and the lamps were encrusted with semiprecious stones. Even with her family's considerable wealth, Emma had never been inside such a luxurious vehicle. Nikolas sat opposite her, and the carriage pulled away with magical smoothness as it passed over the rough London streets.

Temporarily dazzled, Emma wondered about the life Nikolas had led in Russia, and all that he'd been forced to leave behind. "Nikki," she asked abruptly, "do you ever see any of your family? Have they ever come to visit?"

He showed no reaction, but she sensed that he was puzzled by the question. "No . . . nor would I expect it of them. All ties were severed when I left my country."

"But not blood ties. You have sisters, don't you? Tasia once mentioned that you have four or five—"

"Five," he said flatly.

"Don't you miss them? Wouldn't you like to see them?"

"No, I don't miss them. We were virtual strangers to each other. Mikhail and I were raised separately from our sisters."

"Why?"

"Because my father wanted it that way." A bitterly amused look crossed his face. "We were rather like the animals in your menagerie, all of us caged and at my father's mercy."

"You didn't like him?"

"My father was a heartless bastard. When he died ten years ago, he wasn't mourned by a soul on earth."

"What about your mother?" Emma asked tentatively.

Nikolas shook his head and smiled. "I prefer not to talk about my family."

"I understand," she murmured.

Nikolas's amusement lingered. "No, you don't. The Angelovskys are a bad lot, and each generation is worse than the last. We started out as feuding royals of Kiev, then mingled the line with some crude peasant stock, and added a Mongol warrior who thought nothing of drinking blood from his horse's veins for refreshment on a long journey. We've only gone downhill from there—I'm a good example of that."

"Are you trying to frighten me?"

"I'm warning you not to entertain any illusions about me, Emma. 'A corrupt tree cannot bring forth good fruit.' You'd be wise to remember that."

She laughed, her blue eyes dancing. "You sound like Tasia, quoting the Bible. I've never thought of you as a religious man."

"Religion is entwined in every part of a Russian's life. There's no way to avoid it."

"Do you ever go to church?"

"Not since I was a boy. My brother and I used to think angels lived in the tops of the church domes, gathering our prayers and sending them to heaven."

"Were your prayers answered?"

"Never," he said flatly, and shrugged. "But our great talent is to endure . . . that is God's gift to Russians."

The carriage passed a shoddy marketplace filled with stalls of fruit and vegetables, fish stands, and secondhand goods. The noisy crowd milling through the streets caused the procession of horses and vehicles to slow. There was an unusual din in the air, a mixture of bellowing voices and animal cries.

As the carriage came to a halt, Emma leaned forward and looked out the window curiously. "Something's happening in the street," she said. "Some sort of fight, perhaps."

Nikolas opened the carriage door and jumped lightly to the ground. After calling to the driver to wait there, he headed into the crowd. Emma waited for a minute or two, listening to the racket. Perhaps two vehicles had collided, or someone had been run down in the street. Her heart ached in pity as she heard the anguished cries of a horse—or maybe it was a donkey. It was easy to recognize the pain and fear in its screams. She couldn't stand to wait another minute. She sprang from the carriage, just as Nikolas returned with a grim look on his face. "What's happening?" she asked anxiously.

"It's nothing. Go back inside—we'll pass through in a few minutes."

Emma stared into his emotionless eyes, then darted past him in a swift movement.

"Emma, come back—"

Ignoring his curt voice, she rushed through the churning mob.

❧ Three

IN THE MIDDLE of a busy intersection, a cart over-
loaded with bricks blocked the traffic from all di-
rections. A battered old donkey, sharp-ribbed and
swaybacked, strained wildly to pull the cart up a
small hill. Its owner, a beefy little man with arms
the size of ham hocks, was beating the donkey with
a length of chain. The poor animal was bloody and
crippled, its eyes rolling madly.

In the manual Emma had just presented to the
R.S.H.T.A., there was a list of procedures to follow.
She should take down the names of the culprit and
witnesses, the specifics of the crime, descriptions of
the wounds . . . but at the sound of the donkey's
miserable braying, all thoughts of procedure flew
out of her head. A bolt of furious energy went
through her, and she shoved her way through the
crowd. "Stop it! Stop it now, or I'll kill you!"

Startled by the blazing redheaded apparition, a
few people scrambled hastily out of her way. The
thick-necked man paused in his beating and glared
up at her. "Mind your own business, bitch!"

Ignoring him, Emma approached the terrified
animal. Drawing close to his tossing head, she
soothed him until the donkey pushed his nose

against her middle like a child seeking refuge. A wave of astonished exclamations issued from the crowd.

The donkey's owner seemed unimpressed. "Get away from my beast," he bellowed, raising his arm threateningly. "I'll make him climb that hill or send him to hell."

"I'm going to have you arrested," Emma shouted, sliding her arms around the quivering animal's neck. "The cart's too heavy for him to pull, you stupid bastard!"

"Get away!" The chain came whistling through the air, striking the ground near her feet. "Move away, or I'll lay your head open wi' this."

Emma's arms tightened reflexively around the donkey. Looking into the man's purple face, she knew that he was enraged beyond reason. He was deadly serious in his threats. Yet she couldn't back down—she would never forgive herself if she left the animal to be beaten to death. "Sir," she began on a halfway conciliatory note, but he burst out with a flood of obscenities and drew back the chain to strike her.

Suddenly everything happened too fast for her to understand. All at once Nikolas was there, grabbing her with bruising force, shielding her with his body as the chain whipped around in a shining streak. She felt him flinch as the metal links struck him, and she heard the swift rush of air between his teeth. Then he sent her stumbling away with a hard shove.

For Nikolas, the impact of the chain on his back set off an inner explosion he had never expected. All awareness of the present disintegrated; there was only the past, rushing over him, making him blank and crazed and bloodthirsty. In a flash he relived the agony of being tortured by the tsar's officials, his back shredded by the knout . . . *Won't you confess now, Your Highness?* He found his hands clenched around the man's neck, staring into watery blue eyes that were filled with rage and dawning fear. A black, murderous mist surrounded him.

"No," the man whimpered, squirming in fright, his fat little hands coming up to Nikolas's taut wrists.

Nikolas choked him into silence, his fingers digging into the thick, straining neck. The lust for murder oozed like sweat from his pores. Only one sound reached him . . . a woman's voice, low and intent, pulling him back from the edge.

"Nikki! Nikki, let him go!"

He blinked and shivered, glancing in the direction of the voice. Emma was close by. Her dark blue eyes held his. "Let him go," she repeated. Somehow the ecstasy of violence faded, and Nikolas relented, giving in to her quiet command. Reluctantly he took his hands from the man's throat.

Reeling in terror, the man fled into the crowd. He managed to shout hoarse warnings as he clutched his bruised throat. "He's the devil! Look in his eyes—you'll see! The devil himself . . ."

Some people dispersed. Others stayed to complain that their way was blocked and they wanted the intersection to be cleared. A few volunteers organized a group to pull the cart of bricks to the side of the street.

Nikolas's fingers were stiff and coiled. He flexed them, worked the tension from his wrists, only vaguely aware of Emma supervising the unhitching of the donkey from the cart. Her tone was brisk and expert as she directed one of the footmen to tie the scrawny donkey to the back of the lacquered carriage. "We'll bring him to my family's home," she said in response to the footman's muted question. "I think he'll make it as long as the carriage doesn't move too fast."

Nikolas wanted to leave. The confusion of the scene was nothing compared with his inner chaos. He had to be somewhere quiet to think, to compose himself. He sent Emma a commanding look, his gaze boring into her back until she glanced at him over her shoulder. Understanding his silent message, Emma obeyed at once. She seemed calm and unruffled as she made her way back to the carriage. Nikolas entered the vehicle and sat opposite her. To his surprise, he saw that her face was pale, and her fingers were twisted together in a tight knot.

"I see abuse like this all the time," she said in an agitated voice. "I'll never get used to it. Why do people have to be so cruel?"

Nikolas didn't reply, only snapped the curtains shut against the sight of the swarming crowd. Emma stared at him through the darkened interior of the carriage as the vehicle finally began to move. "It must have hurt when the chain hit you," she said tentatively. "Are you all right?"

Nikolas nodded once, still consumed with old and dark memories. How could he have lost control so easily? He never allowed his emotions to overtake him . . . it was a weakness he couldn't afford.

Emma spoke again while she combed taut fingers through the fallen locks of her hair. "Thank you for coming to my rescue. It seems I'm in your debt again."

"Not this time." His attention returned to her slowly. Although her face was averted, he thought that she seemed to be struggling with her feelings. "Do you want a handkerchief?" he asked abruptly. Emma shook her head in refusal, but he fished for one in his coat and held it out to her.

"I'm not crying," she said. "I never do. It doesn't solve anything, and it never makes me feel better." She took the square of soft white linen and blew her nose noisily, shooting a defiant look at him.

Suddenly Nikolas felt his heart pound in a hard rhythm. Other women used tears for purposes of seduction or sympathy, yet they had never moved him. Only Emma, denying her weakness and challenging him to say one word about it, could affect him like this.

Nikolas found himself moving toward her. He took her in his arms, ignoring her unwilling start. After a brief struggle she relaxed against him, her breasts pressing against his side and chest. Her hair was unperfumed, the scent as fresh as if she had been walking in the woods through patches of fennel and crisp green moss. He breathed deeply of the smell, and he hovered at the edge of violence, all his calculated plans threatening to crumble beneath the pressure of overwhelming desire. Somehow he kept his hands impersonal and still on her back, in spite of his desperate need to touch her.

"Stubborn, impetuous little fool," he whispered in Russian, knowing she didn't understand. "I've been waiting for you, thousands of nights. I've imagined other women were you ... I made love to them, always pretending it was you in my arms. Soon you'll know you were meant for me. Soon you'll come to me."

Emma shook her head in confusion at the foreign language. "What did you say?"

Nikolas was transfixed by the dark brilliance of her eyes. He longed to press his mouth to her skin, to kiss the spray of golden freckles on her cheeks, the fiery crescents of her lashes. He struggled with his self-control while it threatened to slip away like sand through his fingers. With all his strength, he locked his feelings away and spoke in a cool, slightly amused voice. "I said there's no need for tears, *ruyshka*. You mustn't be so emotional."

"I can't help it," she said grumpily. "I've always been this way . . . out of place, out of step. I wish I could be like everyone else. My only hope was to marry Lord Milbank."

Nikolas smiled, carefully smoothing her rumpled hair. "The minute you become like everyone else, I'll leave England for good. You weren't meant to be in step with the rest of the world. And if you think Lord Milbank would have given you happiness, you're wrong. I'm familiar with his kind. They exist everywhere. As common as mice."

"I won't listen to any insults about Adam—"

"Did you ever let him see this side of you? Did you ever dare to argue with him? *Nyet*, you adopted a soft facade to please him because you liked his looks and his slippery charm, and you thought he wouldn't want you if he knew how intelligent you are, how brave and ferocious. You were right. He isn't man enough to value those qualities."

"Well, 'ferocious' is certainly a wonderful quality in a woman," Emma muttered, pulling away from him. "One wonders why Adam didn't think so."

"In Russia you would be the most desirable woman in all the land."

"I'm not in Russia, thank God. And stop trying to flatter me—you know I don't like it."

Nikolas caught her jaw in his palms and studied her flushed face. Her skin was tender and soft beneath his fingertips. "The most desirable woman," he repeated, staring hard into her eyes, not letting her turn away.

A shiver went through Emma's body. She must have felt it too, the ineluctable force that drew them together. It was their shared destiny. Nikolas was too much a Russian not to believe in fate. Everything would happen as it was meant to . . . all that was required of a Russian was patience and endurance . . . and God knew he had proved himself on both counts.

A carriage wheel bounced across a hole in the road, jolting the vehicle. Nikolas broke apart from Emma and settled himself opposite her. He continued to watch her steadily, but she kept her gaze on her folded hands. No words were exchanged until they reached the Stokehurst villa on the Thames.

Hesitantly Emma broke the silence. "I'm grateful for your help today, Nikolas. But . . . I would rather you didn't make any further efforts to see me. I don't think we should be friends. I can't see that any good would come of it."

Perhaps she expected him to disagree, even argue. Instead he shrugged and gave her an oblique smile. "Whatever you wish."

Emma escaped Nikolas's presence with blatant relief. With the help of the coachman and stablehand, she lodged the donkey in the stables behind the villa and attended to his abrasions and wounds, discovering that he had infected hooves and a bad case of malnourishment. It seemed likely that the animal would recover quite well. Leaving him in the care of the stablehand, she went into the villa.

The Stokehurst home was of picturesque Italian design, filled with pale marble columns and floors, elegant tile fireplaces, and several splashing indoor fountains. Emma had always liked to stay here, though the villa lacked the comfortable atmosphere of Southgate Hall.

Feeling troubled and out of sorts, Emma took a bath in a huge porcelain tub, in a bathing room lined with hand-painted tiles. Idly she traced the designs of tiny exotic birds with a wet fingertip . . . and thought about Nikolas.

Her encounters with him had become more and more confusing. She had never experienced so many conflicting feelings about one person. He was challenging, charming—and frightening. She had heard the rumors of his affairs, a multitude of discreet, short-lived relationships with society women. That was the kind Nikolas liked—cool, elegant creatures who were bored with their lifeless marriages. Why had he decided to bother with her? What could his motives be?

Well, it was over now. Nikolas was out of her life, just as surely as Adam was. She lifted one long, soapy leg and viewed it with a critical eye. If she were petite and fragile, would Adam have stayed with her? Emma dropped her leg with a splash and sighed. If only she had been beautiful enough, Adam wouldn't have let anything stand in the way of having her . . . not her father, not money, not anything. "If only I were like Tasia," she said aloud.

Tasia was small and delicate, with an exquisite beauty that fascinated men. Suppressing a twinge of envy, Emma scooped handfuls of hot water over her neck and shoulders.

Now that she had lost Adam, she would become a dried-up old spinster, never knowing what it was like to be with a man, to give herself to him in passion and fall asleep in his arms. She could take a lover, but the thought of that filled her with melancholy. How lonely it would feel, sharing a bed with a man she didn't love, a physical exchange in which their emotions and souls were left untouched.

"Lady Emma?" A voice interrupted her thoughts. She glanced at the doorway, where her maid, Katie, stood with an armload of freshly warmed towels and a white linen robe. "Finished with your bath yet, miss?"

"I suppose I am." Emma stood up and reached for one of the towels, wrapping it around her body as she stepped from the tub.

Katie blotted her shoulders with another towel, and helped her into the robe. "Shall I run downstairs and tell Cook what you'd like for supper, Lady Emma?"

"I'm not very hungry tonight."

"Oh, but you must have something, milady!"

Emma smiled and nodded reluctantly. "All right, I'll have tea and toast in my room. And I'd like something to read. Please bring a copy of the *Times*."

"Yes, miss."

Emma walked barefoot into her suite of rooms and sat at her dressing table. She pulled the pins from her hair and unbraided it, luxuriously massaging her fingers over her sore scalp. Methodically she worked a brush through her long, curly hair, smoothing out tangles and snarls until her arm was tired. After placing the brush in one of the dressing table's intricate compartments, she stared at her reflection in the gold-framed mirror.

An ordinary face, she thought. Pale skin with freckles, a straight nose, a sharp chin. The only thing that pleased her were her blue eyes, identical to her father's, except that her lashes were auburn instead of black.

Prince Nikolas had said she was desirable. He had called her beautiful. Had Adam ever said such things to her? Emma couldn't remember such an occasion. Frowning, she went over to her silk-covered bed and curled up on the blue counterpane. She propped her back against a brocaded pillow, lost in thought until Katie arrived with the tea tray.

"Here, milady . . . tea, toast, and the *Times*."

"Thank you, Katie." She watched as the maid set the tray beside her on the bed.

Katie gave her a look of friendly concern. "Everything all right, miss? You seem a bit peaked tonight."

"I'm fine. It was a very long day." Picking up a slice of buttered toast, Emma managed to produce one of her usual impish grins, then took a large bite of toast. Looking reassured, the maid left the room.

Emma poured tea from a tiny porcelain pot into a flowered cup and stirred in a heaping spoonful of crushed sugar. She took a sip, relishing the strong tea. Flipping open the paper, she scanned the long columns and lingered on items of interest. Her attention was snared by something near the bottom of an inside page, an announcement nearly hidden in a sea of lines and letters. She stared at it in mild surprise. As the words began to make an impression on her mind, the ink seemed to grow blacker and spread before her eyes like a bloodstain. A brittle sound left her lips. The teacup shook in her hand, until there were splashes of burning liquid on her fingers and wrist. Somehow she set the cup in its place, and arranged it on the saucer with unnatural concentration. She looked at the paper again . . . no, it couldn't be true; it was some horrible joke, a lie. *During his recent travels abroad, Viscount Milbank became betrothed to Miss Charlotte Brixton, renowned as the American enamelware heiress . . .*

"You couldn't have, Adam," Emma whispered. "It's only been a few weeks. You wouldn't forget me that quickly . . . you wouldn't betray me like this."

But the printed words loomed crazily in front of her, and the pain in her chest kept growing. She needed help. She needed someone . . . some rational voice to keep her from going mad. She had never felt such pain in her life. She couldn't bear it alone. Blinding tears dropped from her eyes. Stumbling from the bed, she rubbed her shaking hands over her wet face, and searched for her trousers and shirt. When she was finally dressed, she pulled on a hooded cloak and strode from her room.

Katie passed her in the hall leading to the main staircase and stopped in astonishment. "Lady Emma, what are you—"

"I'm going out," Emma said hoarsely, keeping her face hidden in the deep hood of the cloak. "I don't know when I'll return. And if you say a word to anyone that I've left, I'll have you dismissed."

"Yes, milady," Katie said, staring at her with dilated eyes.

Emma dragged a sleeve across her damp nose and blinked more tears from her eyes. "Everything will be all right, Katie," she muttered. "Just don't tell anyone."

The maid gave a cautious nod of assent.

Emma hurried out of the house and headed to the stables, taking care that no one else saw her. She saddled a horse herself, abruptly dismissing the sleepy-eyed stablehand, who tried to help her. "I'll do it myself. Go back to your room."

"Going out to save another beastie, Milady?"

She ignored his cheeky question and fumbled at the saddle girth until it was properly snug. Her hands were unsteady, clumsy; they weren't behaving normally at all. "Go away," she said to the stablehand, who was watching her with sudden wariness.

"Can I do something, miss?"

"Please just leave," she said gruffly. He obeyed reluctantly, throwing several glances over his shoulder as he departed.

Emma mounted the gelding and rode through the stableyard into the street, feeling somehow that she had only one chance at survival. She hadn't made a conscious decision about where to go, but it seemed as if the decision had been made for her. Urging the horse into a gallop, she rode west toward the Angelovsky manor, while the humid summer air did little to dry her streaming tears.

When she reached the manor, with its towering white marble columns and classically designed facade, she ascended the semicircular staircase in front and thumped on the door with her knotted fist. An elderly butler with white hair, black brows, and broad Slavic features appeared. She could never quite remember his name, though she had seen him on several occasions.

"Please have someone see to my horse," Emma said. "And tell Prince Nikolas he has a visitor."

The butler replied in accented English. "Sir, you will have to return tomorrow. I will take your card, if you wish."

"I'm not a sir!" Emma cried desperately. She pulled the cloak hood from her head, and a tumble of gleaming red curls fell down to her waist. "I want to see my cousin. Tell him—" She broke off and shook her head with a muffled groan. "Never mind. I shouldn't be here. I don't know what I'm doing."

"Lady Emma," the butler said, his expression softening. "Do come inside. I will inquire if Prince Nikolas is available to speak with you."

"No, I don't think—"

"*Pahzháhlstah*," he insisted, gesturing her inside. "Please, my lady."

Emma obeyed and waited tensely in the entrance hall, staring at the pattern of inlaid wood on the floor. Before a full minute had passed, she heard Nikolas's quiet voice.

"Emma." A pair of gleaming black shoes came into her field of vision. Nikolas slid his fingers beneath her chin, nudging her face upward. His eyes held hers, and his thumb brushed lightly over her tear-stained cheek. His expression was dispassionate, and there was a comforting calmness about him. "Come with me, *dushenka*." He drew her hand into the crook of his arm and pressed it there.

Emma held back skittishly. "Is someone with you? I didn't th-think to ask—"

"No one is with me." He murmured a few quick phrases in Russian to the butler, who nodded implacably.

Emma held onto Nikolas gratefully as he guided her upstairs. His arm was very strong. Her panic began to fade a little, and her breath came easier. Nikolas, with his cool self-possession, his worldly detachment, wouldn't let her fall apart.

They went to the west wing of the manor, where Nikolas's private suite was located. Emma blinked in surprise as they came to a room she had never seen before. It was decorated in rich colors, with a ceiling of blue glass and bronze moldings. The radiance of a rock crystal lamp filled the air with a serene glow.

Nikolas closed the amethyst-studded door, banishing the outside world. He looked at her in the muted light, his features unreal in their stern beauty. The ivory shirt he wore was open at the throat, revealing a scar that twisted across his skin. "Tell me what happened," he said.

Emma pulled a crumpled scrap of paper from the pocket of her trousers. She handed it to him silently. He took it from her, his golden eyes locked on her stricken face. Smoothing the paper flat on a nearby table, he read the betrothal announcement without expression. His lashes cast long shadows on his cheeks.

"Ah," he said softly.

"You don't s-seem very s-surprised," Emma faltered. "I suppose no one is except me. I . . . I thought Adam might actually love me. It was all a sham. And I'm the greatest fool alive for believing his lies."

"He's the fool," Nikolas said quietly. "Not you."

"Oh, God." She put her trembling hands over her face. "I didn't know it was possible to hurt this much."

"Sit." Nikolas nudged her toward a settee upholstered in soft amber leather. Emma curled up at one end, folding her long legs beneath her. Bending her head, she let her hair fall partially over her face. She heard the sounds of crystal and splashing liquid. Silently Nikolas approached and handed her a small frosted glass. Emma took a sip. The liquid was lemon-flavored and very cold, trickling gently down her throat, leaving a path of ice and fire in its wake.

"What is this?" she asked, wheezing slightly.

"Lemon vodka."

"I've never had vodka before." She took a large swallow, closed her eyes against the smooth, searing burn, then took another. Coughing, she held out the glass to be refilled.

Amused, Nikolas poured more vodka for her, and one for himself. "Drink it slowly. It's much stronger than the wine you're accustomed to."

"Do Russian women drink vodka?"

"Everyone in Russia does. It's best when consumed with caviar and buttered bread. Shall I send for some?"

Emma shuddered at the thought of food. "No, I couldn't possibly eat anything."

Nikolas sat next to her, handing her a linen napkin, watching as she blotted her damp face.

"I can't seem to stop crying," she said in a muffled voice. "I think my heart is broken."

"No." He pushed back a straggling curl from her forehead, his touch as light as a butterfly's. "Your heart isn't broken. It's only wounded pride, Emelia."

She jerked back, glaring at him in sudden outrage. "I should have known you'd be patronizing!"

"You don't love Milbank," he said flatly.

"I did! I always will!"

"Oh? And what did he do to earn this great love? What did he give to you? A few smiles, some flattering words, a stolen kiss here and there. That wasn't love. It was seduction, and apparently a poorly executed one. When you have more experience, you'll be able to recognize the difference."

"It *was* love," she insisted, gulping down the rest of her vodka. Coughing, gasping for air, she dried her stinging eyes. "You don't understand anything about it because you're too cynical."

Nikolas laughed as he took the glass from her hand and set it aside. "Yes, I'm cynical. But that doesn't change the fact that Milbank is unworthy of you. And if you're going to give your heart to a scoundrel, you may as well choose one who will give you luxury and freedom . . . one who knows how to please you in bed. That kind of man would be far more useful to you than Milbank."

If she were sober, she would have taken further offense at his bluntness. A gentleman would never have used such words to a girl he respected. But the alcohol had wrapped her brain in a cool white fog, and all she could think was that Adam had been her only chance, her only hope. Certainly no one else was waiting in the wings. "Whom do you have in mind?" she asked bitterly.

His hands gripped her shoulders, then eased

downward. Gently his palms brushed the sides of her breasts. Emma stiffened, her breath catching. She stared at him without blinking, the light from the crystal lamp hovering on her gold-flecked skin. Emotions chased across her face . . . confusion, anger, denial . . . and her mouth trembled as he lifted a hand to her cheek. Gently his thumb touched the edge of her lower lip.

Emma spoke in a scratchy whisper. "I . . . I didn't come here for that."

"Why are you here, then?" he asked softly.

"I don't know. I wanted . . . comfort. I wanted to feel better."

"You were right to come to me, *ruyshka*."

She made a move to get off the settee, but Nikolas held her there in a light, steely grip, one hand at her shoulder, the other at her waist.

"Nikki . . ." she said, half-defiant, half-pleading.

He leaned forward and caught her lips with a light kiss, then spoke with his mouth almost brushing hers. "I can offer you more than your family has, more than Milbank ever could. I can help you, take care of you . . . give you pleasure you've never felt before."

"I have to leave," she said desperately. The vodka had made everything blurry, her thoughts drowning in a tide of feeling.

"Stay with me, Emma. I'll do only what you want. Only what you choose." The tip of his tongue flickered against her lips, and then he nibbled at her bottom lip, his teeth closing gently on the soft curve. He possessed her mouth with slow, seeking kisses, pausing to brush his lips over her eyebrows, her temples, her cheeks. His hand played lightly in her hair, pushing the red curls aside to bare her neck.

Emma shivered at the new sensation. His mouth moved softly over her throat, exciting her nerves, seeming to draw a flush of heat up to the surface of her skin. Gradually she lifted her arms around his neck. Never in her life had she been so aware of a man, the hard body beneath the snowy white shirt, the muscles filled with crushing strength. It was wrong to be here with him, wrong to feel his lips and hands caressing her. But it seemed the perfect act of rebellion against her father, against her unfaithful lover, against all the people who had ever called her an eccentric or a wallflower. Why not let Nikolas make love to her? Her virginity was hers to give—it no longer mattered, since she had lost the one man she had ever wanted. Perhaps this was a sin, but there was undeniable pleasure in it.

Emma raised her hands to his beautiful hair, the tawny locks springing like coarse silk beneath her fingers. At her hesitant touch, he took a sharp breath and pulled her closer, stretching along the settee until they were matched together. Emma pressed close to him, wanting friction, pressure, his masculine weight bearing down upon her. His kisses became longer, deeper, changing from question to demand.

She made no protest as Nikolas unfastened her shirt. The garment parted in front, and his hand slipped inside, fingertips spread wide as they traced the smoothness of her stomach. She had never dreamed a man's touch could be so tender, so reverent. The heat of his palm covered her breast, fitting over the soft roundness. Her nipple contracted and ached sweetly from the warmth.

Opening her eyes, she found his gaze locked with hers.

All at once she was startled by the lack of emotion in the bright yellow depths of his eyes. They were as intent as a tiger's, devoid of emotion. Even now, in this intimacy, his heart and soul were still locked away. She felt the need to reach him, to make him vulnerable somehow. Her fingers trembled as she began to unbutton his shirt. Carefully she eased the white linen from his shoulders. Her gaze swept over his torso . . . over the pattern of raised scars and burn marks.

Even though Emma had known what to expect, had seen the scars as a child, she was still astonished by the legacy of his torture in Russia. Before that, his body must have been beautiful, a work of smoothly sculpted muscle and gleaming golden skin. How strong he must have been to survive such pain. Nikolas held still beneath her gaze, waiting without shame or self-pity for her reaction. She wished for some way to tell him of her compassion and understanding, but there were no words. Instead she leaned forward with deliberate slowness, and held her mouth against the scar at his throat.

Nikolas clenched his fists while Emma's lips pressed on his skin and her hair flowed over him in a blanket of fire. Some women had been repulsed by his scars, some had been excited by them, but no one had ever shown him such a gesture of tender acceptance. His muscles tensed and knotted. He wanted to shove her away, and at the same time he wanted to hold her close until he crushed her. All his life he had feared nothing, not pain, not even death, but this gentle closeness gave him his first taste of terror.

His voice emerged in a rasping whisper. "Damn you, don't be kind to me."

Emma stared at him, her eyes like blue smoke. "I'm not being kind." She lowered her head to his neck once more, and followed the path of the scar to his collarbone.

Nikolas wrenched away in a powerful movement, coming to his feet beside the settee.

For a second Emma thought he was leaving her, but then he extended a hand. She hesitated before taking it. "It's all right," he said softly.

As if she were an outside observer, Emma watched herself reach for him, their fingers tangling in a hard clasp.

Nikolas led her into his bedroom. The furniture was made of gleaming dark wood, adorned only by touches of carved scrollwork. There were no paintings on the walls, only simple mahogany panels and one icon with the figure of a man riding a chariot drawn by red horses, silhouetted against a huge orange-red sun. The bed was covered in cream silk and white linen. A breeze blew lightly through the netting at the windows.

Nikolas took Emma to the wide bed, through flickering pools of moonlight and shadow. She sat on the edge of the mattress, letting him remove her shoes and stockings. He knew she was frightened. He could feel it in her rigid muscles, hear it in the uneven pace of her breathing. Emma made no sound as he finished undressing her. Finally her pale body was revealed in all its sleek beauty.

Emma half-rolled to her side and managed a shaking whisper. "Nikki, I . . . I need more vodka."

He smiled faintly. "You've had enough," he said, removing his own clothes. Emma's eyes squeezed

shut as he joined her on the bed and pulled her
stiff limbs against his. Drawing his warm hand
down her back, he tried to soothe her shivering.
"There's no need to be afraid. I'm going to show
you how desirable you are. You said you wanted
to feel better."

"I felt better with my clothes on," she said in a
muffled voice, and he laughed.

"Put your arms around me."

"I've never done this before."

"Yes, I know. I'll be careful, *dushka*." He kissed
her shoulder, his mouth opening against her skin.
Timidly Emma responded in kind, her tongue tracing a path of moist sensation along his neck.

Nikolas burned with the need to push inside her.
Emma's body was slender and firm, her breasts
more luxurious than he had expected. Her skin was
vibrantly hot, as if she burned with an excess of
life. *There is boundless delight in the possession of a
young, barely unfolded soul . . .* Now, for the first time
in his life, he understood that line by Lermontov,
for he wanted to drown in her innocence, to devour
her as a rare delicacy.

He drew his hands over her, skimming the hollows in the backs of her knees, the fragile structure
of her ankles, the winged shape of her collarbone.
Losing some of her fear, Emma slid her arms
around his waist, fingertips digging into the hollows of his spine. Nikolas brushed warm kisses
over her breasts and pulled the points of her nipples into his mouth, sucking, biting softly, making
her gasp with pleasure. Only then did he touch the
soft cinnamon curls between her thighs, combing
gently through them. She was virginal and closed,

but there was a betraying touch of moisture that made his body throb in anticipation.

The inquiring strokes of his fingers drew forth more dampness, more heat. Gently he pushed his middle finger inside her, stroking the soft, slick inner surface. She whimpered and froze beneath him, her legs stiffening.

"Does it hurt?" Nikolas whispered.

She gave a quick, bewildered shake of her head, robbed of the breath for words.

Nikolas kissed her parted lips and then drew back to watch as she relinquished herself to the rising tension, surrendering to him at last, helpless to whatever he wanted. She arched higher against his hand, inviting more, her head turning to the side as she closed her eyes and let the feeling rush over her. Skillfully he brought her to climax, relishing the involuntary clenching of her thighs around his hand.

When the last delicious spasm had left her, he cradled her face in both his palms. "You're still a virgin, Emma. Shall I stop?"

"No," she said, her voice shaking. "Go on."

Although Nikolas had known what her answer would be, he was still relieved. He lifted his body over hers, fitting his knees between hers, pushing them wide. He had never been with a virgin before, and it was more difficult than he'd expected. She was swollen and small, her flesh opposing his invasion. He pushed harder, forcing himself inside the tight ring of resistance. Her choked cry of pain was smothered against his throat. Suddenly it was easy to slide deeper, and he felt her yield to his slow penetration.

As her warmth surrounded him, he buried his

face against her throat, overcome by the sweetness of being inside her. "Emelia," he murmured thickly, "I've always wanted this ... always wanted you ..."

Her slender hands gripped his head, guiding his mouth to hers. Driven to the edge of his control, he kissed her deeply, while his lower body sustained a steady, driving rhythm. She wrapped her arms and legs around him, holding him tightly, and suddenly it became too much for Nikolas to bear. He shuddered and groaned, his senses unraveling, everything consumed in a bonfire of pleasure. Emma hugged him even closer, her palms slipping on his glistening back. Nikolas moved to his side, pillowing his cheek on her hair while they both tried to regain their breath.

Emma wasn't certain how long she dozed. She awakened with her hand resting on Nikolas's shoulder, her fingertips fanning the ridge of a scar. She felt weak and defenseless, yet oddly peaceful. She tried to comprehend what had happened, that she had gone to bed with a man, with Nikolas. Although she waited for a bolt of lightning, a feeling of disaster, nothing happened. She must have no scruples or principles whatsoever, to have this lack of shame.

Sometime while she had slept, Nikolas must have pulled the bed linens up to her shoulders. Clasping the sheet over her breasts, Emma turned to face him. Thoughts raced through her mind. She had to find her clothes, she had to return to the villa ... but most importantly, she had to make certain he wouldn't tell anyone what had happened tonight. Secrecy was necessary for both their sakes. "Nikki," she began awkwardly.

He touched a finger to her lips. "I want you to consider something, *ruyshenka*. I don't require an answer tonight. You need time to think about what you want. For now, just listen to me."

"All right," she said cautiously.

"There is no one for you now, is there? That is, no one you are hoping to marry?"

The question provoked a bitter laugh from her. "No, and there never will be."

"Then your plan is to live with your father and Tasia for the rest of your life?"

"I don't have much of a choice."

"Don't you?" He used his thumb to smooth away the puzzled crease in her brow. "Why not marry me, Emma?"

She shook her head as if she hadn't heard him correctly. "What?"

"If you became my wife, all doors would be open to you. You would have ten times more wealth and influence than you have now. I would give generous support to your causes and charities. You could spend all your leisure time with your animals if you desire. I'm offering you a life without rules or limits. You'll have anything you want with one snap of your fingers. Think about it, Emma."

Emma's heart beat violently. She stared at him in amazement. A long time passed before she could form words with her stiff lips. "Why me? You could have anyone. *Anyone*."

His hand drifted over her bare chest, one knuckle dipping gently into her cleavage. "You remind me of the women I knew in Russia . . . fiery, blunt, completely without artifice. I respect your honesty. I enjoy your beauty. Why shouldn't it be you?"

"How long have you had this crazy idea?"

Nikolas took a long curl of her hair and coiled it around his finger. "Since you were thirteen," he said casually.

"My God."

"I had never seen a child with such strength of will. You were magnificent. I've watched you mature from a headstrong girl into a beautiful woman. You're the one person who's never bored me. I want you to be my wife."

Emma shook her head in disbelieving wonder. "A real wife?"

"In every way," he agreed, staring into her eyes.

"What if I refuse you? Will you try to punish me? Will you threaten to tell someone about..." She waved a feeble hand at the rumpled bedclothes around them. "About this?"

He looked amused. "Is your opinion of me that bad?"

"Yes," she said promptly, making him laugh. "But even if I wanted to marry you, I couldn't. My father would never allow it."

"I know how to handle your father," Nikolas replied. "The decision is yours alone. If you agree to marry me, you shall."

She frowned skeptically. "I've never met anyone who could handle my father."

"You'll consider it, then?"

"I'll consider it, but I don't believe—"

He shushed her with his lips. "Later," he whispered. "Give me your answer later."

"But—"

He scattered kisses over her face and throat, ignoring her faint protest. Emma quivered and fell silent as he made love to her with astonishing gentleness. She pressed her hands against the scarred velvet surface of his back, and felt the lithe movements of muscle and sinew as he moved over her. For a while it seemed as if she no longer belonged only to herself. Her body was his to pleasure and possess, and he was a tender caretaker, patiently coaxing a response from every nerve. She had never been held so long by anyone. Nothing could have prepared her for the feeling of someone else's naked skin against hers. There were no more thoughts or worries or pangs of conscience ... only the exquisite sensations of being cradled and stroked, until passion gripped her in endless waves.

When they were both sated, Nikolas turned onto his stomach and slept, his face half-buried in the pillow. Only one faintly gleaming brow and one crescent of heavy lashes were visible. Emma reached over to smooth the hair that curled on the back of his neck, touching him so lightly that his sleep wasn't disturbed.

She felt sorry for any woman who would be foolish enough to love him—and there must have been more than a few. A man as beautiful and unattainable as Nikolas could easily break someone's heart. Not to mention his being powerful, mysterious ... and so very much alone. Confused, Emma pillowed her head on her arms. Damn Adam for deserting her, and for letting her end up in this unimaginable situation. But he was gone for good now, and Prince Nikolas wanted her. Would it be so terrible living as his wife? People married without love all the time.

She tried to imagine what kind of relationship they would have. She knew that he wanted her, but he wasn't the kind of man who could ever love someone. "You're not very good husband material," she whispered, watching his peaceful face. "But then, I'm certainly not anyone's idea of a perfect wife."

His fingers twitched as dreams pervaded his sleep, and a tiny frown settled between his brows. Emma realized that Nikolas had never seemed quite human to her until now. More like one of her exotic creatures: safe to admire from a distance, dangerous to come within arm's length. But Nikolas was just a man. He wasn't invulnerable. He was lonely, just as she was.

All at once the choice seemed easier.

She touched the side of his face, stroking the roughness of his night beard until he stirred. "Nikolas," she murmured. "I have to go home now, while it's still dark."

He raised himself on his forearms and shook his head to clear it. "I'll accompany you in my carriage."

"No, I can ride—"

"It's not safe. I'll go with you."

Emma considered the statement thoughtfully, then nodded. "I don't need time to think about your proposal, Nikki. I can give you an answer now. I . . . I will accept your offer."

Nikolas showed no surprise or even happiness, but she sensed his satisfaction. He took her hand and pressed a kiss to the backs of her fingers. "I knew you would," he said, so calmly that Emma almost laughed.

"I think I'd better be the first to break the news to my family. My father's first impulse may be to kill you." Emma shivered in apprehension at the thought of her father's reaction. He would be furious. He would move heaven and earth to keep her from marrying Nikolas. He might even disown her.

"I've dealt with your father before," Nikolas replied, his voice touched with irony. "He won't be a problem."

Emma blinked at that and remained silent. One thought was foremost in her mind—that after she married Nikolas, no one would ever try to tell her what to do again.

❦ Four

EMMA AWOKE IN her own bed the next morning, dream-fogged and puzzled. Daylight streamed in through the parted drapes, until its growing brightness made her head ache. Her body was sore in unaccustomed places. The confusion lasted for a second more, and then memory came flooding back. "God . . ." she whispered, her heart beginning to pound. She felt sick and giddy and afraid. She could not have done those intimate things with Nikolas. It must have been a dream.

But she remembered too many details . . . her desperate flight to Nikolas's home, his lovemaking, his marriage proposal . . .

She had said yes. Emma swallowed hard and closed her eyes. Had Nikolas really meant to propose? Had she been crazy to accept? Fearfully she thought of ways to make it all disappear. She would tell Nikolas she had been drunk, that she hadn't known what she was doing or saying. She would beg him, if necessary, to keep last night a secret. What had possessed her to do something so irresponsible? She had lost her innocence, and given Prince Nikolas the power to ruin her life. "Oh, no," she muttered, feeling nauseated. "Oh—"

"Miss Emma?" There came a discreet knock on the door, and Katie poked her head around the corner. The maid's expression was a study in bewilderment, and she stared at Emma as if her mistress were a stranger.

"What time is it?" Emma asked, rubbing her bleary eyes.

"It's eight o'clock, miss."

Emma rolled onto her stomach. "I want to sleep for a while."

"Yes, miss, but . . . His Highness Prince Nikolas is waiting downstairs. He arrived not a quarter hour ago, and sent me to wake you."

Emma jerked upward with a gasp. Her body protested the sudden movement, and she closed her thighs against the unfamiliar ache. "Tell him to go away—no, no, wait. Tell him I'll see him. Have him wait in the parlor."

Katie nodded and left the room, while Emma scrambled out of bed. Her hand trembled as she poured water from a porcelain jug into a flowered washbasin. She scrubbed herself until her skin was pink, then dressed in fresh underclothes. Wincing at the throbbing ache in her head, she dragged a brush through her hair and braided it in a thick rope that hung down her back. The maid returned to help her into a skirt of pale blue lawn and a delicate white blouse with a sapphire bow at the throat. Emma glanced at her flushed reflection in the mirror and tucked a stray curl behind her ear.

Did Nikolas intend to take back his proposal? Her mouth tightened in offended pride at the thought. Whatever he had to say, she would be ready for him. She would be cool and composed, and if he made any threats or jeering remarks, she would laugh disdainfully.

Squaring her shoulders, she strode briskly out of the room and down to the parlor, where Nikolas waited. She hesitated just before crossing the threshold and turned back to the maid, who had followed her. "You may leave us alone, Katie."

The maid opened her mouth to argue, but as she met Emma's determined gaze, she nodded in resignation.

Emma took a deep breath, closed the door, and turned to face Nikolas. He rose from a chair and stared at her intently. He looked as handsome and remote as ever, his eyes as bright as topaz. Emma had intended to speak first, but suddenly she couldn't say a word. Meeting in such restrained surroundings, after she had shared his bed the night before, was hard to bear. She stood there in silence, her color rising, her pulse racing.

Nikolas approached her and took her cold hand in his warm one. "Have you changed your mind?" he asked softly.

"I . . . I thought you might have," Emma blurted out.

A gleam of amusement showed in his eyes. "There's no chance of that. Not when I've waited so long for you."

She shook her head in confusion. "How can that be true? I could believe it if I were beautiful, or accomplished, or gifted in some way, but I'm only—"

Nikolas slid his hand behind her neck and pulled her to him. His kiss was deep and warm, reminding her of the dizzying passion of last night. After a long moment, he lifted his head and stared into her dazed blue eyes. "I want you. I'll never stop wanting you, even if you decide to turn down my proposal." His hand slipped down the length of her back, coming to rest on the lowest point of her spine. "Consider this, Emma . . . there are many reasons why people decide to marry. Love, loneliness, convenience, necessity . . . and sometimes, as in our case, friendship. That's not such a bad reason, is it?"

His words unlocked an unexpected wellspring of relief inside her. The impulse to take his help, to lean on him, was impossible to resist.

"No," she said breathlessly. "I mean, I'll still marry you. I haven't changed my mind."

"Good." He kissed her again, pulling her hard against his aroused body, letting her feel exactly how much he desired her. Emma wrapped her arms around his neck, her lips parting beneath the pressure of his. She had never felt so overwhelmed by a man, not only by his physical appeal but by the sheer force of his personality. And yet she was not afraid of him. She wanted to meet the challenge he offered, to know and master him as effortlessly as he did her. With an odd little shock, she realized that she wouldn't mind at all if he dragged her upstairs and climbed into bed with her right now.

Nikolas drew back his head and smiled slightly, as if he could read her thoughts. "Shall we go to Southgate Hall and inform your family?"

"They won't give you their blessing," Emma warned.

He laughed, and gently fingered the blue bow at her throat. "I don't intend to ask for it, *ruyshka*."

* * *

They spoke very little on the carriage ride to the Stokehurst country estate. Emma was occupied with her own thoughts, while Nikolas was filled with triumph. He stole swift glances at her determined profile as she stared out the window. The sunlight gave her skin a luminous glow and made her freckles gleam like a sprinkling of gold. He thought of the way her hair felt in his hands, soft and vibrant. Emma had given him more pleasure than he had ever imagined—not to mention the first taste of peace he'd had in his life.

He suppressed a grim smile as he imagined Stokehurst's reaction to the news of the impending nuptials. He and Stokehurst had always disliked each other, not only on a personal level but also on a cultural one. Emma's father openly mistrusted the fatalism and mysticism of Russian ways, considering anything different from Western civilization as barbaric. Stokehurst loved his wife, Tasia, but that love didn't extend to her native country, a country that Nikolas represented at its savage worst. And now Stokehurst's daughter would marry a Russian. Nikolas smiled with a trace of devilish enjoyment.

"I'm not sure I like the look on your face," Emma commented. "Like a cat with a mouse beneath its paw."

He met her gaze and grinned openly. "Who is the mouse? Not you, certainly."

"I feel more like one with every mile that brings us closer to my father."

His gaze narrowed perceptively. "You're not afraid, are you?"

Emma lifted her shoulders in an uncomfortable shrug. "No, but . . . it's not going to be easy."

"Of course it is. There won't be a battle, if that's what you're dreading."

She gave a scornful laugh. "How can you say that, knowing my family?"

"Have some faith. I'm a very persuasive man." There was a sly gleam in his eyes as he added, "You should know that by now."

Emma bristled and glared at him, but he just smiled mockingly.

At last they reached the Stokehurst estate. One footman proceeded to help them from the carriage, while another hastened to alert the butler to their arrival. Emma took Nikolas's arm, her fingers tightening on his sleeve as they ascended the front steps.

She gave the butler a tense smile. Seymour's face was as blank as usual, but Emma thought she detected a flicker of curiosity in his eyes. "Seymour, where are Papa and Tasia?"

"I believe they are in the library, miss."

"Are they entertaining guests?"

"No, Miss Emma."

Words tumbled through Emma's mind as she and Nikolas passed through the great hall and approached the library. How could she tell her family what she had decided? How should she defend herself against their arguments? *This is what I want*, she told herself stubbornly. Besides, it was far too late to back out now.

Her father was at his desk, reading aloud a passage from a letter. Tasia sat nearby with needlework in her lap. They both looked up at Emma's unexpected entrance, a touch of surprise on their faces. It was impossible not to recognize what a well-matched couple they were, both of them attractive and dark-haired. Their closeness was evident even now, as they exchanged a glance that conveyed their thoughts to each other. *That's what I might have had with Adam,* Emma thought, and felt a sudden burst of anger in her chest. *This is your fault, Papa. I'm going to marry a man I don't love, because you wouldn't let me have the one I really wanted.*

"Emma," Tasia said with a bewildered smile, setting aside her needlework. "Why have you returned early from London? What—" Her gaze fell on Nikolas, and words seemed to fail her.

To Emma, it seemed that the frozen tableau lasted for an hour, though it was only a few seconds. Tasia's blue-gray eyes were piercing as she stared at the two of them. Emma sensed that her stepmother, with her uncanny perception, understood that some momentous change had taken place.

"Papa and *Belle-mère,*" Emma said in a stifled voice, "we have something to tell you."

Luke's face turned as hard as granite. He shook his head slightly, already denying what she intended to say.

"Nikolas and I . . ." Emma continued awkwardly, "we want to—" She stopped as she felt Nikolas's light touch on her elbow.

"Allow me," he murmured. He focused on Luke, his gaze unblinking. "Recently the friendship between Emma and me has developed into something quite . . . significant. I have told your daughter of my desire to make her my wife, and she has graciously accepted—"

"No." The word was clipped and final. Luke didn't spare a glance for Emma, only stared at Nikolas. His face had paled beneath its usual bronze. It was clear that his reaction had come straight from the heart, before conscious thought had even registered. "I don't know what the hell is going on. I don't want to know. Get out of my home, while I deal with my daughter."

Emma's temper exploded. "You're not going to *deal* with me, Papa! I'm a grown woman, and I'll do what I want—and if Nikolas leaves, I'm going with him! This time you won't win—"

"Emelia," Nikolas interrupted quietly, turning her to face him. "There's no need to quarrel. Why don't you leave with Tasia and explain things to her? Your father and I need a few minutes alone."

"What should I tell her?" Emma whispered, her cheeks flaming scarlet.

He smiled slightly. "Whatever you like, *dushka*."

Emma nodded and glanced at her stepmother. Tasia's face was blank except for the pinched line of concern between her eyebrows. She walked with straight-backed grace as she preceded Emma from the room. Emma followed her small form with a more uncertain stride.

As soon as the women had left, Stokehurst's demeanor changed, shock giving way to fury. "Why my daughter?" he barked. "You conniving Russian bastard—I should have ripped your throat out years ago, when you first started sniffing around my home and my family!" He gestured with the silver hook on his arm, which shone with lethal brightness. Most men would have been terrified by the sight of Lord Stokehurst in a fury. Even Nikolas was affected, his smugness fading several degrees.

"I won't let you have her," Stokehurst snarled.

Nikolas stood his ground. "I'm afraid you have no choice. If you don't allow this, you'll lose Emma forever. She won't forgive you. Believe me when I say the marriage will take place, with or without your consent. You may as well give us your blessing."

"My *blessing?*" Stokehurst repeated, and laughed harshly.

"You need not fear for Emma," Nikolas continued. "I swear to you, I will never raise a hand to her. She'll have more money than she'll ever be able to spend. I will never interfere with her charities, her social causes, her menagerie. She'll have freedom—which, as you know, is the thing she needs most."

"What she needs is a husband who loves her. You can't offer her a good enough substitute for that."

"But I can," Nikolas said softly. "Ask her. She'll tell you what she wants."

"Your timing was impeccable. You picked the perfect opportunity to worm your way into her life, when she was vulnerable and hurt . . ." Stokehurst paused as a new thought occurred to him, and his rage seemed to double. "Have you dared to touch her? By God, I'll kill you!"

Nikolas kept his face expressionless. "Emma turned to me because she was unhappy. The life you've provided for her at Southgate isn't enough anymore. She's a woman, not a little girl. It's time for her to be married."

"Not to you," came the guttural reply.

"She won't agree to anyone else."

Stokehurst's jaw twitched violently. "I'll find a way to stop this."

"The harder you try, the faster she'll slip through your fingers."

Nikolas watched him in the appalled silence that followed, knowing that of all the suffering Stokehurst had endured in his life, this blow was the hardest to take. Almost, Nikolas was tempted to feel a flicker of sympathy for the man. But life was full of unfairness. He himself had experienced a lion's share of it. "As I said, you have no choice," he said matter-of-factly.

"Why are you doing this?" Stokehurst asked through his teeth. "Do you intend to use Emma as some sort of bargaining chip later on? Are you marrying her as revenge for something I've done?"

Nikolas laughed shortly and spread his hands wide in a gesture of openness. "I'm doing this for a simple reason. I want her. *Dah sveedáhneeya*, Stokehurst. Please inform your daughter I'll be calling on her in a few days." He left the room without another word, satisfied that at last he would get his way.

Emma sat with Tasia in a nearby parlor, both of them occupying gilt chairs upholstered in slick rose damask. Tasia had been calm so far, but Emma could tell that her stepmother was desperately worried. She felt guilty about causing Tasia such distress, but it couldn't be helped. She would marry Nikolas, and eventually Tasia would agree that it had been the best decision.

". . . I'm certain Nikolas must seem like a very romantic figure," Tasia was saying. "He's experienced with women. He has a way of making them feel so desirable that they decide to trust him in spite of their better judgment. But he's not worthy of anyone's trust, Emma. Nikolas is a dangerous man. You don't know about the horrible things he has done, the things he's capable of—"

"Don't tell me," Emma said abruptly. "There's no point. It's too late to change what's already been done."

"What's already . . ." Tasia blanched. "Oh, Emma," she faltered, "you haven't let him . . . you haven't . . ."

Emma's gaze lowered. "That's not important." She didn't look up, even when she heard Tasia's swift intake of breath. "The fact is, I want to marry Nikolas. I want my own life. Whatever I'll have with him will be more than I've got now."

"Don't be so certain. You've been accustomed to living with people who love you, and that's not something to take for granted. You're right—it doesn't matter if you slept with him. We'll never tell anyone. The important thing is to protect you, take you away—"

"I'm not going anywhere—"

"Let me speak," Tasia said with such unusual sharpness that Emma quieted. "Nikolas is a different kind of man from any you've ever known. He'll betray you in a hundred ways without ever stopping to think about it. Everything he does is for his own pleasure, his own needs." Tasia took Emma's hand and held it tightly. "Nikolas wasn't exiled from Russia because of treason, Emma. He killed a man in cold blood. And when he was questioned by the government officials and tortured to the point of death, I believe he lost the last part of his soul. No one can help him. Some things are damaged beyond anyone's ability to repair."

Emma shrugged uncomfortably. "I know about

the man he killed. I don't care what Nikolas has done in the past. I'm going to marry him."

Tears sparkled in Tasia's eyes. "Please don't go through with this. You don't have to throw away all chance of happiness when you're still so young, when you have so much to give—"

Emma pulled her hand away. "I don't want to talk anymore. I've made my decision."

Tasia's pale eyes were so intense that Emma almost flinched from their brightness. "You're doing this to punish Luke, aren't you? You want to pay him back for keeping you apart from Adam. But you'll end up hurting yourself more than anyone else."

Emma hardened her jaw. "Papa made a mistake about Adam."

"What if he did? Oh, Emma, you have so much to learn about forgiveness. Only the young can afford to feel so betrayed, so self-righteous, when their parents make mistakes. What if your father *was* wrong? Can you claim that you've never hurt or wronged him?"

"I never denied Papa someone he loved. I never took away the one person who would make him truly happy."

"By removing yourself from his life, that's exactly what you will be doing. If you don't know how necessary you are to his happiness, then you don't understand anything about him."

"All Papa needs is you, Tasia. Everyone knows that."

Shock crossed her stepmother's face. "You know that's not true! Emma, what in heaven's name has happened to you?" At Emma's mulish silence, Tasia shook her head and sighed deeply. "We'll talk again later, when we've both had a chance to think.''

''I won't change my mind,'' Emma said defiantly, watching Tasia walk out of the room.

Tasia returned to the library and saw that Nikolas had left. Her husband was standing at the window, staring out at the bright summer day. Sensing her presence, Luke spoke in a voice stripped of emotion. ''He said I couldn't stop the marriage without losing her. He was right. If I don't allow it, they'll elope.''

''What if you send her away for a while?'' Tasia suggested. ''Perhaps she might stay with your sister in Scotland. Or your mother could take her on a tour abroad—''

''Nikolas will follow wherever I send her. The only way I can prevent this is to kill him—or lock my daughter in a room for the rest of her life.''

''I'll keep talking to Emma. Somehow I'll make her understand what kind of man Nikolas really is.''

''You can try,'' he said tonelessly. ''I don't think it will do any good.''

''Luke . . .'' She approached him from behind, trying to slide her arms around his waist, but he stiffened.

''I need some time alone,'' he said, facing away from her. ''I need to think.'' He shook his head and made an agonized sound. ''My God, how I've failed Emma's mother. All the things Mary would have wanted for her daughter . . . and I've let it come to this.''

''You haven't failed anyone. You've been the most loving and generous father imaginable. This isn't your fault." Tasia stroked the rigid line of his back. "Emma was born with so much spirit. She's stubborn and hot-tempered, but she has a loving heart, and she does learn from her mistakes."

Luke turned to her then, his blue eyes glittering. "Not this mistake," he said hoarsely. "This one will ruin her . . . and I'll be damned if I can do anything about it."

After returning to the Angelovsky estate, Nikolas spent the afternoon reading the latest reports on his financial investments, then settled in for the evening with a bottle of chilled vodka. Wearing a gray silk dressing robe, lounging on the amber leather settee in his private suite, he paged idly through a volume of writings by Lermontov.

There was a hesitant tap on the door, and the muffled voice of his servant Karl. "Your Highness, there is a visitor from the Stokehurst household."

Nikolas was mildly surprised by the news. "Is it Lady Emma?"

Karl peeked around the edge of the door, his fair Russian face drawn in perplexed lines. "No, Your Highness. Her stepmother, the duchess."

Surprise deepened into astonishment, and Nikolas raised his brows inquiringly. Tasia hadn't paid him a private visit since his illness seven years ago, when she had nursed him back from the brink of death. "This should be interesting," he said. "Bring her to me."

He watched the door intently until Tasia appeared. Her face was as fragile and pale as porcelain. As always, she was perfectly composed, her expression serene, every strand of her shining dark hair pinned smoothly in place. The lavender gown she wore was a perfect foil for the silvery blue of her eyes. She had looked exactly this way at age eighteen, with an otherworldly quality that had never failed to intrigue him.

"You're dressed in the color of mourning," Nikolas said with a touch of mockery, standing as she entered the room. "But this is a time for celebration, Cousin Tasia." He gestured to the refreshments beside him. "Vodka? *Zakuski*?"

Tasia shook her head at the sight of the "little snacks" so dear to a Russian's heart: slivers of buttered bread topped with caviar; tiny meat pies dotted with sour cream; sardines; pickles; all artfully arranged on a silver tray.

"At least have a seat," Nikolas said.

Tasia remained standing. "You owe me," she said quietly. "You admitted it all those years ago. You said the debt would last through your children's children. You believed I killed your brother, Mikhail—and of all the people calling for my execution, your voice was the loudest. When I escaped from Russia, you followed me to England, kidnapped me, and brought me back to St. Petersburg. You intended for me to die, to pay for a crime I didn't commit."

"I was wrong," Nikolas said impatiently. "I discovered my mistake, and I did my best to rectify it."

"And then later," Tasia continued without inflection, "when you were exiled and you came to England half-dead, I took care of you until you were well again. You might have died without my help."

"I would have died," he acknowledged gruffly.

"I've never asked you for anything in return—until now."

"What are you asking, cousin?" Nikolas murmured, although he knew.

"Don't marry Emma. Leave England for good, and never see my stepdaughter again."

"And what will it do to her, to have been abandoned by two men in such a short time?"

"Emma is young. She's stronger than you think. She'll recover in good form."

His lips twisted in a half sneer. "Don't be a fool. If I leave her, she'll be devastated. At the very least she'll never trust a man again. She'll hate you and your self-righteous English husband. Is that what you want?"

Tasia's composure faltered, and a flush of rage crept over her face. "That might be better for her than to be destroyed by you, day by day, piece by piece, until nothing's left of her!"

"I'll be a better husband to Emma than any of the men she was likely to get."

"Oh, a fine husband," Tasia agreed acidly, "who's done nothing so far but manipulate and seduce her. I can scarcely wait to see what comes next. You may have good intentions, Nikolas—you may even have convinced yourself that you'll be an adequate husband—but in the end, Emma will be hurt by you. Because you can't change your nature. You've been shaped by a past filled with such pain and ugliness that it's warped you forever. Much of it wasn't your fault, but that doesn't matter. You are what you are. I understand why you want Emma. She has all the goodness and innocence and compassion you've never been able to feel. You intend to own her, and to keep her here along with all the other beautiful objects you've collected. But I ask you now to honor the debt you owe me. You must leave Emma alone."

Tasia's gaze was so bright and searing that Nikolas was forced to turn away. He recognized the justice in her request. He had always paid his debts when the time came. It was a matter of honor, of self-respect. But to give up Emma . . . no. Anything else he could do, but not that.

His low voice broke the brittle silence. "I can't."

Tasia smiled coldly, as if he had just confirmed the worst she had ever suspected about him. "You selfish bastard," she whispered, and left the room.

It surprised Emma, how little her family argued with her about the betrothal to Prince Nikolas. Certainly they made attempts to "talk sense" into her, which she met with stony silence. If she gave way even an inch, it would be an invitation for them to bully her into doing what they wanted. Her stubbornness appeared to be working. Her father and Tasia seemed to understand that she wouldn't settle for anything less than marrying Nikolas. In her heart Emma believed they would have ample opportunity to make peace later, when she was comfortably settled with Nikolas. They would see that she was content, and that their objections to the marriage had been wrong.

The wedding would take place in six weeks, a date which caused a flurry of gossip for its extreme precipitancy. Emma hadn't expected to enjoy the reactions of others so much, especially the jealousy and astonishment of all the women who came to call. They didn't bother to hide their amazement that Emma had landed Prince Nikolas, one of the most desirable catches in Europe.

"But, my dear, however did you manage it?" asked one of the inquisitive callers, Lady Seaford, a society matron whose own daughter was betrothed to a mere earl. "The prince never gave my Alexandra more than the merest glance—and she was quite the most attractive girl of the Season! Did he take an interest in you because of his kinship with your stepmother? Was that it?"

Emma smiled obliquely. "He did mention that I remind him of Russian women."

Lady Seaford gave her a speculative stare over the rim of her teacup. "I had no idea the Russian women were of such, er, lofty stature. My darling Alexandra apparently never had a chance, being quite dainty and petite."

Tasia interceded then, as Emma flinched at the remark. "Russian women are known for their spirit and strength of character, Lady Seaford," Tasia said evenly, staring hard at the other woman. "Perhaps Prince Nikolas perceived Emma to have more of these qualities than your darling Alexandra."

"Well!" Lady Seaford pursed her lips and settled into an offended silence.

Emma smiled gratefully at Tasia. Although Tasia objected privately to the marriage, in public she was as much Emma's champion as ever. She had even taken Emma to her favorite designer to have the wedding dress made. It would be fashioned of ivory silk, high-necked and trimmed with delicate panels of antique lace. Together Emma and Tasia planned the details of the ceremony, to be held in the chapel of Southgate Hall, and of the reception, in the gold-and-white ballroom.

Many of Emma's days were spent with an architect and a landscape gardener Nikolas had hired. They had designed a set of pens and buildings for her menagerie which would be constructed on the Angelovsky estate grounds. Even Tasia had admitted reluctantly that Nikolas appeared to have gone to great lengths to see to Emma's needs. He was having a suite of rooms redecorated to suit her taste, and had sent a bundle of swatches for her to look at. Emma chose an icy shade of pale blue for the walls, and sapphire brocade for the draperies and bed hangings.

On the days Nikolas didn't come to call, he sent flowers and gifts, ranging from a colored tin of sugar biscuits to an exquisite gold box stamped with the Angelovsky seal. One day he brought a necklace set with twenty diamonds, one for each year of Emma's age. Although Tasia had frowned at the inappropriateness of the gift, she had not suggested that Emma return it.

Emma was bewildered by Nikolas's attentiveness. His manner was utterly respectful as he sat a proper distance from her in the parlor, or watched her tend the animals in her menagerie. He talked to her almost as an older brother would, friendly and gently teasing. But the way he stared at her sometimes, his golden gaze alight with sexual interest as he noted her every move, made her nervous, for she was never certain what he might do. The surface was civilized, but underneath there was a passionate and unpredictable man. She still couldn't quite believe that Nikolas wanted her, but part of her understood the attraction, because she felt it too. Without loving him, she was fascinated by him, with an intensity she had never felt for anyone else.

* * *

The morning of the wedding, Emma was tense and terrified. Unwittingly her father provided the final impetus that pushed her past all indecision. Luke came to her room after she was fully dressed in her bridal attire. Emma turned away from the mirror, where she had been patting down the rebellious curls that had sprung around her face, and she smiled hesitantly.

She was tall and slender in the ivory dress, her hair gathered into a loose chignon and adorned with creamy white roses. She held her mother's tiny Bible in one hand, along with a lace handkerchief borrowed from Tasia. A necklace of three strands of pearls—a gift from Nikolas which had arrived that very morning—was clasped around her throat. Her father appeared to swallow hard, as if there were a lump in his throat. "You look very beautiful, Emma."

"Thank you," she said, her voice nearly inaudible.

"I wish Mary could see you."

Emma blinked in dismay, wondering if her mother would have approved of the match. She had been so young when Mary died, too young to have any distinct memories . . . only impressions of warmth, a musical voice, a wealth of red hair just like her own. Papa had always said he and Mary had loved each other. Perhaps her mother wouldn't have wanted her to marry Nikolas.

"Emma," her father said quietly, "if you ever have regrets . . . if the time comes when you decide this was a mistake . . . you can always come back. I'll welcome you with open arms."

"You're expecting me to regret this, aren't you?" she asked.

He didn't reply, but the way he averted his gaze was answer enough.

"My marriage will be fine," Emma said coolly. "It won't be the kind you have with Tasia, but it will be quite satisfactory for me."

"I hope so."

"Do you?" she asked softly. "I'm not so sure of that, Papa." Her spine stiffened with pride, and she decided right then that *nothing* would stop her from marrying Nikolas Angelovsky. But later, when they walked down the aisle together, there were unshed tears in her eyes.

Locked in her own dolorous silence, Emma remembered little of the wedding, except that it was short and devoid of joy. Nikolas was handsome but grave, making her realize that he considered the wedding nothing more than a necessary duty. For Emma, there was little feeling of spirituality in the ceremony, except for the reading of a passage from Ruth: *. . . whither thou goest, I will go, And where thou lodgest, I will lodge. Thy people shall be my people, and thy God my God . . .* The eternal words of love, of commitment, seemed to carry the echo of a heavy door closing shut.

It was only afterward, at the forced cheerfulness of the reception, that Emma began to breathe easier. There was much toasting and dancing, and a wedding feast of English and Russian dishes. The cake was a towering concoction ornamented with flowers, birds, and cherubs all made from sparkling crushed sugar. Finally, as the evening ripened, it was time for the newlyweds to leave, and they rushed to a waiting carriage in a stinging shower of rice and congratulations.

Once in the carriage, Emma dissolved in a fit of dismayed laughter and shook her head, sending a scattering of rice everywhere. Nikolas combed his fingers through his hair, trying in vain to get rid of the grains caught in his thick blond-brown locks.

"I think we'll be fertile," Emma said, and Nikolas laughed at the unmaidenly comment.

"I never doubted it, *ruyshka*."

His expression made her blush. She ducked her head and asked abashedly, "How many children will you want?"

"As many as God sees fit to bestow."

Emma fingered the ring he had given her, an ostentatious blood red ruby surrounded by diamonds. "Thank you for this," she said. "It's lovely."

"Do you like it? Your expression was rather strange when you first saw the ring during the ceremony."

"I was surprised," she said honestly. "I've never had a jewel this large."

Nikolas smiled, reaching for her slender hand and toying with her long fingers. "You'll own many larger than this. Your hands were made for wearing jewels."

"Yes, I need them to cover all the animal bites," she said, pulling her hand away.

Nikolas bent down and lifted her feet into his lap, forcing her to rest her long legs across his.

"Nikki," she protested, squirming as he removed her low-heeled satin slippers. "What are you doing?"

"I'm making you comfortable until we reach the

estate." He began to knead her silk-covered ankles and feet, ignoring her protests.

"I don't want to be comfortable. I . . ." She winced as he gently rubbed her sore arches, and found herself relaxing back against the velvet cushions. "My feet are too big," she murmured.

"They're enchanting." Nikolas pressed the sole of her right foot into the lee of his thighs. Emma started as she felt the hard length of his arousal against her sole, but somehow she couldn't bring herself to move away.

The blissful interlude ended as they approached the Angelovsky manor, and Nikolas slipped the shoes back onto her feet. Emma was filled with wonder as she realized that this palatial residence was her new home. The huge circular ballroom with its endless rows of columns and mirrors, the spacious rooms lined in gold and precious stones, the countless suites and galleries and glass-paneled rooms . . . all of it was hers, to wander through at will.

"Princess Emma," Nikolas said, as if he could read her mind. "Will it take long for you to get used to the title?"

"I may never get used to it," she answered, making a face.

The carriage stopped in front of the wide staircase leading up to the door. Nikolas assisted Emma from the carriage. There was a sudden flurry of servants: footmen rushing to open the door, the butler waiting to greet them, a view of the maids gathering in the entrance hall.

Nikolas led her to the threshold and gestured to the waiting butler. "You know Stanislaus, of course, from the other times you've visited."

Emma turned crimson at the memory of the last time, when she had stayed the night with Nikolas.

The butler's face remained reassuringly impassive. He spoke in lightly accented English. "Your Highness, the household offers its sincere wishes for your happiness. We hope to serve you well."

"Thank you, Stanislov, er, Stanlisl—" Emma looked up at him apologetically. "I'll practice your name until I can say it right."

Before the butler could reply, Nikolas scooped Emma up in his arms, lifting her high against his chest. She gasped in surprise. "What are you doing?"

"Carrying you across the threshold," Nikolas replied. "It's an English tradition, yes?"

"Only when the bride happens to be smaller than the groom! Don't—I'm too heavy! Please put me down—"

"Stop struggling, or I'll drop you."

Emma groaned in an agony of embarrassment as Nikolas carried her inside the manor and through the entrance hall, past the waiting staff. There were a few murmurs and giggles as the servants watched their master proceed to the staircase that led to the upstairs suites.

"Aren't you going to introduce me to them?" Emma asked, glancing back at the waiting group.

"Tomorrow. Tonight I want to be alone with you."

"I can walk the rest of the way. You'll hurt your back."

"This is nothing," he scoffed. "I've carried deer across my shoulders that weighed twice as much as you."

"How flattering!" Emma was silent with mortification the rest of the way. Nikolas brought her to the new suite he had decorated for her, and set her down in the middle of the bedroom.

"Oh," she said breathlessly, turning in a slow circle.

"If you don't like it, we'll have it changed."

"Change?" she repeated dazedly. "I wouldn't dream of it." The suite, with separate rooms for receiving visitors, changing clothes, bathing, and sleeping, was more beautiful than anything she had ever seen before. It was suitable for royalty, decorated in shades of blue and lined with glass columns. Priceless artwork in heavy silver frames adorned the walls. A Russian heating stove covered with rose-lavender tiles occupied a place in the corner. The bed was enormous, covered in dark blue, embroidered silk and piled high with tasseled pillows.

Opening the door of a mahogany armoire, Emma found it empty except for a few articles of her trousseau that had been sent a few days before. "Where are your clothes?" she asked in surprise.

"My suite is at the other end of the wing."

"We won't be sharing a room?"

Nikolas shook his head, and Emma blushed at her mistake. Her father and Tasia always shared a bed, beginning and ending each day in each other's arms. Naively Emma had assumed that Nikolas would desire the same arrangement. If he stayed in his own separate suite, they would miss all the little intimacies that made a husband and wife comfortable with each other. But apparently Nikolas didn't want such familiarity. Perhaps it was better this way . . . or perhaps someday he might change his mind.

She wandered over to a mahogany table covered with a collection of small, carved figurines. A smile appeared on her face as she picked up one of the objects, a white coral swan with a gold beak and sapphire eyes. There was a malachite frog, a gold lion, an ivory elephant, an amethyst wolf with gold paws, as well as a bear, a fish, and birds, also made of precious metals and stones. She lingered on the most striking figurine of all, a snarling amber tiger with yellow diamond eyes and seed pearls for teeth.

"The collection belonged to my great-great-great-grandmother Emelia. I thought you might like to have it."

Emma turned to face him, her eyes shining. "Thank you."

Nikolas gestured at the tiger in her hand. "That particular piece was said to be her favorite."

Cautiously Emma approached him and placed a light kiss on his cheek. "Thank you," she said again. "You're very good to me, Nikki."

Nikolas stared at her, while the place her lips had touched seemed to burn. A odd feeling came over him, and he stood very still. The look in Emma's blue eyes, the sound of her voice, the way she held the amber figurine in her hand . . . it seemed that it had all happened before. His heart began to thump in a heavy rhythm. The air around him turned hot as an image crystallized in his mind . . .

She picked up the tiger, examining it from every angle. "Look, Nikki. Isn't it beautiful?"

"Very beautiful," he agreed, his gaze on her glowing face. He broke off long enough to tell the jeweler, "We'll take them all."

She laughed exuberantly and threw her arms around

him. "You're so good to me," she said against his ear.
"You'll make me love you too much."

He brushed his lips over her soft cheek. "There's no
such thing as too much . . ."

"What is it?" Emma asked, her brow touched
with concern.

The vision disappeared. Nikolas shook his head
and laughed shortly. "Nothing. A strange feeling."
He took a step back, still staring at her. The thumping of his heart was almost painful. Wiping his
hand across his forehead, he discovered he had
broken out in a sweat. The sensation he had was
similar to that of jumping into an icy river after
having been steamed to exhaustion in a Russian
bathhouse.

"Are you all right?" Emma persisted.

"Ring for the maid to help with your dress," he
said brusquely, turning and heading for the door.
"I'll be back in a little while."

Emma frowned in confusion. Carefully she set
the carved tiger back in place on the table, and
stroked its back with her fingertip. The amber
glowed as if it had a life of its own.

Nikolas had stared at her so strangely. The expression on his face . . . the flash of something like
fear . . . his gaze unfocused, as if he beheld some
unearthly vision . . . where had Emma seen that expression before? "Tasia," Emma said softly. Tasia
looked exactly like that whenever she had one of
her premonitions. Russians were a superstitious
people, Tasia had once explained to her. Their lives
were filled with fantasy and mystery, and they believed strongly in omens and signs. What had gone
through Nikolas's mind? What vision had he seen?

Troubled, Emma rang for a maid, and soon a

small woman appeared. She was Emma's age, perhaps a little older, with thick, braided chestnut hair and intelligent gray eyes. She spoke English quite well, and identified herself as Rashel Fyodorovna.

"I like your name, Rashel," Emma remarked as the maid began to unfasten the complicated scheme of hooks and buttons at the back of her wedding dress. "Is it the Russian version of Rachel?"

"Yes, Your Highness. My mother named all her children from the Bible. I have two brothers, Matfei and Adamka, and a sister, Marinka."

"Matthew, Adam, and . . . Mary?" Emma guessed.

"Miriam," the maid corrected, helping Emma step out of the dress as it collapsed in a heap on the floor. Expertly she lifted the billowing yards of silk and carried it to a nearby chair.

"Are your brothers and sister still in Russia?" Emma held her breath as Rashel unhooked her stays.

"No, Your Highness. They are all here, working for Prince Nikolas. We came with him after . . . after . . ." The maid paused, searching for a tactful way to express herself.

"After he was exiled," Emma said bluntly.

Rashel nodded, the corners of her mouth curving in a smile. "It is good that you speak so plainly, Your Highness. Russians like directness. Shall I unpin your hair?"

"Yes, please." Emma sat down at a dressing table, clad in her linen undergarments. Carefully the maid unfastened the white roses from Emma's ruddy curls and began to unplait her hair, using a silver-handled brush to smooth one section at a time. "Did you *want* to come to England with Nikolas?" Emma asked. "Or did you have a choice?"

"Oh, yes, my family wanted to come. We belong to the Angelovskys, you see. Not by law, of course, since the serfs were liberated by Tsar Alexander fifteen years ago. But my family, the Sidarovs, has served the Angelovskys for more than a hundred years. We felt it was right to follow Prince Nikolas wherever he chose to go."

"I'm sure he appreciates your devotion," Emma said, although she suspected that Nikolas, with all his arrogance, probably took it for granted.

Rashel shrugged cheerfully. "We will always stay with him, if it pleases God. Prince Nikolas is a good master."

"That's reassuring," Emma muttered.

The maid paused in her brushing and sighed thoughtfully. "There are times when I miss Russia. Prince Nikolas never seems to, but I think he must. What a life he had there! He was even richer than the tsar. Twenty-seven palaces, and land everywhere. Once he gave his younger brother, Prince Mikhail, a mountain for his birthday."

"A *mountain*?"

"Yes, a beautiful one in the Crimea." Rashel concentrated on a snarl, brushing gently until it was gone. "We had a life in Russia you could scarcely imagine, Your Highness. Sometimes I ache to see it again. But we have a saying . . . 'It does not matter where you live, just so long as you are not hungry.'"

"That's true," Emma said, and laughed. "I'm glad you're here, Rashel."

When Emma's hair lay in a blanket of ebullient curls over her shoulders, Rashel helped her change into a nightdress of delicate embroidered linen with a matching robe.

"You look very Russian, Your Highness."

Perceiving it was a compliment, Emma smiled in thanks. "I'm afraid I am a hundred percent English."

"My people have very big hearts, and they laugh often. I think you are Russian inside."

Emma was about to reply when her stomach growled loudly, making her blush and laugh self-consciously. "I had almost nothing to eat today," she said, holding a hand to her empty stomach. "I was so nervous . . . the wedding . . ."

"Shall I bring up some soup and *zakuski?*"

"*Zakuski?*" Emma repeated, struggling with the unfamiliar word.

"Small bites of food. You will like them very much, Your Highness. I will bring some for you to try."

The maid left, and Emma wandered through the suite. She shook her head in wonder as she discovered a bathing room fitted entirely with white marble. Four gold spigots shaped like dolphins were poised above the porcelain rim of the tub.

She wondered if her stepmother had lived in this kind of luxury during her childhood days in Russia. So much of Tasia's past was still private, still unknown. For the first time Emma began to realize how much Tasia had suppressed her Russianness, how much of her native language and customs had been left behind. What a different culture it was . . . and how difficult it must be to adapt, as Nikolas and Tasia had.

A soft tap on the bedroom door alerted her to Rashel's return. The maid had brought a large tray loaded with fragrant dishes, including a small tureen of spicy cabbage soup, bits of sausage and smoked salmon, little pies stuffed with mushrooms and ground meat. Enthusiastically Emma followed Rashel into the receiving room, and sat on a small, overstuffed settee. The maid set the food on a nearby table, pointed out a few delicacies she thought Emma might enjoy, and left her in privacy.

The food was delicious, much of it flavored with garlic, pepper, and nutmeg. Emma tried a taste of everything, washing it all down with sips of hearty red wine. The lushness of her surroundings made her feel cosseted and spoiled. "I could get used to this," she murmured, leaning back against the plump velvet settee cushions.

Nikolas's voice came from the doorway. "I certainly hope you will, *ruyshenka*." He wore a dressing-robe of golden-brown silk, a shade or two darker than his hair. His legs and feet were bare. Emma wondered in sudden panic if he was wearing anything beneath the robe.

She tried to camouflage her nervousness with a sunny smile, and raised her wine to him in a toast. "Would you care to join me, Nikki?"

"As long as you don't smile like that again."

"Why not?" she asked, watching apprehensively as he approached.

"Because," he whispered, sliding his hand around the back of her neck, "it makes me light-headed."

Emma's eyes fluttered closed as she felt his mouth press lightly against hers. When Nikolas ended the kiss and sat beside her, she reached awkwardly for a tidbit on the tray and offered it to him, trying to act the part of gracious hostess. "Would you care for a *pirozhi?*"

"*Pirozhki,*" he said, correcting her pronunciation, and lowered his head to take a bite of the filled tart in her hand.

A quick laugh of surprise escaped her. "You're the first man I've ever had eating out of my hand." She waited until he had swallowed, and offered the next bite. Nikolas smiled and took the rest, nipping the end of her finger with his teeth.

Uneasy but intrigued, Emma hesitated before lifting the wine to her husband's lips. He drank from the jewel-encrusted goblet, staring at her over the glittering rim. Slowly he took the wine from her, set it aside, and dipped his fingertip into the fruity vintage. Emma watched him, transfixed. She didn't move as he touched the soft skin of her lower lip, leaving a ruby-colored droplet. Leaning forward, he licked away the bead of wine, gently sealed his mouth over hers, kissed and licked in deepening forays . . . until Emma trembled and reached for him. Her hands slipped on his amber silk robe, skidding over his chest. He wrapped his arms around her, holding her steady against him.

Emma relaxed, dizzy with excitement and pleasure, while his lips moved over hers. It had been six weeks since he had kissed her like this. She had forgotten how good it felt. Suddenly she was hollow with need, wanting to be taken and filled, wanting the same magic she had felt with him before.

Nikolas took one of Emma's hands and urged it down between their bodies. Following his lead, she reached beneath the silk robe until her fingers closed around the hard, silken-skinned length of him. She gasped and pressed her whole body against his, straining to be even closer.

Nikolas buried his face in her hair, dragging the soft curls across his cheeks and forehead, winding his fingers tightly in the gleaming curtain. He didn't know why it should be like this with her, when he had known so many women. None of them had ever affected him as Emma did.

Wrapping his fingers around her wrist, he pulled her to her feet. Emma stood up and pressed her flushed face against his. "Nikki," she whispered, "are you going to visit my bed tonight?"

"Is that an invitation?"

Emma paused in her playful kissing. "Would you like it in writing?"

"That won't be necessary." He eased the robe from her shoulders and arms and dropped it to the floor. Lightly he slid his hand down her front. Her body was willowy and warm beneath the thin linen of her nightgown. "Emelia . . . my wife . . ." Words failed him once more, and he crushed her lips beneath his.

She went with him into the bedroom, where he shed his robe and sat naked on the bed. Spreading his knees, Nikolas drew Emma to the edge of the mattress. She stood before him, holding onto his shoulders, while he pulled the hem of her gown up to her hips. His warm palms coasted up the sleek outline of her thighs, his fingers skimming her taut buttocks. He pressed his mouth to the curve of her breast. Suckling through the delicate fabric of her gown, he felt the small point of her nipple rise against his tongue. Emma moaned and leaned against him, her slender hands coming up to touch his head. Blindly she urged his mouth to her other breast, gasping as he bit the soft peak into stinging readiness.

When Emma could no longer stand, Nikolas lowered her to the bed, stripping away the gown. She put her hands on his back, finding the pattern of scars, stroking lightly as if she could heal all the long-ago wounds. He dragged his mouth over her throat, breasts, stomach, his tongue skimming secret places that made her body tense and trembling.

He kissed the thatch of cinnamon curls, his breath stirring through them. Emma whimpered in dismay and delight, not knowing if she should allow this, not wanting it to stop. Her hands found his hair, her fingers sifting through the thick locks in a shivering caress. The world narrowed down to the flickering movement between her thighs, his expert, teasing mouth. She rose against him in awkward, ardent surges, while each small breath became a plaintive cry.

Nikolas raised his head and lifted his body over hers, spreading Emma's thighs apart. He began to enter her, and she winced at the unexpected tightness. "Careful," she whispered in a sobbing breath. He was very gentle, pushing slowly inside her, waiting until she relaxed beneath him. They began a languorous rhythm, pressing together with increasing hunger. Emma's head fell back, and Nikolas kissed her throat and shoulder, whispering guttural phrases in Russian.

Their long bodies entwined, limbs wrapping around each other, muscles flexing and gripping as they strove for a release that hovered just out of reach. It broke upon them in the same startling moment, a sweet convulsion of sensation. Nikolas thrust deeply and held himself buried tightly within her, while Emma shuddered in aching relief. When the fierce pumping of his blood had subsided, Nikolas rolled onto his back. Emma followed, throwing an arm and a leg across him, pressing her head to his smooth, damp chest. She went completely limp, draped over him like a drowsing cat.

Nikolas lifted a hand to her tumbled hair, stroking softly, while his eyes remained wide open in the darkness. A strange mixture of emotions flooded him; all at once he felt desperate, wanting to crush her in his arms and yet also to shove her away. The peaceful weight of his wife's body, her contented sigh as she snuggled next to him . . . it made his chest hurt. He couldn't let himself relax, couldn't accept the easy affection she offered. If he let himself be vulnerable, even for a moment, the floodgates would open, and everything he had steeled himself to endure and forget would finally overtake him.

Easing himself away from her, he left the bed and groped for his discarded robe.

"Nikolas?" she murmured sleepily.

He ignored her and shrugged into the robe. Quietly he left the room and went to his dark, empty suite at the other end of the wing.

Emma sat up in confusion, pushing her hair off her face. Why had he gone so suddenly? What had she done wrong? She bit her lip to keep from crying. She wasn't a child, she was a married woman, and she didn't have the luxury of tears.

"You chose this," she told herself grimly. "Now

you have to make the best of it." It was a long time before she lay back down again, and longer still before she fell asleep, her body curled in the center of the large bed.

PART II

Who cares if this locked heart holds unforgotten
pictures . . .

—PUSHKIN

❧ Five

NIKOLAS WAS DISTRACTED from his work by the sounds of shrieking outside the library window. He shot up from his desk, although Mr. Meadows and Mr. Bailey, a pair of estate agents he had been conferring with, remained in their chairs with bemused expressions on their faces. Reaching the window in three strides, Nikolas looked outside at the damp October landscape and went still.

"Your Highness?" Meadows asked uneasily. "Has someone been injured?"

Nikolas shook his head. "It's my wife," he murmured. "Taking her daily exercise." He watched with a faint smile as Emma, dressed in a white blouse, boots, and breeches, romped on the manicured lawn with her dog, Samson. Anyone who didn't know her might have been moved to suggest that the princess should be institutionalized. Emma chased the mongrel over flower beds and parterre hedges, her red hair flying in a tangled banner behind her back. In a flash, she whirled around and ran the other way, while the ungainly dog bounded after her.

In the past month of marriage, the Angelovsky household and tenants had become accustomed to

Emma's uninhibited ways, even to the sight of her striding around the estate in men's clothes. Walking through the house hand in hand with an elderly chimpanzee had also become a commonplace occurrence. Frolicking on the lawn with her dog was mild in comparison to everything else.

Nikolas said nothing about his wife's eccentric behavior, for the simple reason that he enjoyed it, especially when it shocked others. He relished Emma's agile and unconventional mind, her straightforwardness, her lack of pretension. She had the boundless energy of a child, working herself to near exhaustion and then releasing her tension by riding her horse at neck-breaking speed, or sprinting across the fields in pursuit of Samson.

Nikolas enjoyed almost every moment of being with Emma . . . except for the times when she turned unexpectedly quiet and sweet, wanting to snuggle close to him and rest her curly head on his shoulder. Then he was forced to pull away from her, before he was consumed with blind panic. Emma had no idea of the way she threatened him, the promise of destruction she brought with every smile. He would not—*could not*—love her. But neither could he ignore his need for her, and so his relationship with her was a complicated balance of attraction and repulsion.

Nikolas was about to turn away from the window when all at once Samson reached Emma and jumped on her, his saucer-sized paws hitting her slender back. She fell forward onto her stomach and didn't move.

Nikolas was filled with a sudden blast of energy. Without a word to the two startled men, he raced across the room and sent the French doors bursting apart as he took a shortcut to the outside grounds. "Emma," he called harshly, running to her still figure. He dropped beside her, his knees digging into the soft green lawn.

She was making choking noises. He turned her over, the blood draining from his face as he saw her struggle to breathe. "Emelia—" He hovered over her, unfastening the top three buttons of her blouse.

"I'm . . . all right," she wheezed. "Wind . . . knocked out . . ." She tried to sit up, and he pushed her back to the ground.

"Quiet. Just relax. Does it hurt anywhere? Are you nauseated?"

Emma shook her head while he checked everywhere for signs of blood or broken bones. "No," she gasped, trying to push his searching hands away.

Nikolas scowled as Samson approached them. The dog whined apologetically and snuffled in Emma's hair. Impatiently Nikolas shoved him aside. Samson retreated a few feet and lay down, moaning anxiously.

"Your Highness?" came the butler's voice from several yards away. Evidently the servants had been alerted to the mishap. "Shall I send for a doctor?"

"Not yet," Nikolas replied, staring at Emma's pale face. "We'll see how she is in a few minutes. Go back inside, Stanislaus."

"Very well, sir."

To his surprise, Emma began to giggle as she regained her breath. "We were playing," she said, taking in weak, rapid gulps of air. "I fell on my stomach . . . that's all."

"Yes, I saw." Nikolas pulled Emma across his

lap, bracing her shoulders. He smoothed back the curls that had fallen over her face. He was quiet, listening intently as her breathing evened out. With one fingertip he stroked the surface of his wife's cheek, which had gone from snowy white to vivid pink. He lingered on a few golden freckles, brushing them with a gossamer-light touch. It crossed his mind that others might be watching the spectacle on the lawn, but he couldn't seem to make himself let go of her. "Do you feel like sitting up?" he heard himself ask.

"Please."

Gently he helped her to sit, his arm locked around her back. "Are you all right?"

"Yes," Emma whispered. Her blue eyes were soft and confused. Their faces were very close, their breaths mingling.

Nikolas meant to admonish her, to demand that she be more careful, but all he could do was stare at her parted lips ... so soft, so tenderly curved ...

"Nikki?" she murmured, her hand fluttering to his chest, where his violent heartbeat resounded.

With a low sound he kissed her, fastening his mouth over hers, yielding to the dark passion that drove him. Emma was pliant and weak in his arms, submitting without a sound, her fingers inching to the back of his neck and sliding delicately into his thick hair.

Nikolas's response was sure and swift, his flesh rising hard against the tight restraint of his trousers. He wanted to pin her to the ground and thrust into her, here, now, grinding her hips into the fragrant earth beneath them. He wanted to make her shudder in climax, until she tore the clothes on his back in an effort to touch his skin. Just as he reached the point of exploding with lust and emotion, he jerked back and pushed her off his lap.

Emma sat on her heels, staring at him in bewilderment.

Nikolas made his voice as crisp as possible. "Spare the household any more of your antics today. I have work to do. In case you intend to spend your afternoon with that flea-bitten mongrel, I advise you to take a bath afterward. At the moment, the two of you share the same remarkable smell."

Emma stiffened with offended pride. "Samson may smell a little strong at times, but he doesn't have fleas!"

Nikolas glanced at the dog, who was scratching industriously with his hind foot. With a sardonic snort, Nikolas stood and left.

Emma leaned over to pat Samson's rough head, and glared at her husband's departing form. "He's an impossible man," she informed the wriggling dog. "Don't pay any attention to him. We don't care about his opinion."

She shook her head as she wondered what had come over Nikolas. One minute he had kissed her passionately, and the next he had pulled away as if burned. After three months of marriage, Nikolas was still very much a stranger to her. It was seldom that he explained his actions or decisions, and rarer still for him to reveal his feelings. But in spite of Emma's exasperation, she was fascinated by her husband.

Nikolas could be devilishly entertaining, provoking laughter, astonishment, and sometimes horror at the stories he told her of his life and the people he had known. He listened patiently when she read aloud her occasional correspondence to and from Tasia, and he was even comforting when she was depressed about her strained relationship with her family. But he could also be callous and unbearably cold, for no apparent reason. She attributed many of Nikolas's nasty moods to the fact that he drank too much. It was his nightly ritual to consume several glasses of wine with supper, and half a bottle of vodka after. Yet she had never seen him drunk. Alcohol made him soft-voiced and guarded, and cuttingly perceptive.

Most of society regarded Nikolas as one of their own, an aristocrat who devoted himself to leisurely amusement and played at business merely to amuse himself. Emma had quickly learned that nothing was farther from the truth. Nikolas was busier than any man she had ever known, even her father. He managed his fortune with assiduous attention, making investments and launching financial enterprises so complex that it almost frightened Emma to see them written out on paper.

The interminable business of entertaining wasn't bad at all, since Emma had to do very little of the planning. The routine had been established years before, and the servants were amazingly efficient as they maintained the house, prepared and served meals, and saw to the needs of every guest. As Nikolas had promised, Emma was able to spend most of her time caring for her animals and working for her causes.

There was an endless parade of visitors at the Angelovsky estate, which seemed more like a hotel than a home. Their dinner table was constantly filled with foreign guests, many from Europe and America and even a few from principalities in Russia. The after-dinner conversation of the men was devoted exclusively to the subject of business, percentages and profit, shares and investment and taxes. Sometimes Emma took a seat at the fringe of the complicated discussions and listened quietly. She was amused by the awe with which others regarded her husband, the way they desired to be his friend and feared him at the same time . . . and she had a touch of sympathy for their dilemma.

Nikolas could be beguiling one moment and incredibly scathing the next. He was cruelest to those who tried to flatter him, and told them with a lethal smile that he cared about no one but himself, and that anyone who believed differently was a fool. He didn't seem to want anyone's friendship, and ironically that seemed to make people even more eager to be close to him.

For her part, Emma had learned to curb her impulses to be affectionate to Nikolas. It seemed to annoy him when she kissed him casually. He was a gentle and skillful lover, but he was never inclined to hold her in the aftermath of their lovemaking. On one of the nights he had visited her, when she had dared to rest her hand on his arm for a minute, he had left the bed with a muffled exclamation of annoyance. Touching, caressing, was acceptable only when he initiated it, and even then it never lasted for long. Emma had come to accept the distance he imposed between them, and had even convinced herself that it was for the best. She was much better off without love, and without all the heartache and longing it brought.

The stale air was stirred as Emma and the two Sidarova girls, Rashel and Marinka, dragged an unwieldy trunk from the corner. Having discovered five locked storage rooms on the top floor of the Angelovsky manor, Emma had asked Nikolas what they contained. He had shrugged indifferently and replied, "Old family possessions from the palace in St. Petersburg. Dishes, carvings, ornaments—nothing very remarkable. Look through them if you like."

Emma's curiosity ran rampant at the idea. She requested the key to the rooms from the housekeeper, Mrs. Evstafyeva, a rotund and cheerful woman who ran the household with remarkable efficiency. "Take the Sidarova sisters to help you," she had suggested. "Whatever you wish to have carried downstairs and cleaned, they will do it. Good, strong girls, both of them."

Emma had liked the suggestion. Rashel and Marinka were remarkably similar. Both girls had chestnut hair, winning smiles, and cheerfully pragmatic temperaments. Using tools purloined from the carriage house, the three of them settled in one of the storage rooms and opened crates and trunks, knocking off small gilt hinges and locks. To Emma's delight, they uncovered some relics of the Angelosky past—a bear rug trimmed with gold braid, a lady's silver toiletry set, a carved wooden box filled with embroidered veils.

"How beautiful!" Emma exclaimed, gingerly unfolding one of the frail lengths of silk. "I wonder what these are for."

The Sidarova sisters exclaimed in pleasure and examined the contents of the box. "They are used to cover a woman's hair, Your Highness," Rashel said. She reached past the veils and extracted a gold circlet that had been bent on one side to form a delicate peak. A single tear-shaped ruby dangled from the point. "Shall I show you how it is worn?" she asked.

Emma nodded and remained sitting on the floor, while Rashel stood to drape the pearl-encrusted veil over her hair. Next she arranged the diadem so that the ruby lay against the center of Emma's forehead. "Married women must cover all their hair, to hide it from a stranger's eyes," Rashel explained, standing back to view her with satisfaction. She gave Emma the hand mirror from the silver toiletry set. "But a maiden arranges the cloth so the top of her head is left exposed."

Emma squinted at her reflection in the cloudy, distorted glass. "I feel quite exotic," she said with a laugh, reaching up to feel the ruby on her forehead.

"It is pretty on you," Rashel commented.

Marinka nodded in agreement. "You look very Russian, Your Highness."

"Let's see what else we can find!" Emma removed the diadem and veil and continued to dig through the trunk. There were beautiful woven shawls and squares of lace, antique combs made of bone, faded silk shoes and purses covered with glinting gems. "Look at this," she said, holding up one of the little jeweled bags. The rose silk was embroidered with a Russian Cyrillic character that resembled the letter *E*.

Rashel examined the purse closely. "That may

have belonged to the wife of Prince Nikolai the First. Her name was Emelia."

"Really? Nikolas mentioned her to me once. She was his distant grandmother, wasn't she?"

Rashel nodded. *"Dah,* Emelia was a peasant woman from a village near St. Petersburg. Would you like to hear the story of Nikolai and Emelia?"

"By all means," Emma said, crossing her legs and settling herself more comfortably. By now she had noticed that the Russian household servants all shared the habit of telling entertaining tales at every opportunity. They always began the same way: *Once, a very long time ago* . . . Or sometimes, *Once, in an age long gone by* . . . Emma looked at Rashel expectantly, waiting for the story to commence.

The maid's eyes sparkled with enjoyment. "Once, long ago, there was an iron-willed prince named Nikolai. He was the most valiant of boyars, and so handsome that even the sun envied him for his brightness. But Nikolai was never touched by love. Over the years his heart grew a shell of hard, cold stone.

"When it came time for Prince Nikolai to marry, he commanded that all the young maidens from Moskva and surrounding lands be brought to him, and he would choose from among them. Five hundred beautiful maidens came in hopes of becoming his bride. He moved among them and dismissed one girl after another, bestowing a gold coin on each one.

"As Nikolai finally despaired of ever finding a maiden to please him, he caught sight of Emelia, a lovely peasant girl. The sun had touched her hair with its rays, and made it shine like the magical gold-and-red feathers of a firebird. The longer Prince Nikolai stared at the beautiful light, the more warmth he felt in his heart, until the stone shell melted away. 'This is my bride,' Nikolai said, and lifted Emelia in his arms, carrying her away to his palace. The rest of the disappointed maidens were sent back to their families. Prince Nikolai and Emelia were married, to the great rejoicing of everyone in the land. They shared a great love, and conceived a child . . . but then the story turns tragic."

"Why?" Emma asked, intrigued in spite of herself. "What happened?"

"Soon after their marriage, Prince Nikolai fell out of favor with the tsar, and many jealous boyars used the opportunity to turn on him. Nikolai was thrown in prison, where he took ill and died. Princess Emelia nearly died also, from grief. She went to a convent to hide from her enemies, and there she bore Nikolai's son in secret. The boy grew to be as noble and handsome as his father had been, and he became one of the most powerful men in Russia—one of the consorts of Empress Elizabeth."

"Is this a true story?" Emma asked skeptically.

"Oh, yes, Your Highness."

Emma stared at the tiny embroidered bag in her lap and toyed with the glinting beads. She was touched by the sad tale, but rather than admit it, she took refuge in a show of mild scorn. "Only an Angelovsky ancestor would be so arrogant. Making all the peasant women stand there for him to choose his wife . . . why, I would spit in his face!"

"Perhaps," Rashel said with a sly gleam in her

eyes. "But it is said that Prince Nikolai was a very beautiful man. Sometimes that makes up a little for arrogance, yes?"

"I don't care how handsome he was. The whole thing sounds barbaric."

"It was the family tradition. Those days were very different. Now, of course, Russians have adopted Western ways, and it is not done anymore."

"Thank God for progress," Emma said. She leaned over and lifted a cloth-wrapped frame from the trunk. With the girls' help, she unwrapped the frame and discovered an old, crumbling landscape. The paint was chipped and coated with decades of grime. Emma was unimpressed by the picture, which was clearly an amateurish effort. "Why would anyone save this?" she asked, wrinkling her nose. "Could it have any value, aside from sentimental?"

Rashel and Marinka gathered behind her to look at the painting. It was a hunting scene of Russian borzoi dogs chasing a wolf through dark fields. There was a country palace in the background, poised on the horizon against a soft lavender sky. "Look," Marinka said, pointing to the corner where the paint had been eroded. "There is something underneath."

Emma leaned close to the canvas and scraped the cracked paint with her fingernail. A large flake fell away, revealing a sheen of copper brown and a touch of flesh-toned paint. "I do believe you're right," she remarked. "Someone has covered up another picture. I wonder what it could be."

She set the painting aside in a pile to be taken downstairs, and continued sorting through the objects in the storage room. After two more hours had passed, Emma was covered with dust and sweat. She grinned at the Sidarovas, who seemed as tired as she was. "Shall we leave off for today?" she asked, and they both agreed immediately. Emma carried an armload of her newfound belongings as she descended to her suite.

Just as she had propped the painting on the velvet settee in her receiving room, Emma heard a knock at the door and Nikolas's voice.

"I came to see if you were ready for dinner. A group of American manufacturers will be attending, and you—" Nikolas broke off as he took in the sight of her wrinkled clothes and dusty skin. A look of annoyance crossed his features, but then he laughed in reluctant amusement. "You've been looking through the attic rooms."

"It's a treasure trove!"

"You must wash and dress for supper at once," he said, casting a dubious glance at the pile of "treasure" she had found. "The Americans—"

"Come have a look at this painting," Emma insisted, gesturing him over to the settee. "Is it familiar? Does it mean anything to you?"

"Nothing at all."

"See where the paint has come off in the corner? I think there's another picture hidden beneath this one."

"Perhaps," he said indifferently. "Now, about supper—"

"Could we ask someone if it's worth restoring? There may be a wonderful painting just waiting to be uncovered."

"If it pleases you, we'll find someone to work on it. Though I doubt there's anything worth seeing.

Emma, you must clean yourself up right away and come downstairs.''

''What could I possibly say to a group of manufacturers?''

''Just sit quietly and smile.'' Nikolas shot her a meaningful glance. ''And no remarks about little animal corpses when the pheasant is brought out.''

A flashing grin appeared on her face. ''Or else?'' She moved to her dressing table and layered the antique Russian veil and diadem on her hair, exactly as Rashel had shown her. Glancing over her shoulder with a teasing smile, she said, ''If I offended all your American guests, would you beat me for it? Exactly how does a Russian prince punish his wife?''

She fell silent as she saw the change come over Nikolas's face. He had turned utterly white, his eyes dark pools of horror as he stared at her. Slowly Emma removed the frail headdress. ''What's wrong?'' she asked.

Nikolas didn't answer. There were no words for the sensation of being jolted into some other place. Something had snatched him away for no more than a second, as if he had been yanked through a door from one time into another. He had a vision of Emma crying, her face red and her hair loose and tangled . . .

''Please punish me,'' she begged.

''You little fool,'' came his own harsh reply. *He pulled her closer in an effort to soothe her, and he stroked her shaking back. ''How in God's name do you think I could leave a mark on you? How could I cause you pain with my own hands? Oh, don't think it's not tempting, my clever one. But even if I tried, I could never lift a finger against you.''*

"Because I'm your wife?" she asked tremulously.

"Because you're mine. You're the only one I've ever wanted, no matter that you'll probably be my downfall . . ."

With a violent shake of his head, he sent the vision spinning away. He didn't understand the strong emotion, sweet, piercing, painful, that clawed at the back of his throat. Aware that Emma was waiting for him to say something, he returned her stare with sudden, baffled anger.

"Nikki," she began, but he had already turned away. He left with the panic of a claustrophobic, unable to put enough distance between himself and his bewildered wife.

Emma welcomed the American guests with a cheerfulness she was far from feeling. She had dressed in one of her favorite gowns, a yellow-and-ivory silk, with a square neckline cut low to reveal the tops of her breasts. Luxuriant fringe trimmed the double overskirt and the elbow-length sleeves. Her hair was gathered on top of her head, two long curls falling down her back. The whole effect was bright and fashionable, and it gave her a boost of confidence that she needed.

Nikolas had fallen into an unpredictable mood after the episode in her suite. He behaved indifferently toward her, but there was a touch of scorn in his attitude that annoyed her. Emma knew that she had done nothing wrong. She couldn't help it if he had occasional "spells"—whatever they were—and she certainly wasn't causing them. He was drinking too much, or maybe he was overworking himself. She might visit Tasia soon, and talk to her about Nikolas's problem. Tasia had always said that Russians had a very mystical and mysterious nature. She might be able to shed some light on the situation. If only Nikolas would help Emma to understand what was happening . . . but she knew better than to question him about it.

The ten guests were seated at the long, linen-covered dining table, with Emma and Nikolas at opposite ends. As usual, the service was *à la russe*, with footmen bringing hot serving dishes from the kitchen and offering a portion to each guest. Turning to her left, Emma smiled at the gentleman seated next to her, a man in his early thirties named Mr. Oliver Brixton. He was far from handsome, for his face was round and plain, and his hair was thinning, but there was a confidence and friendliness in his manner that made him appealing.

"Is this is your first trip to England, Mr. Brixton?" she asked.

"Yes, it is," he admitted in a flat New York accent. "I've never been abroad in my life until now. My tour began in France, then Italy, now England. It isn't nearly as stuffy here as I'd feared."

Emma was charmed by his honesty. "Is England more or less stuffy than New York?"

"A little less, to my surprise. I think it's because Americans have so much to prove, since we live in such a young country. In New York society we muster all the pomposity we can, hoping it will distract others from our raw edges."

Pausing in the middle of lifting her spoon to her lips, Emma glanced at him with teasing speculation. "There's not a raw edge in sight, as far as I can tell."

Brixton smiled, partaking of the herbed and truffled soup. "That's good to hear, Your Highness, since I'll be making many more visits to England."

"Business reasons, Mr. Brixton?"

"Yes, but in addition, I'll want to visit my sister, Charlotte. She's engaged to an Englishman, you know. Charming fellow we happened to meet in France a few months ago."

Emma set her spoon down and stared at him, her mind buzzing with horrified speculation. Brixton, Brixton . . . where had she heard that name before? No, it couldn't be . . .

From his position across the table, Nikolas must have been alerted by her strange expression. His attention broke from the woman on his right, and he focused on Emma's pale face.

Misreading Emma's reaction as one of curiosity, Brixton proceeded to explain. "A week from now, my sister will marry Lord Adam Milbank. Perhaps you know of him, Your Highness?"

Locked in a dumbstruck silence, Emma nodded. Nikolas answered for her, startling the others at the table away from their own light conversations. "Indeed, the princess does know of him. Before our marriage, the princess set her cap for Milbank, but he proved too elusive . . . and so she had to settle for me."

Emma's gaze flew to his. There was a gleam in his amber eyes that betrayed a touch of malicious enjoyment. Had he planned this? Had he remembered that Brixton was the name of the woman Adam was betrothed to? Confusion and outrage tangled inside her. She tried to conceal her emotions by picking up her silver spoon, her fingers trembling slightly.

The sultry beauty to Nikolas's right interceded. She was all dark-eyed flirtatiousness as she spoke to him in a honeyed voice. "Your Highness, I would hardly call that 'settling'! A man as wealthy and attractive as you are would be any rational woman's first choice."

"My only choice," Emma said with poisonous sweetness.

Only Nikolas understood the barb. He acknowledged it with a mocking smile, raising his glass to her. "Let us say that both Lord Milbank and I have been blessed with good fortune—he for attaining the hand of Miss Brixton, and I for winning the beautiful Emelia."

For the next several minutes Emma ate mechanically and listened to Brixton's chatter. Thankfully he didn't seem to require anything more than an occasional smile and nod.

Meeting Brixton tonight was like a slap in the face. In all the activity of her new life, Emma had managed not to think about Adam too often. But seeing this man made it a reality, that there was indeed a woman Adam would make his wife, a week from now—a *week* . . . She steeled herself to keep her eyes from watering, to keep from thinking, *God, I want it to be me* . . . Every time she glanced at Nikolas, she found him watching her, coolly analyzing her heightened color, every flutter of her lashes, every shade of expression. What did he want from her? What did he hope to see in her face?

"You're quite the most enjoyable English lady I've met," Brixton said. "So friendly and open. It's a nice change."

Emma forced her attention back to him. "I'll admit the English have a well-earned reputation for being reserved."

"Why aren't you, then?"

"I don't know," she answered, smiling. "I'm just odd, I suppose."

Brixton gave her a blatantly admiring glance. "Perhaps so, Your Highness. But in the nicest possible way."

Emma blushed and looked across the table. Nikolas stared at her impassively, his lips touched with a mocking smile, as if she were some foolish child he had caught in a lie.

Although the interplay between Emma and Nikolas was never what anyone would call affectionate, at least they had always managed a friendly banter in front of guests. This evening it was impossible. Emma was miserably aware of the strained silences between them. Nikolas was at his most obnoxious, treating her to cold stares and jeering taunts. Emma longed to snap at him that she had done nothing to deserve such treatment. Had Nikolas guessed somehow that she had been affected by Oliver Brixton's presence tonight? Did it annoy him that she still had feelings for Adam? Was he *jealous?* No, Nikolas had never shown any signs of caring for her that way. It must be that his pride had been stung.

Emma suffered through the rest of the evening, profoundly relieved when the guests finally took their leave after midnight. Without a word to Nikolas, she hurried up to her suite and slammed the door. The effort of smiling and eating and making conversation had exhausted her. Trying to calm her jangling nerves, she rang for Rashel to help her undress, and paced around the suite until the maid arrived. Seeming to understand her mistress's fury, Rashel was silent and efficient as she unfastened Emma's gown and unhooked her stays.

"I can do the rest," Emma said shortly, motioning for her to leave. "Thank you, Rashel. *Spahkóy-nigh nóchyee.*"

"Good night, Your Highness," the maid replied in kind, slipping out the door.

Emma donned an embroidered linen nightgown and went to bed, pausing only to jerk the pins from her hair and run her fingers through it. She lay in the darkness with a sheet pulled up to her breasts, and tried to recall Oliver Brixton's face in detail. Did Charlotte Brixton resemble her brother? The same round cheeks, the same light, thin hair? *I hope she has a fortune big enough to satisfy you, Adam,* Emma thought grimly, *if that's what you really wanted.* She remembered Adam at their last meeting, at the Angelovsky ball . . . his warm brown eyes, his boyish smile, the pressure of his lips on hers, his voice saying, *I adore you . . .* A tear squeezed from beneath her lashes, and she buried her face in the pillow.

She had almost drifted off to sleep, her body curled and relaxed, when there was movement in the darkness. Making a drowsy, questioning sound, Emma began to roll onto her back. A heavy body pounced on hers, a spring of coiled muscle. In her drugged confusion she thought she was dreaming and was being attacked by her tiger, Manchu. A man's hot breath pelted against her ear, and she was stunned to realize it was her husband.

"Nikolas?"

He pinned her to the mattress with his weight. Although he was fully clothed, the insistent jut of his arousal was unmistakable as it pressed against her bottom. Emma gasped in surprise, wriggling to free herself as his liquor-soured breath wafted to her nostrils.

"You're a possession to me, do you understand?" came Nikolas's sneering voice. "I own every damn bit of you. I knew what you wanted tonight—I saw the way you flirted and smiled while Brixton looked down your dress. You wanted me to be jealous, my scheming little wife, but it didn't work. I will never be jealous of you."

Emma recovered enough from her astonishment to jab her elbow against his ribs. "Get off me, you drunken ass," she cried in a muffled voice.

Nikolas flipped her over and pressed himself between her thighs. He was breathing heavily, from rage or passion, or from some volatile mixture of both. "You want to tie my soul into knots," he muttered. "But you won't make me feel anything I don't want to feel. I will never love you."

"Who asked you to?" Emma replied hotly. Then she was still, and in a peculiar flash of understanding she knew that Nikolas was afraid, that he was fighting desperately against his own feelings. Wonderingly she reached up to his shadowy figure, her fingers touching the rumpled locks at the side of his head. "Nikki—"

He jerked back with a furious sound. "Don't call me that."

"Coward," she said, the accusation soft but clear. "Why are you so terrified of being close to me?"

Emma felt his tremor of anger as he crouched

astride her hips, anger that made his bones lock and his muscles clench. Then Nikolas gave a defeated groan and bent over her. His mouth sought hers, yearning, passionate, and his hands tore at her nightgown to find her willing body beneath. She moved to help him, pulling at her own clothes and his, ripping his white lawn shirt, yanking at his trousers with such urgency that the buttons popped.

When their clothes were shredded and disarranged, Nikolas pressed his bare skin against hers. He fastened his mouth against the sweet softness of her throat, sucking and licking, working down to her breasts. Moaning in pleasure, Emma opened her thighs and reached down to guide him inside her. He was taut and enlarged, filling her until she quivered with the ecstasy of it. She pushed upward to take more of him, and gasped as he rolled over in an unexpected movement. She rose above him, riding him steadily, pleasuring herself on his aroused body.

Nikolas pulled her down to his chest and hugged her as he thrust straight into her center. Emma moved her mouth against his ear and caught the soft lobe in her teeth, making him growl with desire. Clasped against his long, scarred body, she felt the waves of excitement deepen until she was lost in a searing climax. She sobbed against his neck and writhed in delight. Almost immediately Nikolas convulsed with the same pleasure, his breath hissing through his teeth as he drew a sharp breath. He made a low, helpless sound and pushed one last time, holding himself deep inside her.

Knowing his dislike of being touched too long,

Emma began to roll away. Nikolas gripped her hips in a reflexive movement, holding her against him. They lay together for several minutes, breathing, relaxing, while the cool air dried the perspiration on Emma's back. A new feeling came over her, a sense of calmness and quiet she had never known. Nikolas's heartbeat was steady beneath her ear, his hands gentle as he traced the curves of her hips and bottom. The hair at her temple was stirred into flutters by his breath, and his lips brushed her cheek. It was the most tender gesture he had ever made to her. Soon Emma was lulled to sleep. She was so tired . . . too tired to make anything but the faintest protest as she felt him leave her during the night.

The first thing Emma saw when she awoke was the flattened pillow beside hers. She lay amid the jumble of sheets and experienced a strange feeling of lightness, almost giddiness. Last night with Nikolas had been different from any other time he had visited her. He had been so intense, savage . . . and the moment of intimacy afterward . . . it was as if they had crossed a boundary Nikolas had never intended to reach.

Remembering, Emma turned crimson with an excitement she couldn't explain, even to herself. What would Nikolas say to her today?

She took a long bath and scented her wrists and throat with spicy perfume, then tied her hair at the nape of her neck with a crisp peach-colored ribbon. With Rashel's help, she dressed in a white ruffled blouse and a peach skirt. There was a deep side pocket on the skirt, adorned with a large silk rosette. Pleased with her clean-scrubbed, glowing appearance, Emma went down to breakfast just as the clock chimed nine.

She was gratified to find that Nikolas was at the breakfast table, behind a concealing screen of newspaper. He didn't bother to rise or even glance at her, only flipped a page with meticulous care.

"Good morning," Emma said brightly.

The newspaper lowered a few inches to reveal her husband's expressionless face. His hair was damp and freshly washed, his golden skin gleaming from a close shave. Emma wondered if, like her, he had taken special pains with his appearance this morning. "It's not often we have breakfast at the same time," she commented, seating herself beside him. "I'm usually out with the animals at this hour."

"Why not today?"

"Well . . . there's nothing the servants can't take care of. Just routine chores." For the first time Emma could ever remember, she wanted to spend a morning doing something else rather than tending her animals. Her heart beat a little faster as she thought that perhaps Nikolas might invite her to spend the day with him. They could ride or take a walk together, stroll past a market or through a promenade of shops. "What are you planning to do today, Nikki?"

"I have business in London."

"I could come along with you," she said casually.

"What for?"

"To spend time together."

Nikolas set the paper down. His brows lifted sardonically. "Why the hell would we want to do that?"

"I just thought . . ." Emma began, and floundered into silence.

Reading the disappointment on her face, Nikolas turned caustic. "I hope you're not going to pretend there's more than mere friendship between us. Let's not play that game, Emma. There's no need to complicate things. Surely even you aren't naive enough to have romantic illusions about me."

In the wake of her rapidly deflating pride, Emma's temper began to seethe. "You're the last person I'd ever have illusions about!"

"That's a relief. Don't ever become softhearted, Emma. There's no faster way to bore a man."

"Well, I'd hate for you to become bored," she said, struggling to match his cool, jeering tone.

Just as the exchange promised to escalate into an argument, Stanislaus came to the door of the breakfast room. Although the butler looked and sounded much the same as usual, there was a tension in his face, a line between his slanting brows, that alerted both Emma and Nikolas.

"Your Highness," Stanislaus said evenly, "there are visitors at the front entrance. A farm woman and a small boy. The woman is asking to see you."

"Tell her to take any complaints to the estate agent," came Nikolas's curt reply.

"Sir, perhaps . . ." The butler paused delicately. "Perhaps you might want to hear what the woman has to say."

Coming from a butler, the suggestion was astonishingly bold. Only highly unusual circumstances could have prompted it. The two men exchanged a long stare. Wordlessly Nikolas stood and left the room, brushing by Stanislaus. Emma followed close behind, too curious to resist. They went to the

front entrance of the manor, and down the wide
steps to where the two small figures waited outside.

The farm woman was dressed in simple clothes
and a threadbare shawl that had once been blue
but had deteriorated to a dingy shade of gray. Her
face might have been pretty except for the care-
worn expression and the lines of sun and weariness
around her eyes. The skinny child beside her, a boy
of five or six, wore decent but well-worn little trousers and a corduroy coat with sleeves that were too
short. He had a sullen, tanned face and thick brows
that matched his black hair.

The young woman spoke first, revealing a
mouthful of uneven yellow teeth. "This is Jacob. 'Is
ma died a week ago, of ague. 'Er last words were
for someone to bring 'im to you. No one in the
village wants 'im, anyway. I was the only one who
took the trouble of looking after 'im." She held her
hand out expectantly, wanting recompense for her
pains.

Nikolas's face was blank. Deftly he motioned to
the butler, who gave the girl a few coins. She pock-
eted her reward and started down the road without
a word to the boy, without even a backward
glance.

"What's going on?" Emma asked in astonishment. "Who is he, Nikolas?"

"It's not your concern. Go back inside." Nikolas
turned to Stanislaus. "Find someone to take care of
him," he muttered. "Just for a few days, until I can
make arrangements."

Emma stared at the boy, who waited with unnatural patience, his eyes fixed on the ground. She
approached him as she might venture near a timid

animal. Crouching down, she sat on her heels to be at eye level with him. "Hello, Jacob," she said gently. The boy looked at her without replying. "Is that your name?" she continued. "Or do you like to be called Jake?"

The child had the coloring of a Russian icon, darkness and antique gold, and melancholy amber eyes shaded by bristly dark lashes. She had never seen eyes like that before, except . . . except . . .

Somehow Emma stood upright and stared at Nikolas in disbelief. Her knees shook beneath her. She moistened her lips and spoke hoarsely. "He's your son."

❧ Six

*H*IS SON, HIS *son* . . . Nikolas didn't move as Stanislaus bustled the boy to the kitchen to be fed. He was dimly aware of Emma's questions, but he ignored her as he would a pestering fly. After the child was out of sight, Nikolas made his way back into the manor like a sleepwalker. He went to the library and braced his hands on the mahogany cabinet where liquor was kept. Dully he stared at his own distorted reflection in the silver tray on the cabinet.

He had thought he would never have to see the child. From time to time he had actually managed to forget the boy's existence. To be confronted with him now, without warning, was a tremendous shock. But on top of that, to see resemblance between the child and his dead brother . . . Oh, God, Mikhail had looked exactly the same at that age: the rumpled black hair, the face of sullen and beguiling beauty, the luminous golden eyes. Nikolas fumbled for a glass and a decanter of brandy.

He remembered the countless times in his childhood when he had found Mikhail huddled in a corner or a closet, crying and bleeding after their father had molested him. Nikolas tossed the drink down and poured another. The guilt and rage of those boyhood years were still with him, although he rarely allowed himself to think about that time.

Why had their father made Mikhail an object of such obscene violence? *"I'll find a way to stop you!"* Nikolas had shouted, leaping to attack his father with a small knife after one of those episodes. *"I'll kill you!"* But his father had laughed and twisted his arm until his wrist fractured and the knife dropped away, and then he had beaten Nikolas unmercifully. And the abuse of Mikhail had continued.

It had ruined Misha forever, made him a bitter, empty adult who had eventually met with an untimely death. It had also ruined Nikolas. No matter that his parents and brother were both dead now; the memories were alive, and they had corrupted Nikolas's soul beyond repair. No love, fear, repentance, grief, would ever touch him. He would never be weak. No one would ever have the power to hurt him.

"Nikolas," came Emma's exasperated voice behind him.

Startled from his reverie, he answered without facing her. "This has nothing to do with you."

"I just want to know who Jacob's mother was, and why you never mentioned that you had a son. I don't think that's too much to ask!"

Nikolas turned and looked at his wife. Emma was bristling with outrage and confusion. A few locks of wild red hair escaped her ribbon, and she pushed them back impatiently.

He sighed and answered curtly. "Six years ago I had an affair with a woman who worked at a dairy house on one of my estates. A month after the relationship ended, she came to me with the news that she was pregnant. Since then, I've given her money at regular intervals to care for herself and the child. I never mentioned it because it has nothing to do with you or our marriage."

Emma frowned bitterly. "Hand out some money—that's your solution for everything, isn't it?"

"What would you have had me do? Marry her? Sally was a pretty dairymaid with a healthy appetite for men. I wasn't the first to bed her, nor was I the last."

"And so you decided to let your son become a tenant farmer? Never knowing who he was or about the people he came from? No proper name, no decent education—a life in a thatched-roof hovel? Don't you feel any responsibility for him?"

"I've paid for his upkeep since he was born. Naturally I'll continue to do so. And spare me the speeches about morality and responsibility. Most of the titled landowners in England have illegitimate children. I wouldn't doubt that your own father had a few bastard offspring here and there—"

"Never! My father takes care of his own—and he certainly never went around taking advantage of milkmaids!" Emma's lip curled scornfully. "Is Jacob your only illegitimate child, or are there more?"

"He's the only one." A headache pounded in Nikolas's temples, etching lines of pain across his forehead. "Now, if your display of righteous indignation is over, kindly leave me to deal with the situation."

"What are you going to do?"

"I intend to send the boy away as soon as I find

a suitable family to take care of him. Don't worry, you won't be bothered with his presence for long."

"You mean *you* won't be," Emma said, and left the library with rapid strides. "Cynical . . . heartless . . . *monster*," she said through her teeth.

She had thought more of Nikolas than this. What kind of man would have no feelings for his own son? Her skirts dragged the ground as she went outside. It didn't matter that she wasn't dressed appropriately to go to the menagerie. She didn't care if her clothes were ruined. She needed to be near her animals.

Entering one of the cool whitewashed buildings, she went to Manchu's pen and sat on the floor by the bars. Manchu lay half in, half out of his pool, wriggling like a great tomcat when he saw her. "Hello," Emma said, resting her head against an iron bar. She closed her eyes and fought back tears. "Tasia was right. I wouldn't admit that to anyone but you, Manchu. Nikolas doesn't care about anyone but himself. And the worst thing is, he's never lied to me. He's never pretended to be anything other than the unfeeling bastard he is."

Manchu crept closer and watched her, his head slightly cocked as if he were considering the situation. "What's to be done now?" Emma asked. "Just because Nikolas wants to be rid of Jacob doesn't mean I don't owe him something. Poor little boy without a home, no mother . . . but I'm certainly not fit to be anyone's mother. And I could never look at him without remembering that he's Nikolas's bastard. It's revolting, and unfair. But . . . if Jacob were an animal, I'd take him in without another thought. Shouldn't I be willing to do at least as much for a little boy? He's as much a misfit as you or I, Manchu. I suppose I feel some sort of obligation to him, even if Nikolas doesn't."

The house was quiet when Emma went back inside, except for the mournful notes of a Russian dirge being whistled by a footman as he carried freshly polished silver urns to the dining room. "Vasily," she said, and the footman turned with a start.

"Yes, Your Highness?"

"Where is the little boy?"

"I believe he is in the kitchen, Your Highness."

Emma walked down the hallway into the kitchen complex, which included a scullery, a pastry room, several pantries, a servants' dining room, and the kitchen proper, a barn of a place with a rectangular wooden worktable in the center. Kitchen maids worked in the scullery, washing dishes and polishing pots, while others were busy making cakes and biscuits.

Emma felt a twinge of unwanted pity as she saw Jacob's small form at the wooden table, his short legs dangling from the edge of his chair. There was a plate of stew and lamb dumplings before him, apparently untouched. He stared at the cooling stew without expression while he wiggled one small foot.

At Emma's unexpected entrance, the cook and kitchen maids looked up in confusion. "Your Highness," the cook exclaimed, "is there anything you want?"

"No, thank you," Emma said pleasantly. "Please, go on with your work." She approached the table and leaned her hip on it, smiling as she saw the child's gaze flicker over the dirt on her clothes.

"Not hungry?" she asked casually. "I'm sure the food tastes a little different from what you're used to. Why don't you try one of those white rolls, Jake? They're plain and soft."

Solemn golden eyes stared into hers. He picked up a roll, his small fingers digging into the bread.

"It must be frightening, traveling to a new place and not knowing anyone." Emma watched in approval as he took a bite of the roll, and then another. He appeared to be well nourished. His skin was a healthy golden-pink color, and his teeth were strong and white. What a beautiful child, she thought, noticing the exotic dark slashes of his brows and the bristly crescents of his lashes.

The boy spoke for the first time, in a thick country accent. " 'E doesn't want to be my papa."

Emma tried to think of some lie, some made-up story to comfort him, but the truth was always best. "No, it seems he doesn't," she said gently. "But I'm going to make certain you're taken care of, Jake. And I'd like to be your friend. My name is Emma."

The little boy was silent, picking soft clumps of bread from inside the roll and eating them in little balls.

Emma watched him with friendly sympathy. "Do you like animals, Jake? I have a menagerie on the estate where I keep old and sick animals. There are horses, a chimpanzee, a wolf, a fox—even a tiger. Would you like to come with me and have a look at them?"

"Yes." Jacob put down the hollowed-out roll and slid off the chair, looking up at her curiously. "You're tall," he remarked, and Emma laughed.

"I forgot to stop growing," she replied with a wink. But the boy didn't wink or smile in return, only fixed her with a wary stare. Such a mirthless child, so full of suspicion and isolation. So like his father.

Jacob was an odd child, bright but uneducated, filled with unexpressed emotions. He didn't seem to care for the company of other people, although he tolerated Emma's presence more than anyone else's. After a great deal of effort, she coaxed him to join in one of her romps with Samson, but Jacob was self-conscious, and awkward with the concept of play. He never mentioned his mother or the village where he had grown up, and Emma decided not to push him into talking about his past.

As the days went by, a pattern developed. Emma knew that as soon as Jacob awoke in the nursery, he would dress himself and come to the door of her suite, waiting patiently for her to appear. He shared breakfast with her in the dining room, helped with the chores in the menagerie, and endured her efforts in the afternoon to teach him to ride. He followed her like a shadow, though it was unclear whether he actually enjoyed her company or merely saw that he had no other options. The servants didn't know how to treat him, and Nikolas was determined to ignore him.

"Can't you at least bother to speak to Jake?" Emma demanded at supper one night, on a rare occasion when she and Nikolas were alone. "It's been almost a fortnight since he arrived. Aren't you going to acknowledge him in some way?"

"I plan to find a new situation for him within a week. If it amuses you to entertain the child until then, do so by all means."

"What kind of situation?"

"A family who will be willing to take him in return for an annuity to be paid until he comes of age."

Emma set down her knife and fork and stared at her husband anxiously. "But Jake will know the family only wants him because of the money. The other children will tease him—they won't accept him."

"He'll survive."

Emma set her jaw stubbornly. "I may not want Jake to leave."

"Just what would you like to do with the boy? Keep him here to flaunt him as proof of my past sins?"

"I would never use a child that way!" she said in a burst of fury.

"That's right. You won't have the opportunity, because he's leaving."

More hot words trembled on Emma's lips, but she managed to hold them back. Picking up her fork, she toyed with the cabbage soufflé on her plate. "You seem to take no more notice of Jake than you would any other child," she said, her voice quiet and intense. "But you must have some feeling for your own flesh and blood. That's why you plan to send him away, isn't it? You don't want to love him or even like him. If you only knew how deprived you are, and what a limited life you lead. You live in constant fear, and you try to protect yourself with mockery and sarcasm and coldness."

There was a flash in his eyes, like cold fire. "And what, pray tell, am I supposed to be afraid of?"

"You're afraid of caring for someone. And you're absolutely terrified of someone caring for you in return. But a lack of feelings isn't strength, Nikki. Just the opposite." Emma sensed rather than saw the light quiver that ran through his body, of nerves pulled as tight as a hunter's bow.

Nikolas shoved back from the table. "I've had enough of this for one evening," he muttered.

"If you give Jacob away, I'm going to find him! He deserves better than that. He's an innocent little boy who's been robbed of his birthright. And if this is your notion of being a father, I hope I never bear your children!"

"Keep him, then," Nikolas invited with a sneer. "I should have expected this, knowing of your taste for adopting strays and mongrels. Just make certain he's kept away from me." He left the room while Emma stared after him in speechless fury.

The battle over Jacob was interrupted the next day by the arrival of Mr. Robert Soames. The middle-aged artist had rapidly gained a reputation for his miraculous restorations of artwork that had been damaged by age and mistreatment. Emma liked Soames immediately. He was gentle and unassuming, without any of the pretensions that she expected of people who belonged to the world of art. His lean, pale face was pleasant but unremarkable, except for a pair of piercing blue eyes. The decaying landscape seemed to interest Soames very much, and he accepted the job of uncovering the hidden painting with apparent eagerness.

"It may be nothing very noteworthy," he told Emma with a pragmatic shrug. "Or it may be something quite special. I suspect within a fortnight we'll have a good idea of what lies underneath the landscape, Your Highness."

A guest room was prepared, and Mr. Soames moved a few personal belongings into the manor for the duration of his labor. Emma and Jacob came to visit his workroom every day to catch glimpses of the emerging picture. They never stayed for long, because even with the windows opened wide, the fumes of the solvents Soames used made the air sharp and pungent.

"The trick is in removing the top layers without disturbing the bottom ones," Soames told them, working on the canvas with delicate brushes. "One can't help but lose a bit of the original, even if it's only the smallest fraction of one layer of paint. I must be careful not to rob the portrait of the texture the artist intended."

"Is it a portrait?" Emma asked.

"Oh, without a doubt. See this corner? That is definitely a section of a gentleman's hand."

"I hope it's an Angelovsky ancestor," Emma said, and patted Jacob's small shoulder as he came closer to inspect the painting. "One of your relatives, Jake. Wouldn't that be interesting?"

The boy responded with a noncommittal grunt. He either didn't understand or didn't care for the concept of being an Angelovsky descendant.

"Yes, it would be," Emma said firmly, answering her own question. She wandered over to a nearby window, then half sat on the ledge. "Really, Jake, you're about to talk my ears off. You must try to keep your mouth from running away with you."

Her teasing brought the smallest twitch of a smile to Jacob's lips, and he answered in his gruff country accent. "I can't say nothing when you're always talking."

Emma laughed, swinging one long leg. "It's not

polite to tell a lady she talks too much, Jacob."

"Ladies don't wear trousers," he countered, glancing at her outfit of a man's white shirt, charcoal-colored trousers, and shiny black shoes.

"But I'm a princess, and a princess can wear whatever she wants. Isn't that right, Mr. Soames?"

The artist looked up from his work with a smile as he witnessed Emma's success at drawing the boy into a conversation. "I would say so, Your Highness." His gaze remained on Emma for a moment as she lounged casually at the window with her coltish legs crossed. The sunlight played over her skin until her golden freckles seemed to glitter. With her flashing smile and the tied-back mane of copper curls, she was a magnetically appealing figure.

"Princess Emma," Soames said hesitantly, "if I might make a remark of a personal nature . . ."

"By all means, do. It may liven up my morning."

"You're an extraordinarily attractive woman, Your Highness. I would be honored to paint you someday. Exactly as you are now."

Emma laughed at the notion. "And what would you title the painting? 'The Madwoman'? 'The Eccentric'?"

"I am sincere, Your Highness. You have a rare and original beauty that any artist would want to capture."

Emma smiled skeptically. "I could show you a hundred women more beautiful, beginning with my own stepmother."

Soames shook his head. "Conventional faces and forms are easily found. They are of little interest to me. But you . . ." He paused as a shadow fell across the doorway, and he saw Nikolas standing there.

"I agree," Nikolas said, having overheard the last remarks. "I'd like a portrait of the princess to be painted by someone who appreciates her beauty. The commission is yours, if you can show me some satisfactory examples of your own work."

"Of course I—" Mr. Soames began.

"I don't want my portrait painted," Emma said, scowling at her husband.

"But I want it." Nikolas happened to glance at the small boy, now standing beside Emma, and his smile dimmed. Abruptly he turned and approached the landscape painting. "I came to view your progress, Soames."

"The work will go more quickly now that I've found the most effective way of dissolving the top layers," Soames explained. "So far all I've uncovered is part of a man's left hand."

"So I see." Nikolas stared at the fragment of the portrait, suddenly mesmerized. His own left hand began to tingle and burn. He flexed his fingers and crossed his arms over his chest. A touch of dizziness came over him, and he wrenched his gaze away. "We'll discuss the portrait of my wife later," he muttered to Soames. "For now, don't let them keep you from your work."

"They are no trouble . . ." Soames's voice trailed off lamely as Nikolas strode abruptly from the room. The artist threw a questioning glance at Emma, who answered with a sardonic smile.

"A gracious soul, my husband . . . don't you agree?"

But she left the workroom before Soames could reply, the little boy trotting after her.

* * *

It was on the following night that Nikolas was finally forced to speak directly to his son. He was drinking alone in his suite, sipping chilled vodka in a slow, contemplative way, hoping with each glass that it might numb the uneasiness inside him. Nothing was right anymore. Everything had been knocked off-kilter, and for the first time in his life he felt too slow to adapt to the changing circumstances around him. He hadn't visited Emma's bed in weeks, and his desire for her was beginning to gnaw at him. He wanted to touch her, to kiss her skin and crush her soft red curls in his hands, and feel her slender body quiver in passion as he thrust inside her. But he didn't want her to know how much he needed her, craved her, for she might find a way to use it against him.

It infuriated him that Emma had maneuvered the discovery of his illegitimate child so adeptly, first by playing the role of betrayed wife, then by deciding she wanted the boy to stay. She had no real power to keep Jacob, of course. Nikolas could have him shipped off tomorrow, if he chose. The hell of it was, he was almost grateful—*grateful*—that Emma was so determined to keep the child. Often Nikolas found himself staring at the boy, yearning to talk to him, and at the same time he was tormented by Jacob's likeness to Mikhail.

A strange, soft noise broke into his thoughts. Nikolas set his vodka down and listened intently. It was the muffled sound of crying.

"*Misha*," he whispered in horror, instinct taking precedence over reason. It was not his brother . . . but the sniffling and tears . . . a little boy's sobs . . .

Nikolas rose to his feet and stumbled from the room, gripped by a sense of anguished fear he hadn't felt since childhood. He followed the quiet sobbing along the hall, around the corner, until he saw a small figure huddled by the door of Emma's suite.

"Jacob," Nikolas said with difficulty. The name felt strange on his lips.

The boy looked up with a startled jerk, his face unhappy and tear-streaked. His shimmering gaze reached inside Nikolas to a place of indescribable pain.

"What is it?" Nikolas snapped. "Are you hurt?"

Jacob shook his head and huddled more tightly against the doorjamb, tucking his feet beneath his nightshirt.

"What do you want? Are you hungry? Thirsty?"

Just then the door opened to reveal Emma swathed in her white gown and robe, her face soft and groggy with sleep. She saw Nikolas first, and a question formed on her lips. Her gaze fell to the miserable bundle at her feet. "Jake?" She sank to the floor, pulling the child into her lap, then shot an accusing glare at Nikolas. "What have you done to him?"

"Nothing," Nikolas growled. He watched, his feet stuck to the floor, as Emma wrapped her long arms around the boy.

"What's the matter, Jake?" she asked. "Tell me what's wrong."

Jacob struggled with words, his mouth quivering. A flood of tears welled from his eyes. "I w-want Mama!" He threw his arms around Emma's neck, his small hands knotted in her hair.

"Of course you do, darling," she murmured, holding him tightly. "Of course." She rocked him in her lap, heedless of his runny nose and wet face.

The sight of a woman—especially one of Emma's class—comforting a child was rare for Nikolas. His own mother had abandoned the care of her children to servants and tutors, wanting no responsibility for their upbringing. There had never been an opportunity for Nikolas to share in the private moments of other families, except for occasional visits to the Stokehurst household. The discovery that Emma could be so maternal was unexpected, and it filled him with yearning and unreasoning anger. If only there had been someone like her fighting for him and Mikhail. She would never have allowed anyone to abuse a little boy. She would have comforted and protected Misha.

Nikolas fought a crazy urge to kneel beside her on the floor, to put his arms around his wife and the crying child, to somehow make himself part of the scene. The coldness of his isolation made him shiver. Just then Emma looked up at him as if he were an intruder. Her thoughts were unspoken but clear. *You can do nothing for us . . . you're not wanted.*

Nikolas left without a word, making his way down the hall and around the corner. He stopped there and leaned against the wall, shaking, consumed by memories. He thought of the night in Russia when he had been called away from his mistress's bed and given the message about Misha. *"Your brother was murdered tonight, Your Highness. Stabbed in the throat . . ."* And the long search for justice, culminating in his revenge on Count Shurikovsky. *No, don't think about that*—but the memory came back in a searing flash, and he saw himself walking toward Shurikovsky's drunken form stretched out on a rumpled bed. There had been a peculiar stench in the room, of liquor and stale sweat, and Nikolas's heart had thundered with fear and bloodlust until he couldn't hear anything else above the pounding, not even Shurikovsky's cry as he had beheld the face of his murderer.

Keeping his back against the wall, Nikolas slid down until he sat on the floor. Dazedly he wondered what he had thought about during the time of his arrest, the interrogations, the hours of torture and pain. He couldn't remember much of it. They had asked him about Misha's love affairs, particularly the one with Shurikovsky. It hadn't mattered to Nikolas that his brother had slept with men. After the miserable experiences of Misha's childhood, he had deserved to take his pleasure wherever he could find it.

Nikolas yanked up his sleeves and stared at the scars on his wrists, where restraining ropes had torn open layers of skin and muscle. It had made the government interrogators angry when he wouldn't respond to their taunts about Misha's sexual preferences. *"Perhaps you see nothing wrong in liking boys,"* they had said. *"It must be that you have the same sickness. Do you lust after other men, you perverted bastard?"*

Nikolas had shaken his head, unable to push words through his quivering lips. His whole body had been cold from shock and loss of blood. No, he had never lusted after men; he had always loved the grace and softness of women, the comfort of pillowing breasts, the perceptiveness of a female mind. Older women were always best, for they were less inclined to make demands, they understood about the complications and realities of life, and they were by far the most passionate.

But he had never considered marriage to anyone, until Emma. He had waited seven years to have her, never doubting that she would belong to him. He had wanted her in a way that he defined not as love but as a basic need, like breathing and eating and sleeping. The problem was, she had now become a weakness. He would have to cut her out, or lose himself entirely.

Nikolas rose to his feet and went downstairs, speaking curtly to Stanislaus and a waiting footman. "Have a carriage brought around." He would be going out now, to gamble and drink, and to find a woman. Anyone would do, as long as she wasn't Emma.

After comforting Jacob, Emma carried the boy piggyback to his bed in the third-floor nursery. Covering him with the soft linen sheet, she knelt by the bed and smoothed a cowlick in his dark hair. "I know how it feels to lose your mama," she murmured. "Mine died when I was even younger than you. Sometimes I used to cry because I missed her, and I couldn't even remember her."

Jake rubbed a fist over his eyes. "I want her to come back," he said tearfully. "I don't like it here."

Emma sighed. "Sometimes I don't either, Jake. But Nikolas is your father, and this is where you belong."

"I'm going to run away."

"And leave me and Samson? That would make me very sad, Jake."

He was silent, settling deeper into his pillow, his eyelids trembling with exhaustion.

"I have an idea," Emma continued. "Why don't we run away for a little while tomorrow, and take a basket lunch with us? We'll find a pond to splash our feet in, and we'll hunt for frogs."

"Ladies don't like frogs," he said drowsily.

"I do. I also like bugs, worms, mice . . . everything but snakes."

"I like snakes."

Emma smiled and leaned over to kiss his hair. It smelled fresh and sweet, after the vigorous soaping she had insisted on that morning. She had never felt so protective of a child, not even her own brothers. But they had a loving family, and this little boy had no one in the world, except an indifferent father. "Good night, Jake," she whispered. "Everything will be all right. I'll always take care of you."

" 'Night, Emma," he murmured, dropping off to sleep.

Emma turned down the lamp and left his room quietly. She headed toward Nikolas's suite. A rush of energy filled her. It was time to confront him about the child once and for all. She would make it clear that Jake was going to stay, and Nikolas would be expected to have some sort of communication with him. It wasn't fair that the boy should have to suffer for his parents' past indiscretions. Jacob was an Angelovsky. He was entitled to all that that implied. An education, an inheritance, some knowledge of his heritage . . . those were things he needed and deserved, and Nikolas had no right to withhold them.

She was chagrined to discover that Nikolas was not in his suite. She searched the wing and went down to the first floor, asking Stanislaus if he had seen Nikolas.

No expression registered on the butler's face.

"The prince has left for the night, Your Highness."

"I see." Emma turned away, hiding her confusion and hurt. It was late . . . the only reason Nikolas would have left at this hour was to visit another woman's bed. Even with their petty arguments and distances, he had never been unfaithful to her before. Suddenly she felt like crying. If only she could go after him, and tell him—tell him what? If Nikolas wanted someone else, some other woman's body, there was no way she could stop him. Evidently he was tired of her. She hadn't satisfied him. His Highness was bored with visiting his wife's bed. "Damn you, Nikolas," she whispered. "I'm going to end up hating myself as much as you."

She paced in her own room for hours, until the servants had retired and the manor was dark and shadow-filled. It was finally dawning on her that marrying Nikolas had been a tragic mistake. Their marriage would never get better than this. In fact, it was almost guaranteed to become worse. Nikolas's infidelities would humiliate her, and there would be more arguments, more bitterness, unless she found a way to become as hard and emotionless as he was. Her family had been right about Nikolas, but her pride would never allow her to admit it. She longed for a friend to confide in, someone to turn to.

Making her way to the grand staircase, Emma sat on the steps near the bottom, hugging her knees as she waited for her husband to come home. All she needed was one glance at his face, and she would know if he had been unfaithful to her.

Just before dawn, the sounds of carriage wheels and jangling harnesses awoke her from the half sleep she had fallen into. She sat up on the stairs, wincing at the soreness of her muscles. Blinking hard, she stared at the front entrance. Her spine was stiff with apprehension.

Nikolas came inside, looking disheveled and pale, his golden splendor muted by the darkness. The mingled odors of liquor, perfume, and sex reached Emma across the several feet that separated them. So he had done it, she thought, and flinched at the sudden pain in her chest.

Nikolas didn't see her until he had started for the stairs. He stopped suddenly, a shadow of sullen defiance crossing his features. "What do you want?"

"Nothing from you." Her voice trembled with disgust and outrage. "Nothing at all. I'll try to be sophisticated about this, Nikolas. You don't have to remind me that this sort of thing goes on all the time in upper-crust marriages. But you'd better get used to visiting other women's beds, because it will be a cold day in hell before you're welcomed back to mine!"

"I'll do whatever I want with you," Nikolas sneered, coming closer to her, looming threateningly. "You're my wife. I own you body and soul— and when I snap my fingers, you'll open your legs for me anyplace and anytime I choose."

A violent rage swept over Emma. She struck out with a closed fist, aiming straight for his unshaven, hateful face. The force of it jarred her arm all the way up to her elbow. The punch caught Nikolas by surprise, and he staggered back a few steps. His expression was blank with shock. Emma stared at him with equal amazement, wondering if he would hit her back. She waited numbly, rubbing her sore wrist.

Nikolas was silent. They both breathed heavily as they stared at each other. Lifting a hand to his jaw, Nikolas gave a dry huff of laughter. Emma didn't move as her husband walked by her, going up the stairs to his private rooms. When the last sound of footsteps had faded, she sank back down onto the step and rested her head on her knees. She had never felt so trapped, so hopeless.

For the next week there was no conversation between Emma and Nikolas, except for a few sharp exchanges when they saw each other in passing. It was difficult for Emma to eat or sleep. She felt as if she were living in an enemy camp, barricading herself behind locked doors at night, hurrying through the halls during the day to avoid meeting Nikolas. She knew she was beginning to look haggard even before Mr. Soames asked tentatively if she was feeling well. Nikolas, on the other hand, seemed alert and well rested, making Emma realize with renewed anger that he was comfortable with the situation. He had deliberately put a wedge between them, and he intended for it to stay.

Emma did her best to ignore her husband's comings and goings from the manor, telling herself it didn't matter if he had affairs or not. Not only had he broken their vows, he didn't seem to want even the appearance of friendship with her. Everything had been all right until Jacob had arrived. Why was it so difficult for Nikolas to tolerate the boy's presence? Why did it seem to hurt him to *look* at the child?

Ironically, as Emma's marriage with Nikolas deteriorated, her relationship with Jake grew stronger every day. He was beginning to trust her. She was determined not to betray that trust, even when he began to ask the inevitable questions about Nikolas. Why wouldn't his father talk to him? Why was he always frowning and quiet?

"Your father is a unique man," Emma explained to him, trying to find the right balance between kindness and truthfulness. "He's had a difficult life. Have you noticed those strange marks on his arms, or perhaps the ones on his chest? Those are scars from a terrible experience in his past, when he suffered a great deal of pain. You must try to remember that, especially when he is being cold or unfair. He can't really help the way he is. We're all a product of our experiences. It's like the animals in the menagerie. Some of them are nasty and mean because they've been hurt before . . . because they're afraid."

"Is my father afraid?" Jacob asked solemnly, his gaze locked on her face.

"Yes," she murmured. "I think so."

"Will he ever change?"

"I don't know."

They strolled out to the menagerie together to inspect the chimpanzee's spacious wire pen. Cleo had found a way to unravel the wire and make a space large enough to escape through. "Naughty girl," Emma scolded, surveying the damage. Cleo looked away from her in pointed unconcern, staring at the skylight overhead. After a moment, the chimp picked up an orange and began to peel it with exacting care. Emma exchanged a quick grin with Jake. "What a clever old thing. She must have found one stray end and started untwisting. We'll just have to fix this, Jake. The tools we need . . ." She paused as a strange, unpleasant feeling came over her, and tried to continue. "They're probably in the carriage house . . ."

"Emma." A man's voice came from the doorway.

Emma didn't move for a moment. She kept her face toward the wire pen. Cleo glanced at the newcomer and pursed her lips, making wet kissing sounds.

Finally Emma composed herself enough to face the intruder. "Lord Milbank," she said coldly, and turned around.

Adam looked the same as always, except that his hair was longer, falling almost to his shoulders in silky brown waves. He was handsome in dark striped trousers, a gray vest, and a wool frock coat. His expression was grave, his eyes soft and searching. "You're more beautiful than ever, Em."

Emma's gaze fell to his left hand. The sight of the wedding band on his ring finger was like cold water thrown in her face. "How did you know to find me out here? The servants shouldn't have allowed—"

"They didn't. I stopped my carriage before I reached the estate and walked along the front drive. I knew you'd be with your animals. I waited to make sure no one was watching, then went past the outside gates and through the gardens—"

"The gates should have been locked."

"They weren't." He shrugged. "The menagerie wasn't difficult to find. Quite an impressive set of buildings." Confronted with Emma's stony silence, Adam switched his gaze to the boy hovering beside her. "And who is this? Your little brother William . . . or is it Zachary?"

"Neither. He's my stepson, Jacob."

"Your *stepson* . . . "

Emma watched as surprise, chagrin, and then a trace of pity swept across Adam's features. It was the pity that affected her most, filling her with offended pride. She would die before allowing anyone, especially Adam, to feel sorry for her. "Congratulations on your marriage," she said in a soft jeer that she had learned from Nikolas. "Recently I had the good fortune to meet your brother-in-law. He described you as a charming fellow. He didn't know the half of it."

Adam, who had never received anything but eager affection from her, seemed astonished. "Emma, you don't sound like yourself!"

"I've changed quite a lot in the past few months, thanks to you and my husband."

"Emma?" Jake said, disturbed by her cutting tone. "Emma, what's wrong?"

She softened as she gazed into the child's upturned face. "Everything's fine," she murmured. "Lord Milbank is an old acquaintance of mine. Why don't you go back to the house and ask the cook to give you some sweets? Tell her I said it was all right."

"No, I don't want—"

"Now, Jake," she said firmly, and gave him an encouraging smile. "Go on."

The boy obeyed, dragging his feet and glancing over his shoulder as he left. Cleo settled in the corner of her pen, applying herself to the task of separating the orange into wedges.

"I had to see you," Adam said quietly. "I had to make certain you understood what really happened all those months ago."

"I understand perfectly. I don't want to hear your explanation. I'm married now, and so are you.

Whatever you have to say isn't important."

"The truth is important," Adam insisted, with an intensity that Emma hadn't remembered from before. She had always been the intense one, whereas Adam had been quiet and elusive. "I won't leave until you listen to me, Em. Regardless of what anyone believes, I did love you. I still do. I didn't realize exactly how much until I'd lost you. You're such a special woman. You're so damn easy to love."

"Easy to leave, you mean."

He ignored her sarcasm. "I was threatened into leaving you. I never wanted to, but I wasn't strong enough to stand up to him. I'll regret it every day for the rest of my life."

"Threatened by whom? My father?"

"By your husband. He came to see me the morning after the Angelovsky ball."

"And what did he say?" Emma asked softly.

"Nikolas told me that I was to leave you alone, for good, or he would make my life a living hell. He said I should marry someone else, because I had no more rights where you were concerned. He implied that if I continued to court you, someone would be hurt. I was afraid, Emma. Afraid for both of us. You can hate me for being a coward, but at least you must know that I love you."

Emma felt herself turn white with shock. Adam's story fit in with everything she already knew about her manipulative, lying husband. She thought of the way Nikolas had comforted her after Adam's desertion, making use of her hurt and humiliation . . . seducing her the night she had discovered Adam's engagement. Every move had been calculated. Nikolas had destroyed her love with Adam, methodically taken her life apart, in order to get what he wanted. And he had encouraged her to blame her father for all of it.

"Please leave," she said hoarsely.

"Emma, say that you believe me—"

"I believe you. But it changes nothing. It's too late for both of us."

"It doesn't have to be. We can salvage something of what we once had."

Emma stared at him incredulously. What was there left to salvage? What could he want from her now? "Are you suggesting an affair?"

The word seemed to startle Adam, and she saw that he hadn't expected to have it voiced openly. "As blunt as ever," he murmured, his brown eyes glinting with amusement. "It's one of the things I love most about you. What I'm trying to say is that I want to be some part of your life. I miss you, Emma."

She closed her eyes, remembering how warm and caring Adam had been. She missed him too. If only she could go to his arms right now, and let him kiss and soothe her. But she had lost that particular freedom. Just because her husband had been unfaithful didn't mean she could abandon her own principles. There was no excuse for committing adultery. She couldn't live with herself if she did.

"I don't think there's anything I can give you," she whispered.

"I'll be satisfied with the smallest portion of your heart. You're my true love, Em. You will be until the day I die. No one can change that—not even Nikolas Angelovsky." His face turned hard, as she had never seen it before. "My God, someone

should do the world a favor and get rid of him—
before he ruins any more innocent lives!"

Nikolas heard a knock on his library door and
turned away from his desk with an impatient
growl. He'd had a headache all morning, and it
made his work difficult. Numbers and ink scrawls
seemed to dance before his eyes. Damned hang-
over, he thought, and made up his mind to limit
his after-dinner vodka from now on.

"What is it?" he asked.

Robert Soames poked his head past the door,
looking oddly excited. "Prince Nikolas, I've come
to tell you that I've almost completely uncovered
the painting. Some touch-up work will be required,
of course, but we have an excellent impression of
the original portrait."

"I'll have a look at it later."

"Your Highness, would you permit me to bring
it downstairs for your immediate inspection? I
think you'll be quite astonished."

Nikolas quirked his brows sardonically. "Very
well."

The artist left in such haste that the door remained open. Nikolas scowled and bent over his
work once more, but the lines of accounting
seemed incomprehensible. He heard a little smacking noise, and he glanced at the doorway once
more.

The boy, Jacob, stood there with a sugar-coated
tart in his hands. Crumbs scattered on the carpeted
floor with each small, careful bite.

"What do you want?" Nikolas muttered.

Jacob didn't answer, only continued to look at
him with fearless curiosity.

"Where is Emma? You're usually with her this time of day."

Jacob spoke then, in the rough country accent that never failed to surprise Nikolas, coming from a child with such classic Russian features. "She's in the menagerie. A man came to see 'er."

Nikolas had the feeling the boy had told him deliberately, that he hoped Nikolas would go outside and drive the stranger away. "What part of the menagerie?" he asked in a controlled voice. "Is she with the tiger?"

"No . . . with Cleo."

Nikolas stood and strode from the room, using the French doors to reach the outside grounds. He was halfway through the garden when he saw Emma coming from the stables. The clang of the gates near the house alerted him that someone was heading to the front drive. Torn between going after the visitor and cornering Emma about the incident, he decided on the latter course. He went toward his wife with rapid strides.

"Who was that?" he demanded.

"An old friend. Lord Milbank, as a matter of fact." Emma continued walking. As she passed him, Nikolas reached for her arm, and she flung off his hand. "Don't touch me!"

"What did he want?"

"Nothing."

A wave of blinding jealousy came over Nikolas. He followed her into the house. "I want to talk to you," he said, taking hold of her wrist and yanking her into the library.

"Don't insult my intelligence with this playacting," Emma said scornfully. "You don't give a damn about me, or about anything I do."

"Tell me why he came here."

Her blue eyes flashed with hatred. "Adam told me what you did. The way you threatened him, and made him stay away from me. You kept us apart, and then you manipulated your way into marrying me."

"Milbank didn't have to desert you. He had a choice."

"Adam was afraid of you. And I don't blame him. You're a vicious, selfish creature, and the world would be a much better place without you!" Her voice lowered to a searing whisper. "I despise you for what you've done to me, Nikolas. You've ruined my life."

In spite of his callousness, Nikolas recoiled at the look on his wife's face. It was the truth, he realized bleakly. She did hate him. It was all his doing . . . it had been necessary to push her away, to save himself . . . but still, the proof of his success didn't please him. He was more troubled than he had ever been in his life. His head pounded, and there was a sound in his ears, a jarring, high-pitched tone that seemed to worsen every minute. He rubbed his forehead in an effort to ease the ache. No more arguments for now—he would deal with his wife later. *Get the hell out of here,* he tried to say, but strangely, the words came out in garbled English and Russian. His mind wasn't straight, wasn't clear . . . everything was somehow tangled.

"What is it?" Emma asked sharply, but he shook his head in confusion.

In the charged silence that followed, Mr. Soames came into the library with the canvas he had been working on. "Your Highness," he began, unaware of the scene he had interrupted. He smiled as he saw Emma there. "Princess Emma, I have uncovered the portrait. You must have a look. It's remarkable." Carefully he propped the painting on Nikolas's desk and stood back. "You see?"

Nikolas focused on the portrait, of a man in his early thirties with golden-brown hair, amber eyes . . . high cheekbones . . . a hard mouth, and a sharp-cut jaw . . .

My God . . . It was like looking into a mirror. It was his exact likeness. *That's my face, my eyes* . . .

All at once his head was filled with shooting pain. He tried to tear his gaze away, but he couldn't.

He was vaguely aware of Emma's shocked gasp. "It's you," she said, and the last word echoed in his brain: *youyouyou* . . .

Nikolas made a desperate attempt to escape, but his body wouldn't obey. He stumbled and fell to the floor. The painting seemed to be pulling him inside itself, a magnet for his soul, drawing all the flickering life from his body. He was sinking into darkness, while color, sensations, time itself, shot past him in whirling updrafts.

He was dying, he thought, and he was flooded with panicked regret. What an empty life he'd led, with no one to mourn his loss. Suddenly he wanted Emma: he needed to feel her slim, strong arms around him, her warmth . . . but there was nothing . . . only the torment of his own extinguishing thoughts.

PART III

My pulses bound in exultation,
And in my heart once more
   unfold
The sense of awe and inspiration,
The life, the tears, the love of old.

—PUSHKIN

❧ Seven

1707 November, Moscow

SOMEONE WAS SPEAKING in Russian. "Your Highness, it is time to leave now. Your Highness . . . ?"

The stranger was annoyingly persistent. Nikolas awakened slowly, groaning at the pounding in his head. The taste of wine was strong and sour in his mouth. Blinking painfully, he discovered that he was sitting at a tiled table, his head and arms resting on the hard surface.

"You drank all through the night," the man's voice scolded. "There is no time to shave your face, or even to change your clothes before the bride-choosing. Please, Prince Nikolai, you must wake up *now*."

"What are you talking about?" Nikolas muttered, groggy and perplexed. There was a comfortable and familiar scent in the air, not the sweet wool-and-starch smell of his English house, but one of birch wood and wax candles, and the citric tang of cranberries. It reminded him so strongly of home that he closed his eyes again and breathed deeply. Gradually he recalled what had happened . . . the argument with his wife, the portrait . . . "Emma," he said, lifting his head with an effort. He rubbed his sore eyes. "Where's my wife? Where . . ."

The words died on his lips as he saw that he was in a strange room. A young man, his slim form neatly dressed in antique clothes, waited nearby. His dark eyes, the same chocolate shade as his hair, sparked with exasperation. "We'll get a wife for you as soon as you rouse yourself and go to the bride-choosing, Your Highness."

Nikolas braced his head with his hands and gave the stranger a slitted glare. "Who are you?"

The man sighed. "You must have had even more to drink than I feared! When a man forgets the name of his favorite steward, it is safe to say his brains are pickled. I am Feodor Vasilievich Sidarov, as you well know." He reached for Nikolas's arm to help him up from the table.

Nikolas shook him off with a soft snarl. "Don't touch me."

"I'm trying to *help* you, Prince Nikolai."

"Then tell me where I am, and what happened after—" Nikolas stopped speaking as he looked down at his own clothes. He was dressed in a velvet doublet, narrow breeches, and a white shirt with billowing sleeves, garments that looked as ridiculously old-fashioned as the steward's. He flushed in embarrassed rage, thinking that someone was playing a joke on him. As he took in his surroundings, however, his emotions dissolved in a wash of pure astonishment.

The room was an exact reproduction of one in the private Angelovsky house in Moscow. The parquet floor, intricately fashioned of inlaid wood to resemble a Persian carpet; the scrollwork on the furniture, thickly overlaid with gold; the carved panels on the walls—all of these were things he had known in his childhood. He had left it all behind after the exile.

Nikolas stood on unsteady legs. "What's going on?" he whispered. "Where am I?" His voice shot up several notches. "Emma, where the hell are you?"

Sidarov began to look alarmed. "Prince Nikolai, are you feeling well? Perhaps you need something to eat . . . some bread? Fish? Smoked beef—"

Nikolas strode past him in sudden haste, pausing with a startled jump at the threshold. He began to roam through the halls and rooms like an animal caught in a trap, disoriented, sweating heavily, his heart feeling as if it might burst from his chest. It was all here, the furniture, the wood carvings, everything he had never thought to see again. A few strangely dressed servants regarded him with confusion when they saw him, but none of them dared to speak.

"Prince Nikolai?" came the steward's anxious voice behind him.

Nikolas didn't pause in his headlong rush until he reached the front door and flung it open. A blast of excruciatingly cold air hit him, stinging his face, gnawing through his thin sleeves. Except for a shudder of surprise, he was absolutely still.

All of Moscow was spread before him, in a glittering carpet of gold and white.

The estate was located on a hill near the edge of the city, rising above a sea of shining church domes topped with gold crosses. In between the churches stood houses of wood and stone, their roofs painted with green, blue, red designs. Smoke from thousands of stoves spiraled into the air, mixing with the fresh bite of snow in Nikolas's nostrils. Numbly he watched as flakes the size of down feathers descended gently to the frozen earth. The light covering of snow on the city sparkled in billions of crystalline fragments.

Nikolas's knees shook so violently that he was forced to sit on the ice-laden doorstep. "Am I dead?" he wondered, not realizing he had spoken aloud until Sidarov's sarcastic answer came from behind him.

"No, although you don't look far from it. And you'll certainly catch your death if you sit out here with no coat." Gently the steward touched his shoulder. "Prince Nikolai, you must come inside now. You've appointed me to look after your household and your personal affairs. I would hardly be worth my wages if I allowed you to become ill. Come, the carriage will be readied soon . . . and you will go to the bride-choosing, as you wanted."

Nikolas stood and continued to stare at the city. He felt like weeping in fear and joy, and kissing the hard earth. Russia, his beloved country . . . yet this Moscow was younger, harsher, than he had ever known it. The dark, primitive forest around the city had not yet been cut back and cleared. The streets were filled with the clamor of carts, animals, peddlers, holy men, and beggars. There were no houses or carriages of modern design. The villages in the distance were sparse and isolated, unlike the thick clusters he remembered.

Perhaps this was just a dream. Perhaps it would end soon. How had he come here? What had happened to Emma and Jacob? Disarmed, uncertain, he followed Sidarov back into the house. The steward produced a coat for him, the same shade of dark blue velvet as the doublet. "Allow me to help you with this, Your Highness." The heavy garment enfolded Nikolas in warmth, its line of covered buttons extending high on his chest and reaching to mid-thigh. Standing back to view him critically, Sidarov gave a grunt of satisfaction. "Not quite up to your usual glory, but I doubt the prospective bride will be displeased at the sight of you."

"Whose bride?"

Sidarov laughed, as if Nikolas had just made a joke. "*Your* bride, Prince Nikolai. Whomever you choose to be your mate."

"I'm already married."

The steward began to laugh harder. "I'm glad your sense of humor is back, Your Highness."

Nikolas didn't smile. "I'm not choosing a bride," he said, tight-lipped.

Suddenly Sidarov was flustered and upset. "But, Prince Nikolai . . . you said yourself that it is time for you to marry! You sent envoys to gather beautiful unmarried maidens from every village around Moscow. Now they're all here, waiting for you. Their families have brought them from Suzdal, Vladimir—some from as far away as Kiev and the Ukraine! Are you saying you don't even want to have a *look* at them?" He stared into Nikolas's pale face and clucked disapprovingly. "It's the wine talking. You hardly know what you're saying. As all Russians do, you require one day to get drunk, one to enjoy it, and one to recover."

"I'm not enjoying it," Nikolas muttered, hoping fervently that he *was* drunk. Stinking, filthy drunk. Maybe when he sobered, this would all be gone. In the meanwhile, there didn't seem to be much he could do about the situation.

"Come," the steward coaxed, "we must go to the bride-choosing. At least favor them by walking along the line. Who knows? You may see a beautiful girl and fall in love at first sight."

Wildly Nikolas dragged both hands through his disheveled hair. He didn't want to participate in this ridiculous farce. He had enough trouble with the wife he'd already married. But he decided he would play along until the dream was over. "Let's get it over with," he said gruffly. "I'll go—but I won't choose any of them."

"That's fine," Sidarov soothed. "Just have a look. It's only fair, after they came so far."

A small crowd of servants appeared to accompany Nikolas to the carriage, leading him down the slick steps. Efficiently they tucked fur robes around his legs and lap, placed hot stones at his feet, and pressed a goblet of wine in his hand.

"No more wine—" Sidarov began as he climbed into the carriage.

Nikolas silenced him with a gesture, and glared at him over the rim of the jeweled goblet. He needed a drink badly, and he'd had enough of the bossy little servant. The heated wine was strong and bracing, blunting the edges of his panic.

The gilded carriage was pulled by six black horses and mounted on runners that allowed it to glide swiftly over the carpet of snow. The Angelovsky crest was embroidered on the velvet cushions, and repeated on the ceiling and walls in patterns of jewels, crystal, and gold. "I'm an Angelovsky," Nikolas said tentatively, placing his hand on the crest.

"You certainly are," Sidarov agreed in a feeling tone.

Nikolas moved his gaze to the steward, who was beginning to look vaguely familiar. The Sidarovs had worked for his family for generations, had even accompanied him into exile, but Nikolas couldn't recall anyone named Feodor. Except . . . in his boyhood, he remembered the oldest Sidarov of all, whose name had been Vitya Feodorovich. Perhaps this was Vitya's father? Grandfather?

Then who am I supposed to be? Nikolas gulped the rest of his wine to stave off the sinking coldness inside him. The servant had called him Nikolai . . . Prince Nikolai . . . but that was his *great-great-great-grandfather's* name.

The vehicle passed by the homes and markets of the *posád*, the area of the city between the fortress walls and the outer earthen ramparts that encircled Moscow. People swathed in long coats, bulky robes, and fur hats began to appear on either side of the street and cheer, waving the vehicle on to its destination. The scene reminded Nikolas uncomfortably of the curious crowds that had gathered to watch him depart St. Petersburg at the beginning of his exile.

"Where are we going?" he asked tersely.

"Don't you remember? Your friend Prince Golorkov is the only one in Moscow with a private home large enough to accommodate all the women. He very kindly offered the use of his ballroom and pavilions for the bride-choosing."

"Very kind," Nikolas repeated grimly, gripping the empty goblet in his cold hands. They drove through the city, built in rings like the layers of an onion, with the Kremlin at its center. Some sections contained clusters of noblemen's homes and small, perfect orchards. In others, bunches of gold church domes were gathered like exotic flowers, dwarfing the small wooden cottages nearby. The roads had not been paved or modernized, and the buildings were constructed of wood.

With a dreamlike sensation, Nikolas listened to the pealing of bells as Orthodox churches signaled the approach of morning Mass. No other city on earth rang bells so frequently, filling the air with joyful music. If this was a dream, it was more detailed and vivid than any he'd experienced before.

Finally the carriage-sleigh was pulled up to a great house fronted with slender wooden columns and an octagonal pavilion on either side. People crowded on both sides of the street and at the gates, cheering as they caught sight of Nikolas through the carriage windows. He sank lower in his seat, his face dark and brooding.

"You must be nervous," Sidarov remarked. "Don't worry, Your Highness, it will all be over soon."

"It had better be."

A complement of shivering, brocade-covered footmen opened the carriage door and escorted Nikolas to the house. Sidarov followed close behind, carrying a wooden box with golden latches. Their host, presumably Prince Golorkov, waited in the wide, low-ceilinged entrance hall. Golorkov was a balding old man with a thin gray mustache that curved along with his lips as he smiled. "Nikolai, my friend," he said, a sly gleam in his eyes. He moved forward to embrace Nikolas, and drew back to look at him. "You will be very pleased by the women inside, I assure you. Such an array of beauty I have never seen. Hair like fine silk, breasts like the choicest fruit—you will have no difficulty finding a girl to suit you. Shall we have a drink first, or proceed directly to the ballroom?"

"Nothing to drink," Sidarov interceded hastily, ignoring Nikolas's glare. "I'm certain that Prince Nikolai, in his great eagerness, will want to see the women immediately."

Golorkov laughed. "And who could blame him? Follow me, Nikolai, and I will lead the way to paradise."

The hallways echoed with a roar of excited female chatter that grew louder as they approached the ballroom. Smugly Golorkov reached for the lion's-head door handle, and sent the door swinging open. There was a chorus of gasps, and then an anticipatory silence fell over the room. Nikolas hesitated before entering, until Sidarov and Golorkov pushed him inside.

"My God," Nikolas muttered. There were at least five hundred women in the ballroom, maybe more. They stood in an uneven line, staring at him, waiting for his inspection. Most of them wore smocks and over-dresses of red, the favorite color of all Russians. Each girl wore her hair in the traditional maiden's braid, dressed with a ribbon or scarf, or with a diadem of gold or silver wire. A few of the boldest women sighed admiringly as Nikolas walked nearer.

Nikolas felt a tide of burning color rise from his neck. He turned back to Sidarov, who was close behind him. "I can't—" he began, and the steward elbowed him hard.

"Just glance over them, Your Highness."

"Shy?" Golorkov asked with a mocking laugh.

"This isn't like you, Nikolai. Or is it that you're still reluctant to marry? I promise you, it isn't so bad. Besides, the Angelovsky name must be perpetuated. Pick a wife, my friend, and then we'll share a bottle of vodka."

"*Pick a wife*" . . . uttered as casually as if he were offering a tidbit from a tray of *zakuski*. Nikolas swallowed hard and approached the beginning of the line. His feet felt as if they were encased in lead. Hesitantly he moved past one girl after another, barely able to look them in the eye. He was showered with timid giggles, smiling glances, encouraging whispers—and occasionally, a look of dread from a girl who clearly had no more desire to be there than Nikolas himself. As he walked along the line, spines straightened to display well-endowed figures, and slender fingers plucked nervously at scarves and skirts. For each girl whom Nikolas rejected and passed, there was a word of consolation from Sidarov, as well as a gold coin from the box he carried.

About halfway through the crowd of prospective brides, Nikolas caught a glimpse of a girl with red hair, taller than the rest. She was standing several places down the line, noticeable because of her extreme stillness, while all the others fidgeted. Her face was turned away from him, but the way she stood with her shoulders slumped to conceal her height . . .

He strode directly to her. Sidarov followed in consternation, calling, "Prince Nikolai, you've passed over some of these very nice girls . . ."

As soon as Nikolas reached the young woman, he seized her by the arms, stared into her startled blue eyes, and shook her slightly. Mingled fury and relief coursed through his body. "Emma," he snapped, automatically switching to English. "What's going on? What are you doing here?"

She shook her head in bewilderment and answered in flawless Russian. "Your Highness . . . I don't understand. Forgive me if I have offended you."

Nikolas let go of her as if he'd received an electric shock. Emma didn't speak Russian. But it was *her* voice, her face and body, her eyes. He was quiet, baffled, staring hard at her while the rest of the assemblage broke into questioning chatter.

Sidarov took it upon himself to address the girl. "You with the red hair," he said calmly. "What is your name?"

She replied while still holding Nikolas's gaze. "Emelia."

"I want to talk with you," Nikolas said in a low voice. "Now."

Before anyone had time to react, he swept her out of the ballroom. The crowd of women swarmed in disarray, the line dissolving into a confused mass. Prince Golorkov began to laugh heartily. "Nikolai," he called out, "you're supposed to wait until *after* the ceremony for that!"

Nikolas ignored the group and continued tugging at the girl's wrist. She followed more or less obediently as he led her to the first available room and closed the door behind them. Only then did she pull free of him, twisting her wrist hard in order to break his grip.

"What happened?" Nikolas demanded, looming over her. "We were arguing in the parlor, and Soames brought in the damned portrait, and everything went dark—"

"I'm sorry, I don't understand," she said in Russian, rubbing her reddened wrist. She stared at him apprehensively, as if wondering about his sanity.

Nikolas was enraged by the fluid ease with which she spoke. "The last time I saw you, you knew fewer than ten words of Russian!"

The girl began to back away from him. "I don't think we've ever met before," she whispered, her gaze darkening with alarm. "Your Highness, please let me leave—"

"Wait. Wait. Don't be afraid of me." Nikolas snatched her back and held her stiff body close to his. Wildly he tried to collect his wits. "Don't you know me, Emma?"

"I . . . I know *of* you, Prince Nikolai. Everyone respects and fears you."

Nikolas freed one hand and grasped the vibrant red plait hanging down her back. "The same hair," he murmured. His fingers brushed the pale, downy surface of her cheek. "The same skin . . . the same freckles . . . the same blue eyes . . ." He felt a surge of deep pleasure at holding her in his arms, so beautiful, so familiar. Her lips, parted in dismay, were as full and tempting as ever. He bent and kissed her suddenly. She gasped in shock, offering neither response nor rejection. Nikolas finished the kiss with a gentle brush of his lips and lifted his head. "The same taste," he said hoarsely. "It has to be you. Don't you remember me?"

There was a knock at the door, and Sidarov's anxious voice. "Prince Nikolai? Your Highness—"

"Not now!" Nikolas snarled. He waited until he heard the sound of retreating footsteps. Returning his attention to the girl in his arms, Nikolas pulled her tightly against him. He closed his eyes and inhaled the fragrance of her skin. "I don't know what's happening," he said into the soft space just below her ear. "Nothing makes sense."

Emelia struggled free with a burst of energy. Putting a distance of several feet between them, she stared at him and raised a trembling hand to her mouth. Her eyes were wide and very blue. "Your Highness . . . have you chosen me? Is that why you've taken me aside like this?"

Nikolas was silent, trying to comprehend what was happening.

Somehow reading an answer in his expression, Emelia gave a little nod, as if something she had long wondered about had just been confirmed. "I thought you would," she said gravely. "Somehow . . . I knew if I came to Moscow, you would pick me."

"How did you know that?" Nikolas asked hoarsely.

"It was just a feeling. I heard the things they say about you, and I thought . . . I might be a good wife for a man like you."

Nikolas moved toward her, and she countered with a small backward step. He forced himself to stand still, although he ached to reach for her once again. "What do they say about me?"

"That you are very intelligent and modern. They also say you are in great favor with the tsar because you spent some time in the West and you understand the foreigners. You even shave your face like them." Emelia stared at the hard line of his jaw with open curiosity. "All the men in my village have beards." Slowly she approached him, lifting her hand to his face. She stroked the surface of his chin once, twice, her fingertips soft on his skin. A shy smile hovered on her lips. "It's smooth, like a little boy's."

Nikolas caught her hand and held the palm against his cheek. She was warm, real . . . too real for this to be a dream. "Emma, look at me. Tell me you've never been with me before. Tell me we've never touched, never kissed. Tell me that you don't know me."

"I . . ." She shook her head helplessly, her gaze fixed on his.

He let go of her and prowled through the room in a wide circle, compelling her to turn in order to watch him. "Then who are you?" he asked in a low voice, feeling angry and hollow inside.

"I am Emelia Vasilievna."

"What about your family?"

"My father is dead. My uncle and brother were taken from the village and sent to work on the new city on the Neva. I couldn't live alone in the village, and I didn't want to marry any of the farmers there."

"Why not?"

"Most of the men were taken from the village by the tsar, to build Petersburg. The only ones left didn't want to marry me." Faced with his questioning silence, she continued hesitantly. "My family was unpopular because of my father's political beliefs. But it didn't matter that no one offered for me. They're either too old or too young, and none of them is fit to work. And they're all poor. I wanted more than that."

"More money?"

"No," she protested. "I wanted someone to talk to. I wanted to learn things, and find out what the world beyond the forest is like." She lowered her head and added in embarrassed honesty, "Of course, I wouldn't mind being rich. I think I would like to try it."

Suddenly Nikolas laughed in a flash of genuine amusement. The comment was so much like Emma, a potent reminder of his wife's charming bluntness. "Well, such open ambition should be rewarded."

"Your Highness?" she said, clearly perplexed.

Nikolas took a deep breath. "What I meant was, I'll marry you. I'll go along with this for a time. God willing, it will end sooner or later."

"What will end?"

"The nightmare," he muttered. "The vision. Whatever you want to call this. It all seems so real that I'm beginning to think I've gone insane. But there's not much I can do about it, is there? I choose you, Emma . . . Emelia . . . whoever you are. I'll always choose you, though you may damn me for it later."

"I don't understand—"

"Never mind." He extended a hand to her. "Just come with me."

She hesitated and then reached out for him, her long fingers clinging to his.

Nikolas took her back to the ballroom, where Golorkov and Sidarov and the entire crowd of women waited expectantly. With an extravagant sweep of his hand, Nikolas indicated the blushing woman at his side. "This is my bride," he said in a sardonic imitation of a pleased bridegroom.

Prince Golorkov applauded. "Excellent choice, Nikolai! What a fine-looking female! Surely she will bear you many healthy sons."

Nikolas turned to Sidarov and arched a questioning brow. "When's the wedding?"

The inquiry sent Golorkov into a spasm of laughter. "Such wit!"

Sidarov tried to cover his worry with a thin smile. "Tonight, of course. At the Angelovsky house. Unless Your Highness wishes to wait—"

"Tonight it is," Nikolas said abruptly. "I want to return home now."

"But our drink . . ." Golorkov protested.

Nikolas made an attempt at a friendly smile. "If you wouldn't mind sharing one some other time?"

"Whenever you like," the older man replied, still chuckling.

Nikolas was taken back home in his carriage, with Emelia nestled in the space beside him. Sidarov occupied the opposite seat. Emelia spoke little, except for her refusal to share the fur lap robe with Nikolas.

"I'm not cold," she said.

Nikolas snorted sardonically. "Really? Then why are you blue and trembling?" He lifted the side of the fur and motioned for her to join him. "Your attack of modesty is unnecessary. I'm hardly going to seduce you with my steward sitting nearby— and in any case, we're going to be married in a matter of hours. Come sit next to me."

"I'm not cold," she repeated stubbornly, her teeth beginning to chatter.

"Fine. Don't blame me if you freeze to death before we reach home."

"There is less danger for me out here," she replied, "than under there." She pointed to the lap robe significantly, then turned away to indicate the argument was finished.

Sidarov watched the exchange with speculation

and a surprising trace of satisfaction. "You appear to have chosen well, Prince Nikolai," he remarked. "A strong and spirited woman is what every man should marry."

Nikolas gave him a sour look and didn't reply.

As soon as they reached the Angelovsky estate, Nikolas was separated from Emelia by a troop of servants bent on making preparations for the approaching ceremony. He secluded himself in his suite of rooms and demanded to be given a bottle of vodka and a tray of *zakuski*. The refreshments were brought to him speedily, along with a warning from Sidarov not to become too drunk before the wedding.

Nikolas wandered around the bedchamber, swigging vodka from the bottle in his hand. He could hear sounds coming from the rooms below— scurrying feet and rapid voices, an occasional burst of excited laughter. His mood worsened with each minute that passed.

Investigating his surroundings, Nikolas stared closely at the bed hangings, fashioned of precious Byzantine silk and bordered with gold thread and pearls. A huge Cyrillic *A* was embroidered in the center of the silk coverlet. The carved wooden chest in the corner contained a set of pistols with gold handles and dragon-shaped triggers, a pile of rich fur blankets, and an enameled bow case and gold quiver. None of the objects was familiar to him.

As Nikolas closed the chest and tilted the vodka bottle to his lips, the dull gleam of a painting on the wall caught his eye, the smoky antique gold and the brilliant red glow of a small icon. As he stared at the painting, the gulp of vodka slid down his throat in a painful lump. He had seen the icon before, thousands of times. It had hung on his nursery wall in childhood. He had moved it into his bedroom as an adult, and he'd brought it with him to England after he had been exiled from Russia. "My God," he said aloud, stumbling as he walked toward the icon. "What is this doing here? What's happening?"

The elegant design was of the Prophet Elijah, surrounded by a brilliant ruby cloud as he ascended to heaven in a chariot of fire drawn by flame-colored horses. Nikolas had always cherished the icon for its vivid color and intricate brushwork. He had never seen another like it.

Recognizing the icon, solid and unmistakable, suddenly made it seem as if his other life, the real one, were gone for good. "I don't want this," he said in a whisper that matched the intensity of a scream. "I didn't ask for it. I damn well didn't choose it!" He gazed at the red circle of fire, backed away, and hurled the vodka bottle directly at it. The bottle broke as it struck the icon, knocking it from the wall.

Immediately a servant knocked at the door and asked if everything was all right. Nikolas answered with a forbidding growl, and the servant retreated hastily. Standing over the fallen icon, Nikolas stared at the deep scratch that had just been made, marring the edge of the red cloud. Would that scratch be there a hundred years from now? A hundred and fifty, perhaps more?

What if all this was real? Perhaps he had died and gone to hell. Perhaps hell was having to witness the wretched history of his family from the eyes of his own ancestor.

A new thought occurred to Nikolas, and he felt

his knees turn to rubber. He made his way to the bed and sat down heavily. If he really was Prince Nikolai, about to marry a peasant woman named Emelia, then history was yet to be made. Their son would be Alexei, and his son would be Sergei, followed by Sergei II and Dmitri . . . "And then," Nikolas said aloud, "I'll be born. And Mikhail."

If he could keep from having a child with Emelia, then the Angelovsky line would be broken. The abuse and murder of Mikhail wouldn't occur. And Nikolas's own sinful, pain-filled life would never take place.

A tremor of horror went through Nikolas's body. Perhaps he had been given the power to keep himself from ever being born.

In spite of Sidarov's insistence, Nikolas didn't bathe before the wedding, or shave, or even change his clothes. Barricading himself in his room, he drank steadily in an effort to make the nightmare disappear. It was impossible for him to go through with the ceremony. He might be many things, but a bigamist wasn't one of them. He wasn't Nikolai the First, he was Nikolas Dmitriyevich Angelovsky, and he belonged in London, in the year 1877 . . . with Emma Stokehurst.

Sidarov's muffled voice came through the door. "The guests are here, Prince Nikolai. The ceremony will begin as soon as you decide. You won't keep them waiting long, will you?"

"I'm not going to marry anyone," Nikolas said from his sprawled position in the chair.

There was a lengthy silence, and then Sidarov replied in an agitated tone. "Very well, Your Highness. But you must inform the guests—and the

bride—yourself. I refuse to do it, even if you turn
me out into the streets and I must die a miserable,
frozen death. No, I absolutely will not tell them."

Nikolas lurched to his feet and went to the door,
flinging it open. He glared down at the steward,
who looked pale and upset. "I'll have no problem
telling them," he sneered. "Show me where they
are."

Sidarov's mouth was as tight as a clam. "Yes,
Your Highness."

The steward led Nikolas to the vast gathering
room on the first floor. It had been filled with icons
until there was barely an inch of wall space left
uncovered. A large table at the back of the room
was laden with a mountainous honey cake, dishes
of almonds, figs, and other delicacies, and goblets
of wine. The group of well-dressed guests, including Prince Golorkov, stood around a black-robed
priest and a makeshift altar supporting a massive
Bible. Everyone smiled and exclaimed as Nikolas
appeared. Briefly he glanced over the assemblage,
his gaze centering on Emelia.

His heart sank as he looked at her. She wore a
sarafan of cream silk brocade, and a gold jacket
that was too short in the sleeves. Some kindly ben-
efactor, perhaps Golorkov and his wife, had given
the wedding clothes to her. The pearl-embroidered
veil over her hair was held in place by a gold wire
diadem with a tiny paste ruby glittering on her
forehead. She appeared absolutely calm, except for
the bouquet of dried flowers and pink ribbons she
held. The flowers were trembling visibly, a few
tiny, fragile petals scattering to the floor.

It was that sign of nervousness that was Nikolas's undoing. He couldn't reject Emelia now, in

front of these guests. He couldn't abandon her. She stared at him with a faint glint of hope in her blue eyes and the beginnings of a smile on her lips ... the same way Emma Stokehurst had once looked at him.

Feeling dazed, Nikolas moved forward and took his place beside her. Amid the encouragement and compliments of the guests, Prince Golorkov moved forward to hand Nikolas a ceremonial silver whip, the symbol of a husband's authority to admonish and discipline his wife. Nikolas shook his head as he saw it.

Golorkov frowned. "But, Nikolai—"

"No," Nikolas said curtly, turning from Golorkov to Emelia. He stared into her startled blue eyes. "We'll marry as Westerners do. I won't carry a whip."

Questioning murmurs ran through the crowd, until the priest nodded, his long beard flapping against his chest. "It shall be as the prince commands."

The priest began the ceremony in a tranquil drone. Nikolas and Emelia were each given a small icon to hold and a bite of salted black bread to eat. The wedding rings, heavy gold pieces that Nikolas vaguely recognized from the ancient Angelovsky collection, were blessed and exchanged. He did not look at Emelia, but concentrated on the ceremony, holding his arm steady as their wrists were bound together with a silk cloth. With great dignity, the priest led them in a small, tight circle around the altar, and unwrapped the wrist binding. Following the priest's indication, Emelia began to kneel on the ground. According to tradition, the bride should rest her forehead on the groom's shoe to show the proper submissiveness.

Realizing what was happening, Nikolas caught Emelia by the elbows and hauled her upright before her knees touched the floor. She gasped in surprise and swayed against him.

"The Western custom is to exchange a kiss," Nikolas said in a voice loud enough for everyone to hear. "My wife will not be my slave, but my companion and equal partner."

There was some discomfort and laughter at this, as a few of the guests thought he was making an inappropriate joke. Nikolas didn't smile, only held Emelia's gaze and waited for her reply.

"Yes, Nikolai," she finally said in a stifled whisper. Her eyes closed as he bent his head and kissed her.

Her lips were soft and innocent, parting beneath the hard pressure of his. Nikolas slid his hands around her neck, his fingers splaying across the warm, silken skin as he gathered her closer. The firm weight of her breasts touched his chest. A sound of pleasure caught in Nikolas's throat. He wanted her with sudden, terrible desperation, until his groin and his nerves and his very soul ached with it. Somehow he managed to release her. The priest handed them a red wooden *bratina* cup to drink from, and when that bit of good luck was ensured, the guests applauded the completion of the ceremony.

"Time to celebrate!" someone called, and the assemblage moved as a whole toward the honey cake and the goblets of wine.

Nikolas gazed at his new bride, his blood pumping hard, his fingers flexing as he thought of all the things he wanted to do with her. He was consumed with lust. It didn't matter what her name was. His senses told him this was Emma. Her body, her winsome spirit, and her presence stirred him just as they always had.

Sidarov appeared beside him, giving him a discreet nudge with his elbow. "Your Highness," he muttered out of the side of his mouth, "you may take your bride upstairs now. Is there anything you require?"

Nikolas tore his attention from Emelia long enough to reply. "Privacy," he said meaningfully. "If anyone comes to my room, I'll kill him. Is that clear?"

"But, Prince Nikolai, according to tradition, the guests have the right to inspect the sheets in two hours—"

"Not according to Western tradition."

Sidarov nodded, wearing a beleaguered grimace. "It is not easy to be the servant of a modern man. Yes, Your Highness, I'll keep everyone away."

Nikolas offered Emelia his arm, and she took it at once, bending her head to let the veil hide her fierce blush. A chorus of cheerful farewells followed them as they left the gathering. Conscious of Emelia's nervous grip on his arm, the way she matched her footsteps to his, Nikolas was suffused with hungry anticipation. He wanted her too much to let anyone or anything interfere—it didn't matter what the consequences were. For a few hours the rest of the world would disappear, and he would lose himself in the pleasure of her body. He led her to his bedroom and closed the door. The servants had set out jugs of water and wine, and thick yellow candles that filled the room with amber light.

Emelia stood still, her breath shallow as she watched him with wide eyes. Gently Nikolas removed the diadem from her hair and lifted away the pearl-embroidered veil. He set the articles aside on a small table and returned to her. "Turn around," he said softly.

She obeyed, and he heard her quick indrawn breath as she felt him grasp the braid that hung down her back. He unplaited the thick red locks, setting the brilliant curls free, and he combed his fingers through the loosened mass. Each movement was slow, careful, although he wanted to throw her on the bed and take her at once. Easing the gold jacket over her shoulders, he dropped it to the floor. He drew her back against him and slid his hands over her front, feeling through the layers of her sarafan for the shape of her body. She gasped, pressing her spine against him, while he cupped her round breasts until her nipples hardened from the light caress.

Nikolas was stunned by the trusting way she offered herself to him. He lowered his head over her shoulder, nuzzled his face into her neck, while his heart beat a rhythm of furious need. He let his hand drift over the flat, neat line of her stomach, down to the tantalizing cove between her thighs. Shivering, Emelia leaned harder against him, her breath rushing unsteadily as he pressed his palm over the soft mound, until heat collected between his hand and her body.

Nikolas had always preferred to make love in silence, making the act purely physical rather than an experience of shared emotion. Words said at such a time were too intimate and revealing. But he felt the need to say something to her now, to soothe the tension that had suddenly made her spine rigid. "I'm not going to hurt you, *ruyshka*."

"I'm not afraid," she replied, turning to face him. "It's only that . . . we don't know each other."

Don't we? he wanted to reply. *I've held you in my arms too many times to count. I know you, Emma. Every inch of your body, every expression on your face.* He knew how to manipulate her, how to make her feel pleasure, shame, anger . . . but did all of that mean he really knew her? The secrets of her heart and mind, the things she dreamed of and hoped for, were a mystery to him.

He stared at the woman before him, fingering a cinnamon curl that lay over her shoulder. "You're right," he said quietly. "We're strangers. It's a new beginning for both of us. We'll have to trust each other, *kharashó?*"

"Yes." She smiled hesitantly, reaching for his coat with a bashful murmur. He helped her to remove the garment, and pulled his shirt hem free from the narrow breeches. Emboldened, Emelia worked on the tiny jeweled cuff buttons that fastened the billowing shirtsleeves. When the buttons were free, Nikolas pulled the garment over his head, letting it fall to the floor. He steeled himself not to move as her gaze wandered over his bare chest, and he waited for a reaction to his scars.

But there was nothing in Emelia's face save a flash of timid curiosity. She touched his collarbone and the hard curve of muscle beneath, her fingertips like tender spots of fire. "You're a beautiful man," she whispered.

Surprised by the mockery, for no one with his

scars was beautiful by any stretch of the imagination, Nikolas followed her gaze to his chest. All at once he was wrenched with amazement.

There were no scars, nothing but unmarred skin lighted with the gleam of candlelight. Nikolas lifted his shaking hands to his chest. He looked at his wrists, both clean and perfect. "My God," he said hoarsely, while his legs nearly gave way beneath him. "What's happening to me?"

Emelia retreated a few steps and stared at him in confusion. "Prince Nikolai? Are you ill?"

"Get out," he said, his voice scratchy.

Her skin lost its color. "What?"

"Get out," he repeated numbly. "Please. Find another room to sleep in."

Emelia drew a sharp breath, and wiped at the sudden glitter of tears in her eyes. "What have I done wrong? Do I displease you?"

"It has nothing to do with you. I'm sorry, I . . ." Nikolas shook his head, unable to speak further. Blindly he turned away from her, waiting until he heard her leave the room. There was a sharp pain in his temples, as if someone were driving nails through his skull. "God," he whispered, investing a prayer of fear and wonder into the single syllable. He felt for the scars again, and he was shocked anew when his fingers encountered smooth skin. The lash-marks and burns had been a part of him for years. He had stared at them whenever he needed a reminder of the fiendish cruelty people were capable of. How could the scars be gone? The visible proof of the experiences that had shaped him had vanished, and without them, his identity had been stripped away.

Nikolas moved to a nearby chair and sat in a

tightly drawn heap. He had never felt so isolated. He was disconnected from everything he had known. There seemed to be no way to return to the life he'd once had. He wasn't even certain he wanted to. He had nothing in that life, no one, and he had deliberately destroyed all chance of a relationship with Emma Stokehurst. What was there to go back to?

Reason returned to him with jarring suddenness. It would have been a tragic mistake to bed Emelia. He would do nothing to risk making her pregnant. He wouldn't lay a finger on her. The Angelovsky line would die with him, and the world would be a far better place.

He thought of Emma Stokehurst waiting in the future, of never marrying her, never having her, and he ignored the coldness in the pit of his stomach.

Staring at the jug of wine, Nikolas thought of making himself drunk. But that wouldn't change anything. At best it would provide a temporary respite, from which he would awaken to face the same problem—what was he to do next?

Whether Sidarov knew or merely suspected that Nikolas hadn't bedded Emelia, he said nothing about it the next morning. His lean face was carefully expressionless, but his dark brown eyes were speculative as he gazed at Nikolas's disheveled form. "Good morning, Your Highness," he remarked. "I took the liberty of having a bath prepared, in case you should want one today."

Nikolas nodded and followed the steward to the private bath house attached to the main residence. "You haven't changed your clothes in two days,"

Sidarov remarked, scooping up garments as Nikolas disrobed. "Your bath will be welcome news to the entire household."

The comment reminded Nikolas of the Russians' scrupulous standards of cleanliness. Even the most humble peasants washed themselves frequently. It was one of the few areas in which the Slavs were more advanced than their Western counterparts, especially at this time in history. The English actually feared to bathe themselves too often, believing it made them vulnerable to illness.

The wooden bathhouse was well scrubbed and roomy, with glass windows set high in the walls to allow light from outside. It opened into a comfortable chamber filled with elegant brocaded furniture and large fireplaces. For now, the doors were closed to preserve the warmth of the bath. Steam collected on the windowpanes and ran down in bright rivulets. Nikolas sighed in comfort as he stepped into the bath and sat chest-deep in water infused with herbs. The heat of it permeated his body, soothing tense muscles and a multitude of aches. He closed his eyes and leaned his head back against the rim of the wooden bath.

"Shall I leave you for a while?" Sidarov inquired.

"Yes," Nikolas said, keeping his eyes closed.

"I will return with your shaving instruments when your beard has softened."

For a while there was no sound except the dripping of water from the windows, and the slosh of small waves in the bath as Nikolas moved his foot back and forth. Puffs of steam rose from the tiled stove. Drowsing, luxuriating, Nikolas let his mind drift, until he heard the scrape of a footstep on the floor. "Sidarov?" he murmured.

"No," came a woman's soft reply.

Nikolas opened his eyes. Through the luminous, hot mist he saw Emelia approach the tub. She wore a simple blue peasant dress. Her eyes were red from crying, and her jaw was set with a determination that he recognized. He sat up and stared at her warily, wondering if she had come to reproach him. God knew she had every right.

Her voice trembled a little. "I asked Sidarov where you were. I . . . had to talk with you right away, to ask you . . ."

"Ask me what?" Nikolas murmured, transfixed by her otherworldly appearance, her slender form silhouetted in steam clouds.

"If you're sorry that you chose me." Emelia frowned earnestly and continued in a rush. "I may not be pretty enough, or maybe I seem somewhat odd, but I promise you, I would make a very good wife! I can learn to be just like the Western women—"

"Emelia," he interrupted, "come here." She hesitated and moved forward, leaning her hip against the edge of the tub. Nikolas reached out and enfolded her slender fingers in his wet hand. He forced himself to meet her direct gaze. "I . . . I'm sorry about last night. About sending you away like that." He almost choked on the words. Apologies had never been easy for him. "You did nothing wrong," he added with an effort.

She regarded him doubtfully, her fingers tightening on his. "I hope that's true, but—"

"You were the only woman I wanted. If you

hadn't been at the Golorkov estate yesterday, I wouldn't have chosen anyone.''

A pink blush seeped into the paleness of her skin. ''Is that true?''

''You're a beautiful woman. God knows I find you desirable.''

''Then last night, why didn't you—''

''Things are very . . . complicated for me.'' Nikolas grimaced at his own ineptitude. ''I can't explain it in a way you would understand. Hell, I wish *I* understood.''

Emelia absorbed that for a moment, her gaze locked with his. ''All I would like to know is . . . do you want to keep me as your wife?''

Nikolas was trapped by her intense blue eyes. ''Yes,'' he heard himself say.

She nodded, visibly relieved. ''Then I will stay. And I will abide by your decisions. When you want me to come to your bed, you only need tell me.''

Swallowing hard, Nikolas released his grip on her fingers and busied himself with splashing hot water on his face. Having her in his bed, easing his aching need within her, was not a subject he could allow himself to think about. It was forbidden to him, unless he cared to set off a chain reaction that would culminate in his disastrous future. ''Sidarov should bring in my shaving razor soon,'' he said, swiping at the water that dripped from his face and chin.

Shyly Emelia gestured to the dish of lavender soap beside the bath. ''Shall I wash your hair, Prince Nikolai?''

''No, I'll take care of it.''

''It will be no trouble. A wife should learn to do these things for her husband.'' She picked up one of the buckets of water resting on the tiled stove and brought it to him.

Nikolas hesitated, wondering how to refuse her. He met her expectant gaze and relented with a taut sigh. Why not let her help him with his bath? What harm could it do? He bent his head forward, jumping slightly at the heat of the water as Emelia poured it over his head.

"Such beautiful hair," she commented, pushing the sodden locks away from his face. "The color of dark honey, except for the light streaks on the top."

"It's nothing special." Warily he watched as Emelia pushed the sleeves of her dress to her elbows.

She reached for a slippery cake of soap. "It is good you are not vain." There was a smile in her voice as she continued. "I think many men with your appearance would be." She moved behind him, rubbing the soap over his head, then working the lather into his hair. "Close your eyes, please. I don't want the soap to sting them."

Nikolas leaned back against the wall of the bath as Emelia washed his hair. Her fingers slid over his scalp and the back of his neck, rubbing gently behind his ears. He had always loved her hands, strong and slender and graceful. Suddenly he wanted her so badly he could hardly breathe. If he turned his head, he could reach her breast with his mouth, bite and suck her nipple until it turned hard against his tongue. She would make the feline sound he remembered so well, and arch closer, offering herself to him.

He imagined her naked in the bath with him, her skin sleek and wet, her hair floating in dark crimson skeins around them. He would pump her up and down on his body, until water sloshed everywhere from the force of their passion—

"That's enough," he said hoarsely, sitting up straight. "Are you almost finished?"

"Yes, Prince Nikolai."

He listened as she went to the stove. She returned and rinsed his hair with more hot water, then handed him a dry cloth to blot his streaming face. When he opened his eyes, he noticed her embarrassed but inquisitive gaze focused on the outline of his body beneath the water. A maidenly blush made her cheeks glow. Nikolas was half-afraid he wouldn't be able to control his impulses.

"Thank you," he managed to say. "Find Sidarov now, and tell him I want a shave."

"Yes, but first, would you like me to—"

"*Now*," he repeated gruffly.

Emelia nodded obediently and left, and Nikolas gave a tortured sigh. He sank lower into the water and willed his body to calm down. "I don't know how much of this I can take," he muttered. He was nearly startled out of his wits when a rumbling laugh echoed through the bathhouse.

"Talking to yourself, Nikolai?"

Nikolas turned and stared at the stranger. He controlled his expression, showing none of the amazement he felt inside.

A man nearly seven feet tall, apparently in his mid-thirties, strode to the tub and surveyed him with hearty amusement. "I just saw your new wife," the giant informed him. "A beautiful woman, and of good, sturdy stock, like my Catherine. God grant that you made a wise choice, my friend."

The stranger's face, incongruously small and

round for such a large man, was oddly familiar. A shock of straight, fine chestnut hair fell to his narrow shoulders. A tiny mustache adorned his upper lip, but there was no beard to soften the hard, heavy lines of his jaw. His hazel eyes fairly danced with energy, the same restlessness that seemed to permeate his entire frame. He wore Western clothes but spoke Russian in the thick, rolling tones of a native Slav.

"I brought my entourage for a short visit," the man informed Nikolas. "We're in need of one of your fine suppers and entertainment. Menshikov is back from his command in Poland, and we want to give him an enjoyable time." The man winked. "We owe my Alexashka a lot after his triumph over the Swedes at the battle of Kalisz. Now, if only *you* would accept a command, we would win the war at once!"

"I'm not a military man," Nikolas managed to reply, while his brain worked feverishly. Menshikov . . . the name of Tsar Peter's closest friend and companion.

The man standing in the bathhouse with him was His Imperial Majesty, Peter the Great.

Eight

THANKS TO SIDAROV'S timely arrival, Nikolas was spared having to make conversation until he could gather his wits. He sat in the bath, his heart thumping hard while the servant shaved him expertly. Peter, in the meantime, strolled around delivering an energetic monologue to his captive audience.

Nikolas was both appalled and fascinated. He had always admired Tsar Peter's accomplishments. He had read in his school books about Peter creating the powerful Russian navy, leading the country to victory in a twenty-year war with the Swedes, and building the magnificent city of St. Petersburg. It had taken a mixture of genius and savage will to do all that, and both qualities were evident in the man standing before him.

The tsar spoke at length about the war, the overconfidence of Charles, the Swedish king, and the success of the recent Russian "scorched earth" policy. "The stubborn fools try to press onward through Poland, even though they can't supply their troops with food," Peter said with a grim smile. "They won't last long, the stupid Swedes. They'll have to cut their losses soon, or the winter will destroy them."

"Charles will probably march northeast," Nikolas commented, trying to remember the military history he had studied in his boyhood. "He'll try to outflank your defenses at Warsaw and advance to Lithuania—" His voice was temporarily muffled by the fresh towel Sidarov applied to his face.

"He would never make it past all the rivers and swamps," Peter scoffed. "And even if he did, we would stop him at the border town of Grodno."

Nikolas shrugged, recalling that Charles had made it across Poland and captured Grodno with ease. "Only God and the tsar know," he said, quoting an old Russian proverb. He ignored the way Sidarov's eyes rolled at the bit of flattery.

A smile touched Peter's thin lips. "I have missed you, Nikolai. I will see you often during my stay in Moscow. Two years I have been away from the capital! There is much to be done, enough to keep me here through the Christmas holiday. Unfortunately Menshikov will have to return to his regiments in Poland."

"That's too bad," Nikolas replied smoothly, rising from the bath and donning a robe that Sidarov handed to him.

Peter gave a short bark of laughter, as if Nikolas had made a joke. "There is no need to pretend you'll miss him, Nikolai. Everyone is well aware of the bad blood between you and Menshikov. But you must put your hatred aside, at least for tonight. Menshikov has done well by his country, and he must be respected for his achievements on the battlefield."

Nikolas agreed with a neutral murmur, uncomfortable with the new experience of looking *up* at another man. His own height was not inconsiderable, but the tsar was a giant.

"Besides," Peter continued, "there is no reason the two of you shouldn't like each other. You and Menshikov have much in common. You are both intelligent, ambitious—and willing to break with the old ways in order to make Russia equal to the West. Granted, Alexashka lacks your polish and good looks, but he has talents of his own."

"Especially when it comes to acquiring wealth," Nikolas said idly, remembering Aleksandr Menshikov's historical reputation for greed, and his abuse of power in stealing money from the Russian people and the government. He heard Sidarov's quiet intake of breath at the impudent remark.

The left side of Peter's face twitched as if in annoyance, but a sudden laugh burst from him. He gave Nikolas a warning look. "My Alexashka has his faults, but he has done me great service. And as for *you*, my clever friend . . . how goes it with the Moscow merchants? Have you convinced them to form trading companies similar to the English and Dutch?"

Nikolas hesitated, considering how to bluff his way through the answer. "I doubt they'll do it voluntarily," he said, meeting Peter's gaze directly. "The transition from the marketplace *posád* to industry won't be easy."

Peter grunted in disapproval, though he exhibited no surprise. "It is always this way with my people. They must be forced into progress, for they would never choose it willingly. Well, be prepared to receive a new appointment, Nikolai. From now on I want you to regulate the commercial and financial undertakings of the city. You will advise the governor, who seems to have no understanding of how things are done in the West."

"But I don't—" Nikolas began to protest, having no desire for a government post.

"Yes, I know you're grateful," the tsar interrupted, and strode to the door of the bathhouse. "I must tour the new fortification in the city, and see how the construction goes. I will return later this evening, to enjoy one of your excellent evenings of food and entertainment. I was told you have refurbished your private theater—I look forward to viewing it."

When the surly giant had left, Nikolas sat on the edge of the bath and shook his head in disbelief. "I've lost my mind," he muttered.

Sidarov gestured for him to come and dress in the adjoining room. "After I help you with your clothes, Your Highness, I'll make the necessary arrangements for tonight. There is no time for delay." He paused and added delicately, "You might try to charm the tsar a little more, Your Highness. No doubt Menshikov has been plotting against you as usual. Much depends on your ability to stay in the tsar's good graces."

"Of course," Nikolas said grimly. The Imperial government was always the same, no matter which century. A man's life was at the mercy of the tsar's whims. "I'm supposed to lick one of the tsar's boots faster than Menshikov licks the other. Nobility has its privileges."

Sidarov gave him a shocked glance but said nothing, quietly going about his duties.

The estate swarmed with frenetic activity as the servants readied several rooms in case the tsar and his entourage should decide to stay the night. The estate's private company of actors was summoned to perform a French farce for the evening, while the cook directed the servants in the preparation of an enormous banquet. Sidarov was nothing but a blur as he sped through the house, giving orders to everyone he encountered.

Left to his own devices, Nikolas set about investigating the condition of the Angelovskys' current holdings. He was surprised to find that most of the family's property was poorly documented. Looking through what few papers and account books he could find, he discovered that the family fortune was only a fraction of what it would be in the future. The Angelovsky income was comprised solely of rents from a few private properties, and a minimal interest in an Imperial porcelain factory. It seemed that among Prince Nikolai's interests, making money had not been paramount.

"Nikolai?" Emelia's soft voice came from the library doorway, and he looked up to see his wife peeking around the corner.

"What is it?"

Cautiously she ventured into the room. "Sidarov said that the tsar will eat at our table tonight. Will I have to be there?"

"Yes," he said brusquely, closing an account book. "Western women always eat at the same table as their husbands."

"Oh." She frowned nervously and plucked at the sleeves of her peasant dress. "I . . . I have nothing to wear except a sarafan."

"That will be fine."

"It's not modern. It's not fashionable."

"We'll have some gowns made for you. In the meantime, wear the sarafan."

"Yes, Nikolai."

His gaze remained on her face as he noticed that her skin looked strangely pasty. "Come closer," he said abruptly.

Emelia obeyed with shuffling footsteps, coming to stand by his desk. Nikolas rose to his feet and inspected her face. A heavy application of powder had covered the soft, natural blush of her skin, rendering it dull and chalky. Gently Nikolas drew a finger across her cheek, leaving a silken trail in the white coating. A few grains of powder were caught in the auburn crescents of her lashes.

"Prince Golorkov's wife gave it to me," Emelia said. "All the court ladies use powder. It's to cover my spots."

"Spots?" Nikolas repeated, bemused. "You mean these?" He drew another trail at the crest of her cheek, uncovering a scattering of golden freckles. "I like your freckles. Don't try to cover them."

She gave him a dubious glance. *"No one* likes them. Including me."

"I do." Smiling slightly, Nikolas nudged her under the chin with his finger.

"May I stay and watch you for a while?" Emelia asked impulsively. "Everyone is so busy, and I have nothing to do."

Nikolas sensed that she shared the same trapped, restless feeling that had plagued him all morning. "Would you like to take a ride through the city? I thought I might go to Kitaigorod."

Emelia's eyes brightened at the mention of the Kremlin-area marketplace, where all the finest re-tail shops were located. "I've never been there before!"

He was amused by her excitement. "Then hurry and find your cloak. And wash your face."

Emelia bounded away enthusiastically, while Nikolas instructed the servants to ready the carriage-sleigh. When Emelia met him at the front entrance, she was bundled in old, heavy shawls that were wrapped around her in bulky layers. Nikolas reached out to draw one of the garments more closely around her neck. "Don't you have a cloak, child?"

"No, but these are very warm. I'll hardly feel the cold at all."

Nikolas frowned as he surveyed the collection of tattered shawls. "We'll add a cloak to the list of things you need."

"I'm sorry, Nikolai," she said earnestly. "I have no dowry, no clothes . . . I've come to you with nothing."

"I wouldn't say that," he replied softly, staring into her brilliant blue eyes. The backs of his fingers accidentally brushed against the downy skin of her throat. Nikolas paused, his fingers tingling from the contact. He was achingly aware of the slim, elegant form hidden beneath the layers of cloth. He wanted to take her upstairs and undress her, and hold her naked body against his. His blood raced uncontrollably. But he couldn't make love to her, no matter how much he wanted to. He couldn't risk making her pregnant, or the ill-fated future of the Angelovsky family would repeat itself.

"Come," he murmured, escorting her to the carriage outside. "Let's have a look at Moscow."

Emelia hesitated only briefly before agreeing to

share the fur blanket with him in the carriage. Tucked together in a snug cocoon, their feet warmed by hot stones, they rode through the city toward the Kremlin. Nikolas was amazed at the differences he saw in the ancient fortress. Although the familiar red brick walls were there, as well as the cluster of onion-domed towers, the Grand Kremlin Palace had not yet been built. The Tsar Bell, the largest in the world, had not yet been cast or even designed. Huge icons hung over the gates of the steep red brick walls, in an appeal for God's grace and protection.

"It's quite amazing," Emelia remarked, following his gaze out the window. "To think of what goes on in there . . ." Her face hardened for a moment. "The tsar and the government officials can sit safely behind those walls, and with one stroke they can change the life of everyone outside. Peter wants a war, and so thousands must die in his service. Peter wants a new city by the Baltic Sea—and men like my uncle and brothers are conscripted to work on it. So many have died, doing the tsar's will. My uncle and brothers will probably die there too."

"You can't be certain of that."

"Petersburg is a very dangerous place. There are accidents, disease, even wild animals. Wolves roam the streets at night there, you know. The tsar was wrong to make my family go there against their will. He may be a wise and great man, but I think he's also very selfish!" Emelia stopped and darted a wary glance at him, wondering at his reaction to her impulsive speech.

"That's treasonous talk," Nikolas said quietly.

"I'm sorry—"

"Don't be. You may say anything you like to me, as long as no one else overhears. People are arrested and executed for any hint of rebellion."

"Yes, I know." She stared at him curiously. "You won't punish me for saying things against the tsar?"

Nikolas snorted, thinking of all the suffering he'd received at the Imperial government's hands. "Hardly. Everyone—male or female—is entitled to an opinion."

"You're very strange," Emelia said, a wondering smile crossing her face. "I've never heard a man say such a thing."

The carriage stopped at the marketplace. Many stares focused on them as they descended from the vehicle. Nikolas held Emelia steady as her feet touched a patch of ice. "Easy," he murmured, gripping her arms. "Watch your step, or you'll fall before I can catch you."

"Thank you," she said breathlessly, and laughed as she looked at the marketplace. "Oh, there's so much to see!"

Nikolas kept his hand at her back as they walked past the trade rows, lined with benches and stalls overflowing with goods. Merchants clamored for their attention, calling out the merits of their wares. "Fine leather boots!" "Soft sheepskin blankets!" "Holy icons for sale!" Peddlers strolled by with trays of foodstuffs hanging around their necks: small bottles of honey liquor, *pirozhki* stuffed with cabbage and rice, little salted fish, and occasionally, delicacies such as lemons or apples. Customers both wealthy and poor ate from the same trays, showing no reluctance to mingle together.

Beyond the rows were the more established

shops, housing craftsmen who specialized in gold-smithing, carpentry, and haberdashery. Stonecutters had brought their wares from Ekaterinburg: perfectly cut buttons and charms made of vibrant emerald malachite or bright blue lapis; crystals, topaz, and amethyst made into beads and jewelry. Other shops displayed kegs of caviar and spices, or piles of deep, luxurious furs, including tiger and wolf pelts. Aside from a number of Chinese tea shops, there appeared to be only a handful of foreign-owned businesses, compared with the multitude that would populate the city in the nineteenth century.

Stopping at a lacemaker's, Nikolas drew Emelia inside. She exclaimed in delight at the tables piled with lace of every quality, some of it as fine as spiders' webs. Hunting through the offerings, Nikolas selected a shawl of white lace so intricate it could only have been woven at the rate of an inch per hour.

"Do you like it?" he asked casually, and at Emelia's bemused nod, he flipped a coin to the lacemaker, who waited nearby.

"For me?" Emelia exclaimed, her face glowing with excitement.

"Of course it's for you." A smile tugged at Nikolas's lips. Carefully he removed the dark cloth from her head and draped the fine, soft lace over her hair. "Who else would I buy this for?"

The lacemaker, a little old woman with hands like the twigs of a gnarled tree, nodded approvingly. "Very beautiful. It looks like snow on your red hair."

Emelia reached up and touched the lace gently. "I've never owned anything so beautiful," she murmured. "Even my wedding clothes were borrowed."

The shawl was carefully wrapped in a paper parcel. Next Nikolas took Emelia to a perfumery, filled with incense, oils, and perfumes that made the air sweet. While Emelia investigated the assortment of intriguing flasks and scent boxes, Nikolas spoke to the elderly Frenchman in the corner. "Monsieur, I'd like to choose a scent for my wife."

The perfumer regarded Emelia with bright, dark eyes. "She is a fine-looking woman. Perhaps someday you will allow me to mix a special perfume for her, Your Highness. In the meantime, I have an excellent one already prepared. Rose, bergamot, and a touch of mint." Foraging in the back of the shop, he located a flask of blue glass and removed the stopper. He proffered it to Emelia invitingly. "Your wrist, madame."

Cautiously Emelia extended her arm, and the perfumer rubbed a tiny drop on her skin. Emelia sniffed her wrist and looked at Nikolas with an amazed grin. "It smells just like the meadow in spring!"

"I told you it was excellent," the perfumer said proudly. "I create perfumes for all the women at court."

After a few minutes of negotiations, Nikolas bought the perfume and gave it to Emelia. She received it with an awestruck expression.

"I didn't expect you to buy presents for me," she said, cradling the flask gingerly as she followed Nikolas from the shop. "I haven't done anything to deserve them."

"You're my wife now. You can have anything you want."

"What I *really* want . . ." she began, and blushed up to her hairline.

"Yes?" Nikolas prompted, half-afraid of what she might say.

"I really want—" Emelia tried again, but broke off nervously.

Nikolas stopped at the side of the street, his gaze searching her face. He wasn't certain why he had bought gifts for her, or why it had seemed necessary to show her that she pleased him. She was the one woman on earth he couldn't have. Bitterly he wondered why life wasn't simple for him as it was for other men. He had never been able to reconcile the divided halves of himself, the part that wanted her and the part that feared her.

"We'd better return to the estate," he finally said. "Peter and his entourage will be arriving soon."

The clothes set out for Nikolas, including a long amber velvet coat with brocade cuffs, tight velvet breeches, and a jeweled brocade vest, were the height of fashion for the day. He hated everything about them. The constricting fit, the bright colors, the ostentation—all of it was contrary to his own taste. He was accustomed to the elegant simplicity of black and white for evening, tailored with room to spare in the jacket and trousers, everything crisp and neat. That was the style in the time of Queen Victoria. In the early eighteenth century, however, a man of means was supposed to dress with all the subtlety of a peacock.

Feeling ridiculous in his elaborate attire, Nikolas went to Emelia's room. He found his wife sitting at a mahogany dressing table of French design, staring in perplexity at the blue flask of perfume he had given her that afternoon. Looking over her shoulder at the sound of his entrance, Emelia smiled in admiration. "What splendid clothes, Nikolai."

He made a noncommittal grunt and approached the dressing table. Emelia was wearing the red sarafan, with matching red ribbons wound through her plait in back. She had draped a fragile veil over her hair and secured it with the gold wire circlet. Unable to keep from touching her, Nikolas reached out on the pretext of arranging the tiny paste ruby of her diadem so it lay exactly in the center of her forehead. His thumb passed lightly over one of her eyebrows, smoothing the bright auburn arc. He would have to give her some jewelry—no wife of an Angelovsky should wear fake stones.

Emelia fidgeted with the blue flask. "I've never worn perfume before. How should I put it on?"

"Most people make the mistake of using too much. Just rub a small drop on your wrists and behind your ears." Drawing the stopper from the glass bottle, Nikolas touched the end of the wand to her wrist. He massaged the moist spot with his fingertip, until the heady scent of summer flowers drifted to his nose. "Some women like to perfume the places where the pulse beats strongest . . . the throat, the backs of the knees . . ."

Emelia laughed, holding still as he touched the tender hollows behind her earlobes. "But no one will see my legs!"

The thought of her strong, slim calves, lifting to wrap tightly around him, made Nikolas's mouth go dry. He stared into her smiling blue eyes. If he wanted to, he could seduce her right here, take her to the bed just a few yards away, lift the hem of her sarafan to her waist . . .

With her face at the level of his hips, Emelia couldn't help but notice the change in his body as his flesh hardened beneath the iron restriction of his breeches. She turned pink and cleared her throat before asking, "Nikolai, do you want to—"

"No," he snapped, turning away. He strode to the doorway and paused at the threshold, speaking without looking back at her. "I suggest that you hurry, madam. Like it or not, you're going to play hostess for the tsar tonight. And you'd better make the performance a good one, or there will be hell to pay for us both."

The troupe of six actors performed the comedy by Molière with engaging lightness. A group of approximately thirty guests clustered around the tsar as they relaxed in the private theater at the Angelovsky estate. The theater was small but luxurious, the walls thickly covered with gilt and oval-shaped portraits of family ancestors. Flanked by Nikolas on his left and Aleksandr Menshikov on his right, the tsar laughed heartily at the antics of the actors.

Nikolas was acutely aware of his wife's tension. Emelia was frozen in the seat beside him, darting occasional glances at the tsar. Nikolas guessed that she was intimidated by Peter. Peasants of Emelia's humble background were all taught that the tsar of Russia was the most powerful man on earth, a fatherly and omnipotent figure, and the only being above him was God. To soothe Emelia and keep her attention on the play, Nikolas whispered frequently in her ear, translating the French phrases and jokes into Russian.

When the play was concluded, the guests were led into the dining room and arranged at a long table. Again, Nikolas sat on Peter's left, Menshikov on his right. Emelia was located several places away, looking uncomfortable in comparison to the fashionably gowned court women at the table. Platters of heavily seasoned fish and roasted game were served, and wine was poured into silver goblets lined in pink crystal.

Nikolas said very little, merely sat back in his chair and watched the tsar and Menshikov. There had been few people in his life Nikolas had hated on sight, but Aleksandr Danilovich Menshikov, recently titled Prince of Izhora, was one of them. Perhaps it was because Menshikov so clearly hated him with the same intensity.

A tall, cold-faced man, bone-thin from the hardships of his service in Poland, Menshikov clung to the tsar like a shadow, trying to anticipate all his thoughts and needs. He had unusual turquoise eyes, intense and calculating, and a hard, small mouth adorned with a mustache identical to Peter's. Through a combination of endurance, cleverness, and ambition, Menshikov had risen to a power that often allowed him to speak for Peter himself. A deep sense of comradeship seemed to exist between the two men. Menshikov was fiercely jealous of his relationship with the tsar, and was obviously threatened by anyone whom Peter spoke with or admired.

Menshikov spoke to Nikolas in a catlike tone. "How admirable of you to follow the Angelovsky tradition of marrying a peasant woman! They breed with no difficulty, and it is but a simple matter to train them."

"Alexashka," Peter said in a warning tone, but Menshikov continued idly.

"It was wise of you to marry without love, Nikolai. Nothing must interfere with a man's devotion to the tsar and Russia, especially not love for a woman. Demanding creatures, women . . . they want everything for themselves. As long as a man knows what should come first, he will do well."

"I know what should come first," Nikolas assured him, his voice quiet, his eyes hard. He saw how Emelia flushed in embarrassment at Menshikov's pointed remarks about her background. Turning to her, Nikolas commented blandly, "Just see how far you may rise, *ruyshka*. Our friend Menshikov may be a prince of Russia now, but he began as a pie seller in the Moscow marketplace."

Menshikov twitched as if stung, and Peter laughed uproariously. "You asked for that, Alexashka," he said, still chuckling. "You should know by now not to provoke Nikolai. He's a sleeping tiger. Best not to awaken him."

"We can't all be born aristocrats like the Angelovskys," Menshikov muttered. "How fortunate for Russia that the tsar believes in rewarding a man for his own merits and not because of his noble blood!"

"All I ask is that my people give me loyalty and ardent service," Peter replied. "In this way a peasant may prove himself to be far more noble than a prince." As he followed Nikolas's gaze, Peter's attention alighted on Emelia. "What village are you from, child?"

It was a common question, a courtesy that most Russians exchanged in order to show polite interest. The effect on Emelia, however, was unexpected. She turned very pale, and a clammy sheen appeared on her forehead. Her silence drew out to an almost unbearable degree, until Nikolas thought she might not answer.

Her reply was barely audible. "I . . . it's . . . Preobrazhenskoe."

Peter was still, except for the odd tic that began in his left cheek.

What the hell does that mean? Nikolas thought in worry, before he suddenly realized that Preobrazhenskoe was the site where many bloodthirsty uprisings had begun. It was the home of the Streltsy rebels, who had been responsible for the death of most of Peter's family when he was a child. They had murdered his relatives right before his eyes. The trauma had caused him the lifelong affliction of occasional seizures on the left side of his face and neck. After the second Streltsy rebellion at Preobrazhenskoe, grisly mass executions had been held there until the ground was blood-soaked for miles around. Nothing could guarantee a more negative reaction from Peter than the mere mention of that village.

Menshikov eyed Emelia with barely subdued glee. "And is your family all from Preobrazhenskoe, my dear?" he asked in a delicately malicious tone.

"Yes," she whispered, keeping her face down. She was the very picture of guilt.

A new realization hit Nikolas like a brick between the eyes. He remembered bits of the conversation they had had at the Golorkov mansion, her reluctant answers to his questions . . .

"My father is dead . . . my family was unpopular because of my father's political beliefs . . . "

Her father had probably been executed for being a *strelets* rebel.

Struggling to cope with the new information, Nikolas was only half-aware of the scene unfolding before him.

Peter's face was grim as he moved to alter the course of conversation. "Enough talk for now," he commanded. "Everyone eat!" He cast a stern glance at Emelia. "No wonder you are skinny—there is scarcely a mouthful of food on your plate. And not one scrap of meat!"

"I-I don't like it," Emelia faltered.

Peter's expression darkened. "Not like meat? Foolish girl—no one can live without eating flesh." He picked up a slice of chicken with his huge fingers and tossed it to her plate, where it landed with a splatter. "Here—food from my own hand. Eat it now!"

Emelia took a fork in her trembling fingers while the attention of the entire table focused on her. She picked up a glistening sliver of chicken and regarded it with a sickly expression.

Nikolas watched her with dawning understanding. Emelia was exactly as she would be in the future, with all the same instinctive likes and dislikes. Eating meat went against her very nature. He couldn't let her be abused this way, especially when it would likely result in her throwing up all over the table. He intervened quietly. "*Batushka*, I will send my disobedient wife to her room, where she may go without supper and contemplate her foolishness."

Peter pointed to the chicken. "Not until she eats that."

Nikolas glanced at Emelia. She was lifting the

bite of meat to her lips. Her face had turned pale
green. He knew she wouldn't be able to hold it
down. *"Go,"* he snapped.

Emelia threw him a glance of misery and grati-
tude, and raced from the room in a defeated flurry.

Six hours later, Nikolas ascended the stairs with
a weary tread. His entire body was tense with anger, frustration, and a strong feeling of betrayal. It
had been a hellish evening. After Emelia had left,
Peter's foul mood had poisoned every attempt at
conversation. Menshikov had encouraged him with
a constant flow of sly whispers and insinuations,
while the guests were torn between scandalous
delight and uneasiness. Clearly Peter didn't like
Nikolas's choice of a bride. Nikolas was well on the
way to agreeing with him. After everyone had guz-
zled bottle after bottle of wine and vodka, Peter
and his entourage had left for the night. And finally Nikolas was free to deal with his deceitful
wife.

Perfect, he thought savagely. *All I need in this
damned slippery situation is to be saddled with a woman
whose family was involved in plots to overthrow the
tsar.* He could hardly wait to reach Emelia's room
and unleash his anger on her. He was going to
make her admit that her father was a *strelets,* and
then he was going to make her eternally sorry for
having tricked him into marrying her. She must
have known that he never would have endangered
himself by choosing the daughter of a traitor. Now
the shadow of suspicion had been extended to Nikolas, and from now on his every step would be
watched carefully.

Reaching Emelia's chamber, Nikolas let himself

inside and closed the door with exquisite care. The red-and-yellow glow from the fireplace was the only light in the room. He could barely make out Emelia's huddled shape by the bed. She appeared to be praying. *Good*, he sneered inwardly, *you'll need a hell of a lot of prayer before I'm through with you.* "We're going to have a talk," he said, his voice taut with fury.

Emelia came toward him quickly. "Nikolai," she said in a choked voice. She wore the blank, wide-eyed look of a terrified doe. "You must punish me. I angered the tsar, and now his wrath will fall on you. Here—take this whip—I must be disciplined. Please, I can't bear knowing what I've done—"

"Wait," Nikolas said, interrupting her babble. He saw the gleam of the silver whip handle, and motioned for her to put it aside. "I want to ask you some questions—"

"Here, take it," she insisted.

"Christ, I'm not going to beat you!" He pulled the whip from her grasp and sent it whistling to a corner of the room, where it hit with a solid thud. As he faced his trembling wife and saw the trails of tears that fell from her unblinking eyes, his anger vanished in one startling moment. He cursed himself for being so easily undone.

"But you must," Emelia whispered.

"I'll be damned if I *must* do anything!"

"Please . . ." She bowed her head and shuddered.

Unable to help himself, Nikolas reached out and drew his wife's slender body against his. "Just tell me the truth," he said, his lips on her flowing hair. "Was your father a *strelets* rebel?"

She began to cry violently then, gasping out words in an incoherent torrent. "Yes . . . he was hanged . . . my mother died of grief . . . couldn't tell you . . . I wanted . . . to be your wife, and if you knew . . ."

"If I had known, I wouldn't have married you," he finished for her.

"Please punish me," she begged.

"You little fool," he said harshly, and pulled her closer in an effort to soothe her. He stroked her shaking back. "How in God's name do you think I could leave a mark on you? How could I cause you pain with my own hands? Oh, don't think it's not tempting, my clever one. But even if I tried, I could never lift a finger against you."

"Because I'm your wife?" she asked tremulously.

"Because you're *mine*. You're the only one I've ever wanted, no matter that you'll probably be my downfall. Now stop crying—it's not going to solve anything."

"I c-can't," she sobbed against his neck.

"Stop it," Nikolas said, driven to desperation. He pushed aside the curtain of her red curls and found her wet cheek with his lips. The taste of her tears, the trace of salt on silk, made him dizzy. He moved to the corner of her mouth, the trembling curve of her lower lip, the hint of sleekness inside. He kissed her gently, then harder, harder, until his tongue pushed past the edges of her teeth and he had her in full, deep possession. Her crying ceased magically, and she pressed her body to his. She was so warm, so sweetly compelling, that his desire raced out of control, and he could have taken her right then. Instead he ripped himself away with a tortured groan and strode to the fireplace. He stared into the crackling flames as he fought for composure.

"I can't do this," he said tersely.

Emelia stood unmoving behind him. "Why?" she asked on a little gasp of air.

The notion of explaining to her, and the spectacle he would present, made him laugh sardonically. "There's no way I could make you understand. God, the things I could tell you . . . you'd never believe."

"I might," she said with impossible hope, her voice a little closer than before.

"Oh?" His laughter ended on a savage note. "What if I told you that I could see into the future? What if I claimed that we'll meet again, a hundred and seventy years from now?"

She replied after a long hesitation. "I could believe that . . . I think."

"It's the truth. I know exactly what the future holds. Nothing good can come of our marriage, nothing of any value. The Angelovskys are a corrupt stock. Knowing the pain and misery they'll cause over the next few generations, for themselves and others, I can't let that future happen again. There won't be any children from our marriage because I can't allow the family line to continue."

Emelia sounded bewildered. "If you feel this way, then why did you marry me?"

He shook his head and cursed softly. "I don't know. I can't help being drawn to you."

"It's fate," she said simply.

"I don't know what it is," he muttered. "But it's no damn good." He picked up a fireplace poker and jabbed viciously at a burning log.

"Nikki," she asked, "will there be love between us when we meet again in the future?"

He turned sharply at the use of his nickname.

She looked confused and frightened, her eyes filled with a yearning softness that shook him down to the bone.

"No," he replied, setting aside the poker. "In the future you'll hate me for taking away everything you cherish. I'll end up hurting you, time and time again."

"No harm can come of loving someone," she whispered. "I don't know very much, but I'm certain of that."

"I don't know how to love," he said, his voice thick with self-hatred. "I've never known. And I'm not worthy of it. Trust me."

Fresh tears glittered in her blue eyes. "I could love you. You wouldn't even have to love me back."

"No." It was all he could say, staring at her flushed, emotion-filled face.

Emelia walked straight to him, and slid her long arms around him. She hugged herself to his body, her face into the side of his neck. "I don't care about the future." Her words seemed to burn his skin. "All I care about is that I'm here with you now . . . and I do love you."

"You can't," he said softly, while a white-hot explosion went off in his chest. "You have no reason to—"

"I don't need a reason. Love isn't like that."

In the face of her stubborn, illogical passion, Nikolas could find no defense or retreat. He groaned and sought her mouth with his, kissing her with all the fire he felt inside. He filled his hands with her, cupping her bottom, her hips, her breasts, in greedy and wanton succession. She opened her lips to him, and yielded her body with a tender generosity that devastated him. Locking his arms around her, he held her so tightly that she winced and gasped in pain. He loosened his grip only slightly, and rested his forehead on hers, breathing hard against her mouth.

"I don't know what to do," he said. He'd never made such an admission before.

"What do you want?" she whispered. It was a provocative question, especially when she was clasped so tightly against his aroused body.

He wanted the intolerable pressure in his chest to leave . . . he wanted to be free somehow. "I want there to be no past and no future. I want to be able to tell you . . ."

"Tell me what?"

Nikolas drew back enough to look at her radiant face. His heart thundered with something like terror. He gripped her head in hands that held a distinct tremor, and he stared straight into her glimmering blue eyes. She was so beautiful, so much his.

"I can't," he heard himself say.

"Let the future take care of itself," she urged. "Let the others be responsible for themselves. All you can do is try to make a good life for yourself now, with me."

Nikolas shook his head, wondering if it could really be that simple. He had never lived only for himself, without carrying the burden of his family's dark history. What if he cast all of that aside? It would almost certainly happen again—his father's abuse, his brother's murder, his own corruption. How could he love Emelia now, knowing what would take place?

But he wanted so badly to be with her, and it

didn't seem that he had a choice. How long had he tried to deny his feelings for her? Days, months, years . . . and all of it had been futile. Why keep on trying? He didn't care what price came with loving her. She was worth anything.

Suddenly the emotional upheaval began to subside, leaving a sense of peace he had never known before. "I think I finally know why I'm here," he said hoarsely. "It's not to change my family's history. It's to be with you. To remember a time when I . . . was able to feel this way."

"What way?" she whispered, her hands sliding up to grip his wrists tightly.

His vision blurred, and he swallowed against the sharp pressure in his throat. "I . . . love you." He pressed his mouth to her forehead, for once utterly gentle and humble. A feeling more pure and piercing than he had ever known flooded through him. "I love you," he repeated, kissing her delicate eyelids, and he continued to whisper the miraculous words against her skin and hair. For a long time he wasn't aware of anything except the two of them standing in a pool of firelight, completely absorbed in each other. Later they moved to the bed, although he never remembered if he had led the way, or if she had.

He undressed them both, and he held Emelia's naked body against his, keeping her warm and safe in a cocoon of silk-and-damask covers. With a single fingertip, he traced the lush shape of her mouth, the straight angle of her nose, the bold red slashes of her brows. She moved her hands over his back and sides in tentative strokes. The warmth of her touch filled him with a primitive urgency that took all his strength to contain.

His mouth came to hers, softly ravaging, while his knee slid between her long, silken legs and parted them. He clasped his palms over her breasts until the tips gathered into hard points. Emelia trembled and moved imploringly beneath him, but he kept each caress soft and light. Nothing had ever enthralled him like this, making love at last, *showing* love with his mouth and hands and body. Tenderly he kissed every inch of her, from her head down to her long, narrow feet, returning leisurely to the crisp red spray of curls between her thighs. He pressed his mouth into the softest part of her, licking deep into the sweet cinnamon thicket. Emelia flinched in surprise and pleasure, her fingers tangling in his hair while gasping moans caught in her throat. When she was damp and ready for him, he raised himself over her, matching their limbs length to length.

Emelia slid her arms around his neck and touched her lips to his ear. "I don't know how to please you," she whispered desperately. "What can I do? What can I give you?"

"Yourself. That's all I want." He kissed and stroked her, coaxing her to explore his body as she would. When neither of them could bear any more, he entered her carefully, wincing at her cry of pain. "I'm sorry," he breathed, lodged heavily inside her. "I'm sorry for hurting you."

"No, no . . ." She wrapped her arms and legs around him, pulling him closer, arching in encouragement.

Nikolas began to move, straining to be gentle, while the rising pleasure slowly drove him past the point of sanity. He forget everything he'd ever been, every trace of the past and future. There was only her . . . Emelia . . . Emma . . . driving away all bitterness and anger. His very soul was unlocked, and for the first time in his life, he knew what it was to be happy.

❧ *Nine*

A MONTH WENT by, the winter days passing for Nikolas in a dream. He had been given a new life, a chance to be someone else, and he slipped into the role with surprising ease. Qualities that had always been foreign to him, such as compassion, tolerance, generosity, now seemed to come easily. He envied no one, because at last he had everything he wanted. He was constantly busy, organizing meetings of the merchants in the marketplace *posád*, appointing more agents and stewards to manage the Angelovsky holdings, reluctantly sharing an occasional hard-drinking evening with Peter and the gentlemen of the court. Most of his time, however, was spent with Emelia.

His wife enchanted him, with her high spirits and strength of will. They went on sleigh rides across frozen rivers, summoned musicians and actors to entertain at their estate, or passed hours in quiet companionship as Nikolas read aloud from a novel. They made love for hours, each experience seeming to transcend the last. Nikolas was amazed at how much he needed her, how much closeness he craved after years of solitude. He had never allowed someone to know him so well. Emelia felt free to tease and play and make demands of him, and he was only too happy to indulge her.

He lavished her endlessly with gifts—gowns of vivid silk, velvet, and brocade, with overjackets sumptuously trimmed in lace. There were matching silk stockings, slippers, gilded and tooled leather boots, shoes with raised heels in which Emelia tottered around with awkward pride. For her hair, Nikolas had given her a gold-and-silver box filled with tortoiseshell combs, jeweled diadems, diamond pins, and a rainbow of ribbon.

"It's all too much," Emelia protested one day as they sat in the parlor with Ily Ilych, a wizened, little old man who was known as the best jeweler in Moscow. "I don't need any more jewels, Nikki. I have more than I'll ever wear."

"There is no such thing as too much," the jeweler protested, spreading his wares more invitingly on a black velvet cloth before her.

"Why not a bracelet?" Nikolas suggested, hooking a glittering ruby circlet with his finger.

Emelia shook her head. "I have enough to cover both my arms up to my elbows."

Ilych pointed to other precious objects. "A diamond-and-amber necklace? A sapphire cross to wear to church?"

She laughed and held up her hands defensively. "I don't need anything. Really!"

"The princess deserves something special," Nikolas told the jeweler, ignoring his wife's protests. "Something out of the ordinary. What else have you brought?"

Ilych's wrinkled mouth drew up in thoughtful folds, and he began to rummage through his collection of velvet bags. "Hmm . . . perhaps she

would like . . . yes, I think these will be pleasing.''
He reached deep into one sack and drew out a se-
lection of precious figurines, setting them on the
table, one by one.

Emelia exclaimed in delight as she saw them.
"Oh, how wonderful! I've never seen anything like
them.''

A wondering smile crossed Nikolas's face. "Nor
have I,'' he said, although it was a lie. The menagerie of carved animals was the same set he had
brought with him when he had been exiled from
Russia. The white coral swan with its gold beak,
the malachite frog, the amethyst wolf with gold
paws, and amid all the rest, the centerpiece of the
collection—the amber tiger with yellow diamond
eyes.

Emelia picked up the tiger and examined it from
every angle. "Look, Nikki. Isn't it beautiful?''

"Very beautiful,'' he agreed softly, his gaze on
her glowing face. He broke off long enough to tell
the jeweler, "We'll take them all.''

Emelia laughed exuberantly and came over to
throw her arms around him. "You're so good to
me,'' she said against his ear. "You'll make me love
you too much.''

He brushed his lips across her soft cheek.
"There's no such thing as too much.''

Amid the blissful days of his life with Emelia, a
sinister shadow began to intrude. Nikolas was
aware that whatever his relationship with Peter
had once been, it had disintegrated into a friendship that was at best lukewarm. He had a sense of
distant admiration for the man, but Peter's explosive temper, his ferocity, his unreasoning stubborn-

ness, made it impossible for Nikolas to like him. And only someone in Peter's good graces would survive these precarious times.

Peter was now under tremendous pressure, waging a war not only against the Swedes but on his own people as well. He had conscripted hundreds of thousands of unwilling peasants to serve in the army and build St. Petersburg, earning the wrath of his subjects from every level of society. Discontent and treachery were everywhere, and few people were safe from Peter's suspicion. Secret police were constantly busy ferreting out information about anyone who breathed even one treasonous word against the tsar and the government. God knew how many innocent men had been accused and made examples of, sometimes even without a trial. The atmosphere around Moscow was ripe with intrigue, and Nikolas realized that he himself was the target of much dislike.

"Jealousy," Sidarov, his steward, had explained matter-of-factly when Nikolas had remarked on the cold attitudes of the other noblemen toward him. "In their eyes you have been blessed with more than one man deserves. Your name and wealth, your fine looks—" He was interrupted by a sardonic snort from Nikolas. "Yes, you are very fine-looking, and you married a woman of great beauty as well. You gained the favor of the tsar because of your modern Western ideas, so why should any of the boyars like you?"

"The favor of the tsar," Nikolas muttered. "As far as I can see, that's worth a pail of horse droppings."

"Your Highness," Sidarov protested, his chocolate-colored eyes filled with alarm. "You shouldn't say such a thing aloud. The walls have ears! You will endanger yourself and the princess."

"We're already in danger," Nikolas said softly, lifting a hand to his jaw and touching the outline of a shadowy bruise. It had been inflicted the day before, at the culmination of a meeting among Peter and the eight men whom he intended to appoint as governors of newly created provinces of Russia. Menshikov was to be in charge of St. Petersburg, Prince Dmitry Golitsyn was to have Kiev, Kazan was to go to Boyar Apraxin, and so forth.

Nikolas had infuriated Peter by refusing the appointment as governor of the Archangel region. He had declined to explain his reason, which was primarily that he had no interest in producing more revenue for the government. All Peter really wanted from his governors was for them to prod a virtual army of tax collectors into squeezing more money from the suffering populace. Nikolas had the unpleasant certainty that his refusal of the position would probably have far-reaching consequences, but still, he couldn't bring himself to do it.

Peter's disapproval had fallen on him with full force, and he had pinned Nikolas with an accusing glare that had made some of the men at the long table wince, while a few wriggled in poorly hidden satisfaction. "That's fine—I'll appoint someone else!" Peter had sneered. "But if you feel so comfortable in denying the tsar a request, then perhaps you can tell me what you *have* done, if anything, for my benefit! Tell me why you haven't yet convinced the Moscow merchants to form trading companies." He stood and walked over to Nikolas, leaning down to shout directly into his face. "I want more industry, more development! Why are my people so slow to change? Why won't they give me the revenue I need to make war against the Swedes? I want answers from you now!"

Nikolas was expressionless. He hadn't flinched in the face of the tsar's ear-splitting roar, not even when tiny flecks of spittle flew from Peter's gigantic mouth. Somehow he had managed to reply calmly. "You've found every possible source of revenue and squeezed it dry, *Batushka*. Your tax collectors have drained every kopeck from the people. There are taxes on everything from birth and marriage to drinking water. There is even a tax on mustaches, ludicrous as that may seem."

Nikolas paused, realizing that there was a deadly hush in the room. Peter's eyes had turned into chips of flint. No one could believe that Nikolas would dare to tell the tsar the truth. "On top of that," he continued evenly, "the state monopolies you've created serve to multiply the price of goods at five times their original cost. People can't afford to bury their dead properly because coffins cost too much. Peasants can't even afford salt for their tables. Alcohol, fur, even playing cards are too expensive. The merchants can't make a decent profit under these conditions. They are outraged, and they see no reason to work harder merely to finance your war."

"Your honesty is appreciated." Without warning, Peter had struck him. The blow had landed on Nikolas's jaw with blinding force. Nikolas was nearly knocked to the floor. "But *that* is for your insolence."

The tsar's desire for progress was perfectly in accordance with his Western ideals, but his methods of getting it were not. Blinking hard to clear the bright spots before his eyes, Nikolas had fought to stay upright. There had been a strange ringing in his ears. Rage began to pump through him, and he was consumed with the urge to attack, to defend himself. But lifting a finger against the tsar would be the same as signing his own death warrant.

Slowly Nikolas rose to his feet. "Thank you for the lesson," he said. "Now I know the reward for telling the truth." There were audible gasps at his effrontery, and then they all watched in silence, Peter included, as he strode from the room.

Bringing his thoughts back to the present, Nikolas touched the sore spot on his jaw once more and smiled grimly as Sidarov spoke anxiously.

"But, Your Highness, the tsar strikes everyone. It is just his way. Why, he struck Prince Menshikov once in this very house, so hard that Menshikov began to bleed all over the supper table! The tsar doesn't mean anything by it. The people who are close to him must bear the effects of his frustration—you've always known that."

"His frustration has a hell of a right hook," Nikolas muttered.

"The bruise will fade soon." Sidarov's young face twisted with a frown. "Please, Prince Nikolai, you must try to forget this."

For Emelia's sake, as well as for his own, Nikolas was willing to try.

Later that night, when he went to the room they now shared, he found Emelia sitting at a small table with an odd collection of little mirrors, all positioned to reflect off one another. A candle burned in the center of the mirrors. The soft, wavering light extended to the shadowy wall behind her, making the icon of Elijah and its ruby-colored cloud glow as if lit from behind.

Perplexed, Nikolas stood in the doorway and watched his wife. She was dressed in a pale blue velvet gown, closed up the front with tiny buttons carved from mother-of-pearl. "What are you doing?" he asked.

Emelia jumped a little, and then smiled at him. "You came in so quietly that I didn't hear you!" She returned her attention to the mirrors. "I'm trying to read our fortune. I will stare into the mirrors until one of them reveals our fate. If I can't see anything after a while, then I thought I would melt a candle into a bowl of water, and the drippings will form a figure that will give a clue."

Nikolas closed the door and went over to her, reaching out to tug gently at a ruddy curl. He smiled down at the top of her head. "You don't really believe in that kind of thing, do you?"

She looked up at him earnestly. "Oh, yes, it always works. Don't the Westerners believe in fortune-telling?"

"Some of them do, I suppose. But more of them believe in science than magic."

"What do you believe in?"

He fondled the slender line of her throat. "I believe in both." He drew her away from the table and turned her to face him. "Why are you worried about our fate, child?"

Her gaze moved to the bruise on his face, and she touched it gently with her fingertips. "The tsar doesn't like it that you married me. Everyone knows it."

His jaw hardened. "Has anyone dared say a word to you—"

"I hear the whispers whenever we go out. I think Menshikov and his friends have made certain to spread the news of who I am. It makes you look very bad, to have a wife such as I."

"To hell with them all," he said roughly, and kissed her.

Emelia turned her face away after a few moments. "Sometimes I wish . . ."

He bent his head to her throat and bestowed a chain of kisses against her skin. "What do you wish, *ruyshka?*"

"That we could find a way to make the rest of the world disappear. That it could be just the two of us."

"I can make it disappear," he murmured, dragging his mouth over hers with soft, intimate friction.

Emelia resisted briefly, and stared at him with worried blue eyes. "I don't ever want to cause trouble. I only want to give you comfort and peace."

"You give me so much more than that," Nikolas said, finding the shape of her body beneath the velvet robe. "You make me feel things I never imagined. I love you more than my life, *ruyshka.*" He clasped his hand around the fullness of her breast, until her breathing changed and she clung to him with a pleading moan. Triumphantly he drew her to the bed, intent on giving her such pleasure that all trace of worry would be banished, if only for a little while.

Aware that Emelia's suspicions concerning Prince Menshikov were probably right, Nikolas began to consider the best way to confront him. Strangely, they met by chance in a bookseller's shop, where most of the learned men in Moscow congregated in the afternoons. Picking up some Russian translations of foreign books, Nikolas became cognizant of a cold sensation, and turned to find Aleksandr Menshikov standing a few feet away.

Menshikov's blue-green eyes held a reptilian flatness as he smiled in greeting. "Good day, Prince Angelovsky. Have you found anything interesting to read?" He gestured to a nearby volume. "I recommend this account of the glorious accomplishments of the tsar."

Nikolas's gaze didn't move from the other man's face. "I know all I need to on that subject."

"Perhaps you should read it anyway, to be reminded of Peter's greatness and his formidable will . . . not to mention all he has done for you and the rest of us. You know, he and I had a conversation about you this very morning."

"And?" Nikolas prompted, his muscles clenching.

"It seems Peter is disappointed in you. He had such high hopes, but you chose to squander your talents. Such potential you had, and all of it wasted. You wouldn't accept a military appointment, nor would you do your civic duty by taking the governorship of Archangel . . . and you even decided to marry the daughter of a traitor."

"Not one word about her," Nikolas warned softly, his eyes flashing dangerously.

Menshikov continued in a slightly more subdued tone. "Has she told you about her father, Vasily? I've discovered quite a lot about him from our mutual friend, the chief of the Secret Office. Vasily was indeed a *strelets* soldier, the same kind who schemed against Peter from his birth, and murdered his family. They were supposed to guard his life, and instead they made attempts on it. 'Begetters of evil,' the tsar has called them. Your wife's father was known for making masterful speeches about taking over the capital, killing all the boyars, and restoring the tsar's sister Sophia to the throne. Standing in the middle of a crowd with his hair blazing bright red, shouting incendiary words of treason . . . it led people to call Vasily the red devil. You remember when the Streltsy soldiers marched on Moscow eight years ago? Vasily was a visible and active member of that rebellion. Naturally he was arrested, and he died under torture. But the Streltsy betrayal will never die in the tsar's memory. And every time he sees you and your flame-haired wife, Peter's heart will harden more against you. Emelia is bad for you, politically. If I were you, I'd get rid of her."

Nikolas couldn't restrain himself any longer. He pounced on the other man and shoved him against the wall, clenching his hands around the bastard's throat. "Maybe I'll just get rid of *you*."

The other people in the shop paused to stare at them in astonishment. Menshikov whitened in fear, or anger, or both. "Take your hands off me," he hissed.

Slowly Nikolas complied. "I've had enough of the gossip and rumors you've worked so hard to spread across Moscow," he muttered. "If I hear of any more slander being said against me or my wife, I'll make you answer for it."

Menshikov's lips parted in a jagged smile. "It's too late to repair your reputation, my arrogant friend. Your star has already fallen. You're not in Peter's favor any longer, because you valued your pride and privacy more than you did his affections. It's all a game, don't you see? You refused to play . . . and now you've been cut out."

Menshikov was right, Nikolas thought with a chill. If he wasn't willing to pander to the tsar's whims, then he had no right to expect Peter's good will.

As winter came to Russia in full force, the air was so cold that frostbite was a worry to those who ventured outside for more than a few minutes. Helpful strangers rubbed snow on the faces of passersby who had the telltale white splotches on their skin. No one braved the weather without covering himself in a heavy fur coat, whether it was made of rabbit or sable. The great tile stoves in the Angelovsky mansion filled each room with steady drafts of heat, while the occupants kept their hands warm with steaming glasses of tea, chocolate, or mulled wine. The approach of Christmas was heralded with festive parties and dances, and with carolers who filled the streets with music. Cleverly shaped gingerbread cakes, or *pryaniki*, were baked in every household and offered to all guests.

Caught up in the holiday revelry, Emelia insisted that Nikolas bring her to the ice hill that had been made for the enjoyment of Russian children and adults alike. It was a giant slide constructed of wood and covered with ice blocks and sheets of water. People carried their wooden sleds up to the top of the forty-foot slide, then careened down it at blinding speed, screaming with laughter all the way.

"You want to go down that?" Nikolas asked re-

luctantly while Emelia pleaded and tugged at him
to accompany her.

"Yes, yes, it's the most wonderful feeling . . .
you've gone down an ice hill before, haven't you?"

"Not since I was a boy."

"It's been much too long, then!"

Willfully she dragged him over to the mountainous contraption, and she talked someone into letting them borrow a painted wooden sled. They
ascended the steps to the platform at the top, where
the wind whistled fiercely against their faces.

"I'm going to regret this," Nikolas muttered,
watching the sledders hurtle down the long, im-
possibly steep incline.

Emelia gestured to the sled with an imperious
mittened hand. Her eyes gleamed with enjoyment.
Nikolas groaned and obeyed, positioning himself
far back on the sled with his legs extended. Emelia
sat in the space between his thighs, her body stiff
with excitement. The people waiting behind them
cheerfully assisted, giving the back of the sled a
forceful shove, and off they went.

Air rushed into Nikolas's lungs with a cold, cutting bite, making it impossible for him to breathe
for a moment. The sound of the sled's runners was
a slick hum in his ears. The exhilarating sensation
of speed took over, and they gathered more force
as they crossed the middle of the gleaming slide.
Emelia laughed and screamed, leaning back hard
against him. Faster, faster, racing over the ice . . .
and then they reached the bottom, where sand had
been spread to slow the riders' descent. Nikolas
used his booted feet to stop the sled.

Still laughing wildly, Emelia collapsed against
him. She twisted in an attempt to kiss his wind-

burned face, embracing him with the affectionate clumsiness of an unruly puppy. "I want to do it again!" she cried.

Nikolas smiled and placed a hard kiss on her lips. "Once was enough for me."

"Oh, Nikki!" She struggled to her feet, and threw her arms around him as he stood up. "Well, it's probably for the best. I was afraid my skirts would end up over my head."

"Later," he promised, nuzzling her cold cheek, and she pushed at his chest as she laughed.

That night a Christmas party was held at the home of Prince Golorkov. As they entered the great ballroom, Emelia smiled at Nikolas; both of them remembered the afternoon when he had chosen her from the line of five hundred. "The room looks different now," Emelia said.

"It's the Christmas decorations," Nikolas replied, gazing at the swags of red velvet tied with flowers and gold ribbons that covered every inch of wall space. Long tables were ornamented with fir branches and laden with plates of pastry, dried apples and other fruits, and five different kinds of nuts. One table held nothing but gingerbread, which had been baked, cut, and iced to resemble many important buildings in Moscow, including the Kremlin and St. Basil's Cathedral with its profusion of multicolored domes. The spicy, cheerful fragrance of ginger wafted through the air, mingling with the scents of wax and pine.

Intimidated by the grandeur of the gathering, Emelia swished her billowing skirts nervously. "I look like a peasant dressed in borrowed clothes.

If only you had let me use the powder for my face—"

"You're magnificent," Nikolas interrupted, brushing a kiss over the sprinkling of golden freckles on her cheek. It was true; Emelia didn't resemble an aristocrat in spite of her sumptuous garments. The other women present were pale and chalky, their bodies frail and their gestures languid. Emelia was as vivid as a firefly in the company of moths. The glorious red-amber curls had been interwoven with pearls and drawn to the top of her head, with a few long curls dangling to her shoulders. The velvet dress she wore was a shade of blue that made her eyes gleam like sapphires. A square-cut neckline trimmed with a fall of blond lace showed the generous roundness of her breasts, while a corset had drawn her waist into narrow, compact lines. Nikolas was captivated by his wife's vibrant beauty, and judging from the admiring glances being cast their way, so was every other man present.

Enjoying his admiring gaze, Emelia opened her fan and gazed at him flirtatiously over the scalloped edge. "I know what you're thinking when you look at me like that," came her muffled voice. "You want to take me to bed."

"I'm *always* thinking that," he assured her.

She patted her corseted waist. "I'm tied up with so many strings, you won't be able to reach me tonight."

He smiled and brushed his fingers over hers. "I'll find a way, believe me."

Their banter was interrupted by the arrival of the tsar. But the chatter and excitement that always greeted Peter's entrances were far more pronounced than usual. Wondering what was causing the stir, Nikolas stared at the crowd surrounding the tsar and his entourage, until finally Peter stepped into view. Nikolas shook his head in surprise, while Emelia drew her breath sharply.

In contrast to all the guests dressed in their finery, the tsar wore the simple clothes of a peasant, a red tunic and loose gray trousers, and embroidered felt boots.

"Why?" Emelia breathed.

Nikolas answered tonelessly, without looking at her. "It's a tasteless joke. He's mocking the peasants for complaining about his policies."

The guests chuckled and applauded while Peter did a silly little folk dance, turning so that everyone could view his costume.

"How terrible," Emelia said, flushing in embarrassment and anger.

Nikolas could find no reply. He concentrated on the parquet floor, inlaid with a variety of woods and touches of mother-of-pearl, hoping fervently that the tsar would soon tire of making an ass of himself.

"You don't seem to appreciate Peter's wit," came a man's silken voice from nearby.

Nikolas's brows drew together as he beheld Prince Aleksandr Menshikov. "If that's what you want to call it," he said softly, giving the man a deadly glance of warning. There was an air about Menshikov that made Nikolas uneasy, a sense of malicious triumph.

Menshikov turned toward Emelia with an elaborate flourish. "How are you, Princess?"

"Very well, thank you," she said woodenly, refusing to look at him.

Nikolas took his wife's elbow and began to guide her away. "If you'll excuse us, Menshikov—"

"Not just yet," the other man murmured. "I have a bit of news for your attractive wife. Now may not be the appropriate occasion to impart it . . . but then, there is never a good time for news like this."

Nikolas looked at Emelia, who returned his glance with a confused shake of her head.

"It seems that you have been making inquiries, Princess, about your family—to be more specific, your uncle and brother, who have been sent to work in St. Petersburg." Menshikov emphasized the word "princess" as if it were a term of mockery rather than one of respect.

Nikolas stared at Emelia without expression. What the hell was going on? She had said nothing about wanting to find her uncle and brother—she hadn't mentioned one word of concern to him. Sidarov had been equally closemouthed.

Emelia flushed guiltily and explained in a hushed voice. "I . . . I asked Sidarov to try and find out how my uncle and brother were. They've sent no word since they were conscripted to work in St. Petersburg, building houses and churches. I wanted to find them, and tell them about my marriage, and . . ." She fell into a cowed silence, her gaze darting to Menshikov's face.

"Why didn't you come to me for help?" Nikolas asked. "Did you think I'd refuse?"

"I don't know," she said unhappily.

Menshikov smiled in satisfaction at the turmoil he was causing. "Apparently it takes some time to build trust in a marriage. In any event, your servant Sidarov wasn't able to find out anything. Recently I was informed of his attempts, and I took it upon myself to make my own investigation—as a personal favor." He gave a long, pitying sigh. "Your uncle and brother were fortunate enough to meet their fate together, Princess, although their loss is a pity. They were working side by side when a wall collapsed on them." He shrugged regretfully. "Both dead. But life must go on for those of us left behind, mustn't it?"

"Get away from me," Nikolas sneered at Menshikov, "before I kill you."

Menshikov retreated a few feet, but hovered nearby, watching them intently.

Emelia's long fingers twisted around the fan, clenching until they were white. Her whole body was trembling.

"We don't know if it's true," Nikolas murmured, sliding an arm around her.

"It is true." Tears dropped from her eyes and rolled to her chin. "I knew something would happen to them. Now I have no one left."

"You have me." Nikolas smoothed his hand over her shoulders and back. In spite of his concern for her, he was mindful of the situation they were in and the dangers it presented. "Quiet, *ruyshenka*, people are listening."

"Neither of them wanted to be there," she wept. "They had a right to stay in the village and live with their families and grow old in peace. I hate the tsar for making them go to St. Petersburg! And he's done this thousands of times, to so many other people. He has no right to mock the peasants when he has taken so much from them—"

Nikolas gripped her upper arms, squeezing until she winced. "Hush. You must be quiet now." She nodded, managing to gulp back any further tears and bitter words.

But the damage had been done. Nikolas knew it from the satisfied smile on Menshikov's face and the startled expressions of the people who had overheard them. Halfway across the ballroom, Peter noticed the small disturbance, and he looked over at them, his face thunderous and dark with foreboding.

Emelia was too shocked to notice anything outside of her own grief. She obeyed without a word as Nikolas took her home, and she snuggled against him in the sleigh like a frightened child. Nikolas held her securely, occasionally murmuring against her hair. His thoughts and emotions boiled down to numb resignation.

They had been doomed from the beginning, he reflected. The daughter of a *strelets* rebel and an adviser to the tsar; such a pairing would never have been feasible. But if he had it to do all over again, he would still have married her.

He was no fool, and he was well aware that he was no longer protected by a friendship with Peter. After what had happened tonight, Emelia would soon be forcibly taken to the Kremlin and interrogated about her past and her political beliefs—which would most likely involve some form of torture. Nikolas would kill her himself before letting that occur. Complicating matters was the possibility that by now Emelia could be pregnant. He had to ensure that she would be safe, even if he were unable to protect her himself.

The thought of a baby—his child—filled Nikolas with anguished wonder. A small, perfect being, so

much hope and innocence contained in one helpless package . . .

"My God," he whispered soundlessly, for the
first time letting himself think about Jacob. His son,
alone and unloved in the future, needing a father's
protection . . . "My God, I made such a mistake."
He had never allowed himself to feel anything toward his illegitimate child, and all of a sudden he
ached to hold the boy, to reassure him that he was
safe, that he *belonged* somewhere.

Nikolas kissed his wife's temple, his lips brushing past the wispy red curls. He pressed silent
words on her skin. *If we meet again in the future, I'll
make it up to you. And to him. I'll love you both, I swear
it.*

When they arrived home, Nikolas paused in the
entrance hall long enough to inform Sidarov about
what had occurred. The steward was stricken, his
face turning pale with fear and regret. "Your Highness, I never intended to cause trouble—"

"It's all right," Nikolas said. "You were only trying to serve my wife. Besides, it would have come
to this no matter what you did. It's all in God's
hands, Feodor."

"But what will happen now?"

"I believe they'll come for us soon," Nikolas replied, feeling Emelia's body tense against his. She
shivered and looked at him with startled eyes. He
kept his attention on Sidarov. "Listen to me, Feodor. I will help my wife pack some of her belongings, and then I want to you leave with her
immediately. Take her to the Novodevichy Convent, understand? The same one where the tsar's
sister Sophia was exiled. They will offer Emelia refuge." Nikolas turned to his wife. "You'll be able to

leave there when it's safe. Sidarov will help you to find a place in the country to live."

Emelia's face was horror-stricken. *"No,"* she whispered. It was the only word her shaking lips could form.

Nikolas glanced at Sidarov. "You'll do as I ask?"

The servant nodded and turned away with an inarticulate sound.

Emelia spoke frantically as Nikolas brought her upstairs to their room. "Nikki, please don't send me away! This isn't necessary—"

"If it isn't, then I'll come to the convent and bring you home myself." He kept his hand at the small of her back. "But we're in trouble, *ruyshka.* I want you to be safe."

She began to cry as she trudged up the stairs. "If only I hadn't asked Sidarov to find my family—"

"That has nothing to do with this. I have enemies, led by Menshikov, who have influenced the tsar against me. Perhaps my marriage to you made things a little easier for them, but it would have happened sooner or later. It's fate, Emelia." His own emotions surged in a wave of denial and longing, but he managed to control them. He had to help his wife accept what would happen, or she would blame herself forever.

"I won't go anywhere without you," Emelia said in a low voice. "You can't make me leave."

"What good would that do?" he asked softly. "I can bear anything as long as I know that you're all right. And there is a chance that we've conceived a child by now. Would you put our baby at risk?" He knew from the sound of her indrawn breath that the possibility hadn't occurred to her. "If you are pregnant, the baby will be in danger. As the offspring of a suspected traitor, not to mention the heir to the Angelovsky titles and holdings, he'll be a target for everyone. No one must know about him, not even the rest of the family, until he's old enough to protect himself—"

"Why are you talking like this?" she burst out, weeping angrily. "If you're trying to frighten me, you've succeeded very well! I'm sorry for everything I've done—I'm sorry I ever came into your life and ruined it!"

"No, no . . ." Nikolas drew her into their room and closed the door. He wrapped his arms around her in a tight, comforting hold. "Don't ever say that. You're the only thing that gives my life meaning. Emelia . . . don't regret loving me."

Still crying, she returned his embrace fiercely.

"We have to pack your things," Nikolas said after a moment. "We don't have time—"

She turned her face and pressed her mouth to his, her lips tasting of tears. His thoughts scattered like leaves in the wind, and he responded involuntarily, clasping her body against his until her breasts flattened between them. It was only then that he realized how fast his heart was pounding, had been pounding ever since the Christmas ball. He was terrified for her sake, and equally afraid of the moment when he would have to part from her. He cupped her face in his hands, savoring the shape of her determined chin, her delicately angled cheekbones.

Her fingers curled into the thick amber velvet of his coat, clinging desperately. "Just once more," she said, her eyes glistening. "Please . . . it's all I can have of you."

"Emelia," he began with a shake of his head, but

as he stared into her eyes, his will crumbled and he crushed her lips with his own. She rose eagerly into the bruising pressure, her hands searching over his back and hips. The puffs of her breath struck his cheek in rapid succession.

Nikolas broke the kiss and undressed her with fumbling haste, ripping the fastenings that wouldn't give way quickly enough. The corset was undone, and Emelia gasped in relief, rubbing her palms over the red marks the stays had left. As Nikolas removed his own clothes, Emelia helped to lift the billowing white shirt over his head. Her mouth lowered to the smooth plane of his chest, and she kissed and licked the hollow of his throat, until Nikolas pulled her to the bed impatiently. He pulled the pins and ornaments from Emelia's hair, so that it fell over him in fiery waves.

The minutes ticked by relentlessly while they touched and kissed with frantic intensity. There was no need for words, no thought between them but the shared determination to banish the world for as long as they could. Nikolas warmed Emelia's cool skin with his hands, sliding his palms from her ribs to her slim waist. She lifted her body in encouragement, while her eyes half-closed in anticipation. He was hard with his fierce need of her, aware of each pulse of blood as it coursed through his stiff flesh. When his nerves had been aroused to stinging readiness, he gripped her hips and sank into her. Warmth and moisture surrounded him in gentle welcome. He pushed forward in shallow strokes, then deepened his entry until he had pushed as far as possible.

Nikolas held still, his face close to hers, their gazes locked until he was lost in a sea of shimmering blue. "My redheaded wife . . . you've given me the only happiness I've ever known." His throat tightened with grief and yearning. "Promise me that if we meet again, you'll remember me."

"How could I not know you?" she asked faintly.

He moved inside her, a rhythm of small strokes that made her moan in pleasure. "Tell me you love me."

"I love you, Nikki . . . always." Emelia pressed the words against his throat, his jaw, his mouth, repeating them until the storm quickened and broke in passionate fury. She sobbed against his throat, yielding to the final burst of sensation, pulling Nikolas deeper with her arms and legs until he could no longer hold back his own wrenching climax.

Nikolas wanted to sleep in her arms, abandoning himself to the bliss of unconsciousness. Instead he forced his tired limbs to move, lifting away from her, drawing out of the peaceful cocoon of the bed. He shivered in the cold air of the room and dressed quickly. Emelia was quiet, her gaze following his every movement. Rummaging through the armoire, Nikolas found an array of Emelia's gowns, and he chose a simple dark velvet with a high neck and long sleeves.

Her dull voice came from the bed. "Must I wear a habit when I'm at the convent?"

Nikolas couldn't help smiling. "God, no." He brought the dress to the bed and draped it over the rumpled covers. He paused to cast an admiring glance at her tousled form. She was a tangle of long limbs and a decadent mass of red hair, a delectable witch with a mouth that would entice a priest to sin. "There's no way you could ever look like a nun, *ruyshka*, no matter how you were dressed."

She sat up, holding the covers to her breasts. "What will happen to you?" she asked quietly.

Nikolas was silent, not knowing what to tell her.

"They'll kill you, won't they?" she said. "You're going to sacrifice yourself, because of what I've said and what I am—"

"No," he said swiftly, sitting on the bed and gathering her naked body in his arms. "Whatever happens, it isn't because of you. I made a lifetime's worth of mistakes before I met you."

"I can't bear it." Her hands knotted in his shirt. "I won't let you die for my sake." Her tears splashed on his doublet, making dark splotches on the fine, soft wool.

"If it came to that, I would die a thousand times for you," he whispered. "It's so much easier than being the one left behind."

"Please let me stay with you," she begged, trying to hold him as he pulled away.

Nikolas gestured to the dress and went to the tile stove, which gave off only a feeble heat. Plastering his hands against the lukewarm surface, he spoke gruffly over his shoulder. "Get dressed, Emelia. There isn't much time."

He was businesslike as he helped her stuff a small bag full of clothes and personal articles. Glancing out the small, thick-paned windows of the bedroom, he saw that their sleigh had been prepared and brought to the front of the house, its runners leaving narrow grooves in the snow-covered ground.

He turned toward Emelia. She was wearing the white lace shawl he had given her. Light and exquisite, it covered her hair and left part of her face shadowed, so that all he could see was the gleam of her eyes and the beseeching tremble of her lips. Nikolas was struck by the fact that this one woman could haunt him from one lifetime to another. A hundred images of her flashed through his mind: Emelia, wrapping her long legs around him in bed, romping through the snow like a street urchin, sitting in the bath with her hair dark and wet . . . and as Emma, with all her beguiling smiles and explosive arguments, dancing with him, coming in from her chores dressed in a man's shirt and trousers. He loved her in any guise. And he had lost her twice.

Silently Emelia slipped her hand in his. Their fingers clung in a hard, hurtful grip. Still retaining her hand, Nikolas picked up the valise and carried it as they went downstairs together.

Sidarov was waiting in the entranceway, his brown hair uncustomarily mussed, his face pale. In his arms he clutched one of Emelia's cloaks, a shade of plum wool so dark it looked black. "Everything is ready, Your Highness."

"Good." Nikolas leaned very close to the steward. "Don't let them have her," he said, too quietly for Emelia to hear. "You know what they would do." He drew back and stared hard at Sidarov, leaving the next thought unspoken, that he would rather have Emelia die quickly by Sidarov's hands than be tortured to death by someone else.

The steward nodded, understanding the silent message. "It won't come to that," he said calmly, and Nikolas rested a hand on his shoulder, gripping hard.

"I'm trusting you with everything I value, Feodor."

"I understand, Your Highness."

Nikolas took the cloak from Sidarov and turned to fasten it around Emelia's shoulders. Carefully he pulled the hood over her head, and he tried to smile. The attempt failed, however, and he stared at her in bleak despair. He didn't know how to say good-bye. His throat ached from the strain of holding back his emotions. "I don't want to leave you," he said humbly, reaching for her cold, stiff hands.

Emma lowered her head, her tears falling freely. "I'll never see you again, will I?"

He shook his head. "Not in this lifetime," he said hoarsely.

She pulled her hands away and wrapped her arms around his neck. He felt her wet lashes brush his cheek. "Then I'll wait a hundred years," she whispered. "Or a thousand, if I must. Remember that, Nikki. I'll be waiting for you to come to me."

Nikolas stood at the door, watching as Sidarov took her to the sleigh. The vehicle vanished swiftly into the blue-black night. "God be with you," he said quietly, gripping the doorframe. Eventually he asked one of the servants to bring some vodka to the sitting room. He waited near the tile stove, drinking in apparent leisure as he stared at a blank space on the wall.

After an hour had passed, a servant came to inform him that two agents of the Secret Office had arrived. The Secret Office, established by Peter, had been given jurisdiction over all crimes that threatened the stability of the tsar's government.

The agents had entered the house and followed

the servant directly to Nikolas. One of them was quiet and deferential in manner, while the other, a blade-faced man with a shock of oily black hair, wore a trace of a taunting smile.

"Prince Nikolai," the blade-faced man said, "I am Valentin Necherenkov, and my companion is Yermakov. We've been sent by the Secret Office because of an incident that was reported tonight—"

"Yes, I know." Nikolas moved toward a silver tray and indicated the bottle of chilled vodka. "A refreshment, perhaps?"

Necherenkov nodded. "Thank you, Your Highness."

Carefully Nikolas poured three glasses of the vodka, and joined them in a drink.

Necherenkov stared at Nikolas consideringly. "Your Highness, we've come to speak with Princess Emelia."

"There's no need for you to see her."

"Oh, there is," Necherenkov assured him. "She was reported to have made treasonous speeches within earshot of the tsar tonight. And her background is by all accounts a suspicious one—"

"She's no threat to the tsar, or to anyone," Nikolas broke in with a gently persuasive smile. "An attractive woman, but not too bright, you understand? A simple peasant girl, incapable of forming her own opinions. I'm afraid she was just repeating things she had overheard. In the interest of justice, you should hold the real culprit accountable."

"And who is that, Your Highness?"

Nikolas's faint smile vanished. "Me," he said bluntly. "Even the most casual investigation will reveal that I've had a falling-out with the tsar. Everyone knows it. The lifeblood of the country has been drained for the sake of Peter's self-image—I haven't hesitated to say this even in his presence."

Necherenkov regarded him thoughtfully as he downed more vodka. "We'll still have to question your wife, Your Highness."

"It will be a waste of your time." Discreetly Nikolas fished a black velvet bag from his pocket, hefting its satisfying weight in his palm. "I'm sure you're a very influential man . . . I hope you can see fit to arrange things so that she is forgotten."

Receiving the bag from Nikolas, Necherenkov opened it and tilted some of the contents into his palm. The bag was filled with a fortune in perfectly cut and faceted diamonds, most of them fifteen to twenty carats each, a few of them even larger. They glittered in Necherenkov's broad palm like a pool of white fire. Nikolas resisted the urge to smile grimly as he heard the breathing of the two agents quicken.

Necherenkov spoke quietly. "If she is, after all, a stupid peasant woman, there would seem to be no point in questioning her."

"I'm glad we agree."

Necherenkov met his gaze directly. "But in clearing your wife of suspicion, you've taken all the blame on yourself, and we're obligated to bring you to the Kremlin for interrogation."

"Of course." And in spite of the dark certainties facing him, Nikolas heaved a great inward sigh of relief.

For three days Nikolas was the resident of the Beklemishevskaya Tower, one of a line of Kremlin strongholds on the bank of the Moskva River. The stone fortification was dank and cold, and Nikolas saw his breath in the biting air of his cell. Strangely, no one came to question him. All he could do was sit and wait in silence. Twice a day he was given water and a bowl of boiled wheat. There was no furniture in the cell, not a pallet or even a pile of straw. He had two cellmates, both of them with empty eyes and blank faces. They didn't exchange names or make conversation, except to reply to Nikolas's comment that they should at least have been supplied with a blanket.

"No comfort of any kind is to be given to us," one of them said dully. "The crimes of a boyar are much worse than the rebellion of a peasant, because the tsar expects so much more loyalty of his boyars."

The other man, who remained silent, was clearly ill. The cold, damp air of the tower was making his condition worse, causing him to cough and shiver violently. On the third day the two men were taken out of the cell and never returned. Nikolas heard the distant sounds of someone being tortured, the inhuman cries of pain, and he wondered if it was one of them.

He began to remember what it was like when he had been tortured, and for the first time he began to be afraid, the haze of resignation fading a little. He couldn't go through it again. The damage to his body had scarred over and healed. But the damage to his soul . . . no, he wouldn't survive a second time. Huddling on the bare floor, Nikolas braced his side against the cold wall. He had never felt so alone.

After another day or two had passed, he knew he had fallen ill. He became cold and feverish, his thoughts no longer seeming to make sense. Wrapping his arms around himself, he shivered, slept, and finally let his tears fall. In some moments of his delirium he saw ghosts visiting his cell . . . Tasia . . . his father . . . Jacob . . . Misha, his dead brother, who regarded him with a soul-weary face. He shrank from all of them, but sometimes he asked for Emelia . . . Emma . . . who did not come. He was going to die, he told the ghosts; he wanted his wife, wanted to lay his head on her lap and fall asleep forever.

During one of the periods when Nikolas was lucid, he received an unexpected visitor, the tsar himself. Huddled in a corner of the cell, Nikolas watched as the gigantic figure ventured into the dark, foul-smelling quarters.

"Nikolai," Peter said, his deep voice rumbling against the stone walls. "They told me you were ill. I decided to visit you."

"What for?" Nikolas asked, the words rasping in his dry throat.

Peter regarded him as a parent would an errant son. "I wanted to see if some sense could be talked into you. This isn't like you, Nikolai. You haven't been yourself for months. The love you used to have for me, the deep loyalty . . . what happened to all of that?"

Nikolas turned his face away, not bothering to reply.

"You've let a woman ruin you," Peter continued quietly. "A mere peasant woman. She influenced you to turn against me. She wrought some kind of spell on you. Otherwise she never would have taken the place of everything you once loved."

A fit of trembling took hold of Nikolas, and he

gathered himself more tightly in the corner. "I never loved anyone—or anything—until her."

The tsar sighed and squatted before him. "And now she has led you to ruin. Do such destruction and waste come from something that is good?"

"I haven't betrayed you," Nikolas said.

"Perhaps not yet, but the seeds are there. And *I* must be the most important being to you, no one else. Not even God. That is what I need in order to mold Russia into the country it must become." Peter gazed intently into Nikolas's averted face. "Even now," he remarked softly, "you are one of the most beautiful creatures, man or woman, whom I've ever seen. You've been given too much, Nikolai. I think you were destined for a tragic end."

"What do you want from me?" Nikolas muttered, before he was overtaken by a spasm of coughing so violent that he tasted blood on his lips.

Peter's huge, pawlike hand passed over Nikolas's head gently, smoothing his hair as if he were a favorite pet. "I am willing to offer you a second chance, Nikolai. A chance at life, as well as one to regain my favor. I will forgive everything if you will prove your loyalty to me."

Nikolas stared at him blearily. "How would I do that?"

"Dissolve your marriage by making Emelia take the veil. Send her away, and never see her again. You can choose another wife, one who will serve you much better than she. Come back to the life you once had, and rededicate yourself to my service. Promise me these things, and I will have you taken out of here within the hour. I'll command my personal physician to attend you until you are well again."

Nikolas smiled faintly. "I couldn't stay away from her," he said scratchily. "Knowing she was out there . . . never being able to see her, touch her . . ." He shook his head. "No," he said, beginning to cough again until his lungs were on fire.

Peter snatched his hand back and stood up, glaring down at him. "I'm sorry that you value your own life so little. I was mistaken to offer you a second chance. No man who chooses death and treason over life deserves pity."

"Love," Nikolas whispered, laying his head on the floor. "That's what I chose."

The delirium claimed him again, mercifully before anyone came to interrogate him. He was so cold, his body stiff and frozen. None of the dream figures that wandered through his cell took notice of his pleas for a coat, a blanket, a small fire to warm his hands and feet. He thought of his wife, the way her sleek limbs would twine around him, the fiery red sheaves of her hair. *Emelia, I'm cold,* he tried to say, but she was gone, unable to hear him, and he began to shudder so violently that he feared his bones would begin to rattle against the hard stone floor. Figures from the Russian tales of his childhood crept through his cell—ogres, enchanted swans, witches, a firebird flaunting its feathers of red and gold. And then the bird changed to Emma, her face surrounded by the brilliant cinnamon glory of her hair. Nikolas reached out for her, but she shrank from his touch.

"Emma, don't leave," he gasped, but she didn't want him. She drifted away, while he pleaded for her to come to him. *"Emma . . . I need you."* Time went spinning outside his reach, and his life began to ebb away. He felt the darkness cover him, drowning every thought and memory in its fathomless depths.

PART IV

When the clock's unhurried finger
Rounds its beat and strikes adieu
Bidding strangers not to linger,
Midnight will not part us two.

—PUSHKIN

❧ Ten

1877 London

"NIKKI? NIKKI, OPEN your eyes."

He mumbled a protest, wanting to sink back into the comfortable darkness. But the voice, so anxious and impatient, pulled him out of the deep sleep. Frowning, he rubbed his eyes and opened them to narrow slits. He was stretched out on a bed, and his wife was seated on the edge of it.

He was alive . . . and *she* was there, as vivid and beautiful as ever. "Emelia," he breathed, struggling to sit up. Questions collided on his tongue, and he began to talk in a rush.

"Not so quickly! Relax for a minute." Emma leaned over and covered his lips with her fingers, looking at him oddly. "You're speaking in Russian. You know I barely understand a word of it."

He fell silent, bewildered, while he tried to think in English. "I thought I would never see you again," he said finally, his voice hoarse.

"I was beginning to have doubts myself," Emma replied dryly. "At first I thought you might be shamming, until I splashed cold water on your face. When that didn't revive you, I sent for the

301

doctor. He hasn't arrived yet." She leaned over and laid a cool hand on his forehead. "Are you all right? Does your head hurt?"

Nikolas couldn't answer. All his attention was riveted on her. He was filled with frantic impulses—he wanted to snatch her in his arms and pour out his soul to her, but she would think he'd gone insane. The effort of holding still, of not reaching out to her, made his eyes sting and water.

Slowly Emma withdrew her hand. "Why are you staring at me like that?"

Nikolas tore his gaze from her and cast it over his surroundings. His bedroom was the same as always, the dark wood furniture adorned with scrollwork, the mahogany panels on the walls.

Robert Soames was standing nearby, his lean face drawn with concern. He smiled at Nikolas. "We've certainly been worried about you, Your Highness."

Blinking in confusion, Nikolas returned his attention to Emma. "What happened?"

Emma shrugged. "All I know is that you were looking at the painting Soames had restored—which bears a remarkable resemblance to you, by the way—and you turned ghastly white and fell unconscious. Mr. Soames was kind enough to assist me and the servants in carrying you upstairs. You've been insensible for at least an hour."

"An hour," Nikolas repeated numbly. Looking down at himself, he saw that his shirt had been unbuttoned halfway to his waist.

"You weren't breathing very well," Emma said in explanation, a blush staining her cheeks.

Nikolas spread his hands over his chest, feeling the faint, familiar ridges of healed wounds, rubbing to assure himself they were real. Robert Soames turned away, clearly uncomfortable with the sight of the scars. "Perhaps I should allow you a few moments of privacy," the artist said, retreating from the room.

"There's no need—" Emma began, then rolled her eyes as Soames left. A bitter smile touched her lips. "As if you and I would need privacy," she muttered.

Nikolas's head was filled with a cacophony of pictures and words, the past and the present still jumbled in his mind. Overwhelmed with love and need, he reached for Emma. She jerked away sharply. "Don't touch me," she said in a low voice, standing up. "Now that I know you're all right, you can wait for the doctor by yourself. I have things to do. Would you like a glass of water before I go?"

She poured from a china pitcher, and gave him a crystal goblet. Their fingers touched briefly, and Nikolas felt the warm shock of it all through his body. He drank thirstily, gulping the cool water and wiping his mouth with the back of his sleeve.

"You don't seem quite yourself," Emma remarked. "Perhaps all your vodka-drinking is catching up with you. At the pace you've been going, I'm surprised this hasn't happened sooner . . ." Her voice faded as she saw Nikolas staring with hypnotic fascination at the icon on the wall. "What is it? What's going on?"

Slowly Nikolas set the water glass aside and stood up, weaving slightly as he walked toward the Prophet Elijah icon. Since the eighteenth century, the painting had been decorated with jeweled plates that formed a halo around Elijah's head, covered the body of the chariot, and outlined the red cloud. Nikolas brushed his fingers over the surface of the painting and inserted his fingernails under one of the gold plates. He pried it off, ignoring Emma's bewildered questions. Clutching the small plate in his fist, he stared at the painting.

There was a scratch on the edge of the red cloud ... the scratch he had made a hundred and seventy years ago. Nikolas traced it with the tip of his finger, and felt a sudden hot trickle of tears on his face. "It wasn't a dream," he said thickly.

Emma came up behind him. "Why are you behaving so strangely?" she demanded. "Why are you taking that icon apart? Why—" She stopped with a gasp as he turned toward her. "God," she whispered, backing away a step. "What's the matter with you?"

"Stay here with me." Nikolas dropped the thin gold plate to the floor and came toward her slowly, as if one quick movement might startle her into flight. "Emma ... there are things I need to tell you."

"I'm not interested in anything you have to say," she said sharply. "After what I found out today— the way you ruined my relationship with Adam and tore my whole life apart—"

"I'm sorry."

Emma shook her head as if she hadn't heard him correctly. "Well, that's a first! I've never heard you apologize for anything before. Is that supposed to make up for all you've done to me?"

He searched painfully for words. "Something's happened to me ... I don't know how to make you understand. I ... I've never been honest about my feelings for you. I never wanted to admit them, and when they became too strong, I tried to hurt you and keep you at a distance—"

"Is that why you went to bed with another woman?" she asked scornfully. "Because your feelings for me are so strong?"

Deeply ashamed, Nikolas could not meet her gaze. "I won't do that again, Emma. Ever."

"I don't care what you do with yourself. Have a different woman every night, for all I care. Just leave me alone."

"I don't want anyone else." Nikolas caught her in his arms before she could step away. His heart beat in violent joy at being able to hold her again, and his fingers clenched into her pliant flesh with unconscious force. Emma was still, her body stiff with rejection. She pinned him with a coldly accusing stare.

"I'll make you forget all the things I've done," Nikolas said. "I swear I'll make you happy . . . just let me try. All I want is to love you. You don't even have to love me back."

Emma froze, while the words rang in long-forgotten echoes. "What?" she asked faintly, beginning to tremble.

Casting aside all pride and caution, he laid his heart at her feet. "You have to know the truth. I've loved you for a long time, Emma. I would do anything for you, even give my life—"

Emma wrenched free of him, glaring and shivering. "What in God's name are you trying to do—drive me insane? For weeks you've devoted yourself to being a heartless pig, then suddenly you have a fainting spell in the sitting room, and you wake up and say you *love* me? What kind of perverse game is this?"

"It's not a game."

"You're not capable of love. Your main concern has always been—and will always be—yourself."

"In the past that was true. But not now. Now I've finally realized—"

"Don't you dare try to claim you've suddenly decided to change your ways! Only a fool would believe that of a man who rejects his own child."

Nikolas winced at that. "I'm going to make it up to Jacob," he said grimly. "I'll be a good father to him. He's going to be safe and happy for the rest of his life—"

"Enough of this!" Her face was red with fury. "I never dreamed even you could be this malicious. It's one thing to deceive me with your empty promises, but if you dare lie to that little boy and make him believe you care for him, you'll cripple him emotionally."

"I do care for him."

"You'll abandon him as callously as you do everyone else—and I won't be able to pick up all the pieces. Oh, men are such lying cowards! You make someone believe they can depend on you, and then you leave without a thought. You won't have a chance to betray Jake and me that way—I won't let it happen."

"From now on, you can depend on me. I'll prove it to you a thousand times over." Nikolas took her stiff hand in his and brought it to his mouth, pressing his lips against her hard knuckles. "I won't hurt you again. Believe in me."

Emma stared into his eyes, and whatever she saw made her breath catch. Twisting away, she strode from the room. "Damn you," she muttered, and slammed the door in her wake.

* * *

Emma curled up on a settee in her private sitting room, her arms wrapped around her knees. Questions churned through her brain. She had to give Nikolas credit for finding a way to surprise her. Nothing else would have attained quite this level of mockery and malice. He was trying to make her believe he cared for her, and then he would scorn and humiliate her. What a diabolical mind he had!

But his eyes . . . there had been such a strange vulnerability in them. What in heaven's name had happened to him? She thought back to the scene in the library: one minute Nikolas had been his usual arrogant self, and the next he had seen the portrait of his ancestor and fainted dead away. "It looks like apoplexy," Robert Soames had said as he and Emma had knelt beside Nikolas on the floor.

"But he's too young for that!" she had cried, pillowing Nikolas's head in her lap. "Oh, God, maybe his drinking caused it. Please, go send for a doctor!" She had cradled his head carefully, smoothing his sun-streaked hair. The servants had been enlisted to help carry him to his room, and Emma had stayed by his side every second. She wasn't certain why she had been so afraid. After all, it wasn't as if they had a real marriage. There was no love between them. And yet . . . when his eyes had opened, she had been overwhelmed with relief.

What had happened during that still, silent hour to make him behave so strangely upon waking? He had said he loved her. She laughed incredulously, feeling close to tears.

"I swear I'll make you happy . . . just let me try. All I want is to love you. You don't even have to love me back."

Those words had shaken her badly. Nikolas had a talent for cutting through people's defenses, especially hers. "Tasia warned me about what you were like," Emma said softly. "She said you would lie, manipulate, and betray me, and she was right. Well, I'm going to put a stop to your game-playing, Nikki, for Jacob's sake as well as my own."

She went to Nikolas's room, squaring her shoulders as she approached the partially open doorway. Dr. Weide, a small, thoughtful-looking man with gray hair and spectacles, was replacing instruments in his medical bag.

"How is he?" Emma asked briskly, entering the room.

"Your Highness," the doctor murmured with a smile, coming forward to kiss her hand. "From the haste with which I was summoned, I expected to find a man on his deathbed. However, your husband appears to be in extraordinarily good health. Not a thing is wrong with him."

"What could account for his fainting spell?" she asked, frowning. "He was unconscious for approximately an hour."

The doctor shook his head. "I can find no apparent physical reason for it."

"Well, he wasn't playacting," Emma said. "I did everything short of sticking pins in him to make him wake up."

"There are many things we don't understand about the mind," Dr. Weide replied. "As I understand it, the sight of a particular portrait caused Prince Nikolas to faint. One could speculate that perhaps it reminded him of a traumatic event in his past."

Emma stared at her husband speculatively. His

expression was closed, secretive, and she sensed his impatience to have the doctor leave. "Traumatic event," she murmured. "Well, you've had enough of those, haven't you?"

Nikolas concentrated on fastening his shirt buttons. "It won't happen again."

"Please inform me if it does," Dr. Weide said. "In the meantime, my best wishes to both of you."

"I'll see you out," Emma said.

The doctor shook his head. "Please stay with your husband, Your Highness. I'm perfectly capable of finding my way through the mansion—I think." He winked and departed quietly.

Emma folded her arms as she regarded her husband. "How do you feel?"

"Fine. There was no need for the doctor to examine me."

"A little poking and prodding never hurt anyone."

Nikolas snorted. "Wait until you're the one being poked." He stood and tucked his shirt into the lean waist of his trousers.

Emma shifted her weight from one foot to the other, uncomfortable with the intimacy of watching her husband dress. "I came to give you a warning," she said brusquely. "I may very well leave here soon, and take Jake with me."

He looked at her suddenly, his gaze searing. He made no reply, but his rejection of the notion was evident in every tense line of his body.

"I haven't yet made my decision," Emma continued calmly. "However, the first moment that I feel you're doing harm to Jake or to me, I'll take him away in the blink of an eye."

"Try it," Nikolas said softly. "See what happens." His tone was casual, but it had a chilling effect on her. "Jake stays here. He's my son. And you're my wife."

"The all-powerful Prince Nikolas," she mocked. "Perhaps everyone else is afraid of you, but not me. I'm not some helpless creature you can bully and take advantage of. And you can't make me stay here."

"I can make you want to stay."

There was still power in his arrogance, so pure and distilled that it took Emma's breath away. She didn't reply as he must have wanted, by asking how or why, or by trying to argue with him. Instead she began to retreat. "I've told you what I intend," she muttered.

That line should have marked her exit. Nikolas came after her, however, and loomed over her until she felt physically intimidated. For a woman who played with tigers and wild creatures, that feeling was alarmingly rare. "Before you leave, let me tell you what I intend," Nikolas murmured. "I'm going to be back in your bed soon. I'm going to be the husband I should have been from the beginning."

"The devil you are!"

"I won't let you go. I need you too much."

He had never been like this before, direct and shockingly sincere, his emotions unveiled. It was far more threatening than his customary insouciance. "You don't need anyone," she managed to say.

"That's not true. Look closer, Emma. Look at me, and tell me what you see."

She couldn't obey. She was too afraid of what she might see in his eyes. Ducking her head, she shouldered her way past him and fled. He let her go, thank God, although she felt his hot gaze trained on her until she reached the end of the hallway and disappeared from sight.

Nikolas remained alone for a few minutes. He wanted a drink, something sharp and bracing, but he would not have one. There would be no more pleasantly soothing numbness, no inviting alcoholic blanket over his emotions. He needed clarity. He hated the bleak existence he had fashioned for himself, and he couldn't stand the hostility in Emma's face. If only she could give him the understanding and trust that she had bestowed so long ago. He must find a way to make her love him once more.

"Emelia," he whispered, yearning to know what had happened to his wife. Had she suffered after his death? Had she found some source of comfort? Had there been another man for her? The thought filled him with fury and jealousy. He needed to know what had become of her, or the unanswered questions would drive him mad. He went to the library and fumbled through old books and records, scavenging what scraps of information he could find. There was nothing about the fate of Emelia Vasilievna, and precious little about their son, Alexei.

It was written in one family volume that the young man Alexei Angelovsky had appeared suddenly in Moscow after a childhood spent in seclusion in a village east of Kiev. Apparently he had led a good life, amassing land and wealth for the family. He was helped in these endeavors by a long-lasting affair with Empress Elizabeth. Prince Alexei was known as a charming and cultured man, a patron of the arts who played the violin. He had married eventually and produced two children, both of them surviving into adulthood. But what of his mother? What had happened to Emelia?

Nikolas shoved the pile of books aside with a curse. He would hire a historian to find out, and send him to Russia with a troop of translators, if necessary. He rested his arms on the library desk and dug his fingers into his thick hair. Perhaps he had gone mad, to search so desperately for the history of a woman who had lived a century and a half ago. Had it really happened? Was the scratch on the Elijah icon a coincidence? Perhaps his tormented mind was conjuring fantasies in order to keep from focusing on the wreck he had made of his life.

Springing up suddenly, he headed upstairs to the nursery. He needed to see Jacob, to make things right with his son. God grant that the boy would forgive him for abandoning him. Nikolas's feet slowed on the stairs, and he came to a halting stop. He forced himself to admit the truth—that he was afraid of his own son. He hadn't the vaguest idea of how to be a father. His own father had been an abusive brute. His memories of childhood were so pain-ridden and bleak that he had no wish to see reminders of it in the eyes of his own child. He didn't want to hurt Jacob, and yet he already had. "I've denied and neglected him," Nikolas muttered. "God knows a parent can't do worse than that."

How should he talk to the boy? How could he make Jacob understand that he could depend on him as a father? Now it seemed incredible that he had actually planned to send the child away. He hadn't let himself care about Jacob then, but now he couldn't stop himself. He wanted to take care of the boy, to give him everything his heart desired. There were so many delights in the world to show him. The sprawling estate in the south, where they could build sand castles and collect shells on the beach. Or his castle in Ireland, where they could ride across the moors, eat picnic lunches, and fish and swim in the river. He would take Jacob sailing on one of his yachts, or hunting at one of his estates in the country.

I could have done all that for him already, Nikolas thought wretchedly. *I could have given him a good life, and instead I turned my back on him.* He continued up the stairs and reached the nursery. Hesitating at the door, which was ajar, he tapped on the panel before entering.

Jacob was sitting on the bare floor, surrounded by odds and ends: a pot from the kitchen, an assortment of stones, a tree branch, and a piece of wood carved in the shape of a bear. Nikolas recognized the wooden figure as the handiwork of his carriage driver, who was fond of whittling in his spare time. The thought that one of his servants had provided a toy for his son, when he had given him nothing, wrenched Nikolas's heart. He glanced around the nursery, which had long been in disuse. Except for a small bed, an old trunk, and a dusty, antique rocking horse, the room was painfully empty.

Jacob stared at him curiously, with eyes exactly like his own.

He reminds me of Misha, Nikolas thought in a flash of agony, but somehow he managed to smile.

"Hello, Jake," he said quietly. "I thought I would visit you up here. Is that all right?"

The boy nodded and began to play with his wooden bear.

"Did you know the bear is the Russians' favorite animal?" Nikolas remarked, sitting cross-legged beside him on the floor. "We used to worship the bear as a god. There is a superstition that the presence of a bear drives away all evil spirits."

Jacob stared at the carved animal in his hands, then reached over to nudge the pot nearer to Nikolas. "What about frogs?"

Lifting the piece of mesh that covered the pot, Nikolas saw that it had been filled with a half inch of water and a large, flat stone, all for the comfort of a slick olive-colored frog. Nikolas smiled and deftly picked up the frog, whose legs thrashed a few times. "A handsome specimen," he said, giving it an admiring glance. "Where did you catch him?"

"In the garden pond, yesterday. Emma helped me."

"I'm not surprised," Nikolas said wryly, replacing the frog in its temporary home. He would have liked to see his wife splashing in the formal estate garden pond in pursuit of a frog.

"Emma says I have to set him free tonight."

"You like Emma very much, don't you?"

Jacob nodded, carefully setting a stone on top of the mesh to keep it secured over the pot. He glanced at Nikolas with a troubled expression. "You were sick today. I saw you fall on the floor."

"I'm all right now," Nikolas said firmly. "I feel better than I have in a long time." In the silence that followed, he gazed around the room and shook his head in displeasure. "You need some toys, Jake. Some books and games, not to mention furniture." He reached over to the trunk and lifted the creaking lid. There were some faded children's books printed in Russian, a box of playing cards, and an old wooden box covered with scars and nicks. A faint smile touched his lips, and he pulled the heavy, rattling box out of the trunk. "I haven't seen this since I was about your age."

While Jake watched with increasing interest, Nikolas unwound the leather strap that secured the box. Inside were two complete armies of painted metal soldiers, and a lacquered board that unfolded into a battlefield. It was a Crimean War set, complete with cannon, horses, wagons, and a tiny bridge. "These are the English," Nikolas said, holding up a figure dressed in red, "and the ones in blue are the Russians. My brother, Misha, and I used to play with these. In real life, the English won that particular war, but when Misha and I played, the Russians always triumphed." He handed the soldier to Jacob. "Now they belong to you."

Jake carefully examined one figure after another. "Will you play with me?" he asked. "You can be the English."

Nikolas grinned as he helped his son set up the battlefield in neat rows of men and artillery. He stole frequent glances at the child, filled with pride that Jake was his. He was a handsome boy, his features bold and finely drawn, his eyes shaded with thick black lashes and heavy, winged brows. There was a touch of the exotic about him, a hint of the Tartar ancestor that had given the Angelovskys their stubborn will.

"Jake," Nikolas said quietly, "there is something important I want to talk to you about."

The boy paused and looked at him, one small hand clutching a toy horse far too tightly. As if he were afraid of what Nikolas would say.

"I'm sorry about your mother," Nikolas continued slowly. "I should have told you that before. I know how difficult it is for you. But now that you're here with me, I would like us to spend time together, and come to know each other. And . . . what I want above all else is for you to live with me from now on."

"Forever?"

"Yes, forever."

"You're not going to send me away, then?"

Nikolas swallowed hard. "No, Jake. You're my son."

"Does that mean I won't be a bastard anymore?"

The word was a cold shock to Nikolas. It filled him with acute remorse . . . and fury. "Who called you that?"

"The people in the village."

Nikolas was silent for a moment. He reached out to smooth his son's rumpled black hair with a hand that wasn't quite steady. "That's because I didn't marry your mother. That wasn't your fault, Jake. I should have taken responsibility for you. If anyone calls you a bastard again, you tell them you're an Angelovsky, a Russian prince. You're going to have the finest of everything—education, homes, thoroughbred horses—and damn anyone who says I'm spoiling you."

Absorbing the speech, the boy stared at him with those unnerving eyes. "Why didn't you come for me?" he asked in a small voice. "Why didn't Mama tell me about you?"

"I . . ." It took all of Nikolas's strength to meet the child's gaze and answer honestly. "I've made many mistakes in my life, Jake. I've been selfish and bitter, and I've caused everyone around me to suffer. But I promise you, I'll try to be a good father. I'll give you the best of myself . . . whatever that's worth."

Emma went for a hard ride one morning, catapulting through the local village and ignoring the startled stares of the people she passed. She knew she was an odd sight: a red-haired virago, an amazon on horseback, racing at top speed as if the devil were chasing her. She didn't care whom she shocked—this was the only way she knew to vent her emotions.

She rode until the horse was tired, and then she headed back to the Angelovsky estate. The exercise had helped, but it had provided only a temporary escape. The fact was, she was living with a stranger. He still looked like Nikolas, gestured and moved and spoke like Nikolas, but no one could deny that he had changed profoundly. She didn't know why, or what had caused it, and the mystery frustrated her to no end. Two weeks had passed since his fainting episode, and he still showed no sign of reverting back to his old self. The servants could barely do their work, their astonishment plain as they witnessed the transformation of their master.

To begin with, Nikolas had cut back his business dealings, and devoted a part of each day to Jake. The boy seemed to blossom under his attention.

Nikolas took his son with him everywhere . . . on walks through London, on carriage rides in the park, on visits to the sawmill, the carriage-house, and any other place Jake found interesting. Jake no longer took his meals alone but ate with Nikolas and Emma in the formal dining room, and when Nikolas worked at his desk in the library, Jake sat nearby with a pile of toys. Most astonishing of all, Nikolas's drinking had stopped, except for an occasional glass of wine at night.

Emma was invited to join them on every excursion, but she refused most of the invitations. She was bewildered by what was happening, and she was doing her best to cope with the way Nikolas had turned their life at the Angelovsky estate upside down. He bought a shiny black pony for Jake—named Ruslan, after his favorite fairy-tale hero—and also a little lacquered carriage to pull behind it. He filled the nursery with toys and furniture, and played cards or board games with his son in the parlor each night.

Emma was disgruntled at how quickly Jacob had taken to Nikolas. Children gave their trust with such frightening ease, and Jacob was clearly beginning to adore his father. There was a bond between them, albeit fragile, that came from an intrinsic likeness. Both of them were independent, perceptive, mistrustful of the world; both of them seemed to crave security. And they apparently found it in each other.

Lately Nikolas had begun to interview a parade of nannies and tutors, consulting Jake in a way that offended or amused almost everyone. Adults were never supposed to ask a child's opinion about anything, especially significant matters, but Nikolas didn't seem to know or care about that. Jake reveled in his new life, laughing, yelling, becoming more unruly with each day that passed, but he was so endearing that no one was inclined to complain about it. Finally Emma decided to suggest that Jake needed some discipline.

Privately she approached Nikolas, after Jake had been put to bed at ten o'clock in the evening. "I just want to point out that children need some regulation in their lives," she said, hovering in the doorway of her husband's bedroom. "It would be better for Jake if he had a consistent bedtime. Last night he went to bed at nine, and tonight, ten. And not only that, you let him eat three helpings of cake at tea this afternoon, and he had no appetite at supper—"

"He's had enough limits in his life. For a while he's going to enjoy himself."

"You're thinking only of your own guilty conscience, and not of Jake's welfare," she snapped. "That's a disservice to everyone involved. You must stop indulging him like this!"

"But then I'll have no one left to spoil," he said softly, his eyes suddenly touched with small twin flames that disconcerted her terribly. "Unless you're volunteering for the position."

"Don't be ridiculous."

Nikolas smiled slightly at her confusion, and gestured toward the pair of velvet-upholstered chairs next to the glowing fireplace. "Come in, *ruyshka*. We'll talk and have a drink—"

"No," she said, trying to look anywhere but at her husband. He wore a velvet robe of rich mink brown, and his sun-streaked hair was in disarray. Rotten husband or no, he was still one of the most attractive men she had ever seen in her life. "I'm tired. I'm going to bed."

He moved even closer to her, and picked up a long red curl that lay over her shoulder. "Don't worry about Jake," he murmured, toying with the lock of her hair. "He'll be fine."

Emma wet her lips nervously. It felt as though her hair were a living rope, a conductor of sensation. She imagined his hands on her skin, the caress of his fingertips, and her heart beat madly. "I can't help but worry," she said. "It's been very confusing, watching you spend so much time with Jake when you couldn't stand the sight of him before."

"Yes, I know." He wound the red coil around his fingers and held it tightly. "When I first saw Jake, all I could see was how much he looked like Misha. It hurt to look at him and remember my dead brother." His gaze became shadowed, the thick gold lashes concealing his emotions. "Do you remember when I told you how my father abused us? The worst of it was done to Misha, perhaps because he was more helpless than me. I would try and console my brother when I found him crying and bleeding after my father's attacks. You can't imagine the rage and guilt I felt, seeing such a vulnerable creature being hurt—" He stopped and smiled crookedly. "Well, perhaps you can. Anyway, I could do nothing for Misha. I was too young to protect him. But I can take care of my son, and give him everything he needs to be happy. It's like having a second chance."

Emma didn't move, imprisoned by the silence between them, the yearning that hung heavy and warm in the air. Nikolas had always known how to make her respond to him. She hated him for this charade, and at the same time she desperately wanted it to be true. He was pretending to be the kind of man she could have fallen in love with, the kind of man she had once dreamed of. And he was so damn good at his performance that every now and then she caught herself believing him for a few moments. Her heart ached from the strain of wanting to love a man who wasn't worthy of it, who would scorn and betray her when it suited him.

"Why are you doing this to me?" she asked in a pained whisper, betraying tears coming to her eyes.

"Emma," he said softly, releasing her hair.

She jerked back and stared at him, shaking her head. Before he could say a word, she strode away rapidly, trying to keep herself from breaking into an outright run.

After midnight, when Emma was sleeping soundly, Nikolas entered her sitting room. He stared at her bedroom door, left partially ajar. He imagined he could hear the soft sound of her breathing. Slowly he sat on a velvet-covered chair and picked up one of the carved animals in the little menagerie he had given her. The amber tiger, its small, sleek body warming in his hands. Drawing his finger along the polished back of the figurine, Nikolas continued to stare into the shadows of his wife's bedroom. He was transfixed with lust and loneliness, knowing her warm body was so near. But he wouldn't take her until she welcomed him, loved him, as Emelia had.

"Emelia, what happened to you?" he whispered in Russian, closing his hand around the tiger in a tight grip. He had questioned the family servants, including the Sidarova sisters, to find out if they knew anything about Emelia beyond the familiar old tale, but they had no more stories to impart. Subsequently he had hired one of the curators of the British Museum, Sir Vincent Almay, to travel to Russia and examine both private and public records to determine the fate of Princess Emelia. Nikolas didn't believe his family would interfere with Almay's search. Perhaps one of his sisters might even help in the quest. Until he knew what had become of his wife, Nikolas would never be at peace.

If only he could have done more for Emelia, protected her . . .

He forced himself to stay in the chair, though he ached with the need to go to Emma and wrap her in his arms. *You promised you would remember*, he thought fiercely, staring into his wife's room. *You said you would know me.*

The next day Emma received a surprise visitor while Nikolas and Jake were away on one of their rambles through London. As she enjoyed a last cup of tea after a hearty breakfast, she was approached by the butler, Stanislaus, who presented a silver tray with a calling card positioned exactly in the center. Emma's eyes widened as she saw Lord Milbank's name on the card.

"Shall I send him away, Your Highness?" Stanislaus asked.

"No," she said distractedly. "Show Lord Milbank into the drawing room."

The butler's Slavic features showed no expression, but his black brows inched upward toward his shock of white hair. "Very well."

Emma smoothed her hair, which had been

braided with green silk ribbons and pinned to the nape of her neck. She yanked her forest-green velvet dress into place, straightening the bustle in back and the silk draperies in front as she hurried to the drawing room. Why would Adam call on her, especially considering his loathing of her husband? Perhaps he wanted to discuss the past with her, or even reestablish his friendship with her, though for what purpose she couldn't fathom. It didn't matter—his presence here suited *her* purposes without a doubt. Nikolas would find out about it, and he would be infuriated. She wanted her husband to feel some of the hurt and wounded pride he had made her feel in the past. Perhaps it was wrong to use Adam toward that end, but she didn't care. She had been used by both of them, Adam and Nikolas, and it was time the tables were turned.

Stanislaus guided Lord Milbank to the drawing room, and inquired if there was anything Emma required.

"Tea, please," she said, and the butler left them with a quiet murmur. Emma approached Adam, the man she had always considered the love of her life, with outstretched hands. "Adam," she said with a smile. "I had intended to write you a letter and invite you to tea. How nice to see you!"

Clearly surprised by her welcome, he took her hands and gripped them lightly. His boyish face looked troubled, but his brown eyes were alight with hope. "I had merely intended to leave a card—"

"No, stay and have some tea with me," she insisted. "If you have time, that is."

"There could be no better use for my time." Adam walked farther into the room, carrying his hat and riding whip. He shook his head in wonder as he glanced at his surroundings. "All this luxury, and yet you look quite at home here."

"It *is* my home," Emma said with a light laugh. "But I haven't changed all that much. I spend most of my time in the menagerie with the usual bill of players—Manchu, Cleo, Presto—"

"How are your animals?"

"Oh, they've taken to their surroundings quite well."

"And you?"

Her smile faded, and she seated herself in a chair with embroidered cushions, carefully arranging her skirts. "I still have some adjusting to do," she said honestly. "Nikolas is very . . . confusing. He's not easy to understand, or to live with."

"Does he make you happy, Emma?"

It was far too intimate a conversation for a man and a woman married to other people to be having. However, their past relationship made it far too easy for Emma to slip back into the habit of talking to Adam comfortably.

"No . . . but I'm not as *un*happy as I thought I might be. It's impossible to explain."

Adam sat beside her, his brown eyes melancholy as he looked at her. He took a long breath. "I've thought about you quite a lot after our last conversation. There were other things I wanted to tell you, but there didn't seem to be time. All I could think about then was how much I wanted you to know the truth about what your husband did to us. Before I saw you again, I wanted you to have a chance to reflect on it."

"Oh, I've reflected on it," Emma said grimly. "I've also told Nikolas exactly what I thought of his manipulation."

"He ruined both our lives, Em. I'm married to a woman I don't love. It just seemed to be the only thing to do. I knew I couldn't have you, there was just too much opposition from your family and Nikolas, and then I met Charlotte—"

"Please," Emma said with discomfort, holding up a hand. "I don't want to talk about her."

"Certainly. But let me at least tell you . . . we're not happy together, Charlotte and I. We don't suit. Not as you and I did." Adam ran a hand through his long, silken sheaves of brown hair, looking impatient and perturbed. There was an edge to his voice, as well as a glint in his eyes, that was unfamiliar to her. "I keep thinking about what we might have had," he said bluntly. "Do you ever wonder what it would be like if you and I had married each other?"

"I used to wonder all the time," she admitted. "But lately . . . no, I suppose I don't allow myself to think about it anymore."

"I can't stop dwelling on what was taken from me. Your husband slithered into our lives and took away everything I wanted. I have the damnedest fantasies about the things I'd like to do to him, various ways to cause him incredible pain and degradation—" He stopped in astonishment as Emma began to laugh.

"I'm sorry!" She tried to stifle her gasps of amusement. "It's just . . . you're not the first, believe me! I think almost everyone who's ever known Nikolas has felt that way about him."

"I don't think it's amusing," Adam said with extreme dignity, color etching across his cheekbones.

Emma sobered somewhat, though a few bubbles of laughter were still trapped in her throat. "You're right. Nikolas is an absolute scoundrel."

"It tortures me to think of you with him—the way he must abuse you, the way he has humiliated you by forcing his bastard son on you—"

"No," she said quickly. "I *want* Jake to live here. I care about the boy—and so does Nikolas." She paused as the truth of her remark resounded in her very bones. "I thought Nikolas couldn't love anyone," she continued in a wondering tone, "but he adores his son. Either Nikolas has changed, or . . . there's something in him I never noticed before. Either way, he's the most caring father I've ever seen—aside from my own."

"Your father!" Adam said indignantly. "You're talking about the two people who both managed to keep us apart! Domineering, manipulative men who like to control everyone around them!" He took her hand and squeezed it tightly. "Em, don't you remember how it was? We loved each other so much, and we were torn apart by those two and their own selfish need of you. They did it so carelessly, so *easily*—" He broke off with a frustrated sound.

"Yes," Emma murmured. "Why was it so easy? If we truly loved each other, why were they able to separate us?"

They were both silent then, thinking back to that time just six months ago.

Emma didn't feel any of the pain she had expected, talking about the past. No heartache or longing. To her surprise, it was doing her good, helping to free her from the bitterness and hurt.

Even more astonishing, Adam had lost some of the magic sparkle that her memory had endowed him with; he was a little less handsome, a little less perfect, than she had thought. In fact, he seemed rather *ordinary* in some ways. The revelation perplexed her greatly. Adam no longer made her heart throb with joy, or filled her with intoxicating delight.

I no longer want him the way I once did, she thought.

"You've become so beautiful," he murmured, staring at her. "So queenly and elegant."

"I haven't changed a bit," she said self-consciously.

"Yes, you have. You used to have the most endearing touch of uncertainty, a look in your eyes as if you wanted to hide away from the rest of the world. Now that's gone, and you're so polished . . . mature . . . indomitable."

Emma wrinkled her nose and laughed. "Indomitable? That's a word I would use to describe a statue or a big ship—or a mountain!"

Adam smiled back at her. "You're like a full-blown rose. Is that better?"

"Much."

He seemed to treasure the moment between them. "Both of us smiling and comfortable with each other," he mused. "Just like it used to be. Do you remember how it was . . . how happy we made each other? I've never felt like that before or since."

"Let's look at it honestly," Emma said, staring at him steadily. "You also wanted me because of my family's money. If I hadn't come with the promise of a significant dowry, you would never have been interested in me."

"I wanted *you*, first and foremost. If you came with a large dowry, so much the better. Was that such a terrible attitude? Why shouldn't I like having money, and all the security and comfort it brings?"

"You have money now. You've married into quite a nice little fortune."

A strange look came into his eyes, something hard and bright and pained. "It doesn't make up for losing you. Nothing will."

Emma tried to think of some comment to ease the sudden tension between them, when she became aware of someone else entering the drawing room. Expecting it was a maid with the requested tea tray, she looked up with a trace of relief. To her dismay, she saw her husband standing a few feet inside the doorway.

She should have been pleased at this bit of good luck. She had never dreamed the timing would be so perfect, having Nikolas see her in the midst of a cozy chat with her former suitor. Instead she was seized with cold worry. She had meant to stir up trouble, and now she wasn't so certain she wanted it.

Nikolas's face was flushed. Strange, he was usually so adept at hiding his feelings—but he looked absolutely furious, as if some demonic frenzy were about to be turned loose. Adam Milbank stood up with his fists clenched, looking not defensive but equally enraged. Hatred seethed in the air like a living thing. Emma was amazed by the explosive silence. Once she might have provoked a fight between the two of them, and taken great pleasure in it, but now she tried to defuse the situation.

"Nikki," she said with a shallow smile, "you're back early. I was just having a conversation with Lord Milbank, waiting for some tea to be brought in—"

"I'm afraid I don't have time for tea," Adam interrupted, his gaze locked with her husband's. "I've just recalled a pressing engagement. I must leave at once."

"Oh, that's too bad," Emma said instantly, and tried to usher him toward the door. "It was pleasant to see you. Please give our regards to Lady Milbank."

Nikolas spoke then, his tone simmering with belligerence. "This is the last time you'll come sniffing around my wife, Milbank. Don't try it again, or I'll rip you limb from limb."

Rather than fear, the statement provoked a flash of malevolent defiance from Adam. He stopped near the door, his arm like steel beneath Emma's tugging grip. "This isn't the last you'll see of me," he said in a low hiss. "You were once able to smash my dreams to bits because I was afraid of you. I'm not afraid any longer. I'm going to even the score, and I promise you won't have to wait for long. I owe it to Emma as well as myself."

Emma's hand fell away from Adam, and she stared at him in surprise. She had never heard him speak like that before. He strode away rapidly, leaving her to face her husband, who watched Adam's departure with a contemptuous curl to his lip.

"Where is Jake?" she asked, trying to appear relaxed, even though her stomach was pierced with needles of anxiety.

"When Stanislaus told me that Milbank was here, I sent Jake upstairs." His gaze traveled over her in a quick sweep. "Did you invite him here?"

"No, he was making a social call—although I *will* invite him or anyone else I choose, and I won't ask your permission!"

Nikolas took a step toward her, his expression darkening. "I won't abide his presence in my home."

"After all you've done to me, you have no right to complain about any of my friends or anything I choose to do with them."

"I'm not complaining. I'm telling you to stay the hell away from him."

"You arrogant, conceited— You can be a petty dictator with everyone else, but not me! And stop treating me as if I'm a fool, putting on this jealousy act when I know perfectly well that you don't give a damn about me—"

"I love you," he growled. "Damn you for not believing it!"

She laughed sharply. "You have such a sweet way of showing it."

"I do love you," Nikolas said through his teeth. "So much that I'm going to explode. Do you have any idea of how much I need you? I nearly go insane every night, knowing you're so damn close, alone in your bed—"

He broke off and seized her in an unbreakable grip, leaving her no chance of retreat. "Emma," he murmured, pulling her close until she could feel the tremor in his body, the tightly leashed power that strained to be free. He was intensely aroused, the taut ridge of flesh burning against her loins. Emma was startled to feel a throb of response in her own body. Her pulse thrummed as if a resonant chord had been struck within her. Suddenly she knew she wanted him to hold her like this—she had wanted it for weeks.

She felt his lips on hers, eager and hard and sweet; felt the pressure of his hands as he urged her higher against his body. His lungs shuddered with a breath of relief, and he kissed her more deeply, greedily searching the warm interior of her mouth. She could smell the cold outdoor air on his clothes, and the scents of wool and tea that mingled in pleasantly familiar harmony. She flexed her body around him, arms tightening and legs pressing to hold him in her sphere. Her breath came fast, driven by pleasure and excitement. Nikolas had never kissed her like this before, not with skill or technique, but with raw feeling. The sensations climbed too far, too fast, and she broke away with a fearful sob.

Nikolas released her without a struggle, staring at her with hot golden eyes.

Emma fought to catch her breath, and clasped her arms around her middle. She had never felt so defenseless, so horrifyingly vulnerable. In that moment she discarded all plans of pitting herself against him or putting him in his place. She had to stay away from him if she was to have any chance of keeping herself whole. "Don't bother me like this again," she said shakily. "If you need a woman so badly, find someone else. *I don't want you.* Even if I did find pleasure in it, I would hate myself afterward." Her throat clenched, not allowing any more words, and she fled the drawing room.

Nikolas followed Emma purposefully. He wasn't finished yet. He wanted to know exactly what had been said between her and Milbank, and how Emma felt about her former suitor. She headed outside toward the menagerie, her green skirts swishing along the cold ground and billowing in the blustering wind.

"Emma," he snapped, and she glared at him over her shoulder.

"Go away! I don't want to talk to you!"

"Why did Milbank call on you? What does he want?"

"He wants to be friends with me," she said scornfully. "Nothing more."

"Like hell," Nikolas muttered, following her into the menagerie.

"Do *not* come in here, Nikki!" Emma's voice floated from the direction of the tiger's pen. "I want to spend a few minutes of peace and quiet with my . . ."

Suddenly there was silence.

"Emma?" Nikolas frowned, walking cautiously into the building. Then he understood why Emma was quiet. His heart stopped as he saw Manchu's pen.

Jake was in there with the tiger.

❧ Eleven

NIKOLAS COULDN'T BREATHE or think, his body frozen with a kind of fear he had never known before. The locking pin to the pen's opening had been pulled out, and Jake had lifted the latch to walk inside. The boy stood at one side of the enclosure, while the tiger crouched in the center. Manchu grumbled in confusion and annoyance as he watched the small creature intrude on his territory.

Slowly Emma turned to look at Nikolas. Her face was pale, her eyebrows standing out in glowing red arcs. Her stiff lips twitched as if she wanted to say something, but she too seemed robbed of the power of speech.

Emma's thoughts clicked at a speed a hundred times faster than usual. She forced the terror back and stared at the tiger, trying to assess his mood. She didn't like the intense focus Manchu maintained on the child. Such keenly patient attention could precede a sudden attack. His spray of white whiskers bristled as he approached the boy cautiously, one paw at a time. Although Manchu didn't have claws, he still had teeth—fifteen on each side of the skull, including long canines that pierced the neck vertebrae of prey to kill with speedy efficiency, and bladelike carnassials. A tiger had powerful jaw muscles to clamp down on struggling prey, either biting at the nape of the neck to sever the spinal cord, or crushing the throat until the victim suffocated.

For a creature of Jake's small size, Manchu would probably use the nape bite. But Manchu seemed ambivalent, and Emma realized with fearful hope that he hadn't yet committed to the attack. She attracted his attention with a cheerful whistle, striding to his empty scraps bucket and lifting it as if it were heavy with meat.

"Manchu!" she called, carrying the bucket to the far end of the pen, away from Jake. She stayed outside the enclosure, calling to the tiger. "Come over here, you handsome boy ... come see what I have!"

The tiger obeyed slowly, padding toward her with a low-pitched, whiny meow. At the same time, Nikolas darted to the pen, lifted the latch, and slipped inside. Aware of the sudden entrance of yet another person in his enclosure, Manchu growled in frustration and whipped around, ignoring Emma's voice. Nikolas snatched his son in a bruising grip and carried him out, slamming the door shut just as the tiger reached it.

"Papa," Jake cried indignantly, squirming to be free, "I didn't want to come out yet! Papa, let go!"

But Nikolas couldn't let go, only held the small body tightly and shuddered in relief. Emma dropped the bucket and leaned against a nearby wall, dizzy from the pounding of her heart and the flood of fear in her veins.

When Nikolas could speak, he set the boy down and sank to his haunches, staring intently into the small face. "What are you doing in here?" he asked, his voice thick. "I sent you upstairs to the nursery."

"I didn't want to go there. I wanted to see the tiger." Jake wore a defiant but unhappy expression, still not understanding the danger he had been in.

"You've been told never to visit the menagerie without Emma or me."

"Manchu wouldn't hurt me, Papa. He *likes* me."

Nikolas looked pale and grim. "You disobeyed me, Jake. I don't want to punish you, but you've left me no choice. You're not allowed to visit the menagerie for a month." While the child protested and struggled, Nikolas turned him over his knee and delivered three resounding spanks to his backside. Jake howled and began to cry from surprise. Standing the child up before him, Nikolas spoke hoarsely. "That tiger is dangerous, as are the rest of these animals. You scared the hell out of Emma and me. I don't want anything to happen to you— that's why you must follow the rules we set, even if you don't always understand the reason for them."

"Yes, Papa," Jake sobbed, ducking his head to hide his tears.

Nikolas pulled him close, holding him tightly, and the child's arms came around his neck. "All right," he murmured. "Everything's forgiven—just remember to do as I tell you."

"Can I go play in the nursery now?"

Nikolas nodded, giving him one last, fierce squeeze. "Yes, you may go."

Jake stood back and rubbed the tears from his eyes with small fists. He stared at his father curiously. "Why are *you* crying, Papa?"

There was a brief silence, and then Nikolas answered gruffly. "Because I hate having to spank you."

A small, grudging smile crossed Jake's face. "I hate it too." He ran to Emma and locked his arms around her hips, hugging her. "I'm sorry, Emma."

Too moved for words, she ruffled his hair and kissed the top of his head before he scampered away. When the rapid footsteps faded, Nikolas stood and rubbed his hands over his face, sighing tautly.

Emma approached him hesitantly. "Nikki, I thought I had made it clear to him—"

"He knew he shouldn't have come here alone," Nikolas said, turning to face her. "He's a willful child, full of curiosity. I should have expected this."

Emma wondered why he still looked so ashen, and why there was such a haunted look in his eyes. "Well, everything's fine now, thank God. No harm done."

Nikolas didn't seem to agree with her. He dragged his sleeve over a clammy brow, and pushed back a lock of sweat-dampened hair. "I've never struck a child before."

Then Emma understood. The episode had reminded him of Misha, his brother, and all the times their father had abused him. "You didn't *strike* Jake," she said quietly. "It was a spanking, and a very mild one at that. You did it to make certain he wouldn't put himself in danger again. Jake understood that, Nikolas. You didn't hurt him . . ." She paused and continued in a very soft tone. "And you're not like your father."

He was silent, his gaze unfocused, as if he were lost in memories of another time and place.

"It's not easy being a parent, is it?" Emma asked softly. "There are so many things to worry about, things you never expect, and you're tortured by the decisions you try to make for their own good—" She stopped speaking as thoughts of her own father caused a wave of sudden longing and guilt. Lucas Stokehurst had always been a loving, if overprotective, parent, and she had virtually cut him out of her life. She missed him. She was tired of punishing her family and herself—she wanted to make peace with them. "Don't feel guilty," she murmured, too occupied with her thoughts to notice Nikolas's reply, or if he made one.

That evening, Emma went upstairs to the nursery at eight o'clock. She intended to explain to Jake that although she often referred to Manchu as a beloved pet, he was a dangerous animal, and by no means domesticated as a dog like Samson was. Manchu should be loved but feared, because his nature would always be unpredictable. She felt guilty for not having made that clear enough to Jake before.

As she neared the top step, she heard the boy's sleepy, relaxed voice float through the nursery doorway. "Papa, will you tell me stories even after we hire the nanny?"

"Of course," came Nikolas's reply. "Although I imagine she'll have some stories of her own to entertain you with."

"I like the Russian ones best."

"So do I," Nikolas said with a smile in his voice. "Now, where were we?"

"Prince Ivan just met the gray wolf."

"Yes." The pages of a book rustled. " 'It so happened that this was an enchanted wolf, who knew all about Prince Ivan's search for the magical firebird. "I know where the firebird is," the wolf cried, and offered to take Ivan there. Climbing onto the wolf's back, Ivan rode swiftly through the night until they reached a garden surrounded with high golden walls. This was the palace of Tsar Afron . . . ' "

Quietly Emma crept away, envisioning Jacob curled up in bed listening to his father's soothing baritone. She felt lonely, unhappy, wanting something she couldn't name. She drank a glass of red wine without tasting it and retired early to bed. Wearing a thin cotton gown, huddled under a pile of blankets, she waited for the icy bed linens to warm. The room was still and dark, voices coming to mock her from the shadows.

She remembered Tasia's appeal: *"He's not worthy of anyone's trust, Emma. Nikolas is a dangerous man."*

Her father's quiet anguish: *"You can always come back. I'll welcome you with open arms."*

And Nikolas's plea: *"I won't hurt you again. Believe in me."*

The memories troubled her for hours, until finally the mist of sleep drifted over her. But there was no respite for her even then. One of the most disturbing dreams of her life seized her with a detail and vividness that chilled her to the bone.

She was in a cold, dark cell with wooden walls, a stone floor, and a tiny rectangular window. Crosses and icons hung on the walls, somber painted faces staring down at her, reflecting her grief. She sobbed desperately as she paced the small room, her dark gown trailing the floor. She knew that Nikolas was suffering, and she couldn't go to him. All she could do was wait here in

*helpless agony. Two other women—one of them a nun
in gray garments—were trying to soothe her, but she
shrugged off their gentle hands and turned away from
their compassionate faces. "He's dying," she wept. "He
needs me, and he's all alone. I must go to him! I can't
bear it, I can't—"*

Emma jerked awake with a gasp, sitting upright
in bed. The familiar room of her suite was eerily
silent. "It was just a dream," she told herself, wiping at the tears on her face. But for some reason
the tears kept coming, and her heart ached as if
someone truly had died. She didn't know how to
make the pain go away. She slipped out of bed and
found herself walking toward Nikolas's suite. Using the long sleeve of her gown to blot her face,
she went to the doorway of his bedroom and stood
there, a slender ghost hovering uncertainly in the
darkness. Moonlight drifted through the window
and puddled on the carpeted floor.

"Nikki," she whispered.

She heard the sheets rustling and Nikolas's
groggy voice. "Who is it? . . . Emma?"

"I had a nightmare," she whispered. She had
never known such desperate grief. Surely he could
feel it, like another presence in the room with them.

"Tell me," he said.

"You were dying . . . you wanted me, but I
couldn't come to you. I was in a convent room, and
they wouldn't let me leave."

He made no reply to that. Inexplicably, he murmured her name in Russian.

Struggling with tears and words, Emma was silent for several moments. Then the anguished questions, born of weeks of frustration and yearning,
burst forth. "Why have you changed so much?

What happened to you on the day you fainted in front of the portrait?''

Finally she had asked. Nikolas couldn't speak at first, filled with such eagerness and desire that he knew his explanation would come out in an incomprehensible stutter. In the back of his mind he had rehearsed hundreds of ways to tell her, searching for the right words to make her accept, believe . . . but it seemed hopeless. How could she understand when even he didn't?

His voice was nearly inaudible as he replied. ''During the hour I was unconscious, I dreamed I was in Russia. I dreamed that I was my ancestor Nikolai.''

''Nikolai,'' she repeated hesitantly. ''The one who chose his wife from among the five hundred maidens?''

''How did you know that?'' he asked with sudden intensity.

''Rashel Sidarova told me the story. How Nikolai married one of the maidens—''

''Yes. It was all there in the dream. You were the bride. Your name was Emelia Vasilievna, and I fell in love with you.''

''What happened then?'' she asked uneasily.

''We were together only a short time before I was imprisoned on suspicion of treason. To escape the same fate, you went to the Novodevichy Convent, where you bore my child. I don't know what happened to you after that.'' He added quietly, ''I'm trying to find out.''

She was stunned by his tone, so absurdly matter-of-fact. ''My God . . . you believe it really happened, don't you? You think it was more than a dream.''

"It was real."

His admission startled her. She put her hand up to her mouth, holding back a frightened, incredulous laugh. "You're talking like a madman!"

"I loved you a hundred and seventy years ago. Now I've found you again."

She began to tremble in confusion. "No."

"Don't be afraid," he said softly.

"This doesn't make sense!"

"Why did you dream you were in a convent, Emelia?"

"Don't call me that! It was just a coincidence!" She breathed rapidly, fear pulsing through her body. "This isn't like you, Nikki. You've always been rational above all else. To hear you spinning such a story and claiming it's real . . . you must be trying to scare the wits out of me! It's not going to work—"

"It's the truth."

Emma saw him rise from the bed and come to her, his lean body touched with the intimate gleams and shadows of nakedness. Although she tried to flee, her feet wouldn't obey, and she stood there in frozen bewilderment.

His hard, hot arms slid around her, one hand pushing beneath her hair to grip the back of her neck. She flinched and gasped, her body shaking. "I don't believe you," she whispered. "I don't believe in your dream."

Nikolas was overwhelmed with the relief of being able to tell Emma. The scent and nearness of her, the things he needed to communicate to her, came over him in a rush. He had to have her now. He spoke to her in Russian, soft, guttural words she didn't understand.

"What are you saying?" she pleaded.

He translated for her, his breath burning the skin of her neck. "I don't care if you believe me. I want you in my bed tonight. I want to be inside you, and feel your arms and legs around me."

Emma arched away from him, but his strength was so much greater, his muscles tight with determination. "I want you," he said, his accent thicker than usual. "I want to make love to my wife."

She felt his mouth on her breasts, heat blazing through the fragile fabric of her gown. He found her nipples, biting and sucking the hard points until she stopped struggling and moaned in protesting pleasure. His hand slid between her thighs, caressing the soft cove through the thin cotton layer that covered her. "Emma," he groaned, pressing her hard against his engorged flesh, his fingers clenched into her buttocks.

"Yes," she whispered, consent and desire tangling inside her.

Nikolas took her to the bed and bent her over it, snatching feverishly at the hem of her gown. She turned her face into the tangle of linens and spread her thighs as she felt him settle over her. He pushed against her in aggressive seeking and made a sound of pleasure when her body contained and shielded him, drawing him deep inside the dark sweetness. He impaled her strongly, answering the backward push of her hips in a rhythm that drove her to a wrenching climax. She sobbed and held still for him, shivering with delight as she felt him flood her with his seed.

Slowly they curled together on the bed, weak-limbed and exhausted. Emma felt the warmth of him all along her back, his legs tucked beneath hers, his arm beneath her neck. Small aftershocks still rippled through her. It was a long time before she spoke in a thin whisper.

"I'm afraid."

"Why, *dushenka?*"

"What does that mean?"

"My little soul," he answered readily, smoothing her wild hair. "Why afraid?"

A tear slid down her cheek and trembled on the tip of her chin. "Because I don't want to love you," she said with a gasp. "Then I'll be at your mercy, and you'll tear me to pieces. I won't let that happen, Nikki."

He hushed her with a soft murmur and pushed her hands aside. He began to kiss her throat, where the edge of lace met her skin . . . nuzzling kisses that made her breath quicken and her nipples rise against the veil of cambric. He moved over her, his heavy shoulders lit with a silvered gleam as a shaft of moonlight crossed them. His hands, capable of such cruelty and power, slid gently from her hips to her breasts. He whispered to her, sometimes in English, sometimes in Russian, his words spilling over her body. Lifting the hem of her nightgown inch by inch, he celebrated her newly revealed skin with gentle bites and kisses. Emma reached down to grip the muscles of his back, finding the familiar texture of his scars.

The gown was pulled over her head, leaving her completely naked. Emma twined herself around him, embracing him fully. They kissed ardently, rolling once, twice across the bed. Nikolas groaned at the caress of Emma's hands, the gentle flex of her fingers around his stiff flesh. His head dipped over the taut plane of her stomach and moved to the soft cove between her thighs, until his tongue expertly located the tender place where all pleasure centered.

Shaking with need, Emma touched his hair, her fingers delving into the silken locks and twining tightly. "Now," she whispered urgently, writhing in response to the demand of his mouth. "Please, now . . ."

Nikolas levered himself over her and entered slowly, gliding low and full until she gave a cry of satisfaction. They were still, utterly joined. Emma saw the glitter of his eyes in the darkness, the mysterious outline of his face. He was a stranger to her, more gentle and passionate than she could ever have imagined. "Who are you?" she murmured.

"I'm the one who loves you," he whispered. "Forever, Emma." He pushed even deeper, seeming to relish her helpless sob of pleasure. She clung to him in surrender, reckless and open, yielding all of herself. And he gave the same, letting the fire rage out of control until all memory had burned away and the world was clean and new.

For the first time, Emma awakened in the morning with her husband's arms around her. She waited through the initial moments of confusion, then shifted to look at Nikolas's face. His amber eyes were open, his gaze searching. "Good morning," he said, his voice sleep-scratchy.

He had held her all night, occasionally interrupting her dreams by kissing her face and throat. They had made love once more as morning approached, their bodies moving in languorous rhythm until they had both dissolved in shuddering release. What could she say to him after a night of such unguarded sensuality? She looked away from him, her cheeks burning, and she made a move to roll out of bed.

He stopped her, pinning her down to the mattress. He stared into her eyes. "How do you feel?"

"I don't know. I have no idea where to go from here, or how to *be* with you. It's easy to argue all the time—it's what I'm used to. But to be at peace . . . I don't know if that's possible for us."

His warm hands covered her bare bottom, squeezing the firm curves. "It's simple, *ruyshka*. We'll take it day by day."

Emma felt him stirring between them, the insistent throbbing that betrayed his awakening passion. He gripped her bottom, keeping her on top while his mouth wandered in a moist path over her breasts.

She protested breathlessly. "No, Nikki. It's time for breakfast—"

"I'm not hungry."

"—and I haven't seen to the animals this morning—"

"They can wait."

"Jacob might come looking for you—"

"He won't. He's not my son for nothing."

She tried one last time to divert him. "I'm sore . . ."

"I can fix that," he whispered, rolling until she was pressed flat on her back. He pushed her thighs apart and applied himself toward convincing her to stay. Emma succumbed with a moan of pleasure as his hands and mouth made promises he was more than ready to fulfill.

* * *

Nikolas seemed to take it for granted that he would be welcome in her bed after that, and Emma did not deny him. A week passed swiftly, while Emma awoke each day with a sense of discovery. She was learning things about her husband that she had never guessed in all the previous months of their marriage. There were moments when he could be astonishingly tender, helping her take down the heavy mass of her hair at night, his fingers massaging the sore spots that hairpins and combs had left on her scalp. He would rub salve into her hands where they had been chafed or scraped during work, or interrupt her bath and wash her as if she were a child.

One day his mood took a predatory turn, and he cornered her in the menagerie. Ignoring her startled protests, he unfastened her trousers and took her against the wall, until they were both sweat-drenched and gasping with satisfaction. He teased her unmercifully, provoking her and at the same time making her laugh, until she didn't know whether to kiss him or kill him.

In the afternoons when Robert Soames painted Emma's portrait, Nikolas came to watch the sittings, staring at her with such absorption that she finally banished him from the room. "I can't sit still and look dignified when you're watching me," she informed him, shoving him toward the doorway. Nikolas obeyed reluctantly, scowling as she closed the door in his face.

He talked about his dream once more, on the day they took a walk across the snow-dusted land around the estate. Snowflakes descended gently from the sky, and Nikolas stopped to kiss the melting patches on Emma's face. "You look like an angel," he murmured, touching the snowy points that had caught in her hair.

"So do you," she replied, and laughed as she brushed at the snow on his tawny locks. "A fallen one."

Suddenly Nikolas was quiet. Emma saw that he was staring at her, transfixed. "What is it?" she asked warily.

"You looked like this before, in Russia. I gave you a white lace shawl, and you wore it over your hair."

I was never in Russia, she wanted to say, but she held the words back as she contemplated her husband. How often did he think of that mysterious hour when he had been lost in his dream of the past? She sensed the craving behind his closed expression, the desire to recapture what had been taken from him. Nikolas truly believed they had known and loved each other in a past life. Certainly she wouldn't encourage him in that belief, but neither could she bring herself to mock him for it.

"You loved the woman in your dream, didn't you?" she said quietly.

An indistinguishable emotion flared in his eyes. "That woman was you."

"Even if that were true, it has nothing to do with us now," she said. "It makes no difference to our situation."

"It makes all the difference to me. I remembered how it felt to love you, and to be loved in return."

"I'm sorry if that's what you want from me," Emma said stiffly. "It's not possible. Can't this be enough for you? Being friends of a sort, and finding pleasure in each other's company?"

"No," came his grim reply. "It's not enough."

They continued their walk in silence until they came upon a small stone structure, the estate chapel which had been converted for the use of the Russian servants.

"I've never been in there before," Emma said. "What does it look like?"

Nikolas regarded the chapel without expression and accompanied Emma to the small, arched doorway. He pushed open the door and held it for her as she went inside. Covering her hair with her blue woolen scarf, Emma glanced around the chapel. It was filled with icons and altars laden with candles. A few of them had been lit recently, their tiny flames sending soft light through the air. It was a sad and solemn place. The walls seemed to have absorbed the confessions and appeals of all those who had been there before them.

"Shall I light a candle?" Emma asked in a hushed voice.

Nikolas didn't reply. His golden features were as still as the icons that surrounded them.

"Well, it couldn't hurt," Emma remarked, selecting a long taper. She lit it from a burning flame and placed it carefully in one of the holders before the Mary-and-child icon. Turning, she glanced at Nikolas, and her breath stopped.

Nikolas's eyes were flooded with burning wetness. He was unable to control his reaction at the sight of Emma surrounded by Russian paintings and candlelight. He had never known such torment. It seemed that she had the power of life and death over him. He didn't know what would happen to him if she never came to love him. He was afraid of what he might become.

It seemed an eternity before he spoke with inhuman self-control, his voice low and even. "I don't know what happened to me on that day. I'm not certain what's real anymore. All I know is that I need you."

Emma stood there in helpless confusion, gazing at the man who had seduced, married, betrayed her . . . the most complex and disturbing man she had ever known. It would take courage to stay with him. She felt as if she were standing face-to-face with a tiger, with no bars between them. She had so many feelings for him . . . fear, desire, anger, tenderness. Would anyone ever fascinate her as he did? Was it worth the risk to find out if he truly did care for her?

She moved toward him and laid a gentle hand on his jaw. She felt the tremors in his body, a tension too great to bear. "Perhaps I need you too," she whispered.

His hand tangled in her hair, a tightly possessive grip, and he pulled her to him, compressing and crushing her against his body. He pressed muffled words to her lips, then kissed her savagely, holding her as if he would never let go.

"Where are you taking me?" Jake asked the next day, his small hand locked in Emma's as they went out to the carriage on the front drive. "And why are we wearing fancy clothes?"

Emma had dressed him with exacting care in little black breeches, a blue vest, and a blue cap pulled over his heavy, dark curls. For herself she had chosen a smart gray frock trimmed with violet-and-gray-striped silk. Her hair had been neatly braided and pinned, and topped with a gray felt hat trimmed with grosgrain ribbon and a gauzy lavender scarf. A velvet hooded cape with a shawl mantle covered her shoulders.

"We're paying a call on my family," she told Jake. "My stepmother wrote to me, saying they will be staying in the city for a few days."

"You have a stepmother too?" he asked in surprise.

"Well, yes." Emma adjusted his cap carefully and smiled at him. "You don't have a monopoly on stepmothers, you know."

"What is yours like?"

"She's Russian, like you and your father."

"Does she know Russian stories?" There was a flash of eager curiosity in the boy's eyes.

Emma smiled. "Probably hundreds of them." She was grateful for Jake's happy chattering, the way he settled in the carriage and pulled toy soldiers from his pocket, engaging them in a mock battle. Any distraction was welcome, helping her to ignore the fluttering nerves in her stomach.

She had refused to see her parents since her wedding to Nikolas four and a half months ago. There had been little communication, aside from a few stilted letters exchanged between her and Tasia. She wondered how they would react to seeing her. Would their reception be warm or cold? What would they say about Jacob? Perhaps it would have been best to go by herself, but Emma needed the boy's company. And she wanted them to know about the child—it would help them understand the things she would try to tell them. Jacob seemed to be an integral part of the change that had come over Nikolas.

"You'll probably meet my brothers, William and Zachary," she said as the carriage proceeded down the long front drive. "William is exactly your age, Jake, and you're cousins of a sort, although so distant that it's very difficult to trace. Russians are very keen on the idea of family, and very proud of their relatives, so I imagine William will be quite pleased to claim you."

Jake looked wary. "Will I like him?"

"You will definitely like him," Emma said firmly. "He's a nice boy, Jake. He's not the kind who calls names or makes fun of others."

"But I talk like the villagers . . . and I'm a bastard too."

Emma hadn't realized the boy was conscious of his rough country accent. "You don't have to tell people that, Jake. Your heritage is nothing to be ashamed of, and certainly nothing you could help. Second, William won't think anything about your accent. And as you grow older, that will soften a bit."

"Will it?" Jake looked vaguely pleased, and went back to playing with his soldiers.

Emma's nervousness increased during the drive to her family's Italianate villa on the Thames. The lovely, familiar trio of round towers with cone-shaped roofs and surrounding loggias came into view. The carriage stopped in front of the villa, and footmen dressed in heavy brocaded livery came to assist her and Jake from the carriage. Perhaps sensing her apprehension, or sharing it, Jake slipped his hand in hers as they walked to the front door. Emma glanced quickly at him and at herself to make certain they looked their best.

The butler met them at the door, a small smile cracking his usual composure as he recognized her. "Miss Emma," he said, welcoming them to the entrance hall just as Tasia hurried to meet them.

"I saw the carriage through my window," Tasia exclaimed, rushing to Emma. Her face glowed with delight. "How wonderful it is to see you!" She threw her arms around Emma, and they both laughed in joy, the embrace none the less hearty for being muffled by Emma's mantled cape. Emma's anxiety began to fade as she basked in the familiarity of home, of Tasia's loving presence.

Tasia pulled back and surveyed her appraisingly. "Stunning," she said. "Smiling, radiant, splendidly fit . . . you seem to be thriving, Emma." Her gaze moved to the small figure at Emma's side, and her blue-gray eyes widened a little. Surprise caused her face to pale a shade or two. The soft lines of her mouth trembled, and she whispered something in Russian. Finally she appeared to gather her wits. "Who . . ." she said unsteadily. "Who is this?"

"This is Jake," Emma replied, keeping her hand on the child's tense shoulder. "Nikolas's son."

Exercising a great amount of self-control, Tasia managed to hide her surprise. "Of course . . . there is no mistaking the look of an Angelovsky. The eyes, especially." She met the boy's gaze and summoned a smile. Her voice was very kind. "Nikolas's son . . . I suppose that makes me your grandmother, doesn't it?" She knelt in a rustle of silk and perfume to enfold him in her slender arms.

"You're too pretty to be a grandmother," Jake said frankly, accepting her embrace. He added in a muffled voice, "And you don't smell like one either."

Tasia laughed. "And you, my lad, have a way with women—just like your father. You may call me *babushka*, if you like. That's the Russian word for grandmother." She stood and removed the boy's cap, smoothing his dark hair. "Would you like to sit with my son William and his tutor while they finish a lesson? Come with me, and we'll look in on them."

"What about Zachary?" Emma asked.

"He's in the nursery—it's naptime for him." Tasia reached down for Jake, who took her proffered hand obediently.

The three of them went through the halls, lined with marble and columns, to the stairs, which were bordered by priceless tapestries depicting social scenes of medieval life. Tasia encouraged Jake to talk, and he eagerly told her about the menagerie on the Angelovsky estate and all the things he did with his papa. They reached the schoolroom, a cozy place filled with toys and books, the walls covered with maps and framed engravings from children's stories.

William, who was sitting at the table with an earnest, scholarly-looking young man, looked up at the visitors. His gaze fell first on Emma, and he crowed in delight, hopping off his chair. "Emma!" he cried, flinging his arms around her excitedly. "Emma, you're back!"

She laughed and hugged him tightly. "Oh, William, you've grown at least an inch." Her dark-haired brother was as wonderfully sturdy and energetic as ever. Glancing down at Jake, she saw that he had drawn back a few steps, watching them with a mixture of curiosity and possessive jealousy. She let go of her brother and drew Jake forward, keeping both her hands on his shoulders. "William, this is your cousin Jake. Nikolas's son."

The boys regarded each other closely, while the

process of appraisal and acceptance occurred in the space of a few seconds. "Are you an Angelovsky, then?" William asked.

Jake nodded with wary pride. "I'm part Russian."

"So am I," William replied, and they exchanged a shy smile.

"Look what I have." Jake pulled a handful of soldiers from his pocket, and William examined them with great interest.

Tasia interceded then, talking briefly with the tutor and asking that Jake be included in the study session. When both boys were seated side by side at the table, Tasia and Emma left the schoolroom and walked together toward the parlor.

"Is Papa at home?" Emma asked.

"He's at a board meeting at the railway company. He'll arrive soon, I expect." Tasia slid an arm around Emma's narrow waist. "Now, tell me about Jake."

"Nikolas had never seen him until a few weeks ago. The mother worked at a dairy on one of Nikolas's farms. Recently she died, and someone from her village brought the child to us. Nikolas has decided to keep Jake and openly acknowledge him as his son."

"I find that surprising," Tasia said frankly. "I don't recall that Nikolas has ever liked children. Not only that, but the boy looks so much like Mikhail—it must cause Nikolas a great deal of discomfort."

"Yes," Emma said earnestly, "the whole thing has been a tremendous shock to him. At first he could barely stand the sight of the boy. But now he adores Jake. It's amazing to see them together."

Tasia shook her head in bewilderment. "I suppose children can bring out the best in people. Even in a man like Nikolas." She paused for a moment. "You look so healthy and happy, Emma. I hope that means Nikolas is treating you well?"

"He didn't at first," Emma admitted, coloring slightly. "But lately..." Her blush deepened. "Lately things have been better. He's different now. I can't even be certain the change is permanent. All I can do is hope."

They sat in the parlor together, talking while Tasia attended to some needlework. Her hands were delicate and deft as she repaired the torn cuff of her husband's shirt. Finding it a relief to unburden herself, Emma told her about Nikolas's strange behavior of the past months. "At first he had these odd episodes in which he had a feeling of seeing something familiar. He had visions he didn't like to talk about, and they seemed to disturb him greatly."

"Visions," Tasia repeated, setting the mended shirt in her lap and staring at Emma intently. "What kind of visions?"

"I don't know exactly. But every time it happened, there was such a strange look on his face, such fear and anger ... and then I found the painting. Do you remember one of the letters I sent to you in which I mentioned that we were having an old landscape restored? It turned out that underneath it was a portrait of an Angelovsky ancestor ... Nikki's distant grandfather, actually. It's a mirror image of him. When he got his first good look at it, he turned white and fainted dead away. We couldn't revive him for an hour. And when Nikki finally awakened, he was ... different."

"Different?" Tasia was startled and intrigued.

"It was like the flip of a coin. One minute he wanted nothing to do with Jake or me, and the next, we were the most important things in the world to him. Later he said that he had remembered a—a past life, in which we were married to each other. For him it seems to have changed everything." Emma frowned self-consciously. "No rational person would believe such a story. The surprise is that Nikolas, of all people, would invent something like this. Tell me, *Belle-mère*, is my husband going mad, or is he trying to make me out as the greatest fool alive?"

Tasia was quiet for a while, concentrating on her needlework. "I suppose I could believe Nikolas's story," she finally said.

"You must be joking!"

"It's a Russian's nature to believe in such things. We're a people full of contradictions. Intemperate, mystical, superstitious . . ." Tasia shrugged and smiled slightly. "Perhaps we have all led past lives. Who am I to say we haven't?"

"But you're so religious! You know the Bible by heart!"

"For Russians, religion is an elastic thing. It encompasses many different beliefs and ideas."

"I'm not like that. I can't allow myself to believe in something so extraordinary. But I do know that Nikolas is convinced his experience was real, and it seems to have influenced him for the better."

"Then perhaps you don't need to question it too much, Emma. You might try to accept what has happened and simply go on from here."

"But *how*—" Emma began, and suddenly she became aware of someone's entrance into the room.

She looked up, and her heart jumped as she saw her father. Lucas Stokehurst looked the same as always, tall and distinguished, his blue eyes bright and piercing. A change came over his face as he stared at her, his features softening with hope and love.

"Emma—"

She sprang up and ran to him, throwing her arms around him. He was so comfortingly solid and dear. A wave of happiness rushed over her, and she lowered her face to his shoulder. "Papa, listen to me," she said rapidly, her arms locked hard around his neck. "I've realized so many things lately. I've always demanded so much of other people, expecting them to be perfect. And I was the hardest on the people I love, so angry when they disappointed me by being human. You were trying to protect me and help me, and you were absolutely right about Adam Milbank. Forgive me for things I said. I was in such a rage, I didn't mean any of it. I love you, Papa. I've missed you so much."

Her father couldn't answer, only pressed his chin deeper in her hair and swallowed hard, while his arms threatened to crush her. Emma brushed away her own tears of happiness. She was with her family, and everything was finally all right.

Emma sat and talked eagerly with her parents, telling them a carefully edited version of her life at the Angelovsky estate. She took pleasure in the way her father reached over to squeeze her hand. Tasia beamed at them both, delighted by their renewed closeness. After a while the boys came to the parlor to have tea and cakes. William and Jake were becoming fast friends. Zachary, still drowsy from his nap, sat on Tasia's lap.

"I want to visit Jake and see the menagerie," William announced, his fingers and cheeks sticky from the iced cakes he and Jake were devouring. "When can I go? Will you take me there, Emma?"

"You must come soon," Emma replied, smiling. "The animals would love to see you, William." She hesitated before suggesting to her parents, "Now that the holidays are here, perhaps you might come to our Christmas Day party, and share supper with us afterward."

Tasia agreed immediately, smacking her lips at the thought of the Russian delicacies the Angelovskys' cook would undoubtedly prepare. While they were in the midst of making plans, the butler arrived with the announcement that a police inspector was waiting at the front entrance. "I've been expecting him," Luke said. "Excuse me. I must talk with him privately for a while."

William and Jake suddenly found an excuse to leave the room. Emma was certain they were going to get a look at the visitor.

As the parlor emptied rapidly, Emma stared at Tasia with wide-eyed surprise. "Why in heaven's name is a police inspector here?"

Tasia grimaced. "The house was robbed the night before last, while we were sleeping! It has unnerved me and the children terribly. Your father's been in a fury." She lowered her voice confidentially. "It hurts a man's pride to have his property stolen from right under his nose. Luke has set Scotland Yard on its ear—they sent two sergeants and an inspector yesterday—and he won't let anyone rest until the culprit is caught."

"I pity the poor thief when Papa finds him," Emma said dryly. "What was taken?"

"Some jewelry, a cashbox, a case of pistols." Tasia frowned and shook her head. "The ease with which it was accomplished suggests that the thief was familiar with the house plan and the location of our valuables."

"Then it's likely we know the person who did it?"

Tasia nodded, kissing the top of Zachary's head and holding him protectively. "Our servants are all old and trusted ones, so we believe the culprit has probably been a guest of ours in the past. We might even have entertained him at supper or a party."

Emma shivered slightly. "I don't like that at all."

Tasia shrugged, turning pragmatic as usual. "Life is always full of surprises, praise be to God."

When Emma and Jake returned to the Angelovsky estate, Nikolas was in the process of ushering out a small group of estate agents, accountants, and lawyers, all of whom had delivered semiannual reports on his holdings. The last of the visitors departed, and Nikolas took his son on his knee, asking how the day had gone. Patiently he listened to Jake's excited account of his newfound cousins and grandparents. "Then you like the Stokehursts?" Nikolas asked quietly.

"Oh, yes," Jake assured him. "I never met anyone like them before."

"That I'm sure of," Nikolas replied dryly, with a sideways glance at Emma. He grinned at her faint scowl and turned back to his son. "Why don't you go up to the nursery, Jake? There might be a new toy waiting for you."

Jake ran upstairs to investigate, leaving with such unseemly haste that Nikolas and Emma laughed.

Nikolas stood and arched a tawny brow quizzically. "How was it?"

Impulsively Emma went over to him and slipped her arms around his lean waist. "Tasia was as sweet and kind as always, and Papa and I managed to iron out all our differences. Before I left, he even admitted that you couldn't be such a bad husband if I looked so well. I think Papa would like to make peace with you, Nikki. Don't be surprised if he wants to talk to you privately someday soon—I think he might be ready to accept you as his son-in-law."

Nikolas smiled sardonically. "Why does that thought give me cold chills?"

She bit his ear lightly. "If Papa decides to be nice to you, I expect you to do your utmost to charm him. For my sake."

Nikolas removed Emma's hat and smoothed his hands over her head. "I don't like it when you braid and pin your hair so tightly."

"I'm trying to look respectable."

"You weren't meant to be respectable. You were meant to be unbound and natural, like your animals. No, don't bite me again . . . I have a present for you."

"What kind of present? Where is it?"

"You'll have to find it," he said, smiling as she began to search his pockets. "Not so roughly, *ruyshka* . . . you may damage something of value."

Triumphantly Emma located a heavy velvet pouch and pulled it out. Loosening the drawstring, she shook the object into her palm. "Oh," she said softly, her breath catching. It was a ring, a single sapphire mounted in gold. The rich, glittering stone was the size of a robin's egg, seeming to contain every shade of blue in its glowing depths. Emma turned her stunned gaze to her husband's face.

"Try it on," he said.

Emma watched as he slid the enormous sapphire onto her finger. The ring fit perfectly, a ball of blue fire balanced on the surface of her hand. "Why did you buy this for me?" she asked in awe.

"Because it matches your eyes."

"It's so incredible, but . . ." She stroked his chest, tracing the hard curve of muscle. "Why did you buy this for me?"

"It gives me pleasure to see you wearing beautiful things . . . almost as much pleasure as seeing you with nothing on at all." He whispered endearments to her, lightly fondling and stroking her body, unfastening the neck of her dress. His lips caressed her exposed throat, his tongue tickling the hollow where her pulse fluttered.

Emma sighed and closed her eyes. "Nikki, don't—"

"Let's go upstairs."

"Not before supper," she exclaimed, blushing.

"I want to see you naked—except for the ring."

"You're impossible," she said, letting him tug her from the room.

A week before Christmas, Emma was busy decorating the mansion with bells, acres of red ribbon, holly, and mistletoe. The Sidarova sisters and two footmen climbed ladders to hang ornaments on a towering pine tree situated in the central hall. As they worked, they entertained Emma by singing Russian Christmas carols.

"If only this place weren't so large," Emma lamented, tying clumps of holly to the banister. "It takes three times as many decorations to make any sort of impression."

"Yes, but it looks so wonderful," Rashel exclaimed, carefully affixing a gingerbread man to one of the pine branches. They had baked gingerbread in a variety of shapes, and were already having problems with encroachers daring to nibble at the spicy treats. Samson was a constant threat, venturing forth to gobble the gingerbread hanging from the lowest branches of the Christmas tree. He reclined beneath the fragrant boughs, occasionally scratching at the festive red bow tied around his neck.

The butler approached Emma with a perplexed expression on his hawklike face. "Your Highness," he murmured, "I just discovered this package on the doorstep."

Abandoning her work on the banister, Emma came down the steps and took the object from him. It was a small white box with a red bow, bearing a card that read, simply, *Emma*.

A smile flitted across her face. "I wonder who would deliver a gift in such a way."

She untied the ribbon and opened the cold, slightly damp pasteboard box. It contained a scrap of velvet, a fresh bloodred rose, and a small card with the initial *A* on it. Her smile vanished, and her forehead creased. Who would send her a gift like this, and in such a mysterious fashion? Could it possibly be from Adam? Once, long ago, he had given her a red rose just like this one. She touched the rose, and jerked her hand back as a thorn pierced the tip of her forefinger. "Ouch!" She sucked on the sore spot, tasting the salty tang of blood.

Stanislaus's black brows drew together. "Your Highness, if you will permit me . . ." He took the box from her and unrolled the velvet scrap, dropping its contents into Emma's palm.

She gasped as a pair of pearl earrings, strung in loops, fell in a cool, heavy tumble into her hand. The Sidarova girls came to view them, exclaiming in admiration. "Very beautiful," Rashel said.

Emma was aware of a cold, uneasy feeling. She had once read that pearls meant tears. A box with a red rose and pearls . . . blood and tears. She dropped the earrings back into the box. "It's a good thing Nikolas isn't here," she murmured. "I don't think he'd appreciate my receiving gifts from other men."

"No, Your Highness," Stanislaus agreed.

Emma glanced at the gift distastefully. "Please return that to Lord Milbank. I suspect he is the one responsible for sending it to me." She paused and looked at the servants around her. "There's no need to mention this to Prince Nikolas. He would be jealous or angry, and I would prefer our first Christmas to be free of trouble."

They all agreed immediately and went back to work, trying to recapture the light mood of a few moments before. Emma was disturbed by the unexpected gift, but she resolved to put it out of her mind. What could Adam have meant by his gesture? To let her know that he still cared? That he wanted something from her, perhaps even an affair? How silly some men were, only desiring what they couldn't have. Or perhaps the gift was intended to express a heartfelt good-bye. It didn't matter—she intended to concentrate on the future, not on the past. She had a good life with Nikolas, and it only promised to get better. Nothing would spoil their chances. She would make certain of that.

❧ Twelve

IN THE MORNING Stanislaus came to Emma while she was taking tea in her private sitting room.

"Your Highness," the butler said, and paused, as if wondering how to continue. His black brows were drawn together, and his mouth was tight.

"What is it, Stanley? You have the strangest expression on your face."

He ignored her nickname for him. "Your Highness," he answered, "I have discovered this on the front doorstep." He held out the object in his hand.

Emma set her teacup aside and stared at it in astonishment. It was the same bloodred rose that had been delivered to her yesterday. "Didn't you send it back?"

"Yes, Your Highness, along with the pearls. Apparently the flower was left by itself this time."

She shook her head, staring at the slightly bedraggled blossom. "Whoever the giver is, he's remarkably persistent."

"Shall we tell Prince Nikolas?"

Emma thought for a moment. She was certain the rose had come from Adam. Mischief-making, probably. He would be glad to provoke Nikolas, and cause trouble between them. "No," she said brusquely, "It's just a silly gesture. Please dispose of the thing—we'll forget all about it."

It was Christmas Eve, and the scent of pine emanated from the small tree in the corner of the family parlor, a cozy room lined with tapestries and golden oak paneling. Hangings of burgundy velvet framed the windows, and were parted to reveal a trace of the evening starlight. A fire in the fireplace burned with crackling vigor, sending out a wavering yellow glow to relieve the darkness of the room.

Nikolas lounged amid a pile of velvet pillows on the floor, watching his wife stir about the room. Jacob was asleep in his bed in the nursery, dreaming of the morning to come. And they had the whole night ahead of them.

"Come here," he said lazily, drinking wine from a glass-lined goblet, its silver and gold exterior glittering with inset diamonds and rubies.

"Soon," Emma replied, adjusting strings of cranberries on the tree. "I'm not finished yet."

"You've done nothing for two days except retie ribbons and move garlands up or down a mere inch—"

"With nearly two hundred guests coming tomorrow, I want everything to be perfect."

"Everything *is* perfect." Nikolas poured more wine and admired the shape of his wife's bottom as she bent over in her trousers. "Come here now—I have a present for you."

"I have one for you too," she replied pertly. Reaching behind the settee, she pulled out a large, square object that was the right size and shape to be a framed picture. It was covered with a length of dark cloth.

Nikolas sat up straighter, eyeing the object with interest. "Is that your portrait?"

"Yes, Mr. Soames worked night and day to have it finished in time."

"Let me see it."

"My present first," she said, coming to sit beside him. She crossed her long legs Indian-style and accepted a goblet of wine.

Obligingly Nikolas slid a wrapped package from beneath one of the tasseled pillows. Emma reached for the fist-sized box with childish glee. "Oh, good, I like the small ones best." She tore the paper and opened the velvet-lined box and stared at the object inside with delight. Carefully she lifted it out, and it glittered richly in the firelight. Nikolas had commissioned a brooch to be fashioned in the shape of a tiger, with stripes of black onyx and yellow diamonds. "Thank you," she said, flashing a smile at Nikolas. "It reminds me of you."

"It's supposed to remind you of Manchu."

"You and he aren't so far removed," she commented, reaching out to stroke the hair at the nape of his neck. "You're both solitary creatures who have been wounded in the past, and neither of you will ever be completely domesticated."

His eyes were bright yellow gold as he looked at her. "You wouldn't want us to be."

Smiling wryly at the truth of his statement, Emma retrieved the nearby picture. "Now for your present." She paused before unveiling the painting and frowned. "It's rather . . . unconventional."

Silently he gestured for her to proceed.

"All right, then." With a flourish, she whipped

the cloth from the portrait. "What do you think of it?"

Nikolas stared at the portrait in silent absorption. Robert Soames had painted Emma half-sitting on a windowsill. She wore a white shirt open at the throat and light beige trousers—and in an oddly sensuous touch, her feet had been left bare. The length of her red hair, made brilliant by the filtering sunlight behind her, cascaded to her hips. A dreamy, slightly serious expression on her face was the perfect counterpoint to the abandon of her posture. Nikolas found the portrait riveting and erotic.

"It's very odd, isn't it?" Emma asked, watching closely for his reaction.

Nikolas smiled and pulled her onto his lap, turning his gaze back to the painting. "It's beautiful. Thank you, *ruyshka*. I'll value it more than any work of art I possess."

"I don't know where we'll hang it," Emma said, leaning against his chest. "Some people would be offended by the sight of a princess in trousers."

Gently he drew his hand down her coltish legs. "The only kind of princess I want, *ruyshka*."

She smiled, pleased by the compliment, and began to fiddle nervously with his shirt buttons. "Nikki, I've been thinking ... there's something you should be aware of."

"What is it?" Nikolas sensed her sudden change of mood. He waited quietly, holding her as she struggled for words.

"I don't know how to tell you," she finally got out.

Nikolas cupped his fingers beneath her jaw and tilted her face upward, staring into her deep blue eyes. Something trembled inside him, a chord of awe and disbelief. He knew what it was, the sudden certainty resounded through his core, but he had to hear the words. "Just say it, Emma."

"I . . ." Her fingers clenched in the soft linen of his shirt. "I think I'm . . ." She paused and gazed at him wordlessly, unable to finish.

He moved his hand to the flat surface of her belly, and he held her gaze questioningly. She gave him a small nod in answer, her cheeks turning carmine.

Nikolas drew in a deep breath. His child with Emma, a part of himself inside her . . . The thought caused, not elation, but instead a kind of astonished humility that he had been given such a chance. He had been haunted by three children in his life: Misha, the brother he had been powerless to save; Jake, the boy he had failed and denied; and Alexei, the son forever lost to him. To be able to see his child born, to take part in his—or her—life, to wipe away the wreck of his past with a new beginning . . . Nikolas bent his head over Emma's and buried his face in the vibrant mass of her hair.

"You're pleased, then?" Emma asked, her arms locked around his neck.

For a while he was unable to reply. "You're my whole world," he finally said, his voice hoarse with emotion.

After a lively Christmas morning, during which the servants exchanged presents in the great hall and the Angelovskys held their private celebration in the family parlor, the house was filled with torn paper and ribbons. Knowing that the guests for their lavish Christmas party would arrive soon, Emma changed into a blue silk dress trimmed with narrow black braid. The skirt was simple, with no flounces or ruffles, only a wide trim of black fringe. She wore no jewelry except for the tiger brooch, pinned to the froth of white lace at her throat.

Maids were dispatched to clean the colorful clutter of discarded boxes and wrappings, while the cook and kitchen staff bustled to prepare a Christmas feast for approximately two hundred guests. Appetizing English smells of roasted stuffed turkey and goose mingled with the Russian dishes of mushrooms and cream, seasoned cabbage, and the rum-soaked yeast-and-raisin cake called baba au rhum. Jake raced around the house in unrestrained glee, brandishing his new toys and asking impatiently when his cousins would arrive.

"Soon," Emma promised, unable to keep from laughing at the contrast between Jake's happy expectation and his father's resigned air. She knew that Nikolas wasn't looking forward to meeting with the Stokehursts, especially Luke. The two men had never been on good terms, and since the wedding, Nikolas had been more than happy to avoid his father-in-law.

Catching Emma's amused glance, Nikolas managed a grimace that almost passed for a smile.

She went over to him and kissed his cheek. "It will be painless," she murmured. "Everyone will be in a festive mood, and my parents are quite pleased to be attending. Stop looking as though you're about to have a tooth extracted."

"Are you planning to tell your family about the baby?"

"I'd like to keep it private for a while."

He nuzzled the soft tendrils of hair near her ear. Before he could answer, Rashel Sidarova appeared in the doorway. "A parade of carriages is coming along the drive," she said breathlessly.

"Thank you, Rashel." Emma clapped her hands in excitement and pulled Nikolas along to welcome their guests.

Soon the house was filled with conversation and merriment. A score of children gathered around the large Christmas tree in the central hall, while the adults congregated in the drawing room to sip spiced wine, eggnog, and a Russian beverage flavored with fermented honey. Lord Shepley, a guest with well-known musical talent, played Christmas carols on the piano while others lent their voices in song. Emma relaxed as she saw how well the afternoon was progressing. Her father and Nikolas were polite to each other, keeping their respective distances and taking refuge in watching the antics of the children. Tasia, who looked lovely in a gown of plum silk, caught Emma's gaze and winked.

Deciding to check on the cook's progress with the first course of dinner, Emma slipped discreetly out of the parlor. She hummed a few bars of "Deck the Halls" as she walked toward the kitchen. Suddenly a hand grasped lightly at her elbow. She whirled around in surprise and saw Nikolas. Her lips parted to ask a question, but he caught her face in his hands and kissed her passionately.

"Why did you do that?" she asked when she had a chance to speak.

Nikolas gestured toward the ceiling, to a sprig of mistletoe that someone had hung in the hallway. "I could use that as an excuse. But I would have done it anyway."

A smile curved Emma's lips. "You should be entertaining the guests."

"I'd rather be entertaining you."

She laughed and pushed at his chest, but he tightened his arms around her. "I want to be alone with you," he said, his mouth descending on hers.

All at once they were interrupted by an unexpected sound—the naughty giggling of children. Emma stiffened and broke the kiss, turning to the intruders. Hot color flooded up to her hairline as she saw the group of three children: Jake and her half brothers, William and Zack . . . and they were accompanied by her father.

Luke's face was expressionless, but one dark brow lifted quizzically.

Jake broke the silence. "Don't mind them," he said, rolling his eyes. "They're always doing that."

Blushing, Emma wrenched free of her husband's embrace and yanked at the waist of her bodice to settle it in place. "Where are the four of you going?" she asked, trying to cover her discomfort.

Jake grinned cheerfully. "I'm taking them to see my pony, Ruslan."

"Don't let us keep you," Nikolas muttered.

Emma pinched him discreetly for the rude remark and cleared her throat. "Perhaps Nikolas will accompany you."

Luke regarded Nikolas speculatively. "Yes, why don't you?"

Jake and the other children began to clamor for Nikolas to go with them, and he complied reluctantly, giving Emma a deadly glance. She smiled sweetly in return, hoping that her father would find an opportunity to say a few private words to Nikolas. At the very least, it would be good for both of them to spend time together.

Crossing through the central hall, Emma continued toward the kitchen. All at once a strange feeling caused the back of her neck to prickle, and her steps slowed. She felt as if there were something wrong, as if a shadow were descending on the house. Throwing a glance over her shoulder, she saw Stanislaus welcome a trio of guests into the hall. The first person she recognized was Mr. Oliver Brixton, the American enamelware manufacturer who had once been a guest at the Angelovsky manor. He was the brother of the woman Adam Milbank had married. Then a small, plain-faced woman appeared, dressed in expensive silk and lace, her hair arranged in a neat, practical style. She was on the arm of a dark-haired man with very familiar features.

Adam had come to the Christmas party . . . and he had brought his wife.

Emma was motionless, while her thoughts raced in wild confusion. How was it possible? An invitation had been sent to Mr. Brixton, more as a courtesy than as an actual expectation of his attendance. But he had decided to come, and in an astonishing breach of etiquette, he had brought the Milbanks with him. Brixton was smiling easily, clearly having forgotten about Emma's former relationship with Adam. But Charlotte, Lady Milbank knew. Curiosity and mistrust shone in her gray eyes as she stared at Emma.

Emma's heart began to pound so heavily that it seemed to knock against her ribs. A light sweat broke out on her face. Why was Adam here? What did he intend? People would be watching and wondering, holding their breath to see if there would be trouble between Adam and Nikolas. She forced a smile on her lips, and went forward to welcome them. Mr. Brixton's homely but kind face lit up, and he kissed her hand.

"Happy Christmas, Your Highness."

Emma murmured a reply and lowered her gaze to Adam's wife, who was at least a head shorter than she.

Charlotte Milbank surprised her by speaking first, in a tone that was well modulated but threaded with steel. Her deep voice was incongruous, coming from a small, pudgy woman. "I hope you are able to accommodate an extra pair of guests, Your Highness. I'm afraid I insisted on accompanying my brother to your party. Ever since I moved to England, I've heard everyone talking about Prince Nikolas and his magnificent estate—not to mention his wife and her menagerie."

Emma kept her gaze on the woman, not daring to look at Adam. "You and your family are quite welcome to share Christmas with us, Lady Milbank."

Even as the name left her lips, it sent an odd feeling down Emma's spine. Lady Milbank—the title she had once longed for more than anything else.

Charlotte Milbank's face was round and boneless, but her skin was flawless, a beautiful milk white with just a hint of pink in her cheeks. Perhaps if she were possessed of a vivacious personality, she could be considered attractive, but there was accusation in her flint-gray eyes, and her small mouth was tight and unsmiling.

Emma had the strange urge to console the woman. *You have nothing to fear from me,* she longed to say. Instead she smiled politely and drew Char-

lotte toward a nearby group of guests in the drawing room, introducing her to each of them. Brixton
and Adam lingered behind, while Brixton admired
the huge tree in the central hall.

Emma left Charlotte Milbank's side and began to
mingle with other guests, but her gaze darted rest-
lessly around the scene. Nikolas would return
soon—she had to find him. He must be warned
that Brixton and the Milbanks were attending. She
refused to look at Adam, although she sensed that
he was staring at her. *Damn you, Adam,* she thought
angrily. *Why must you make trouble for me? What's
done is done. You left me and married someone else, and
I managed to recover from the hurt. Now let me get on
with my life!*

Moving through the crowd, Emma played the
part of hostess, and finally took a moment to glance
at Adam. He wore a pleasant expression, but he
seemed tense, his smile forced. His wife was at his
side, her round white hand poised on his arm.
Emma overheard a brief portion of their conversation as she walked near them. Adam was at-
tempting to tell a story.

"... friends of ours employed a rather haughty
footman dressed in the most splendid blue livery—"

"Black livery, dear," Charlotte interrupted gently.

Adam continued as if he hadn't heard her.
"—and we were walking in their garden, beside
the yew hedges—"

"They were fruit trees, darling," Charlotte corrected.

"—when we heard the most frightful yelp, and
splash! The footman had slipped and fallen into the

fish pond on his way to the carriage house. I've never laughed so much."

"It was quite vulgar," Charlotte added primly.

Emma felt a touch at her elbow and turned to find Tasia beside her. Tasia's face was soft with concern. She indicated the Milbanks with a flicker of her gaze. "I see you have unexpected company," she said quietly.

Emma made a comical face and sighed. "When Nikolas sees them—"

"Nikolas won't make a scene," Tasia assured her. "He has too much self-control."

"I hope so."

"Adam seems rather henpecked," Tasia observed.

"Yes, I noticed that." Adam was a sensitive man with touchy pride. Why had he married a woman like Charlotte? Perhaps she was reacting out of insecurity, trying to assert herself by badgering him. "The poor woman," Emma said suddenly. "I know what it's like, trying to hold onto an elusive man. I tried for a long time, and finally recognized the folly of it."

"Whom are you referring to?" Tasia asked. "Adam or Nikolas?"

Emma smiled ruefully. "Both, I suppose. But Nikolas has changed, and Adam hasn't. I think Adam thrives on keeping a woman slightly off-balance, never letting her feel that she can entirely depend on him."

"And you feel you can depend on Nikolas?" came Tasia's soft question.

"Yes. Everything I've seen during the past few weeks has convinced me I must take that chance.

I've made up my mind to trust and believe in Nikolas, until he proves me wrong."

Tasia's gaze was searching. "Have you come to care for him, Emma?"

Emma hesitated, debating her answer. Out of the corner of her eye, she saw Adam disentangle himself from his wife and wander through the crowd, stopping at the French doors that opened onto the garden. He turned and gazed directly at Emma.

Adam wanted to speak with her privately. Emma looked away from him, her brow marked with a troubled frown. Soon she would slip away and join him.

"Are you certain that's wise?" Tasia asked, reading the situation accurately.

"It may not be wise, but it's necessary. I must settle things between us, once and for all."

Nikolas returned to the drawing room with a sense of relief. The boys had delighted Jake with their admiration of the pony. Stokehurst had been polite and even marginally friendly, murmuring that he would like to talk with him over a snifter of brandy sometime soon. Nikolas had agreed dutifully, perceiving that Emma had been correct— her father did seem to want peace between them.

As he crossed the threshold of the drawing room, an unfamiliar woman approached him. She was small and plump, with startlingly hawklike eyes set in her round face.

"Your Highness," she said in a deep voice. "I am Lady Milbank. Your wife and my husband both seem to be missing. Since I am unfamiliar with your estate, I must prevail on you to help me locate them."

* * *

The garden was dark and rustling with winter breezes. The ground was hard and the hedges laced with frost. Emma's breath blew in ghost-puffs as she walked through the freezing night air.

The garden was the only place she and Adam could be guaranteed the privacy they needed. It seemed appropriate that they should meet here, the last place they had truly been together before Nikolas had intervened in their lives.

She found what she was looking for, a small clearing behind the border of Irish yews. Adam was waiting there, his longish hair blowing gently around his face and neck. He seemed so much older, as if years instead of months had gone by. Emma felt as if she had aged as well. How could it be that they had both changed so greatly?

She no longer saw them as young and impetuous lovers, and she realized they were separated by more than their marriages to other people. She had never really loved Adam. Real love was accepting people's faults, and forgiving them when they failed. Understanding their weakness, and loving them better for it. What she and Adam had shared was an illusion—it had crumbled at the first real challenge they had faced.

She stopped a few feet away from him. Her lips trembled from the cold. "Why did you come, Adam?"

He held out his hand, his palm filled with the white gleam of pearls. "I wanted to give these to you."

The earrings she had sent back to him. Emma shook her head and folded her arms across her middle. "I can't accept them."

"Why not? Aren't they as fine as the jewels he gives you?" His gaze dropped to the tiger brooch at her throat.

Emma swallowed hard, uncomfortable at being alone with him. "What do you want from me?" she asked in a mixture of impatience and pleading.

"I want to go back to the night you and I were here in this garden. I would do it all differently. I wouldn't let myself be intimidated into leaving you this time. I didn't realize until it was too late that you were my only chance at happiness."

"That's not true."

"Isn't it? People say that Nikolas has changed, that marriage to you has made him into a better man. You might have done that for me had I married you. You would have defied your family and the whole world to become my wife. You would have loved me."

Once, this moment might have given Emma great pleasure, seeing how much Adam regretted having abandoned her. But now she didn't want his regrets—she wanted them both to find peace. "Adam, it does neither of us any good to dwell on the past."

"What if I can't stop myself?" he asked fiercely, casting the earrings at her feet with such force that one of the loops shattered, sending pearls flying around her skirts. "I wanted to see you wearing these tonight . . . wearing something of mine."

"You should have given them to your wife."

"I don't love her," Adam said, his eyes dark with intense misery. "After I gave you up, I sold my soul. I thought Charlotte's fortune would be adequate consolation. Do you know what I learned?" He laughed bitterly. "My newfound wealth comes with obligations that turn my stomach. Charlotte treats me as if I'm a trained monkey. She expects me to do her will, and she rewards me only when I please her. I've lost all pride, all self-respect."

"Oh, Adam," Emma whispered sadly. "You mustn't tell me such things. I can't help you."

"But you can."

Emma had opened her mouth to argue when she heard the sound of footsteps on the hard ground and the movement of someone brushing by the garden hedges. A few seconds later, Charlotte, Lady Milbank appeared. Her pale face was expressionless, but her eyes gleamed with angry triumph. "We've found them," she announced to her companion, who stepped onto the path beside her.

"Nikki," Emma said, her heart sinking.

Her husband spoke very quietly to Adam. "Get off my property or I'll kill you." For some men the phrase might have been a figure of speech, but Nikolas was in deadly earnest.

"No," Emma intervened swiftly. "Let them be, Nikki. Don't give the gossips more fodder. Besides, you have business concerns with Mr. Brixton and his American crowd, don't you? You mustn't offend Brixton by turning out his sister and her husband."

Nikolas's tigerish gaze fastened on her. "Why do you want Milbank to stay?"

"We must be leaving now anyway," Charlotte Milbank murmured, coming forward to take Adam's arm. "My head is beginning to ache. And I've seen what I came here to see. Come along, dear."

At first it seemed doubtful whether or not Adam would move. The silence became excruciating. Finally he obeyed his wife's imperious tugging and left the garden with her.

Nikolas stared at the scattered pearls on the ground by Emma's feet.

She felt defensive, when there was no reason to be. Angry at her own uneasiness, Emma took the offensive. "What now, Nikki?" she asked crisply. "Arguments? Accusations?"

"Did you invite him?" He was still looking at the pearls.

"Do you think I wanted him here?"

"Perhaps you did. Are you testing me, Emma?"

The question sent her into a sudden fury. "I won't defend myself. Believe what you like."

"I want your explanation."

"Do you really?" she asked, all sarcastic innocence. "How wonderful that you've decided to be fair with me, after you've already drawn your own conclusions! You and Adam are exactly alike—a pair of dogs fighting over a bone. Well, I won't be pushed and pulled and manipulated by the two of you. How *dare* you look at me with suspicion when I've been trying so damned hard to believe the best of you! Don't I deserve the same consideration? The same blind trust?"

There was no sound, no words exchanged, nothing but stillness. Nikolas seemed occupied with an inner struggle that required all of his concentration. Emma gazed at his austere profile, the lines of his nose and cheekbones etched with silver moonlight.

Nikolas drew a deep breath and let it out slowly, seeming to relax. "I know you didn't invite him," he said gruffly. "When I saw you here with him, I wanted to strangle you both. I was . . . jealous."

Emma felt her temper subside. "There's no reason for that."

"Isn't there?" He was quiet for another long moment. "Six months ago I stood in this garden and heard you tell Adam that you loved him—words you've never said to me."

"Didn't I tell you in your past life?" she asked in a feeble attempt at humor.

"Yes," he replied, utterly serious. "And I want to hear it again. It's the only hope that sustains me, Emma."

To everyone's relief, the holidays passed without further incident. The Milbanks faded from Nikolas's mind as he occupied himself with the needs of his family, tenants, and business. Once he had finally found a highly qualified candidate to be Jake's tutor, Nikolas summoned him to the Angelovsky estate in the afternoon. The elderly man was shown to the library, where Nikolas and Jacob waited.

Nikolas gestured for the elderly man before him to have a seat. "Mr. Robinson, my son and I would like to offer you the position of tutor. Your credentials are excellent, and after meeting with you last week, we both agreed you were the right man."

Robinson, a portly, gray-haired gentleman, had taught at Eton for the past forty years, and had now come to desire a simpler life as a private tutor. There was a kindness and gentle humor that Nikolas liked about the man, but also a thread of steel that suggested discipline and good sense. More importantly, Jake approved of him, regarding him as a grandfatherly figure.

Robinson's neatly trimmed beard split with a smile. "I accept," he said without delay. "I might add that it was quite unusual to allow the boy to have a say in such a decision—but also refreshing." His eyes twinkled as he glanced at Jake. "I believe Master Jacob and I will do well together."

"We'll provide excellent accommodations for you wherever the family happens to be staying. We would also like you to travel with us on occasion."

"I'll look forward to that, Your Highness. Traveling is always an excellent opportunity for learning. Even for a man my age."

"That's good—" Nikolas broke off as he saw the butler appear at the library door. "Yes, Stanislaus?"

"A carrier just brought this to the door, Your Highness." The butler brought him a folded and sealed note on a small silver tray, then departed from the room.

"Excuse me," Nikolas murmured to Mr. Robinson, breaking the wax seal and scanning the note, which had been addressed exclusively to him.

Nikolas—

I want to discuss a matter of great importance with you. It involves Emma. Meet me at the old gatehouse at Southgate Hall, at four o'clock this afternoon. I would prefer that you mention this to no one.

Stokehurst

"What the hell . . . ?" Nikolas muttered, reading the note once more. The cryptic message didn't seem in Stokehurst's usual straightforward style. But perhaps that was because the man was concerned about his daughter. Nikolas had no choice except to comply with the summons. He wanted to be on good terms with Emma's family. And if that meant going to extra lengths to please her father, it was worth it.

Jake stared at him curiously, while Mr. Robinson looked mildly concerned. "Bad news, Your Highness?"

"No," Nikolas said thoughtfully. "Just unexpected." He doubted that Emma knew anything about the message her father had sent. She was gone today, attending a meeting of the Royal Society for the Humane Treatment of Animals. Often such gatherings were an all-day event, so it was unlikely that she would return before supper. If he left at once, he would make the journey to the Stokehurst county seat, meet with Stokehurst, and reach home before Emma did.

Nikolas slipped the note into the corner of his desk. "In-laws," he commented dryly. "They never seem to be satisfied until they've put a man to a great deal of trouble."

The older gentleman smiled. "I agree, Your Highness. My dear wife passed away ten years ago, and her family still plagues me."

Nikolas smiled and ruffled his son's dark hair. "Jake, I must leave now, so perhaps you would show Mr. Robinson the schoolroom." He turned to the tutor. "Stanislaus will help make the arrangements to move your belongings here by week's end. Give him the list of supplies you'll need."

"Thank you, Prince Nikolas. It is an honor to be entrusted with Master Jacob's education."

Jake tugged impatiently at Nikolas's sleeve. "Where are you going, Papa?"

"I'll be back in time for supper."

"I want to go with you."

"Not this time. You must stay here, and act as the man of the house until I return."

"Yes, Papa." Jake's reply was obedient, but there was a frown of displeasure between his small black brows.

Emma returned from the R.S.H.T.A. glowing with the success of the day. The meeting itself had been routine—dull, really—and with few noteworthy news items and no developments in ongoing projects, it had ended quite early. What had been different was the way she had been treated by everyone. As Nikolas had once promised, her social influence had been multiplied at least ten times, simply because she was his wife.

By now all the members of the Society were aware of the legendary fortune Emma had married into, as well as her impressive new title. Everyone had fawned over her, agreeing to all her suggestions and praising her intelligence and charitable nature. Today she had been declared by the president of the organization as the Society's most prestigious member. Emma had been embarrassed, pleased, and also slightly annoyed that all her previous work had not gained her the recognition that being Nikolas's wife had.

She entered the house and shivered pleasantly at the contrast between the warm air inside and the arctic temperature outdoors. "Hello, Stanley," she said to the butler, allowing him to help with her cloak. She removed her gray felt hat and gloves. "Where is my husband? In the library?"

"He left the estate a few minutes ago, Your Highness."

"Really? Why?"

"He didn't say, madam."

"Emma!" came Jake's voice, and she turned to see him bounding down the grand staircase, an elderly and well-dressed gentleman following at a more sedate pace. "This is my tutor, Mr. Robinson."

Emma gave the man a wide smile. "My husband told me about you, Mr. Robinson. Have you decided to accept the position?"

"Yes, Your Highness."

"I'm so glad." Glancing down at Jake, she asked casually, "Did Nikolas say when he would be back?"

"Before supper."

"Do you know where he went?"

"Yes."

When no further information seemed forthcoming, Emma smiled and asked patiently, "Would you like to tell me?"

"I can't *tell* it—I have to show you."

Puzzled, Emma followed the boy to the library, while the tutor stayed in the entrance hall with Stanislaus. Going to Nikolas's desk, Jake riffled through a few scraps of paper until he came up with a folded note pinched between his small fingers. "Here."

Emma shook her head reprovingly. "It's not right to look through other people's letters, Jake."

"But you wanted to know."

"Yes, but . . ." She stared at the note, longing to read its contents. "Hell," she said softly, and took it with a grin. "It's very bad to do what I'm doing, Jake. We must always respect others' privacy."

"Yes, ma'am." He watched as she read the note, his eyes as golden and luminous as a cat's.

Emma was immediately confused. "How strange." It wasn't at all like her father to send such a message. Why would he do it, and why— "But this isn't his handwriting!" she cried. There was a spasm of nerves in her stomach. Something was wrong—this was Lord Milbank's penmanship. Her eyes blurred for a moment, and the black ink seemed to crawl like vermin across the page. She had seen his handwriting before, when he had sent her love notes, and that final letter of good-bye.

Milbank wanted to see Nikolas alone.

The note dropped from Emma's hand, falling gently to the floor. She remembered the things Adam had said about Nikolas, his words tumbling through her mind . . .

"I can't stop dwelling on what was taken from me. Your husband slithered into our lives and took everything I wanted . . .

"I'm going to even the score, and I promise you won't have to wait for long. I owe it to you, Emma as well as myself . . .

"My God, someone should do the world a favor and get rid of him—before he ruins any more innocent lives."

"No," Emma said, her fists clenching. "This is crazy. He wouldn't do such a thing."

But in her heart she knew that Nikolas was in danger. Ignoring Jake's confused questions, she strode to a wooden cabinet where Nikolas kept crystal decanters of liquor and a few valuables. "You were right to show me that note, Jake," she said, hunting through the cabinet. "Now please go out to the entrance hall."

"But why—"

"Do as I say, Jake." She threw a reassuring smile

over her shoulder. "It's all right," she said lightly.
Jake obeyed reluctantly, his feet shuffling on the
carpeted floor. Emma found what she was looking
for, a set of finely wrought pistols in mahogany
cases. She pulled out a French pinfire revolver
made of gold and silver with ivory grips. Its weight
was heavy and reassuring in her palm. She checked
to see if it was loaded, and discovered that the
chambers were full.

She slipped the revolver into the pocket of her
dress, its lump concealed by the heavy folds of her
skirts. Walking back into the entrance hall, Emma
gestured for her cloak. Although she thought her
expression was calm, there must have been some
betraying hint of what she was feeling, for the two
men looked at her strangely.

"Stanley, have the carriage brought around
again," she said abruptly. "I'm certain they haven't
yet unharnessed the horses."

The butler hesitated, as if tempted to question or
delay her, but as his gaze met hers, he nodded.
"Yes, Your Highness."

A carriage was already waiting at the old gatehouse, the horse's breath puffing white in the cold
air. The small, centuries-old gatehouse was located
miles away from Southgate Hall. It was poised at
the edge of a thick forest, on a winding path that
used to serve as the original drive leading to the
main residence. Now it was in disuse, after a new
gatehouse and a more direct road had been established years ago.

Nikolas left his own one-horse carriage and patted the chestnut's steaming neck before walking to
the gatehouse. The weather was cold, but nothing

like the wicked bite of the Russian winters he had known for most of his life. Still, he wanted this meeting to be finished soon so he could return to home and Emma. Damn his father-in-law for wanting to be humored this way—yet Nikolas supposed he owed it to the man.

Pushing open the heavy wooden door, Nikolas walked into the dank structure, illuminated by the daylight that shone through the small, square windows. Adjusting to the change from the brilliant white outdoors, Nikolas blinked several times. "All right, Stokehurst," he muttered. "Tell me what this is about."

But the voice that replied wasn't Stokehurst's. It was soft, gloating, hostile. "You're not used to surroundings as humble as these, are you? Only the best for Prince Nikolas. A fine home, luxury, a beautiful wife . . . but now it's all going to be taken away. By the man whom *you* robbed of everything."

The speaker stepped forward, and Nikolas recognized the features of Lord Milbank.

Startled, disoriented, Nikolas stared at him without blinking. "What the hell do you want?"

Milbank gestured with his hand, displaying a heavy-barreled pistol. "I want revenge, and I'm going to take it with this. You were jealous of what I had with Emma, and you took her for yourself. You think you're a better man than me, don't you? Well, there is precious little difference between us, Angelovsky. Neither of us is worthy of Emma." Adam took careful aim with the weapon in his hand, using his thumb to ease back the hammer. "This is Stokehurst's pistol. I'm going to kill you with it and leave you here on his property. You and Stokehurst conspired against me. Now it's time for justice."

"You fool," Nikolas said softly, staring at the pistol. It was trembling in the man's grip, betraying his tremendous agitation. "No one will believe that Stokehurst did it."

"At least it will cast a shadow on the fine name he's so proud of. And the world will be better off without you—selfish Russian bastard!"

"What do you think will happen afterward?" Nikolas asked, switching his gaze to Milbank's sweating face. "You'll only end up in the hangman's noose. And you still won't have Emma. She doesn't want you."

"She wanted me until you tore our lives apart!" The gun jerked, and Nikolas flinched in reaction. Milbank laughed harshly. "You're right to be afraid, Angelovsky. I mean to do this. I'm going to kill you with no more regret than I would feel swatting a fly. But first, get on your knees." As Nikolas hesitated, Milbank's rage seemed to double. "Kneel on the floor! For once I want to see you humbled."

Slowly Nikolas sank down to his knees, staring at the other man while rage and denial rushed through his body.

"I began to plan this the day I heard you had married Emma," Adam said. "Your life hasn't been worth a shilling since then."

Nikolas licked his dry lips. "You'd sacrifice your own life for revenge? What about your wife?"

"My wife," Adam repeated, then laughed bitterly. "Fat little hen, always pecking away at everyone around her. Every time I look at Charlotte, I remember that it's your fault I'm with her. And you have Emma . . . *you*, who deserve her less than any other man on earth."

"That I don't deny," Nikolas said quietly.

"Emma will thank me for the rest of her life for what I'm about to do."

"No, Adam." A new voice broke in on the scene, startling them both. They had been so intent on the exchange, neither of them had noticed the slim figure that had slipped through the partially open door. Emma stood there, the hem of her skirts damp from the ground, her face angular in the shadows. Nikolas had never seen her eyes so fixed and brilliant, as if she were in a hypnotic trance. She moved forward, holding a revolver in a grip that was far steadier than Adam's. "This is insane. Stop pointing that thing at Nikolas. If you harm a hair on his head, I'll put a bullet in you."

"Emma, get out of here!" Nikolas snapped, his entire body cold with sudden terror. His wife, his child . . . they must not be harmed, no matter what became of him.

Adam barely spared Emma a glance. "I don't want to kill him in front of you. But I will if I have to."

"For God's sake, why are you doing this?" Emma asked tautly. "Are you trying to frighten Nikolas? Well, you've succeeded in scaring the hell out of both of us. Now put the gun away."

Adam looked grim and increasingly anxious, the pistol wavering in his hand. "You should be grateful that I'm getting rid of him. Isn't that what you want, Emma? You couldn't love such a monster— you want to be free of him."

"I don't want this." Her jaw trembled visibly. "You must stop this nonsense, Adam!"

"Damn you, Emma, please go," Nikolas said in desperation. Dear God, it couldn't be his fate to be ripped apart from her once again. After all he'd gone through, everything he had learned, would he lose her one final time? The past echoed in his ears, Emelia's grieving whisper... *"I'll never see you again, will I?"*

"Not in this lifetime."

"Emma, get out of here," he said harshly.

"Not another word from you!" Adam shouted, his eyes gleaming with hatred. His tormented gaze returned to Emma. "I never understood how I really felt until I lost you. I must do this. I can't let him win. I'll never feel like a man again, as long as I let him go unpunished. No one has ever believed that I loved you, Emma—not even you. This is the only way I can prove it. Then you'll know."

"You don't need to prove anything," Emma said. "I do believe you." She felt tears prickling at the corners of her eyes, while a voice inside cried with terror, *Please don't hurt him, please...* She blinked the tears back and kept the gun steady on Adam. "But I didn't love you, Adam. I was lonely, unsure of myself, and you flattered me and made me feel wanted. Through my own immaturity I mistook that for love—"

"He's tricked you into believing his lies," Adam said hotly.

"You and I were friends who cared about each other. That's not the same as love. Now we've each made a good life for ourselves with other people. You don't have to destroy all of that. You'll accomplish nothing by doing this. Just put the gun away and we'll leave. I-I'll go with you somewhere and we'll talk—"

"No," Nikolas said swiftly.

"You have no say in this," Adam sneered. *"I'm in control, not you!"*

"Put it down now," Emma said. "I mean it, Adam."

"I can't," came his stubborn reply.

"Now."

Adam didn't appear to hear her, his gaze locked on Nikolas. "It's too late."

For the rest of her life Emma would remember the events taking place outside of time, seconds turning into hours, each move slow and visible and understandable. Whatever Nikolas saw in Adam's eyes, it convinced him that he was about to die. He turned his face toward Emma for one last look, his eyes pale and piercing.

She squeezed the trigger of her revolver. The shot seemed unnaturally loud, echoing repeatedly through her mind. *"Nikolai!"* came a high-pitched scream, and much later she realized it had been hers. Adam was twisted around by the blow, the upper part of his shoulder opening with a red burst. His pistol went off, the shot flying wide. Instantly the bullet buried itself in the wall behind Nikolas.

Nikolas didn't move as Adam fell in front of him. He was frozen, his mind still numb with the expectation of death. He was curiously blind and deaf, lost in a dark void. Gradually his senses were restored, and he found himself still kneeling on the floor, with Emma crouched before him. Her hands were on either side of his face, and her breath was warm on his skin.

"Nikki," she whispered, her blue eyes glittering with tears. "God, I love you!" She kissed his eyelids, his cheeks, his lips. "Look at me," she said, weeping openly. "I can't ever lose you, do you understand? I love you."

Nikolas wrapped his arms around her as the roaring of blood in his ears subsided. He glanced at Milbank's prone body. The wound seemed to be located in the upper arm or shoulder; the bastard would probably live. Returning his attention to Emma, he tried to wipe at the tears that streamed down her cheeks. She seemed so vulnerable, a tigress suddenly cowed and seeking comfort. There were no more defenses between them. They clung together, whole at last, while the past fell away in vanquished tatters.

"How did you know—" he managed to ask.

"I saw the note. I knew it was Adam's handwriting, and that he meant to harm you. I had to come find you."

His hold became punishingly tight. "Don't *ever* put yourself in danger like that again. Not for any reason."

A wobbling smile touched her lips. "You can't tell me what to do," she said, blotting her face with her sleeve.

"Don't cry," he whispered. "It's over now. We're both safe."

"When I realized Adam might kill you, I knew how empty my life would be without you. I need you." Her jaw trembled as she tried to master her emotions. "So you'd better stay with me forever, Nikki . . . or I'll make your life hell."

"You called me Nikolai," he said, stroking the curve of her wet cheek.

"Did I?" Emma looked startled at that, and thought for a moment. "Yes, I did," she said slowly. "I wonder why. Perhaps . . . I'm beginning to believe in your dream."

He didn't care about that anymore, not when the future was hanging ripe and sweet before them. "It doesn't matter. Just as long as you love me now, *ruyshka*."

"Yes," she whispered, pulling his head down to hers.

❧ Epilogue

I<small>N THE MONTHS</small> following Lord Milbank's formal indictment and trial for attempted murder, his wife, Charlotte, found the scrutiny of the public, as well as the disdain of high social circles, too much to bear. She fled to her family and home in America, where the other Brixtons closed their protective ranks around her. Found guilty by a jury of his peers, Adam was sentenced to a brief term of imprisonment, and the loss of most of his land and property.

In her private moments Emma thought about Adam with a feeling of guilt, wondering if she could have done or said something that would have kept him from making an attempt on Nikolas's life. Like her, Adam had fallen in love with an illusion, and he had blamed others for his disappointments in life. Thank God she had finally learned better, or she would never have been able to find her hard-won happiness with Nikolas.

During the last months of her pregnancy, Emma's world was narrowed to her own estate and the homes of family and close friends. Women in her condition were discouraged from appearing in public, except in the early stages when they could conceal their bodies with shawls and heavy shrouding. Tasia and a few other women came to visit her regularly, easing the boredom of confinement, but still, there were no trips to the theater, no parties or dances, no riding through the park or walks through London; and worst of all, her work in the menagerie was all but forbidden.

Nikolas had almost carried her bodily from the stables on the afternoon a new horse had been brought there. The bad-tempered animal had been mistreated by his previous owner until he had no trust left in humans. After he had kicked a stablehand who had tried to attend to his festering foot, Emma had gone to try to calm the animal. Nikolas, who had been alerted by a tattletale servant, came to the stables immediately.

Emma had first been guilty and then defiant as her husband had locked his arm around her back and steered her out of the building. "Just let me have a few minutes to gentle him," she said angrily. "I do it all the time with other animals—you've seen me!"

"That damn horse has bitten and kicked everyone who's come near him," Nikolas replied curtly, pulling Emma along too fast for her to dig her heels in.

"I can make decisions for myself," she persisted, although she knew he was right.

"Not while you're carrying my child."

It had taken a long time for her temper to cool that afternoon. Her anger was directed mostly at herself, and at the fact that for the first time in her life, she was physically dependent on others. She tired so easily these days, and her usual free stride was now beginning to resemble the waddle of a duck.

"It won't last forever," Nikolas murmured, coming to rest beside her as she settled in bed for an afternoon nap. He cuddled behind her spoon-fashion, his hand sliding gently over her burgeoning stomach and breasts. Emma felt him smile against the back of her neck. "Soon you'll be back at work in the menagerie, getting bitten and scratched, and happily raking up manure."

She sighed longingly at the thought. "It's not easy, you know, having the servants do the things I want to do myself. Not only that, but I'm getting so awkward and *fat*—"

He laughed softly, his palm settling high on her abdomen. "You're slender everywhere but here, *ruyshka*. Not fat, but pregnant. Russians believe there is nothing more beautiful than a woman in your condition."

"We're not in Russia," she grumbled. "We're in England, where an expectant mother is decidedly out of fashion." Nikolas began to knead the lowest point of her spine, finding sore places and massaging the stiffness out, until Emma sighed in contentment. "Oh, I do love your hands," she murmured, arching slightly.

"Only my hands?"

"Well, your hands are all I can feel at the moment."

"What about this?" He pressed his loins against her backside, making her aware of the hard length of his arousal. "I find you enchanting, beautiful . . . and very desirable," he said, kissing the side of her neck. "What do you think of that, little mother?"

Emma smiled and wriggled slightly. "I think

you're a strange man with perverse tastes." She eased onto her back and circled her arms around his neck. "And I'm very lucky to be your wife."

Two months later, Emma sat in bed and cuddled her infant daughter, while Nikolas sat beside her. With the tip of her forefinger, Emma brushed back the tiny fluff of red hair on the baby's head. The crescents of her red lashes fanned the pink curves of her cheeks. "What shall we call her?" she asked. "Somehow not one of the names I considered seems appropriate."

"I have one to suggest." Nikolas's hand settled on the blankets, covering the shape of Emma's knee. "I'd like to call her Mary, after your mother."

Emma was silent for a moment, bending her head over the baby. When she looked back at Nikolas, her eyes glittered with tears of happiness. "Yes, I would like that. Her name will be Mary Nikolaievna Angelovsky. God knows she'll never learn to spell it."

They were interrupted by a gentle tap on the bedroom door. "Yes?" Nikolas asked, turning to regard the maid who had appeared in the doorway.

"Your Highness, a parcel was delivered for you not five minutes ago. Mr. Stanislaus said it was from Sir Almay. Shall I leave it in the library, sir?"

Emma watched as a peculiar blankness came over her husband's face.

"No," he said. "Bring it here."

"What is it?" Emma asked when the maid had left. "Who is Sir Almay?"

Nikolas seemed not to hear, but after a few moments he replied distantly. "The historian I hired to research the Angelovsky records in Russia."

"Oh." Her gaze traveled from his expressionless face to the restless clenching of his fingers in the bedclothes. Then she understood. "You asked him to find out about Emelia."

"I had to."

"Yes, of course." Emma reached for his hand, stroking the taut backs of his fingers. She could only guess what this meant to him. That time was still so real to him, affecting him in countless small ways; he would certainly grieve if he discovered that harm had come to Emelia Vasilievna. "Nikki, whatever happened to her . . . it wasn't your fault. You know that, don't you?"

Nikolas didn't answer, staring at the door as if he half-expected a ghost to appear. The maid returned with the parcel, coming forward to hand it to Nikolas. At Emma's gesture, the maid took the baby and carried her to the nursery for a nap.

Slowly Nikolas slid the strings from the parcel and parted the layers of brown paper. Emma leaned forward in eager curiosity. The package contained a folded letter, two or three volumes with Cyrillic characters on the covers, and another object Emma didn't have a chance to see. Nikolas reached for it and turned his back to her, staring at whatever it was he held. Silently he rose and walked to the window. She saw him lift a hand to his face, whether to blot sweat or tears she couldn't tell.

Emma picked up the letter and saw that it was written in English.

To His Highness Prince Nikolas Dmitriyevich Angelovsky:

Having completed the research you requested, I would like to thank you for the experience of traveling to Russia. The accommodations were superb, and I found the translator, Mr. Sigeyov, most effective. Should you have questions regarding the materials I have sent, I would be happy to meet with you and provide further details. Most of the information regarding the fate of Emelia Vasilievna was contained in personal correspondence written by her son, Prince Alexei Nikolaievich Angelovsky. The letters were in the possession of your oldest sister, Katya, a charming woman who gave them to me along with her affectionate wishes for your well-being. There was also a mention of Emelia's residence in her latter years, a small Moscovian estate which Empress Elizabeth reputedly visited in the company of Alexei—

"What happened to her?" Nikolas asked hoarsely, still facing the window.

Emma scanned the letter rapidly, jumping forward a page or two. "Emelia left the convent seven years after you . . . after Nikolai died," she said. "Angelovsky relatives kept her and the child with them in St. Petersburg for a brief time. They were harassed by city officials and agents of the Imperial government, until Emelia virtually disappeared with her son for the next ten years. It's possible they lived in her former home of Preobrazhenskoe—one year the village church listed an unidentified woman and her fatherless child in its register. That could have been Emelia." Emma found another significant passage from Almay's report and read it aloud.

Two years after Tsar Peter's death in 1725, Emelia and her son finally came out of hiding. At that time Alexei was around nineteen or twenty years of age. He claimed complete ownership of all Angelovsky holdings, and assumed his place as Nikolai's rightful heir. Apparently no one in the family was able or willing to contest him. Alexei established Emelia in a palace outside Moscow, where she lived in comfort for the rest of her days. For the next twenty years, he applied himself to increasing the Angelovsky fortune. There are several letters preserved from this period, written in Alexei's own hand and addressed to his mother at her home. These are included in the materials I have sent. From this correspondence it is apparent that Emelia objected to her son becoming the private consort of Empress Elizabeth, Peter's daughter. However, she lived long enough to see her son marry a Russian noblewoman and produce two children, Sergei and Lida. Emelia's death was recorded in 1750. She was sixty-three years of age. Among your sister Katya's collection we discovered a miniature of Emelia Vasilievna, painted not long before her death . . .

Emma's voice faded as she realized what Nikolas was holding. ''Nikki?'' she said quietly, setting aside the letter. She rose from the bed and joined him at the window. At first the glare of daylight made the image impossible to see. She touched his hand, and he tilted the miniature until the face became clear.

Emma stared at the tiny portrait of an old woman with silvery-peach hair. Her face was weathered but regal, her mouth unsmiling, her eyes of an indistinguishable color. She looked as though she were staring wistfully at something— or someone—very far away. "Does she look like me?" Emma asked, her fingers curving around Nikolas's. Her throat became very tight. "Yes, I suppose she does."

"She never married again," he murmured.

Emma looked up and saw the glitter of tears on his cheek. "No, it appears she didn't."

"She had no one."

"She had her child," Emma said. "She took comfort in Alexei, as well as her memories of Nikolai. Most of all, she knew they would meet again . . . and they did."

Emma sensed an easing in him, a relief that made his fingers unclench. "Did they?" he asked, turning to her with the miniature clasped in his hand. "How can you be certain?"

Emma smiled and leaned against him, until his arms closed around her. "I just know."

Nikolas rested his face against her hair, whispering his love to her, while they stood together in the healing warmth of the morning sunlight.

*At Avon Books, we know your passion
for romance—once you finish one of our
novels, you find yourself wanting more.*

May we tempt you with . . .

- **Excerpts** from our upcoming releases.

- Entertaining **extras**, including authors'
  personal photo albums and book lists.

- Behind-the-scenes **scoop** on your favorite
  characters and series.

- **Sweepstakes** for the chance to win free books,
  romantic getaways, and other fun prizes.

- Writing **tips** from our authors and editors.

- **Blog** with our authors and find out why they
  love to write romance.

- **Exclusive content** that's not contained
  within the pages of our novels.

Join us at
www.avonbooks.com

AVON

An Imprint of HarperCollins*Publishers*
www.avonromance.com

"Another solid Jack Ryan novel by author Marc Cameron, who has this series down perfectly. It starts off fast and never lets up on the action. He does Tom Clancy proud with every book he writes." —Red Carpet Crash

PRAISE FOR THE BESTSELLING NOVELS OF TOM CLANCY

"Heart-stopping action . . . entertaining and eminently topical. . . . Clancy still reigns." —*The Washington Post*

"Brilliant." —*Newsweek*

"Highly entertaining." —*The Wall Street Journal*

"[Clancy] excites, illuminates. . . . A real page-turner." —*Los Angeles Daily News*

"Exhilarating. . . . No other novelist is giving so full a picture of modern conflict." —*The Sunday Times* (London)